ABOUT THE AUTHOR

Harper Ford is an author, much of the time. She started out as a writer of historical novels, then found out she was funny during lockdown so decided to write contemporary romcoms too. She's also a Fellow of the Royal Literary Fund, based at the University of Lincoln.

Divorced Not Dead is her debut in the women's fiction space.

www.harperford.co.uk

Praise for *Divorced Not Dead:*

'I want Frankie to be my new BFF! This book is like a (very big) glass of wine with a friend – honest, unfiltered, hilarious. Your cheeks will hurt from laughing so much.'

Louise Pentland, author of *Time After Time*

'Brilliantly observed, hilariously documented, a vivid commentary and celebration of life at fifty . . . Personal, funny, relatable and motivational.'

Shazia Mirza, award-winning stand-up comedian and writer

'It's a blast – full of verve and vinegar, defiantly funny and a terrific shot in the arm. We need more books like this!'

Georgie Hall, author of *Woman of a Certain Rage*

'Get ready to learn a whole new dating vocabulary as we follow Frankie – fifty, fabulous, freshly divorced – as she steers her way through dating etiquette in the 2020s. Funny, entertaining and enlightening . . . Sex education was never like this the first time around!'

Julie Ma, author of Richard and Judy selection *Happy Families*

'I laughed out loud . . . loudly out loud, to be precise!'

Reader review

'Absolutely raced through this irreverently funny, clever and thoughtful book. A whip-smart novel with a clever heroine!'
Reader review

'Better than *Sex and the City*! I loved it and you will too!'
Reader review

'Definitely a book to read before you sign up for any dating apps!' **Reader review**

'Frankie's experience of online dating is hilarious and priceless . . . A fabulous, funny five-star read for me.'
Reader review

'I can't think of a character I have liked as much as Frankie! She's the friend you want and need in your life. I absolutely adore her!' **Reader review**

'A heart-warming and relatable romance novel that celebrates second chances . . . ' **Reader review**

'Ford has perfectly captured the online dating world - warts and all!' **Reader review**

'It's so empowering!' **Reader review**

'This is a novel that instantly feels totally relatable. Frankie is an "everywoman" in the 21st century!' **Reader review**

'An irreverent tale of friendship and life after divorce . . . '
Reader review

HARPER FORD

divorced (not dead)

avon.

Published by AVON
A division of HarperCollins*Publishers* Ltd
1 London Bridge Street
London SE1 9GF

www.harpercollins.co.uk

HarperCollins*Publishers*
Macken House, 39/40 Mayor Street Upper,
Dublin 1, D01 C9W8, Ireland

A Paperback Original 2023

1

First published in Great Britain by HarperCollins*Publishers* 2023

A catalogue copy of this book is available from the British Library.

ISBN: 978-0-00-865130-5

Typeset in Sabon LT Std by Palimpsest Book Production Limited, Falkirk, Stirlingshire

Printed and Bound in the UK using
100% Renewable Electricity at CPI Group (UK) Ltd

This book is dedicated to my two Fionas –
McKinnell and Cooke.

They know why . . . 😉

CHAPTER 1

Fuck You, Mars

If you'd asked me ten years ago how I'd feel about being newly single and online dating at fifty, I'd have said I'd rather use a cactus as a dildo. Except I probably didn't even know what a dildo was back then, let alone sexting (and flexting) or ghosting (and zombieing) or catfishing (and kittenfishing). Or anything else found in the parallel universe of dating apps. I'd have been content to stay with my dementor-ex until doomsday because I thought that's what middle age was all about. Being somewhere between vaguely and violently unhappy. Making do; putting up; sticking it out. Staying for the sake of the kids. Sleepwalking through midlife in a general malaise.

But, somewhere along the way, I woke up.

There's that bit in *When Harry Met Sally* where Harry says, 'When you realise you want to spend the rest of your life with somebody, you want the rest of your life to start as soon as possible.' Well, that's how I felt the day I left the marital home and moved into the flat above my shop. Except that the somebody I want to spend the rest of my life with is me. She's been missing for a while, you see. Me, that is. Frances Brumby. More commonly known as Frankie. And I just found her again.

So, it's a Sunday evening in mid-January a couple of weeks after I left my home of over twenty years – originally my ex Gareth's house north of Lincoln, where I moved in with him during our hopeful early thirties and married him and then raised our lovely boy, Jay. Now I've moved out again, two decades later, into my tiny new flat. It was the lockdowns that did it for me. Seeing Gareth rarely meant I could just about scrape through my daily existence, but being holed up with him and Jay for weeks on end drove me and the kid insane. I'd planned to drag myself through one last Christmas together, but it didn't work out that way. I cracked on Christmas Eve Eve. My son James (or Jay as I've called him since day one when he lay on my boob looking drunk after the caesarean) already knew it was all going to happen and he was the one who said, 'Fuck this, let's get you gone before and have a nice, quiet Christmas in the new flat.' This morning, I put Jay on the train, off to his second term at Manchester Uni. There's nothing left to do now. I've packed everything away and sorted the shop and I'm done. I'm alone in my flat and I'm sitting here brooding.

I can't stand the silence so I message my best friend Bel and she immediately replies, telling me to get my sad ass over to hers, stat. Not long after, we're sitting in Bel's shed in her garden, freezing our tits off as it's snowing outside, the snowflakes fat and feathery as they drift past the grubby little shed window, while her husband is warm and cosy inside the house with their new baby who is asleep, hopefully. Well, we can't hear him screaming like he often does about this time (the baby, not the husband. Not usually.) The shed is a proper potting one, with bags of old compost, stacks of terracotta pots on shelves and gardening implements hanging on nails on the wall. We're wrapped up in winter gear, me in my duffel coat and woolly accoutrements and Bel in her Mountain Warehouse puffer jacket with fleecy pyjamas underneath, her curly red hair like a copper halo around her head. I always knew Bel liked to smoke weed and for years I've wanted to try it out, but Gareth had always slagged off Bel to high heaven, saying she was a druggie and how dangerous it was. BUT now I'm a free woman, I have to admit, I do want to try it. I've always been curious about what it would feel like but been too scared to give it a go. We can try a mild one and then progress, Bel tells me. So we're sharing a small joint and after a few puffs, I must say, I think I'm a natural. It just makes me giggle and feel chilled out and nicely buzzy and I've not instantaneously morphed into *Withnail and I*, as my ex described it. The most extreme part of it is an overwhelming urge to snack on Mr Kipling's French Fancies. As we're passing a joint back and forth, Bel says: 'Have you ever seen *The Martian*?'

'What, the little guy with the Roman gear on?'

'No. What? What guy?'

'You know, with the little . . . thing and the thing on his head and the skirt. The . . . centurion . . . thing.'

'No,' tuts Bel. 'No, the movie. With the bloke.'

'What bloke?'

'The bloke from . . . *Good Will Hunting*.'

'Ben Affleck.'

'Yeah. No.'

'The other one?'

'Yeah.'

'*Mork and Mindy*?'

'What? No.'

'Matt Damon.'

'YES. Matt Damon.'

'No.'

'No what?'

'I haven't seen *The Martian* with Matt Damon.'

'Oh. Right, well . . . I forgot why . . .'

'Okay . . . Is it good?'

'Listen to me, Frankie.' Bel looks dead serious now and I pull myself together and try very hard to listen very properly, sort of.

'I'm listening,' I say. Bel sits up really straight and I can tell she's going to have a monumental moment of lucidity.

'There's this bit where Matt Damon is recording his video diary, right? And he's just realised he's stuck on Mars and he's gonna run out of food and oxygen and all that. So he has to figure out how to survive. So he sits there, really quiet for a minute, and then looks straight into the camera and says: "Fuck you, Mars."'

'Nice.'

'Yeah, right? Fuck you, Mars. So that's what you need to do, babe. Whenever it gets to you. All this . . . shit. All this shit you're going through, babe. Whenever it all gets on top of you and you're feeling so angry and sad and full of . . . you know, RAGE. When you get like that, you just gotta say, "Fuck you, Mars".'

'FUCK YOU, MARS!' I shout, then cough.

'Yes! Or FYM for short. Just text me those three letters when you're really going through it. FYM.'

'FYM.'

'Yeah.'

'That's genius.'

'Innit, though?!'

'Yeah,' and I look at Bel and I'm so grateful for her at that moment, so glad she's in my life, that she's my friend. (And that she has this shed in her garden, because there's nowhere else we could smoke weed and get away with it.)

'So . . .' says Bel and I wonder if she's going to come up with some other moment of brilliance. 'Who's the little centurion guy?'

'In the Bugs Bunny cartoons. The little martian guy.'

'With Bugs . . . Oh my God, yes! With the funny voice!'

'YES. Marvin the Martian! Weird as fuck!'

And we laugh a lot for a long time.

I love Bel.

Thank heavens for Bel. I never would've got through this thing alive without her.

Thank heavens for my boy Jay. Thank the *stars* for him. I mean, he's eighteen and supposedly an adult now, off doing biology, and I know I'm supposed to be helping him through all this. And I do. My God, I do my best. But he helps me too. He may not realise it, but he helps me get through the week with his texts checking up on me.

And thank heavens for my shop. For my little quilting shop and the flat above it, because without that, I'd be sleeping on a quilt on the shop floor at night. So, thank heavens for the shop and the little flat – one bedroom for me and the sofa-bed in the living room-diner-kitchenette for Jay when he's home from uni, and thankfully a separate WC and bathroom so we never have to bother the other person if we just want a wee. These things matter.

Downstairs is my quilting shop. I sell sewing supplies and material and all the stuff you need to be a quilter and seamstress. Hence the name: *Sew What?* I like its vibe. It tells you what the shop sells, but it does it in a sarcastic, kick-ass way. You wanna sew? What do you wanna sew? And so fucking what if you do? Don't let your other half give you a hard time about spending all your money on sewing stuff. It's nobody's business but yours, so fill your boots. If they give you any grief, just tell them: Sew What? If I could have, I'd have called it *Sew Fucking What?* But I can't see the elders of Lincoln letting that one through committee . . .

Thus, I'm fifty, soon to be divorced, I've sunk all my savings into my shop and I live in a shoebox. And my ex – soon-to-be officially ex-husband, whenever the goddamn divorce comes through – dropped a bombshell when we started divorce proceedings: after the sale of the house, there would basically be no money left, as he had massive secret debts from a bad investment into a friend's start-up, which I knew nothing about. So, I've left my marriage with basically zilch. But, as Bel said to me the night I decided once and for all to leave my ex, 'Whatever happens next, it can't be as bad as being with that total twatface.'

I immediately changed his name in my phone from Gareth to Twatface. It's so gratifying to see Twatface pop up whenever he sends a passive-aggressive little missive about the divorce or the house sale or Jay – or James as he always calls him, in that weird formal way he has, the pompous financial advisor even at home, talking to Jay and me like minions at his office.

And Bel was right. She's always right. All of my friends listened to me try to make sense of why I was so dreadfully unhappy for years, and they were so careful, so politic about how they approached criticising him – because it's so hard, isn't it, when you know your friend's partner is a wanker? You can't risk saying it in case they don't split up and then you have to face them every time you go round. But Bel told me that she hated Gareth, that she hated the way I looked when he was around – fearful, cowed, eager to please – that he was a bloody nasty piece of work and that I'd be much better off if I left him.

Hearing those words was the push I needed to face my future alone. I'm so grateful for her honesty. I'm so grateful for a friend who'll tell you unpleasant truths, but with love.

I look across the smoky space between us in her shed and we're talking about her baby boy Barney now and how bloody difficult new motherhood is. Bel is finding it particularly hard, as she's nearly forty and doesn't have the energy she used to. I had Jay at thirty-two and I was knackered enough then. She's looking through the shed window and says, 'I'm glad the snow's heaving it down as it'll cover up my shit-hole of a garden in a pristine swathe of white and I can pretend it's as lovely as it used to be.'

'Don't beat yourself up,' I say. Bel's gardening has always been exquisite, wherever she's lived, even when she had no more than a windowsill. She grows plants from seed on her dining room table and fills the pots and borders with vegetables and flowers, year on year. Or at least she used to, before a difficult pregnancy and Barney. 'You'll get back to it. In the meantime, you should hire a hunky young gardener and ogle at him from the French windows; get all Lady Chatterley on his ass.'

'Hey, I'm married, you may recall, very happily.' And I do recall indeed. Bel and Craig are a gorgeous couple, madly in love, still having sex all the time despite the baby and so sweet and nice to one another, as well as having a healthy dose of sarcasm towards each other and life in general. They met later in life than some, when they were both in their late thirties, both teachers (her, maths, and him, design and technology – or as he calls it, the Department of Colouring In) and while they were both recovering from crappy previous relationships. Baby Barney came along pretty soon and was very much wanted and adored. It's the marriage I never had and always hankered after, but never begrudged for Bel, because I love the bones of her, but also she's had her fair share of arsehole boyfriends to contend with over the years and deserves the fairy tale ending.

'Yeah, you're married, Bel, but you're not dead.'

Then Bel sits up and looks excited and says, 'Oh Frankie, you're gonna have such a *laugh* when you start dating. I will live vicariously through you!'

'Oh my God, no. I'm not dating.'

'Why not?! For fuck's sake, Frankie, you're divorced, *not dead*. Or you soon will be. Divorced, that is. Not dead.'

'I never want to have anything to do with men ever again!'

'Everyone says that. But you'll change your mind.'

'Well,' I say, and take a deep toke before passing it over, 'I must admit, I've not had a decent shag in decades.'

'There, you see? You're free now for the first time in twenty-odd years and there's a whole world of men out there. You have your new life ahead of you, definitely some random shagging to begin with then who knows, perhaps love will come along.'

'There may well be shagging but there will *not* be love. I'm telling you now: I will never love a man again.'

'A-ha, well, we shall see . . . Now gimme your phone.' I squint suspiciously at her and drag it out of my dungarees pocket, handing it over. 'Scooch over here then, babe, and let's get cracking. As you know, I am the goddamn MASTER of online dating. It's how I caught Craig, of course. And I mean caught. There was nothing random about it. The thing you need to know about online dating is it's all a giant game. You have to *out-date* the dating apps. And you have to learn the rules and use them to your advantage. Then you win.'

'I've never been very good at games,' I say miserably, moving over to shove up beside Bel on the potting bench. 'I always get shafted on Mayfair with hotels on it.'

In the short space of time it takes to utter those words and park my butt next to Bel's, we've lit up a new smoke – fuck, it's so good to smoke a joint and know I'm not going to get the third degree from Twatface about it when I go home; smoking weed is one of my first rebellions against his dictatorship – phone-whizz Bel has downloaded two new dating apps: eHarmony (sounds nice) and Plenty of Fish (sounds rough).

'Right, here we go!' says Bel, her eyes gleaming.

'You're enjoying this far too much,' I say, feeling a little sick with nerves. Can I do this? I haven't dated anyone for over twenty years and never online. What horrors await in these virtual dens of iniquity?

'And so will *you* be, imminently, mark my words. Now shut up and listen. I'm starting you on two contrasting apps. eHarmony is for relationships, POF is for sex.'

'Can't I have both at the same time?'

'In an ideal world, yeah. But to begin with, you'd be best off separating the two goals. They just confuse things. So, look. Here's eHarmony.'

The app is set out with background images of lakes

and mountains, empty beaches and cycle rides, making everything look chilled and homely, middle-aged and non-threatening.

'This one's for old folk, isn't it,' I state.

'You got it. But I figured you might want to talk to some civilised gents.'

'Oh, I do. I think . . .'

'So, look. You upload a few photos of yourself here and type in your profile here. You then answer all these questions about yourself and it gives you suggestions of eligible chaps based on your answers. Do all that later, at your leisure. It's all terribly nice on there, although the only downside is that in order to reply to any messages and see the guys' pictures, you have to pay. Set that up later on your card too. But don't forget to change automatic renewal in your settings straight after, or the bastards will charge you for another month or whatever, without telling you.'

'Crikey, it's a minefield.'

'It is!' says Bel emphatically. 'You've got to have your wits about you. You are so . . . babe in the woods, babe. You are so Bambi, prancing into the meadow, before his mum gets shot – BLAM!'

'Bloody hell, all right. No need to dredge up childhood trauma.'

Then Bel swipes off that app with nimble dexterity and brings up the other one, a totally different kettle of fish. POF looks like the Wild West in comparison. No lakes, no cycling. Black, blue and white, with harsh, basic text marching across the screen. Bel sets me up a quick profile, just my first name, and ignores all the details. Pictures of random men leap out in lurid colour and Bel starts swiping left, left, left, right.

'What does that mean? What are you doing?!' I say in horror.

'Okay, listen. POF is a whole different story. eHarmony is like The Wig and Mitre on a Tuesday evening and Plenty of Fish is Sugarcubes on a Saturday night.'

'Jesus CHRIST!' I say and facepalm.

'Look, you want sex, don't you?'

'Well, yes.'

'Then POF is what you need. Tinder too, though you have to wait to match before they can message and you have to pay to see your likes. On POF, anyone can message you at any time.'

'Anyone?' I say, aghast. 'Is that . . . safe?'

'No! That's why you have to get with the programme, babe. Grow up. You've gotta ditch the Bambi act and take control. Filter out the weirdos by blocking them. Keep on the good ones. Test their veracity, then choose who you want to see, where and for how long. If you play the game, you can have any kind of man you want, any kind of sex you want, any time of the day or night. You don't believe me, do you?'

I shake my head and pass over the joint I realise I've been hogging. 'No.'

'Well, you shall see, my pretty. Okay look. Now you're set up, next step is to fill out your profiles. Nice and elegant for eHarmony, fun and flirty for POF. Then do some selfies. Tasteful and beautiful for the old guys, high-class hooker for the fish. I'd say we'll do some now, but . . . you know, you look like Captain Oates about to leave the tent.'

'I've got a couple of recent photos, from Craig's birthday bash the other month. Gareth was away for that business weekend thing, so I was allowed to put on make-up.'

Bel makes a sad face and gives me a quick rough one-armed hug. 'Jeez, woman. The shit you put up with before you rode up on a white charger and rescued yourself.'

I feel momentarily desolate at the thought of the person I was, only weeks before, frightened to express myself, treading on eggshells, never right, never good enough. But not anymore . . .

'I like the sound of Plenty of Fish,' I say and grin.

'That's the spirit! It's a madhouse but an absolute hoot, as long as you take care and don't be a naïve fool.'

'Okay, so give me the low-down. What are the rules of the game?' I say, taking my phone back to look for a couple of pics from our night out. I find a nice one of me smiling, where the rosy lights of the pub have my face a little bleached out so you can't see all the wrinkles around my eyes. Nice. I pop that one on eHarmony. After some scrolling I find another option, where Bel and I are linked arm in arm, looking up at a very drunken Craig who'd said, 'Smile, you sexy biatches!' and we gave him proper foxy looks and you can see a bit of my cleavage. It's not exactly high-class hooker, but it's about as foxy as I've dared to be in recent years. Though, maybe all that is about to change. I crop out Bel and pop that one on Plenty of Fish.

Bel stands, pushes her hands deep in her pockets and stares at me. That's her I-mean-business stance.

'Now look, I don't want you turning up as a re-enactment on *Crimewatch*, so listen up. Don't give away any details about yourself that could reveal where you live, where your shop is. Don't tell them your surname or your kid's name or any names that could easily be traced back to you. Don't give out your phone number or any other contact details. No links to your social media. Nothing, not yet. Stay on the app. Just chat in a general way, about general things. Have a laugh, flirt and so forth. But don't tell them your bloody life story, as you are wont to do.'

'I really am wont to do that. I'm a terrible blabbermouth.'

'I KNOW! So, none of that. These aren't just strangers in a pub. They're worse than that. Loads of them won't be who they say they are, or the guys in the pictures. Have you heard of catfish?'

'With the whiskers? I think they use them for navigating or something.'

Bel rolls her eyes then reaches for the joint, which I've been hogging again. 'Oh gawd . . . all right. Now, catfish is youth parlance for liars online pretending to be someone else. They use fake pictures, fake names, fake profiles. They're usually scammers who want money, but sometimes they're just sad fucks who hate themselves and want to lure you in with their fake persona.'

'I'm kidding, you idiot – of course I know what catfish are. I had to be savvy about some of this stuff, raising a kid. Plus I get them on Facebook all the time and I just delete them. But why do it on a dating app, though? As soon as you meet, it'd be obvious.'

'Nah, these arseholes don't want to meet. They just want sexting.'

I grimace, then look sheepish.

'Oh blimey, you've never sexted, have you?'

'Nope. I mean, Bel, I've been in a relationship with a frigid sociopath for decades and it began when phones were in their infancy! Sexting wasn't really a thing back then.'

'Well, it probably was but you've always been late to the party, babe. We'll circle back to the art of sexting later. Now then, let's get on your phone and go fishing.'

Bel rubs her hands together with glee, then we settle back down on the potting bench and she starts swiping through the profiles. And what a motley crew they are. So. Many. Ugly. Men. I've literally never seen so many ugly men in one place, except perhaps lurching out of Sugarcubes at 2am in my dim and distant youth.

'Ah nice, here we go,' says Bel and stops on a gorgeous blond bloke, looks around early thirties, lovely muscly arms with some tasteful tats, square jaw, perfect tan. And those green eyes . . .

'Yes please . . .' I say, all but drooling.

'A-ha, wait and see,' she says.

She clicks on the picture and up pop a couple more, one where he's pulling up his T-shirt to show perfect abs with a lascivious look in his sparkling eyes. Behind him is some holiday destination, palm trees and white square buildings.

'Catfish,' declares Bel.

'Why? How do you know?'

'Nobody actually looks like that. Well, addendum – some men do. I've had the odd one with abs like that, in my dating days. But in general, only models look this good and pose in places like that.'

'He could be on holiday. He could be a gym rat.' I want to take my phone back, so I can message this muscled Adonis and take my first steps into the brave, new world of random online sexting.

'Highly unlikely. Okay, so to ascertain further, we look at his name. Read that out.'

'*Steven John*.'

'Dead giveaway. Two first names. Catfish so often use two first names. I've no idea why! It must be in the Wankers' Playbook, page one.'

'Gosh,' I mutter, looking back at the gorgeous one with a newly critical eye. 'How else do you know it's a catfish?'

'Okay, so assuming that we'll give him the benefit of the doubt, that he's unfeasibly good-looking and called by two first names, let's look further. He lives in Lincoln and claims to be forty-eight. Does he look forty-eight to you?'

'Not like any forty-eight-year-old I know.'

'Exactly, they do that because they want to prey on older women. They think they're more desperate, the arseholes. Now look at his profile text. Read that.'

i am honest men no lie or cheating my wife die trajic and i look for longtime love of life give all cash for her tight nestegg i swearing you

We both burst out laughing. 'Holy fuck,' I say, crying with laughter now. 'He's allergic to grammar. Oh my God, this swiping business is the best entertainment I've had in ages.'

'See?! I knew you'd love it. Now does that sound like Steven John, forty-eight, from Lincoln?' says Bel, taking hold of my duffel coat lapels and shaking me to attention while I'm still wheezing with laughter at *tight nestegg*. 'Or rather does it sound like a scammer whose first language is not English, perchance? And he's pretending he speaks English fluently to go with this fake English name?'

'Okay, okay. But even if their English just isn't that good, that's not a good enough reason to block someone, is it? Come on!'

'No, it's not just that. As I've said, there's a bunch of other tell-tale signs of a catfish, like they're immediately crazy about you, or they want to get you off the dating app onto another chat app like WhatsApp straight away. Plus they might use a real person's photo, like David Gandy or even Paul Hollywood, though God knows why anyone would want to pretend to be the latter. And their jobs are usually humanitarian or butch or both, like UN surgeon or US military. But about the language, it's not about their English not being great, it's about the fact that they often pretend to be English and can't carry it off. Or they may well pretend to not be able to speak English very well to play the sympathy card!'

'Ah, right, yeah. That could well make sense then. I've seen these bot things on Facebook, that include a web link or phone number in their comment or message.'

'Yeah, you'll get those on dating apps too. So, once you get good at spotting the scammers, you can either block and report immediately or you can chat with them a while before you block them, string them along a bit, for shits and giggles – it's great fun! Waste their time a bit just like they're wasting the time of countless women. But be safe. Catfish and liars are not always as obvious as this idiot. Go with your gut: it's always right, ALWAYS. And don't believe a word any of these fuckers say until you've verified them and even then . . .'

'But how on earth do you verify them?'

Suddenly we hear Barney launch into screaming mode and although Bel knows that Craig is perfectly capable of dealing with it, she always feels guilty about leaving them alone, despite me telling her not to.

'Time to be Mum again,' she says and stubs out the joint. We both hop off the potting bench. 'Look, message me tomorrow night and I'll give you the low-down on verification et cetera. Get tarted up a bit and take some new selfies. The best profiles have a few photos, not just one. I've turned your notifications off on your phone for those apps, otherwise the DING-DING-DING will drive you insane, what with all the millions of messages you'll get. And you *will* get millions, you'll see. You're a total fox.'

'Thanks chick,' I say. 'For everything.'

'Ah, it's nothing. Got me out of the house, even if it's just to the shed. Back we go, back to reality.'

'Back to the acting,' I say and open the door, the night's chill rushing in on the wintry air. We step outside onto the crunchy fresh snow, then Bel grabs my arm and pulls me in for a hug.

'You've got this, girl,' she says quietly in my ear and we hug. At this comforting human contact and the blast of cold air, the real world feels all too present once again. My fear and loneliness grip me and I start to sniffle a bit. Bel checks me out and knows I'm about to get all emotional. I look at her worried face and her care makes my eyes fill with tears.

'Don't be nice to me!' I say, knowing it'll make me sob.

'Don't be sad, be angry. Fuck you, Mars, remember? FYM!'

'Yes! FYM,' I repeat and stamp my feet in determination, yet also trying to keep warm.

'Shout it. Shout it out to the night sky, you badass bitch!' shouts Bel and laughs.

I stand with my arms outstretched, tip my head back and yell up into the night sky, 'FUCK YOU, MARS!'

Barney's screams have now reached a crescendo to match me. We look over and Craig is watching us from the window, the bairn wriggling in his arms, Craig's face nonplussed at why I'm hollering a quote from *The Martian* into the night.

'He'll be thinking, *Those mad bitches are at it again*,' I say and we snort with laughter as we trot over to Bel's back door. A quick final hug and I'm off round the side of the house to walk home. We live around the corner from each other in Lincoln, in the historical bit, where the cathedral and the castle are. She lives in a little cul-de-sac off Cecil Street. Her house is a very sweet detached cuboid, with four windows and a door, just like a child's drawing. She has pots full of plants and a bench outside, with a little fence and a gate to the street. I totter off up the street, then trudge my way down Bailgate. I only live down the road from here, my shop occupying the ideal spot for punters on Steep Hill (which, if you've never been to Lincoln, you won't know is the most literal name of any road ever).

I plod along through the snow, the cold night air soon sobering me up, as well as the thought of going back to that pokey little flat, alone. It's late, nearly midnight and the streets are mostly empty. I quickly begin to feel sorry for myself, moping about being truly alone in the world at this moment. No house, no husband, no money, no kid around and no mum. When she died ten years ago, all sense of security left with her. Dad was living abroad, had been for years, with little contact. But I'd had my son and my husband and we had the house and I felt safe, sort of. I felt at least that I had my own family to take care of and that would keep me busy and stop me missing Mum too much (which it didn't, but I'd got through it, though the grief still shocks me sometimes, as real and sudden as a burglar in your home).

But now it's just me. I feel my mouth turn down and my eyes prick with self-pitying tears. I start down Steep Hill towards my shop, when my feet skid and skitter and I slip up and land on my arse, then tip backwards and there I am, lying on my back in the street, staring up into the snow-speckled sky on a Sunday night in January, with nobody to rush outside and find me, take care of me, dust me off and settle me down with a cuppa and ask if I'm okay. So I don't move. But then, lying there, I realise that even when I had someone, when I had Gareth, he would not have been so caring as to do that small thing. He would've stood and stared at me, shaking his head at my foolishness. Even the boyfriends I had before him weren't very nice. I seemed to have an innate ability to pick out men who had something missing in their brains, in their genes, I suppose – the caring gene, the one that makes you look at another person and empathise with them.

The boys and then men I typically fell for were charming and witty, clever and impressive, luring me in with their patter. I'd always fallen in love fast and not had time to question their validity, heartily ignoring the veritable carnival of red flags each one was waving. In fact, nobody talked about red flags the last time I was single, over two decades ago. People are savvier about narcissists these days and about coercive control and all that abusive shit that so many partners have to deal with in their relationships. And once you're in love, you put up with that crap because you love them. And because they do it gradually, at least, the clever ones do.

It's like the frog in the pan: as the water warms slowly, you don't realise you're being cooked. It happens so steadily, in tiny increments, over years – the little comments putting you down, the mockery, the control, the denigration of family and friends, the increasing isolation and dependence – that by the time the water is hot, you had no idea it was even happening. You'd become acclimatised to misery.

Until you get out, that is. And now I'm out, I can look back on those two decades with Gareth and think, how did I never see it? How did I think that being sad and scared in my own home was normal? It was a gradual process at first, my escape: inklings of standing up to him, then more arguments as I did so, then a realisation that this didn't have to be it, this didn't have to be the rest of my life. I first told him last summer that I was going to be leaving him as soon as we could get things sorted, just before Jay went to uni. I was pretty sure Twatface was seeing someone by that point, but he never admitted it. We put the house on the market and I started looking for shops to rent and we engaged solicitors for the divorce. The first couple of weeks of September it went okay and I thought, yeah, we can do this amicably. But something snapped in him and, as letters and emails mounted up about the divorce and selling the house, he got increasingly angsty and erratic, to the point where I was even more frightened there than I had been all those years living Under his Eye, as it says in *The Handmaid's Tale*. By December, I'd got my shop lease sorted and I was going to do my best to drag us through one last family Christmas together, for old times' sake, but no. I had to get myself out to somewhere that felt safe. And even then, once I was free, expecting the house sale to set me up for the next phase of my life, I find out he had secret debts, which will leave us with nothing left after the house sale. So after all those years together and living in that house together and improving it and bearing him a son, I'm left with nothing. Not a penny. Yes, the frog jumped out. And thank heavens for that. But this frog has sod all security for its little froggy future.

I'm lying on my back in the snow in the street, staring

at the sky and thinking about myself as that frog, boiling to death, slowly, so slowly. But at least I did eventually jump out. I may be on my back in the street, vastly alone and with no nest egg or pension, insignificant beneath the indifferent stars with snowflakes falling casually on my face, but at least I am free.

'Fuck. You. Mars,' I say with a croaky voice. I'm not that person anymore. I'm the one that got herself out. And now I'm finally liberated, I'm going to enjoy myself. I'm going to get on those dating apps and have some fun. Once I get off my arse in the snow, that is.

I drag myself up from the ground and stagger down the alley beside my shop. I make my way up the back stairs to the door and let myself in. It's nippy in the flat, as the heating went off hours ago. I'm wet from my snow-bed and shivery cold, so I fall onto the sofa fully clothed in dungarees, jumper, mittens, scarf and bobble hat, then make the mistake of reclining, my head on the sequinned cushion Jay gave me for my last birthday, which looks silver one way then when you smooth out the sequins the other way spells out WHAT THE ACTUAL FUCK beneath a picture of Winnie the Pooh looking confused. Within seconds, I'm asleep.

And that's where I wake up in the morning, as the sound of someone knocking insistently on the door to the flat drags me out of my slumber. I struggle to open my eyes and my left cheek feels prickly. I've slept on the sequinned cushion with the little bastards digging into my face all night. I must've been exhausted (and wrecked) to sleep so soundly.

The knocking persists so I sit bolt upright and stumble to the front door, vaguely perceiving that it's Monday morning and my shop is closed on Mondays, so at least I'm not late opening up. The knocking is louder now and my mind starts racing through all the possibilities. (Is it the police? Are they here to tell me that Jay is missing or injured or dead?? Or is it the Amazon driver with that book I ordered called *How To Be An Optimist*?) I fling open the door and there is my ex, Twatface, suited and booted, looking perfectly in order. And here I am, in dungarees, jumper, mittens, scarf and bobble hat. He looks at me as if he's just found a pubic hair in his carbonara.

CHAPTER 2
Slide Into My DMs

'What the hell have you done to your face?' he says, with a superior smirk.

I reach up with my mitten, a wholly useless gesture.

'What do you want?' I say in a monotone.

'You've got little circles all over your cheek and you stink of dope. Been sleeping on that dumb cushion have you, on the sofa, fully clothed, stoned on a Sunday night? How . . . bohemian.'

It takes all my strength not to tell him to go fuck himself. I know that's what he wants – not to go fuck himself (or actually, he might do, knowing his capacity for self-admiration) but for me to lose my cool. I know I look utterly ridiculous but I hold myself up as straight and tall as I can and I repeat, 'What do you want?'

He's standing there, smirking. Mid-brown-grey hair perfectly coiffured with a crisp side parting, tamed by gel (but sticks up in clumps when he's just woken up). He's the same height as me, five foot seven, which is fine by me. I mean, I dated shorter men than me before I met him, but he's always had a chip on his shoulder about it, a Napoleon complex, I reckon. Then he pushes past me – yes, he actually shoves me with his elbow – and walks straight into my flat, heads for my armchair (the purple one Mum gave me all those years ago) and plonks himself down. He reaches over for the little mosaic table Bel gave me and drags it from its position towards him, then throws his keys down along with a balled-up, snotty tissue. He sits back, shoving his feet under the table, far too comfortably.

I take a deep breath. He's not been in the flat since the day in December that I leased the shop and then it was just a cursory glance. I don't know what excuse he'll come up with for why he's here now, first thing on a Monday morning. But I know him better than anyone and I know exactly what he's doing. This is all about control. He's pushed his way in here, into my territory and he's literally got his feet under the table, as the saying goes. It still riles him that I actually escaped, used my own savings to set up this shop and get myself away from him. He cannot bear it that I saved myself.

'Don't move my furniture,' I say, calmly.

He stares at me, pretending to be bemused.

'Don't. Move. My. Furniture,' I repeat, my voice still low and steady.

He looks blank and takes the keys and the snot-rag off and shoves them in his pocket, then pushes the table back to roughly its place. It's a small victory, but it gives me some strength.

'Why are you here?' I continue.

'I've come to inform you about recent events of which you ought to be privy.'

Jesus Christ, to think I used to be impressed by the way

he talks. What a pompous ass. I wait for him to go on. I'm not going to participate in a conversation with him if I can help it. I want to get him out as soon as possible.

'I've told James by text this morning and now I'm telling you, that I'm in a committed relationship with Melissa Pridgeon.'

Melissa Pridgeon??

Melissa, who lives at number 9 with her three kids? Who, one night seven years ago, we saw behind the bins during her husband's birthday party snogging his brother then getting discovered and shouting across Willows Close, 'Think about the kids, Paul!' before pushing the brother into the bins whereupon he fell over and so did the bin, the plastic and glass recycling spilling out all over the close and getting whipped up by the wind. Meanwhile, she rushed around trying to pick it all up and me and Gareth were standing at our window watching the whole sorry farce unfold. THAT Melissa Pridgeon? Well, let's face it, Pridgeon is such a weird name, like someone trying to say pigeon with their mouth full. There can't be more than one Melissa Pridgeon in Lincoln, surely, if not the entire world. I didn't know it was her, but I KNEW he was up to something! It's good to be vindicated, to know that my gut was right. But to be actually confronted with the truth of it . . . well, it hurts like hell. It feels like shit.

I know he's examining my face for shock, that same self-satisfied smirk playing around his lips.

'And?' is all I say.

'And as my partner, I will be moving in with her for the foreseeable future and then, once all this business is concluded, we will be buying a house together.'

'And her three kids?' I was determined not to show any

interest in his ridiculous news, but now I'm too curious to stop.

'The older two have left home by now, as you know, while the younger one will be living with their father much of the time.'

He looks at me defiantly, as if urging me to comment on this. All I can think is, the poor bastards. All of them, her included and especially the youngest kid, a girl, around twelve or thirteen now, I think. To escape from a narcissist feels like a triumph. But when you're confronted with the next poor woman who's fallen for their charm, it sours into a hollow victory. If only I could go over to number 9 Willows Close right now and say, 'Run away, Melissa Pridgeon! Run very far away and don't look back!' But, of course, I'd be seen as the crazy ex, trying to ruin Gareth's life out of spite. She'd never believe me. I don't know Melissa really, just the odd comment when we put the bins out, or when our kids careered past each other on bikes or rollerblades in the close, but she always seemed all right, nice enough, rather acerbic when she told her kids off, but generally a bit harried by life.

I felt for her, with her husband gone (who knows what happened with the brother, but he never came round) and three kids and a full-time job to cope with. And now, she's shacking up with my ex, or rather, he will be shacking up with her, in her house, at her expense, no doubt. And when they buy a house together, God knows what he'll be contributing towards that, if anything. Poor cow. Then, the next question came to me. *How long has this been going on?* During the last few years of our relationship, I'd become convinced he was seeing someone. I was sure I heard a phone in the house go off once, a message sound that I didn't recognise. But he made up some excuse to explain it about an old SIM card, but it was too much information and sounded like bullshit. And he'd be gone for hours and talked about meetings, but I never had any evidence of where he'd been. He always kept home and work so separate, so I didn't have anyone I could call to check on him. So yeah, plenty of signs of an affair were there. But he never admitted it, though I told him over and over it would be okay, that it was time for us to call it a day anyway and if I knew he was in love with someone else, it would all make more sense and help us to make a break, finally. But he never, ever admitted to it. I look at him now and his eyes are willing me to ask him more. Well, I'm not going to play that game, or any of his games anymore.

'Anything else?' I say.

'No. I just thought you should be informed.'

'The only thing you should've informed me about years ago was that you'd pissed away our future on your dodgy mate's dodgy start-up.'

He scowled at me and began, 'That business had every chance of—'

'Don't start all that again with me. I don't want to hear it.'

I have so much more I want to say, but it has all been said before. And it would be as much use as pissing in the wind and if you're a woman who's pissing in the wind, all you get is a wet leg. The damage is done and he'll never take responsibility for his actions. He over-invested in a friend's new business using a massive re-mortgage, all without my knowledge. When we were first together, he had his own house and I'd moved in. Later, we married and had Jay, but we never got round to putting my name on the mortgage. So, when he decided to invest in this start-up, he went to one of those new online mortgage lenders and got them to give him a big loan to invest, using the house as collateral. He was so sure about his mate's business, he even agreed to an interest-only loan. But the new business utterly collapsed and he lost all his money, and once the house sale process began, of course, the online mortgage company wanted their money back. Once divorce proceedings began, even though my name wasn't on the mortgage, I'd expected to receive 50% of the house sale, as we'd been married for a long time. But then I found out the truth, that all of the money for the house sale would go on paying back this crazy loan and all the fees associated with the divorce. There'd be little to nothing left. And in one fell swoop, Twatface had fucked our financial futures. It's as simple and awful as that. I could rail against it till the cows came home, but it won't get me our money back. A lesson to be learnt there: never trust anyone with your financial future. Nobody. Not even your partner, husband, wife, whatever. You must be involved at every step. I learnt this too late, unfortunately.

'When it comes to investments, nothing is—'

'I said I don't wanna hear it!'

He looks at me coldly. That icy stare used to frighten me. Now, sitting in my mum's chair with his sad little tale of broken homes, he just looks small.

'Don't you wish to discuss the arrangement with Melissa Pridgeon?' he says, trying to reel me back in. I hate this game-playing shit he does so much and I hate that I still have to deal with this wanker in my life. I want to say, *I'd rather play water polo with an orca*. But no, he isn't going to have the satisfaction of my humour. He isn't going to have the satisfaction of anything. He's going to leave.

'No. And text next time. You've no need to come here, ever.'

He ignores that and ploughs on, 'I've informed James because he needs to know the situation at home, for when he comes to stay in the holidays. You realise that this pathetic little flat you have here is far too small to be a base for him at any time. I'd be surprised if he even visits, especially if he wishes to bring a friend or girlfriend with him. You'll have to make other arrangements to see him when you can. For Melissa's daughter, we will have a bedroom for when she stays with us and James will always have a bedroom for himself, as long as he needs it. This place you've ended up in . . . and seeing the state you are in presently . . . well, I'm sure you'd agree that neither are suitable for James or his requirements these days.'

The look of twisted triumph on his face is goading me, but I hold my resolve.

'You need to leave now.'

He watches me for a few moments, clearly a little surprised I haven't taken the bait. And at last, he gets up and goes to the door. As he steps over the threshold, he turns to say something and I shove the door with my shoulder and it slams in his face.

I immediately message Jay on Instagram, the only place I can guarantee he'll be online at most times of day.

Just had a visit from your dad. He said he texted you about Melissa Pridgeon?? Just checking you're ok, honey. Here if you wanna talk about it all. <3 <3 <3

I wait a few minutes and there's no reply. He must be in lectures, I guess. I sigh, willing him to respond. I'm worried about how Jay will take it. Then I think, *How am I taking it?* I should feel triumphant. I handled Twatface so well! I didn't break under the mudslide of his superiority. I didn't rise to his petty jibes. But, oh God, I feel empty. I don't know whether to scream or cry. Then I catch sight of myself in the mirror. I look just like the time before Jay was born when Bel and I camped out under the stars at Avebury Stone Circle in our sleeping bags and when we woke up in the morning a bunch of American schoolkids were standing around staring at us and one said scathingly, 'When did you last wash your hair? Ten million years ago?'

What a bloody shitshow of a mess I look and to think I stood there in all dignity against Twatface's nasty little newsflash and I looked like THIS?

I tear off my mittens and hat and scarf and coat and throw them on the floor. Then I start crying, blubbering like Baby Barney with a shitty nappy, all snot and tears. I feel terrible, I'm in shock and I feel hollowed out inside, like a Jack-O'-Lantern, except I'm not the happily evil pumpkin, I'm the slimy thready seedy gunk left on the counter in a sticky mess.

Gareth has a girlfriend. Not just a girlfriend, but a 'partner' in a 'committed relationship'. (Urgh, the almighty prick and his affected terminology.) It's not that I'm at all jealous of her, of him, not a scintilla of envy for the whole sorry mess of it. But he's got one over on me and he knows it. He sat here in my flat with the gold medal of his superior situation shining brightly i.e. *I'm fucking someone else and there's nothing you can do about it, you sad middle-aged bitch in your silly little shop and your no-sex-life and your duffel coat.* I slope back into the living room-diner-kitchenette and slump down on the sofa. I carry on crying for a while, letting it flow out. Then, the mosaic table catches my eye, the one he moved, then moved back, but it's out of place, the invisible handprints of his crass attempt at ownership all over it. And I stare at that table and I think, that bastard took up twenty years of my life. And now he wants to take up space in the only place I could ever call my own in all that time. Well . . . fuck that. Fuck that and fuck him and FUCK YOU, MARS.

I'm not going to let him get me down, let him beat me or let him stop me. I get up, go to the shower and wash away the night, the morning, the tears and all the sticky pumpkin-entrailed-misery of it all. I get dressed in my favourite combo of joggers (black and yellow Batman ones) and sweatshirt (cornflower blue with TELL YOUR CAT I SAID PSSPSSPSS on it). I blow-dry my hair so it looks really great (*at least I have good hair*, I think, as I brush it through, long and thick and dark with some nice toffee-coloured highlights. My hair is my crowning glory, as Mum used to say). I am a free woman with people to talk to and places to go (but not the places and the going quite yet, because I've no bra on right now). But people to talk to? Namely, fresh new guys? Oh yeah, baby. I make a sandwich with healthy stuff like houmous and avocado and purple lettuce leaves then ruin it all with a big handful of roast chicken crisps on the side. Sod it, the Get Fit plan starts tomorrow. I get comfy on the sofa and start munching, then I pick up my phone – still no reply from Jay and my message is as yet not Seen – and now I'm ready to dive into the fun and fucked-up world of online dating.

Holy SHIT, I've got dozens of messages already! On both apps! I start on POF, as something tells me it's going to be more fun. The first few I read are minimal, to say the least.

One or two words from each guy and not exactly inspiring or even personalised.

Hey
Hey
Hi
Hey
Hey gorgeous
Hey sexy
Hey sexx
WYD
Wanna shag c

Then the first one with more than one line: his first message reads:

How are

And his second:

How are you

Well, he nailed it eventually.

The next profile has only one pic of a guy called Roger, forty-two, dressed in a navy-blue onesie with every body part covered in skin-tight lycra, including his entire head, taken in the mirror of a hotel bedroom, with beige walls, beige vertical blinds and beige padded headboard on a wall. His message reads:

Wanna meet me here?

Do I wanna meet him there? Well, obviously his outfit is fine but the hotel décor is a disgrace.

The next two have the best usernames so far, *Lickylady53* (whose profile reads only '*Nice guy not looking for a slag*') and *PeckerUp69*.

It really is a wayward wilderness on POF . . .

So I go over to eHarmony to see if the quality improves. And I find this magnum opus from Terence, aged fifty-four:

Hello Frankie.

The question of whether or not a friend can also be a lover is one that has engaged my mind for many years off and on, more on than off, and more in the mind than in the heart or loins. Can friendship truly win out over passion and can long relationships ever sustain themselves over time, or instead, like a body lacking in vitamin C, can we eventually find we have scurvy of the heart and do not instead wish for grace and another idea is to do with coastal shelves eroding, yes? For is it possible to maintain a true yet bloated connection of

Yes, it finishes halfway through a sentence. Wow. Years of psych study right there. Either that or he's high as a satellite. He should've stuck to Hello Frankie. It all went downhill from there, like a fucking avalanche.

The next one is from Reginald, aged seventy-nine:

I'd like to start with an apology, as I wanted to message you this morning, but unfortunately the boys in blue flagged me down and told me off for using my phone while driving. But when I showed them your beauteous profile picture, they were so impressed, they told me that if you messaged me back, I would avoid points on my licence or a fine. Could you help a fellow out, my dear?

Well, it's original, I guess. And the guy can use punctuation. But I reckon he's sending that message to everyone on the site, plus he's nearly thirty years older than me at seventy-nine, and – not to be ageist or anything – but my love life right now will not be including the number seventy in it, sorry Reginald. A silver fox is all very well, but I need one who has the energy for a decent shag and I'm not sure seventy-nine is gonna cut it.

That's it for eHarmony so far, a grand total of two messages. Plenty of Fish has about fifty messages, more coming every minute, no word of a lie. I trawl through them and most are the *Hey* variety, quite a few ask for my WhatsApp or phone number, then I come across this little beauty and see from the app that he's online right now:

Hey beatifull lady I want taking u to most wonderful vacation of ur life give me your whatsapp so I can know you better dear and show you most beatfully place in the earth

His profile pic is of an unfeasibly good-looking guy in his twenties against a tropical backdrop and says he's fifty-one. We have a catfish, ladies and gents!

'Come to Mama,' I whisper and dying-fly my fingers like Tom Hanks going in on *You've Got Mail* and I reply:

Why, where are you?

Instantly, he replies!

I show u where give me whatsapp

I'm not on WhatsApp.

Why not how about insta

Sure, darling. My Insta is: @youareacatfish

I try find u on there but cant so pls send me messg

OK, try my other account: @stopwastingmytime

O no again I cant find messg me baby

Now this is a mystery. Try my Snapchat: Youareatwat69

By this point, I'm laughing so hard, I can't see my phone. I screenshot the whole thing to send to Bel later, then block and report him as a scammer. I could've gone on all day, but I'm sure there will be plenty more of these wankers. I think I've found my new hobby: catfish-fishing.

So I peruse more and find a couple on POF that don't seem insane, are within ten years of my own age, can string a sentence together and are vaguely nice-looking. The best so far is a guy called Guy (yes, really) whose message is a GIF of a kid sliding down a slide and falling off the end onto his head, and he's put *Me sliding into your DMs like . . .* It's very silly but it makes me laugh. He's very nice-looking too and he's forty-eight. I reply with a friendly ***Hahahaaa that's the best message I've had all day. But that's not saying much. How are you?*** But he's not online, so no more banter as yet. Then I set about paying for eHarmony so I can reply to messages – if I ever get any decent ones on there – and writing my profiles. I keep it simple, sticking to Bel's advice about not giving away too much detail, then it's time for some selfies. I look down at my attire and decide that 'Got up at midday' is not quite the look I'm after, so I put on some slap and a nice dress I used to wear before Gareth vetoed it as 'too revealing'. It's barely low-cut, just shows a tad more in its V-neckline than an Elizabethan ruff. My hair is good, make-up is acceptable and the dress fits well. I take a few pics by the open window, in front of my bookcase and then my bedroom curtains, because they have green leaves on them and my hair always looks great against green. Yeah, they're not too bad. I sculpt a couple of these on Insta drafts, before screenshotting and popping on the dating apps. Not bad for fifty, gal. Not bad at all. I look at myself on there and think, *You haven't seen yourself as desirable for nearly twenty years now, pet.* Time for a change. I go on ASOS and order some cheap, fun outfits and then make a hair appointment for later this week. Once I've done all that, I've had quite enough of online dating for one day and decide to pop down to the shop.

As I walk in, the multi-coloured, busy, crowded splendour of materials and designs and tools and threads fills my view and lifts my spirits. As the snow outside reflects bright morning light into the room, I stand in the middle of my shop and I absolutely beam with joy. Every single time I walk into my shop, I feel peaceful and yet excited at the possibilities. I absolutely bloody love it. It's my ultimate happy place. It's my nirvana, this little shop and, most importantly – after years of feeling like a lodger in my own life – it is mine. I am a woman with a business who is going to make it a success. My top triumph in life has been Jay, my beautiful, funny, kind, clever, brave, genius boy. But coming a close second in my very short list of accomplishments is my shop, *Sew What?*

It's a treasure trove of quilty gorgeousness. You might know nothing about quilting, you might have never sewn a button in your life, but I defy you not to be struck with the visual deliciousness of a well-organised, well-stocked sewing and quilting shop. Mum got me into quilting to start with, but she died not long after, so I didn't have the chance to learn all her secrets. But she got me going and from there I taught myself, with a stack of books, found in second-hand shops and Amazon Marketplace, as well as a few hundred YouTube videos to help along the way. And I inherited all of her quilting supplies; a small selection of which I could bear to part with were the first stock I put in the shop. What I love most about quilting is that it's mindful – you're doing something that requires work and thought and design. It completely takes your mind off your troubles and submerges you in another world, a practical world filled with colour. Secondly, it produces something beautiful and useful at the end of it, something that can be kept in the family or gifted to another to become part of their family history. Quilts are special, made by love, skill and care and handed down from mother to child to mother to child and so on. Scraps of your family's clothes or other meaningful materials can be sewn into a quilt, to make it more than just an heirloom, instead becoming a part of the family itself. Quilts are amazing. I mean, sex is great. Cake is even better. But quilts? Quilts are life.

So, here I am in my shop. My brand-new shiny shop, full of brand-new shiny stuff. I'll never forget the day last year, when I had a call from my mum's brother down in Suffolk, to say that their auntie who'd emigrated to New Zealand decades ago had died and had left a will. It turns out that she lived a simple life, Great-Auntie Margie, and while she was doing so, she was an absolute wizard at the stock market. And she'd left me a chunk of money, bless her ever-loving heart, about £40k. It wasn't a life-changing amount of money as such – I mean, I couldn't retire to Benidorm on it – but it came at the perfect time. Immediately, I knew what I wanted to do: to invest the money in starting my own quilting shop. I was a school secretary at the time (the school where Bel teaches when she's not on mat leave). A nice enough job I'd had for years, but not my ambition, never was. This was in the dying days of my relationship with Gareth and, though I hadn't yet made the conscious decision to leave him, my subconscious was strongly urging me to make other plans for my future.

I've been open for two weeks and I've had very few customers. It's a specialist shop, I get that. But some days, maybe only one or two people come in. We're in a post-pandemic, cost-of-living-crisis, climate-changing, warmongering disaster zone these days and, of course, this is the time in my life, at fifty years of age, when I decide to open a niche business. I must be mad. I've sunk all my savings into it. I have a five-year lease and pay rent and rates to a landlord, so I used all of my windfall on equipping and refitting the shop, as well as the first quarter's rent, plus my commercial solicitor and accountant's fees. So I don't have any money left to play with now. It's sink or swim. I simply have to make this shop a success or I am absolutely, one hundred per cent up shit creek without a paddle and totally, royally fucked if I fail. Even more than the financial ruin, another thing drives me inexorably towards making this shop a booming success and that is being able to thumb my nose with sheer delight at Twatface, who I know will be willing me to fail. Even when these controlling bastards don't want you anymore, they need to know you can't cope without them, the sick puppies that they are.

So, I needed to spread the word about the new shop far and wide, but I can't afford expensive advertising. I do have a social media presence. I blog about quilting and have a few followers, but they live all over the world. I need more customers in the shop and I need them now, or yesterday even. So, a couple of weeks back, on the day I stood in my finished shop for the very first time, I thought, how can I start building local, regular customers who want to come in often and buy up my stock? Then, it came to me. A quilting group. That's what I need. Why have I never joined one already, I hear you ask? Well, the truth is, I have the social confidence of a naked mole-rat. I find social situations about as appetising as drinking bin juice. Faced with making small talk to mums on the school run, I'd rather have a drug-free root canal. So, joining a group, any sort of group, fills me with horror. I have a laugh on social media and can share a mean meme, yet I'm not half as confident IRL. But needs must. I got on Canva and made some colourful ads, using pictures of my creations and stock that I'd saved on Pinterest. I shared them all over social media. I joined TikTok because Jay told me to, but I have posted diddly squat on there. I mean, really, could I ever see myself making videos starring me and having to actually talk and be seen by the actual public? Not today, Satan, not today. So, the Canva ads were out there and a few likes and hearts and so forth began to trickle in. And I arranged for ads to go in all the local papers, then put up posters in local libraries and community centres. By the weekend, I'd had a few messages from women all over Lincoln and nearby villages saying they might come. They MIGHT come. No definites yet.

I sit and think about how embarrassing it'll be if nobody turns up tonight, but instead of letting my anxiety about this imminent social catastrophe drown me, I realise I'm knackered from the late night/early morning, as well as the worry and stress of having faced Twatface. I decide to snuggle down on the sofa for a nap. I'm soon absolutely out of it and, hours later, I wake up with a start at my phone alarm, an hour before the quilters are due to arrive. I check my phone for Jay; still no reply. I do a quick change into my customary dungarees, clean up the sleep-smudged make-up from earlier and I look nice enough. I scoff down some Uncle Ben's Golden Vegetable rice. Then I get a text from Jay:

hey mam all good bout dad n MP

i guessed about those 2 anyway

Did you??

yeh i saw them in Spar chattin a few times
she was tossing her hair n LARFING at all his shite jokes

dead giveaway

didnt tell u as didnt wanna stir shit up or upset u

Aww honey, it doesn't upset me. I wish them no ill will – especially her, if you know what I mean . . .

yesssss indeed i do kwym

poor cow

id rather get chicken pox than be her having dad movin in tbh hahahahaaaaa

ME TOO!!

And I feel all proud that Gareth's jibes about Jay only wanting to stay at his house in the holidays was the nonsense I thought it was.

OK sweetie, just checking you're all right. You can talk to me about all this stuff anytime yano . . .

yeh yeh ikkkkk no worries mam

oh hey its ur 1st nite with quilty club tonite innit

Yes! Thank you for remembering!

good luck w them wild quilters mam & may they beat down ur door in the manner of barbarian hordes

I LOVE the way you text seamlessly between youth speak and articulate adult! :-D

Multitalented me

jus checkin u ok

I smile at his care for me and message back:

Aww check you out checking in on your crusty old mam.

Then, because we mostly communicate through many-layered strata of sarcasm, I want him to know I truly appreciate him thinking of me:

Thanks sweetie. You're quite nice really. I might even stop chatting shit about you.

He replies in Oscar Wilde style:

Theres only 1 thing worse than being talked bout n thats not being talked bout
ILU

And I reply:

ILU2 <3

Jay's messages cheer me up a treat and bring on a surge of optimism. But as the time of the class arrives and no punters have turned up yet, my confidence starts to spiral down the plughole.

It is the Mondayest Monday in the Januaryest of Januarys. It's 6pm and tonight, Matthew, I'm going to be a sad, single, middle-aged business failure who can't even get a bunch of women to show up at her place for a very small sewing bee.

It gets to 6.10 and I want to cry. I'm literally standing at the door of my shop looking expectant and I feel like such a tit. I'm contemplating locking up in defeat and illegally breaking into Bel's shed (she's away tonight visiting her mum with Baby Barney) stealing her weed and giving it another go on my own this time by rolling a joint the diameter of a Cadbury Mini Roll and smoking myself to oblivion, when a young woman with blue hair stops in front of the shop, looks up at the name of the shop then looks at me (as I'm staring through the glass door at her like a salivating

Dickensian orphan), then she gets her mobile out, checks something, then knocks on the glass door.

I hurriedly open it and say, 'Yes?' just stopping short of bagging her with a net like the Child Catcher.

And she says, 'Is this the quilting thing?'

And I say, 'Yes! Yes, it bloody is!'

And she laughs and says, 'Well . . . can I come in then?'

I welcome her with open arms, which is awkward AF. After a minute of stilted chit-chat where I cannot stop admiring the absolute blueness of her blue hair, another woman turns up, then a pair of women together, then two more. And by 6.25 we have seven members (including me) of the brand new, hot off the press, très exclusive coterie known, for now, as the *Sew What?* Quilting Club (yeah, I know, we'll need a better name than that). There're only seven of us, but standing there, with this band of seamstresses in my very own shop on Steep Hill in the beautiful cathedral district of historic Lincoln . . . I tell you what: *The Great British Sewing Bee* can kiss my arse.

CHAPTER 3
A Hotbed Of Quilters

Meet the quilters. We're all sitting down now at a large folding table I've set up in the shop. There are seven chairs around it, but actually only four people stayed. No, the other two didn't take one look at me and scarper. They were dropping off loved ones: a daughter of one, the mother of another. It's a small band of seamstresses but they're all smiling and looking expectant. Two of the women are picking up and looking at the jelly rolls of material I've put on the table, while the others seem a bit nervous about touching anything yet. We've done all the 'Did you find the shop okay?' and 'Where did you park?' small talk and now it's time to get cracking.

'I'm Frankie,' I say. 'I've been quilting for a few years now, inspired by my mum. She was an excellent quilter. She's not with us anymore, but I feel sometimes like she's here in spirit, as I still use patches of materials she gave me in my quilts. That's a thing I love about patchwork: it keeps those memories alive in a really tangible way. I'm recently separated from my ex, starting life again at fifty, single for the first time in twenty-odd years. I even joined some dating apps last night. God knows why, but I live in hope. I have one son away at university: Jay. He's doing biology and he's the best thing I ever made, patched together mostly from my side of the family, I'm happy to say, with little of his dad in him, except his dad's academic brain and work ethic, the best parts. *Sew What?* is my new business. I worked as a school secretary before that. If it doesn't work out, I'm screwed financially. So . . . well . . . it *IS* going to work out. If I say it aloud, hopefully it'll happen. Anyway, that's me. It'd be lovely to hear a bit about each of you, unless anyone hates doing that introduction thing? I mean, I do, to be honest. But since I've done it now and it wasn't too dreadful, maybe someone else would like to jump in and save us all from an embarrassing silence? I mean, I get it. Normally, I bloody hate social situations. I'd rather have a colonoscopy than introduce myself.'

That gets a ripple of laughter from the quartet. And hopefully, it seems to have chilled everyone out a bit. I've actually surprised myself by doing that. It wasn't in the plan. I was just going to go straight into the sewing talk, but something about having them all here in my space, because I brought them here, and I'm responsible for them being around my table, made me feel I needed to explain myself a bit. But I'm shocked I said so much. Why on earth did I tell them about my ex, my son, my single status?! I've no idea. But now I've said it, I actually feel a lot better. There's something liberating about being frank with strangers. You don't know them, you may never see them again, so why not just say it how it is? So, finally, one of the women speaks up.

'Hello everyone. I'm Linda.'

She pauses and everyone waits, then waits, then realises maybe that's it, then one woman says, 'Hello Linda' and another one says a weak 'Hi.'

Linda carries on, 'And I'm an alcoholic.'

I burst out laughing, which seems to give everyone else permission to laugh too. Then, for a horrible moment, I wonder if she's being serious and she's caught the confessional bug from me.

'Oh shit, sorry, you're not really an alcoholic, are you?' I say, aghast.

Pregnant pause.

'No,' she says and laughs and we all laugh and it's all right again. 'So, I'm sixty-four and, it seems, the grandmother of this group. I'm a TEFL tutor at Lincoln College. That's English as a Foreign Language, if you weren't aware. Also called English for Speakers of Other Languages. My students are lovely. And fascinating, from all over the world. Asylum seekers, refugees et cetera. They desperately want to learn. Humbling, that, truly. Anyway, I digress.'

Everyone is rapt. Linda is a tiny little person, very small and slight, birdlike, yet she looks strong, tough as wire. Her cropped grey hair is boyish and a bit playful, as it looks like there's a bit of product in there making it sit up at sculpted angles. She looks like a mature elf who'd break your arm rather than mend your shoes. No make-up, slacks and a sweater on. She's casual AF and looks completely at ease with herself. I hope I get that nonchalant when I'm her age, which is not that far away. Everyone else is gazing at her, taken in by her confidence. I'm really glad I did the introduction thing, because now Linda is doing it too, and I'm keen to hear this little summary from everyone. Wouldn't it be nice if we just did this all the time? With strangers, anyone you bump into or have to deal with: a quick potted history of themselves, the bits they want to draw out, the picture they want you to have of them, made of patches they've chosen to show you.

Linda continues, 'I started sewing years ago, when my kiddies were small. Mending things, making their clothes. I have a daughter, who you met earlier. My eyes aren't behaving themselves these days, so she drives me around sometimes, when I can't get the bus. She has two little ones under five – a "geriatric" mum as the hospital called her, she didn't find the right fellow until she was in her late thirties. Two girls, and a full-time job at a nursery, so I don't want to bother her too much. She's kind though, like her brothers. They live away: one in Edinburgh, the other in the Middle East right now, in Oman. I raised them there, for a while, when their father was in the Army. We lived all over the place, covered a lot of ground. I started quilting to keep myself busy when they went to school. What else? Well, I do yoga every day. My father was Indian and my mother was a white English woman. I grew up backstage at an Indian restaurant. I'm a very good cook. Regarding the quilting, I haven't done it for years. So I want to take it up again. Hence my appearance here tonight. Will that do?'

That captivating snapshot of Linda's life gets a smattering of applause from our group, which makes us all laugh again. We need to move on, because this evening is supposed to be about quilting, and I'm not Eamonn Andrews doing *This Is Your Life* (although I really hankered after that job as a kid, getting to meet all those famous people's unfamous friends and relatives and asking them what the big cheese was really like, behind the scenes, when they were at school, before they were a celebrity and became a name instead of just a person they knew. I'm a big fan of flashbacks in stories: I always get a thrill when you see an old person as a kid in a movie.) I'm picturing Linda's past, raising her children in Oman, sewing in a cool white-walled house while the heat was baking outside. I have questions . . . but I need to get on.

'Thanks Linda. That will do brilliantly. Would anyone else like to have a go? No pressure, if you'd rather not.'

'I'm up for it,' says our blue-haired young woman, grinning a bit sheepishly, but with a friendly, open face. 'I'm Paige. I'm twenty-four, so it looks like I'm the baby of the group. Erm . . . not sure what to say about myself as I haven't lived much. I'm still at my parents' place, 'cause I can't afford to move out. I'm a hairdresser, specialise in colour. As you can see. I'm trying all the colours of the spectrum, one by one. Blue is my favourite so far. Feel like a mermaid.'

'It looks fabulous,' says Linda and everyone nods. Paige's hair is a lovely layered, curled bob that looks cheeky yet soft at the same time. She's obviously a very good hairdresser, or whoever cut her hair is. I always say, if your hairdresser has shit hair, don't trust them with yours. Her clothes are effortlessly cool: ripped jeans and a loose grey top that's slipped off one shoulder, revealing a green bra strap. Enormous purple DMs on her feet.

Paige grins and says, 'Thanks! Anyway . . . so, what else? I'm five foot nine and wish I wasn't . . . Erm . . . Oh yeah, quilting. Well, I've always been a bit crafty, y'know . . . tie-dye and stuff like that. I did knitting and cross-stitch for a while, taught by my nan. When I was little, she'd let me turn the handle on her old sewing machine and she told me her granny let her do that too. I spend a lot of time with my nan. She's gorgeous, a really lovely person. I like sitting with her – she's in one of those assisted living places and it's a bit depressing. But we like sitting together in her easy chairs and we like sewing and nattering about this and that. She's got all her memories around her, photos of her brother who died in the war, and her husband who died when I was little. And photos of my dad and me and my brother. And photos of her as a young'un, playing golf or in a swishy dress on a dancefloor, that kind of thing. It's like that bit at the end of *Titanic* when the camera moves across all those pictures of the old woman when she was Kate Winslet, horse-riding or being a pilot. That's what my nan's like. She's lived a full life. And she's shown me a bit of quilting. But not much yet, so I'm more or less a beginner. So yeah, that's me.'

Another little clap from everyone.

'That's fab, Paige. Thank you.'

'Shall I go next?' says a lady a bit older than Paige and definitely younger than me.

'Sure,' I say. I glance at the remaining member of the group, a woman who looks to be in her forties or so and – blimey – she looks terrified. Maybe when this one is done, I'll tell her it's okay if she wants to pass. She can just say her name, no pressure. I'm wondering now if this was a bad idea, suggesting we all do this. But actually I can't regret it. It's so bloody interesting! I'm such a nosey cow, I can't resist.

'Well, hi everyone. I'm Kelly. I'm thirty-five, nearly thirty-six and can't quite believe that. I'm not an alcoholic . . . or am I?'

She looks like she's genuinely considering this.

'You'd know if you were,' says Linda. 'We all know who we are, deep down.'

Well, things have taken a philosophical turn. 'That's a bit bloody wise, Linda,' I say and we laugh. I nod at Kelly, who still seems to be deciding if she's an alcoholic or not.

'Well . . . yes, so I like a glass of wine or two. But I don't want one when I wake up or anything.'

Kelly seems fixated on the whole alcoholic thing, but it reminds me that I bought red and white wine and forgot to bring it down. I got biscuits too – nice ones from Co-op, but not too chocolatey, as we don't want all that melting everywhere, getting the fabrics grubby. I'll go fetch them in a minute, when we've finished with the Parky-style interrogation. I'm still not sure if it was a good idea, but we've gone too far now to turn back. And I'm loving it.

'How did you get into quilting?' I ask, to nudge her onwards.

'Oh, well, I've been doing it a while. I saw a magazine in Smiths a year ago, or so. It gave you a bit of material every week and you started to learn skills and assemble patches, you know. I just caught the bug. And I don't have a telly. Or an iPad or anything like that. I'm not very keen on technology. And I live on a narrow boat with my boyfriend and our dog, a fat little Scottie called Dylan, after Bob Dylan. I'm a musician and teach and perform. We don't have kids. No reason. Not a tragedy or anything. Just never wanted them, either of us. We're happy as we are, with Dylan and Bessie, our boat. It's all we want, really.'

There's a pause as Kelly considers this too. She seems to think a lot, between utterances.

'What do you play?' asks Paige, looking genuinely interested.

'Oh, a few things. Guitar. And I do some drumming. And the handpan. You probably won't have heard of it, but it's a bit like a steel drum but smaller, and it's shaped like a UFO and you have it on your lap or a table-top. I'll bring it one night, if you like.'

'Yes please!' I say and everyone else agrees. Kelly smiles at this, a lovely smile that really lights up her face. She frowns a lot when she's thinking and it's nice to see her relax a bit. Her clothes remind me of the stuff I'd wear when I was a teenager in the nineties, bought from what we called The Hippy Shop, which had flowery shirts and suede waistcoats and joss sticks. Her hair is long and dark with a few streaks of grey, tied back in a plait. She has exceptionally large eyes and blinks them rapidly when she's listening to others. She seems a bit awkward in her own skin, so I'd love to see her play. I bet she transforms when she's holding an instrument.

'Okay I will. So yes, on the boat, we listen to the radio and music. My boyfriend – he's Canadian and a swimming teacher – he likes building models and Lego and things like that, so I wanted something to be doing with my hands. So I started quilting. All self-taught, with books from the library. I want inspiration, that's why I came to the class. And to meet other quilters. So yes, that's me. And I really could do with a glass of wine right now, because I haven't said that much about myself to anyone in years! I think I need a glug of red to get over it!'

Another round of applause and smiles and now I glance at our last lady and she's still looking stricken. She's dressed very demurely – not quite twin set and pearls, but close enough: a pair of chocolate-brown slacks, court shoes and a black jersey with white Peter Pan collar. Her hair is mid-brown, perfectly blow-dried in a Claudia Winkleman style but not as mad with the fringe. She's very neat, very trim, everything just so. I'm trying to think of how I can put her at ease, when she suddenly says in a clear, quite posh, southern accent, 'I could fucking murder a glass of red about now.'

We all fall about laughing, in a surprised and delighted way, because nobody expected that to come out of her mouth. Nobody also seems to have minded her swearing, which makes me feel a bit comfier about saying, 'It's a good job I bought some fucking wine then, isn't it!'

'Oh brilliant!' says Kelly, eagerly. Then frowns again, as if checking herself, after the whole Am I An Alcoholic thing earlier.

'I'll pop upstairs and get it in a minute. But shall we finish our intros?' I look at posh, sweary lady and say, softly, 'But not if you don't fancy it. No worries at all. Just your name would be nice to know though.' And I smile, hoping she'll see there are no rules here, no pressure to conform.

'Now I feel like the last and the least, if you don't want to hear my life story too.'

She's not smiling. Shit. Have I made a big faux pas, made her feel like we weren't bothered about her? But the others are making nice noises of *no, not at all etc*. And I realise she's a bit prickly. A complicated one, this one, I reckon.

'Absolutely not,' I say. 'I can't bloody wait to hear what's going to come out of that mouth next!'

It's a gamble, but I say it light-heartedly and I think the group are starting to vibe with my sense of humour and know that I'm basically fuelled by sarcasm but a nice version of it, which is a bit edgy but not horrid to anyone. And she smirks, which I think is her way of showing approval. So I reckon my gamble paid off.

'I'm Michelle. I'm forty-four, if we must do the age thing.

Married, two children – twins, a boy and a girl. I work at Marks and Spencer's, my husband's a sales manager at a Honda dealership. So my job is boring, my house and family are average, I don't play any musical instruments, I haven't lived abroad, I don't even have interesting hair, so I'm a bit bloody drab and dull and dreary all round.'

A silence descends, as awkward as watching *Basic Instinct* with your parents. Michelle looks round at us blankly, almost willing us to say *Oh no, not boring at all.* But actually, everything about her looks middle-of-the-road, yet she's clearly got an absolute rage boiling under that coiffed exterior.

'You couldn't be boring if you tried, Michelle,' I say and I mean it absolutely. 'You're a total mystery wrapped up in a riddle and inside an enigma, or whatever Churchill said.'

I smile at her and there's another brief silence, then Linda adds, 'I'm with Frankie. I find you very intriguing. I just hope you come back next week.'

Michelle's accusatory eyes and folded arms relax a little and she smiles, actually smiles. Her first proper smile of the evening.

'Well, I want to. I've been quilting for ten years and never met another quilter. I have a quilting room at home and it's my . . . my . . . sanctuary.'

'I wish I had a quilting room,' says Paige, dreamily. 'I just have a bed in the box room. All my crafty stuff is in boxes under the bed.'

'Me too,' says Kelly. 'No room on the boat. I dream of a quilting room. Do you have a photo?'

It seems such an odd question, not to ask Michelle for pictures of her kids, but instead for a room in her house. But we are all quilters, new and old, and we all understand the dream of a quilting room. That's why I adore my shop, because it's the desired quilting room writ large, full of everything a quilter or seamstress could ever want.

'Yes, I do, as it happens. I'm on Pinterest and put quilting ideas up on there.' Michelle gets out her phone and starts efficiently tapping her way to her page, which she holds out. We all crowd round to look. 'Hardly any followers. But I enjoy filling up banks of pages on different colour themes and styles of quilting. Look, here's some pictures of my room.'

It's beautiful. Stunningly neat and organised. Rows upon rows of transparent drawers full of quilting goodies, stacks of other materials and tools hung up on the wall, as well as examples of her quilts framed behind glass. We all coo over it, just like we're looking at a new baby, or puppies, or anything else that elicits joy. Because quilting is our joy.

'You've done a beautiful job there, Michelle,' I say.

She shakes her head swiftly and says, 'It's just organised, that's all. I can't stand mess.' She puts her phone away in her handbag and we all move away, then she says, 'And your shop is beautiful too.'

I turn to look at Michelle and she's giving me that odd, lopsided smirk that's meant to be a smile and something melts in me about Michelle. I mean, she's awkward as hell. But there's something soft in there, something yearning about her. I'm not sure what it is, but I'm dying to find out.

'Thanks. It's my happy place.'

'Yes,' Michelle says and looks around it. We all stop and look around at the shop. There's a quiet moment where we drink it all in with our eyes. There are the stacks of fat quarters – squares of materials in every colour of the spectrum, in every design you can imagine, tied up in neat bundles, to pick up and pore over at your leisure. There are the rolls of batting – the inner wadding that lies between the top and back layer of the quilt, that gives a depth to your stitching and makes the finished quilt toasty and warm on your bed. Then there are the tools of the trade: the quilting threads in every shade, the strips of interfacing to hold pieces of batting together, the straight pins, machine needles, blue tape for marking up a stitching line, seam rippers for redoing mistakes, marking pencils and chalks for drawing on lines and designs, rotary cutters and sewing scissors of all types, cutting mats and rulers, spray glue and basting pins for holding the quilt sandwich together while you sew it, thimbles and hoops and needles and gloves and other sundries. The complex loveliness of a quilting shop.

Kelly audibly sighs. 'It's all so gorgeous, quilting stuff, isn't it?'

'It really is,' says Paige, while Linda and Michelle are both nodding and catch each other's eye and smile.

Gosh, we really are a little band already.

I clap my hands together to break the quilty spell and say, 'Anyone want some of that fucking wine now?'

I leave the ladies while I pop upstairs and grab the bottles of red and white, plus the packets of biscuits, and bring them down. We all get stuck in and then turn our attention to the reason we're here tonight, somewhat waylaid by the unintended therapy session earlier. We have a range of skills here in these ladies, from Paige the beginner to Michelle the expert, so I say to the group that I think it's best if we start a new project with some skills-based activities, just to remind ourselves of the important skills we need for good quilting, as well as provide a good basis for Paige and allow more experienced quilters in the room to show off their techniques.

We start with a simple task: to make a pin cushion in the shape of a turtle. It's dead cute and makes everyone smile. It's not too difficult, mostly constructed from pentagons. It's a good early task because it shows clearly how to use templates and patterns. I use cereal boxes to cut out the templates – a nice cheap way of doing it. (Kellogg's Crunchy Nut Bites, if you must know. I can't stop eating them, they're so damn good. The crack cocaine of the breakfast cereal world.) Michelle and Linda work quickly, while Kelly does a reasonably neat job and Paige struggles on, but with plenty of help from me and Michelle's guiding voice now and again, which is surprisingly soothing, now she's not as jagged as she was earlier. Once we're all settled and hand-sewing, we talk and sew, sew and talk.

Give a bunch of women some needlework and a glass of wine and they'll be telling you all their business, as disparate as how bloody great their air fryer is, to that time they had their Mirena coil tugged out and it got stuck up there and it was bloody agony. Don't get me wrong, they're just as likely to be discussing the economic consequences of Brexit or the climate crisis, but something about sewing can bring out the confessional in you. You're all looking down at your hands, no awkward eye contact, and hidden things just slip out of people's mouths into the safe space of the sewing circle. At one point, after leaning over Paige's work to help her, I collect up biscuit wrappers and tidy away some cut scraps of material and then just stand there, watching my little band of seamstresses, grinning away to myself.

Linda looks up and says, 'It's not time to go, is it?'

And indeed it is, so we all start tidying away. Quilters often seem to be neat by nature – it's something about the intensely precise work needed in quilting, everything having to be measured just so, or the pattern will fail. So everyone helps and soon the shop is looking ship-shape again.

We've just time in the last five minutes to finish off the last bit of wine. Then, I remember, we don't really have a decent name for our group yet.

'We need a better name than the *Sew What?* Quilting Club. Any suggestions will be gladly accepted. Then we can vote.'

'Quilty McQuiltface?' says Linda and I snort with laughter. She's such a wag!

'That's bloody tempting, Linda.'

'How about looking up the collective noun for quilters?' says Kelly.

'What's a collective noun?' says Paige.

'Words you use to name a collection of something,' I say. 'Like a herd of elephants or a school of fish.'

'Or a murder of crows. Or a huddle of walruses,' adds Linda.

'Ooh, I love that walrus one,' says Kelly.

Michelle gets out her huge iPhone again and says, 'I'm on it.'

We all watch her and wait. She says, 'The only thing that comes up is . . . a hotbed of quilters!'

'Aye, that'll do nicely!' I say. 'Now then, ladies. Let us raise a glass, of thanks and camaraderie, to fat quarters and charm squares, to thimbles and rippers and chalk. Cheers, to our hotbed of quilters.'

'Cheers!' we all cry.

With that, our first quilting group session is done. Time for a quick mention of homework, to finish off the pin cushion at home and bring some fabric scraps they might want to use for some quilting squares for next week. Everyone is getting their coats on and moving to the door and saying goodbye and it's so nice, like we've known each other ages, not just met on an icy winter's night in my cosy, warm shop two hours hence. Then, the door shuts, the jingle of its bell signalling the last guest has gone and I'm left in the shop alone, but not lonely. I feel buoyed up. As, fuck me, if it wasn't a thousand times better than I thought it would be! *You're not such a loser after all, eh?* I tell myself. Then I chide myself for calling myself a loser. I really need to have a word with myself about confidence. And about changing old habits, of living under the shadow of disappointment and criticism. That shit needs to go, right sodding now. I think of that bit in *Babe*, when the farmer reserves his greatest praise for the piglet as he says, 'That'll do, pig. That'll do.'

Well, Frances Brumby, that'll do.

I go upstairs to the flat and settle down on the sofa, all pleased with myself yet quite worn out from all that social interaction. I have dozens of dating messages but I really can't be bothered to reply right now. But then I spot a catfish who's currently online and think I'll have a bit of fun before I curl up with the telly until bedtime.

His so-called name is Harry Larry (for real hahahaaaa) and his profile pic is a young hunk holding a fluffy white dog. He certainly ticks off some of the catfish Hall of Fame. Let's see what other bullshit he's peddling tonight . . .

Hi my dear how u are doing

Hi Harry Larry

Thank you so much for answering to me

No worries. What job do you do?

I am a military

You are a military?

I am a military yes

What kind of a military are you? And where do you live?

I am a military general and I am from Manchester and I am born in Manchester

Wow, a general!

Yes but I need money to pay for my plane trip back to home in Manchester

Do you now? Where are you based then?

Singapore

That's a long way from home! What do you miss about England?

I miss so many about England. What is your job

I'm a chef. My specialty is fish.

Oh really which fish you like

My signature dish is roasted catfish.

Ok you are single no or married wife

Single. Most guys don't like the fact that my life is full of catfish.

I doesn't matter for me as catfish is very good fish for wellness and I like eating catfish much

Manchester of course is famous for its catfish due to its mangrove swamps. Did you ever go boating in the

Manchester swamps? I love it there.

Manchester swamps are nice thing in Manchester

Oh, they're the best! What else did you love to do in Manchester?

The beach is good for playing sports of many type

The beach in Manchester is so beautiful. Did you ever harvest coconuts from the palm trees there?

Yes I do that everytime in Manchester

You clearly know Manchester very well.

Yes I know well also what is your spare time doing

In my spare time, I like to string along scammers online until they prove beyond doubt that they are liars, then I report them for the time-wasting catfish idiots they are. How about you?

A pause. I screenshot to send to Jay. He'll appreciate the local knowledge this joker has of Jay's university city. Then I report this wanker and block him before he has a chance to block me first. Ah, to be in the Manchester swamps in springtime . . . And bitchin' surf at Manchester beach. You can't beat a Manchester coconut. I do hope he tells the next woman he's a Manchester coconut farmer. I tell you what, not all heroes have capes, you know. This is a goddamn public service.

CHAPTER 4

Sons And Lovers

The rest of the week after the triumphant Monday night passes in a bit of a blur, as I have a few new customers, including Paige (blue hair) and Kelly (boat-dweller), who pop in separately to buy a bit of quilting stuff, which feels like a further victory. New, regular clients! I decide to work on my own sewing projects at the cash desk during the day, so that when people come in, they can see a work in progress and I can tell them about the hotbed of quilters. But, if I'm honest, most of the time when customers aren't in the shop, I'm glued to my phone, armpits-deep in the world of online dating. Holy cow, it's addictive.

The messages keep coming, without end, just as Bel said they would. There are numerous reiterations of *Hey*s from random POF people. I decide I'm not going to answer any message that starts with simply *Hey*. Bel informs me that this even has a name in dating lingo – The Hey-ter. I'll do the same with *WYD* (What You Doing), a similarly lazy opener. I mean, if they can't make an effort with the first message, what hope do we have going forward? That cuts out a huge swathe of randoms. eHarmony is more erudite, as expected, and I have a few conversations with nice-seeming chaps, but I wouldn't say there was any spark, know what I mean? I'm looking for something electric, something that gets the heart beating faster. I haven't felt that way about a man in years and I'm searching for it now. That quick banter, witty repartee. That to me is far more alluring than a nice set of abs (though some decent abs would not go amiss AS WELL, if that's not too greedy . . .) The only person I've had some of that spark with so far is Guy, remember him? The one who slid into my DMs. We've been chatting a bit during the week. He's funny and clever, proper makes me laugh; he's a dad with three sons in their teens and an ex-wife he gets on pretty well with; he's a university lecturer in neuroscience, which is fascinating and I love quizzing him about it. But he's a bit on and off with his messaging. I'm thinking this is probably normal in the dating app world, as we all know everyone on dating apps is talking to multiple people. Plus nobody can be on these things 24/7, as life has a habit of intervening in the far more important business of flirting. And Guy's methods of flirting – basically telling jokes – is light relief after the plethora of clumsy flirting I get from the majority of POFs. And the stuff they tell me! You would not fucking believe it!

I'm bloody amazed how much personal stuff these people will spill, after only a few hours of messaging, or sometimes less! One guy (not Guy guy, a different guy) tells me he steals knickers from his one-night stands or previous girlfriends. He's literally pulled them off washing lines or rifled through their knicker drawers. I tell him, ***I bet you don't steal the cheap Tesco pants, do you? I bet you go for the pricey, frilly, lacy stuff*** and he says ***Yeah, obvs. I only***

want the finest stuff. I tell him, ***Have you any idea how expensive that stuff is?! Leave some cash for those poor women if you're going to steal their fancy kecks FFS!***

I know quite a lot of women would block a man for this, but do you know what? Quite apart from keeping my eye on the prize of getting a first date with a halfway decent chap, I'm absolutely fascinated by the weird ones and I don't block them, unless they get aggressive or something, because I want to quiz them about why on earth they are the way they are. I mean, here we are, on these dating apps, and men are sharing their deepest, darkest sexual desires with me, a complete stranger, with no shame, no embarrassment. They don't give AF! I feel like I've started a new job as a psychiatrist and it's utterly compelling. And Bel wants in on it too, hearing updates and being sent screenshots of all the major players. I find I'm renaming some of these guys with their particular peccadillo, as a shorthand for Bel. So there's ANDREW KNICKER THIEF and GERMAN GUY SKI SOCKS. Yeah, that one was wild. German Guy Ski Socks is called Dieter and lives in Scunthorpe and he is into women having pigtails in their hair, wearing floral waist-high pants and ski socks, or any long woolly socks. They have to be woolly. He says it's the wool that gets him off. I say, Do you have a thing for sheep then? And he blocks me! Maybe too close to the bone. He comes back again later though and wants to keep chatting. I get the impression from some of these guys that they get blocked a lot. But for me, I feel like I've stumbled into a confessional and I'm a new priestess. First week on the job and these guys are telling me all sorts. I could block all these blokes and flounce off disgusted, but hell no, it's far too enthralling. Ski socks is just the tip of the iceberg; one man wants to come round my house, dress himself up as a French maid and tidy my whole flat. I mean, I'm seriously tempted – I don't give a stuff about the maid outfit, just the free clean. Another tells me he wants to call me Mummy. In fact, I've had a few say this, including a six-foot-seven pole vaulter (yes, that was his job description) who says he's into sniffing the armpits of mothers, and only mothers, of any age. What. The. Actual. Fuck? One says he wants me to wear his mother's dirty knickers while we shag. I say, ***Sorry, honey but I'm not into that.*** I start to get the feeling that he's sad about what he needs, that he hates the fact that's the only thing that turns him on. I find I'm doing a bit of psycho-analysis – completely unqualified – and I ask him why he thinks he feels that way about his mother's dirty underwear and he says he doesn't want to talk about it. Then I feel a bit bad, that I've pried into his soul a bit too much. But he doesn't seem to mind and just asks me again if he can call me Mama instead, as if it's just the word that's the problem, not the whole mother/son sex concept . . .

Are these guys just watching too much weird porn? All of the ones who profess unusual sexual preferences are in their thirties or twenties. Either they're just more open than men nearer my age and all men have these bizarre kinks. Or maybe it is a generational thing. Are we finding a whole new cohort of men that were raised on internet porn and can't get turned on without these highly specific somewhat left-field triggers? MAMA MAN blocks me too, then comes back a few days later, but he's like a broken record about the used maternal knickers, so I block him. Wow, who'd have thought I'd end up acting as a kindly listening ear to all these guys? I learn quite quickly that many of these men do not find their sexual preferences weird, however laughable they may sound to a Bambi in the meadow like me. They take them deadly seriously and that's exactly what they're looking for, which of course suggests that there are women out there who want some of these things too. I'm Googling constantly when I'm having these conversations and find out a phrase I've not heard before and that is 'kink-shaming'. Laughing at people for their particular thing they like, that turns them on. So, at first, I'm screenshotting this stuff I find weird and having a laugh with Bel about it. And I still do that, I mean, some of it is comedy gold. And it's just between Bel and me. We're not going to name and shame these guys on Twitter, or anything. But as the days go on, I find I'm listening more and asking more, and realising that everyone has their thing that they like, that everyone is weird in their own weird way. I mean, if I were to ask you right now to think about what turns you on, what absolutely gets you going . . . It might be innocent-sounding or generic, or it might be something very specific and weird-sounding that you'd never tell a soul, except a lover, and even then . . . it might just reside in your mind, hidden forever. And I realise that I have no idea what turns me on. It's been so long since sex has been an important part of my life, that I need to explore this aspect of humanity, find out what the hell is going on out there in people's minds and loins. Maybe that's why I'm so interested in all these guys' weirdness. Sex is weird, attraction is weird, we're all weird! But what is my particular brand of weirdness?

Bel is hooked on the stories but she's scolding me too, for my lack of progress. We're back in her shed on Saturday night and I'm sharing some puffs of her joint, at the end of the first week of dating, and we're having a post-mortem of my progress. And she tells me off, for getting too involved with the weirdos.

'Hey!' I say. 'Don't kink-shame!'

'Ooh, hark at you, getting all in with the lingo. Look, it's a messy, mesmerising world, dating. You'll get caught up in all sorts of bizarre characters. And I'm talking about *you*, Frankie, because you're too nice. You're not brutal enough. I didn't listen to those cry-babies whining about their fucked-up sex lives. And neither should you.'

'But it's so INTERESTING! I could write a book about this shit. It'd be a bestseller!'

'Look, it's all very fascinating. But it's not real. The online world is not real. I had a friend at work who was online dating during lockdown, so she only had the online bit and couldn't meet anyone. And that's when the whole thing becomes like a parallel universe, where hardly anybody is who they say they are, because they can get away with it, because you're not going to meet, for weeks, months maybe, probably ever. So the weirdness goes on and on. And they can tell you all sorts of stuff they wouldn't if you were sitting opposite them in a pub. Some people excel online too, but in real life, they're hopeless. Take it from me, some of the best sexters are often the worst lovers. All mouth and no trousers, as they say. And we're not in lockdown. There's no excuse now. The online world is alluring, but ultimately it's not what you're there for.'

'Okay, okay. I get it. I'm just finding it such a blast. It's such an insight into human nature.'

Bel points the smoking joint at me and narrows her eyes. 'Listen, lady. This is not a social experiment. This is dating. And the goal is to get laid, or to get a relationship. Either/or, perhaps both. You're not their social worker-slash-psychologist-slash-nanny, okay? Get with the programme. You haven't made any dates yet, have you?'

'Nope. Well, would you? With the KNICKER THIEF or MUMMY ARMPITS?'

'Exactly. You're talking to the wrong guys. Ditch the weirdos and focus on the possibles. Don't forget, dating is a game.'

'Yes, yes.'

'So, what about this Guy guy? He sounded the most likely so far.'

'He's hit and miss. Sometimes goes AWOL for days. I dunno, I don't feel like he's that interested.'

'Then, ditch him. You don't chase these fish. They come to you, you play with the line, then reel them in. Guy might be benching or breadcrumbing you.'

'Translation please.'

'Benching is when they text just often enough to keep your interest, but meanwhile they're spending the lion's share of their time pursuing more interesting options. Breadcrumbing is where they're just playing about with you, sending the odd text or meme to keep you hungry, but really they have no intention of meeting up. Classic online dating bullshit.'

'Well, yeah, could be. But we're all doing that to a certain extent, aren't we, while we're juggling all these online randos?'

'Yeah but you should only be meeting up with the ones who seem genuinely keen. You're nobody's also-ran, babe. You're a thoroughbred. Anyone else talked about meeting up yet?'

'Yeah, a local man who works in IT, Gerry. And a plumber called Lee. I mean, they sound okay. They're both in their forties, nice-looking. They're keen. They both want to arrange a date.'

'Good, good,' says Bel, her face lit up. I can tell she's

ready to impart more illuminating wisdom. 'Right, it's time for your next lesson. Last time, we mentioned verification, remember?'

'Oh yeah, how do I do that?'

'Right, so, there are various ways. A quick upfront way you can do with any guy on the apps, is to get them onto Snapchat.'

'I'm not on Snapchat. That's for kids, isn't it?'

'No, no. It's very useful. It means you can swap photos and audios and video chats, without giving them your phone number. I'll set you up an account in a minute, show you how to use it. You must turn your location off on there, or the bastards will know exactly where you are.'

'Urgh, information overload. Too many new apps for an old bird like me!'

'Get with the plan. If you're going to meet up with someone, you need a way to verify them before you do. That's rule number one. Gone are the days when you turn up to a date to find they're a totally different person, or ten years older than their profile pic. All of that can be verified before you waste your time meeting them. And you need to do that off the dating app.'

Bel hands me the joint and takes my phone. She talks me through Snapchat and it's got a lot of confusing terminology that makes my head hurt, but I get the general point that you can talk on there and send pictures and so forth, and each message disappears, plus you know if someone's taken a screenshot.

'Why would I want to do that?'

'Well, if someone's sending nudes, that's what people do. So be warned. Anything you send online can be copied, even on Snapchat.'

'I'm not going to send nudes!' I gasp, truly horrified at the thought. I mean, I've seen myself naked. And it ain't pretty. But would men look at me and think that? All I see are the lumps and bumps, the wrinkles and stretch marks. But that's a real woman, isn't it? Do men look at us that critically? Or are they just happy they've got a naked woman in front of them, like a dog with a bone? Sex is one thing, but committing one's naked image to a digital likeness and sending it to a stranger . . . do I want to do that? And a little thought creeps into my head that it might actually be fun, it might be hot, it might be . . . liberating? Or it might be a bloody nightmare. That's dating for you, it all seems to be one extreme or another.

'Well, you might surprise yourself. But that's another lesson, for the future. Don't send any until we've had a shed session on Nudes 101, all right?'

'All right. So, verification.'

'Yes, so, as the Mandalorian might say, *This is the way*. Firstly, give them your Snap – that's your Snapchat name – and get off the dating app, onto Snapchat. If they whine they're not on Snapchat, tell them to download it. No excuses. Verification trick number one: tell them to take a selfie holding a piece of paper with *Hello Frankie* written on it. Or they can send you a video saying "Hello Frankie". Either way, if they're legit, they'll be only too happy to do it. If they're lying about any aspect of themselves, then they'll immediately find an excuse not to do it. You can give them the benefit of the doubt if they're at work, but only till their lunchbreak or early evening. If they're proper keen, they'll do it ASAP, so they don't lose you. Any hesitation to verify, block them there and then. There is absolutely no reason on earth why they should object to this. So don't let them soft soap you with any excuses. They might ask you to do the same, and that's fine, you can do that first, if you like, to show willing.'

'That's really good advice,' I say. 'You are clever at this.'

'I told you, babe, it's just a game. These are the rules. But they're not written down in any handy rulebook. You have to live it to learn it. Okay, so once they've verified, and you're happy with the results, then you can arrange a date. Public place – pub, restaurant, bowling alley etc – never go to their house. If it's just for sex, then meet at a busy hotel, preferably in the bar first. Never go straight to the room.'

'I can't afford hotels! I can barely afford my own rent!'

'Well, as long as you don't go to their place. You never know. Be circumspect, always. Most of these guys are just guys who want to get laid. Or who want a girlfriend or whatever. But there will always be psychos out there. And I don't want you to fall foul of those bastards. You're too lovely.'

'Aww, honey. Thanks,' I say and give her a hug. She looks tired. I stub out the joint and squeeze her arm. 'Listen, that's enough about me. How are you? How's Barney and everything?'

Bel glances out of the window, across the garden towards the house. The snow is still out here, but it's mushy and depressing now, nearly rained away. Bel's eyes instantly fill with tears.

'Oh, love! What's up? Come here,' I say and pull her in for a hug, our bulky winter clothes affording us a well-padded cuddle.

'Oh, it's silly really. I'm all right really,' she says and brushes away tears. 'Let's talk about dating again. It's much more fun.'

'No, no, let's talk about you. And the baby. What's going on? Anything particular or just general motherhood madness?'

Bel looks up at me with hopeful, tear-filled eyes. 'Is that a thing?' she says, in a small voice. 'Motherhood madness? Cos that's what it feels like. I feel like I'm losing my mind. I feel like I'm not . . . me anymore. Just this thing, this mother thing, this object made to feed and clean and soothe ad infinitum, forever and ever, amen. It's so hard to explain. Am I going mad?'

Bel is so knowing about some things, about the dating scene and all that, where she's the master and I'm the apprentice. But when it comes to motherhood, now that's where I can help my friend a bit, I hope.

'You're not going mad, okay? Motherhood is insane. Parenthood in general. Kids are bonkers. Absolute nutters, the lot of them. Babies are tyrants. And they can't explain themselves, so you're trying to read this little bastard's mind the whole time you're exhausted from lack of sleep. They sleep whenever they like, for as long as they like, and they carry on sleeping through their full cycles and feel rested. You, meanwhile, are woken up whenever they're ready, but you've probably not had a full sleep cycle in months.'

'I haven't! I'm so . . . tired, babe. I'm just so, so tired.'

And then it comes, the floodgates open and she's sobbing on my shoulder. I let her just cry it out. That's what she needs right now. And once she's done that, and is sniffling and wiping her eyes, then she needs a bit of a pep talk.

'Listen, darling. You are doing brilliantly. You'd do anything for your son, anything. You'd die for him. I'd die for my son. None of that is in question. But that doesn't mean it's easy. I remember times when Jay was little, where he cried and cried and wouldn't sleep, and I was on my own for hours on end with him, and remember imagining booting him out the window like a football. I remember picturing, so clearly, the arc he'd make as I kicked him out! Or I'd think, maybe if I put his crib in the airing cupboard and shut the door, he'll be nice and cosy in there and then he'll shut the hell up and fall asleep and I can get some bloody rest at last. Like, I remember literally thinking that might be a good idea, before the awake part of my brain was like, WTF, woman? That's mental!'

Bel laughs through the tears and says, 'I can't even tell you what I think about doing.'

'Ah yeah, you can. I bet you I've thought of worse.'

'Well, it's nothing very creative. Largely involves dumping the car-seat in the hospital car park, or wrapping him up in a basket and leaving him on the orphanage steps, like a Catherine Cookson novel. Or sometimes it's just the idea of leaving him in the house with Craig and getting in my car and just driving, driving, driving. For hours, days. Wherever I wanted. And never coming back.'

'Oh, I used to have that one all the time. The urge was so strong! The means of escape parked right there, in front of my house. If it weren't for this darned baby! The little twat!'

'Yes!' Bel laughs a bit. She's brightening up now.

'So, you see? You're not alone. We all have dark thoughts about them sometimes. It's the madness of motherhood.'

'And to think,' Bel says, warming to her theme, eyes dry of tears now, 'I used to long to have a baby, when I didn't have one. I'd be so jealous of everyone who had one, like a terrible tug in my stomach. And now, I look at everyone who DOESN'T have a baby, and I'm thinking, I'm so jealous of you I can't see straight!'

'Oh, blimey, yes. I remember that too. Watching Gareth go off to work, standing at the door holding Jay and thinking, *You lucky, lucky bastard.*'

'Yes! God, I never thought I'd miss work. And it's not so much the work I miss, as the freedom from the house, from this. All this. But then when I have had a day off, when Mum's taken Barney or whatever, I enjoy it, yeah, sort of, but I miss him so much. And I think of all the stuff I'm missing out on, that he might be doing, developing, learning, changing. And I'm not there. So it's nuts. Can't live with my son, can't live without him. Why can't we be happy with what we've got? Am I just a spoilt brat?'

'No, you're a normal mum. Motherhood is never what you think it's going to be. You see all these images of perfect mothers everywhere, smiling beatifically at their perfect, cherub-cheeked babies. You don't see them at 4am, tearing their fucking hair out as they've had no more than forty minutes' sleep in forty-eight hours. That's the truth of it, that the media doesn't tend to show us. I hated Jay for a good few weeks at this age! Hated him! Thought I was a terrible mother and if anyone knew, they'd take him away from me. But at the same time, I loved him to distraction, I did everything I could think of to nurture him and love him. That's the madness of motherhood. It's all normal, darling. All of it.'

Bel smiles at me and says, 'You're so wise, Frank.'

'Yeah, yeah, I'm wise about some things and you're wise about some things, and that's friendship. That's the true love story of life, your friends.'

And I give her a quick hug and a peck on the cheek. I've said it to myself many, many times, but thank the stars for Bel.

'Too right. We can tell each other anything with zero judgement, two kickass women helping each other through life's ups and downs and ins and outs (literally).'

'That's it, Bel. Men aren't worth a damn compared to my friendship with you. And most of them are weird anyway.'

'Not all men are weird. Craig isn't and my dad isn't. Your dad is though!'

'Too right. My dad's an iceman. Never gave a shit about me.'

'Yeah, so listen, babe.' Now it's Bel's turn to give me a peck on the cheek. This is what we do for each other. One's weak while the other is strong. And vice versa. 'Truth is, you've had a bunch of shitty role models in the men you've known. And the weirdos you're talking to right now. But that's not the whole story. There are good men out there, I promise you. And don't forget your beloved grandad. He was a good man too, remember? You just need to get out there and meet them.'

'Oh, don't mention Grandad, or I'll cry.' I really will though. I haven't seen him since I was a teenager but I still think of him, a lot. 'They don't make 'em like him anymore. But you're right. I'll make dates with these two guys then,' I say and *almost* mean it. What if they're boring? What if I don't fancy them? Suddenly, I realise why I've been spending the whole week talking to these way-out, unreal guys. I've been hiding in all this online weirdness, because actually I'm terrified of going on a real date. I'd rather lick a nightclub floor than meet a new man and make conversation for an hour or two. The very thought brings me out in a rash. But Bel is right. It's the only way forwards. I'll have to swallow my fear of social embarrassment and grasp the nettle of real-life dating. It's time for shit to get real.

'Yes, get on it, babe.'

'I will. But look, honey, you're exhausted. Is Craig doing his fair share? How about I take Barney for a night soon, so you guys can have a break?'

'Yeah, Craig is great. Really, he is. And I may well take you up on that sometime, darling. I mean, Mum's offered as well. But I'm not quite ready for that yet. But when I am, I know where you are.'

'Yeah, I'll be on the sofa quizzing some kinky fucker about why he wants to wear my dirty knickers on his head.'

CHAPTER 5

First Dates

So here's a list of some of the first dates I go on within my first week of hurling myself head-first into the real-life dating pool, beyond the virtual.

Lee the plumber passed the verification test – sending me an immediate pic of himself holding a napkin with *HELLO FRANKIE* written on it – and here we are. We've met at Lincoln Castle on Monday afternoon for a nice walk around as it's a sunny day. When I first spot him as I walk through the gates, I think, *Oh shit, I don't fancy him.* Like it's an instant thing, the moment I see him. He looked great in his photos – short, spiky hair and a good body for his age – but seeing him there standing and then turning and walking towards me, his body is fine, nothing wrong with it, but I realise immediately that seeing a photo of someone and watching them move in real life are two utterly different things. The same goes for his smile, which is just too . . . cheesy. I don't know why. What does that even mean? Wow, am I that fickle? *Give the guy a chance, Frankie.* And then, maybe he feels the same way seeing me. Urgh, I hate dates already.

'Hi, hi! Frankie, yeah? Hi!' he says, very excitable.

'Hi, yeah. Lee, I presume?' I *presume*? What is he, Dr Livingstone? *FFS, Frankie.*

'Great. Shall we?' He motions for us to start walking. I realise that walking was a good plan actually, as we're side by side and don't have to stare at each other. But I need to get some more glimpses of him, to check him out. So, I keep glancing round as we're walking and my first impressions don't improve, as yet. He has a goofy face. Oh God, that's so unfair. I mentally slap myself. *Stop being such a judgy cow! Listen to the guy.*

So, he's talking. That's good, right? A date with a strong, silent type would be hard work. But he's talking and talking and talking. He's telling me about his family. Here's an extract:

'So my sister-in-law – the fat one, not the fit one – she's a right cow and she's having a go about it all and going on and on and my brother kicks off and my dad tells him he should never hit a woman and I'm all like, that's obvious, isn't it? I mean, if you have to tell someone to never hit a woman, then what the hell is the world coming to, you know? And so it's like the worst bank holiday ever and everyone wants to leave the caravan but my mum won't let us because of the flapjacks and everyone's got to have one, but the kettle's bust and you can't have flapjacks without a cuppa, I mean, because they can be a bit, you know . . . in the mouth. What's the word?'

He pauses for breath.

'Claggy?' I say.

'Yeah, claggy! That's it! That's the perfect word. Yeah and my mum's flapjacks are always claggy. I mean, they're nice, don't get me wrong, but they are claggy. Yeah, claggy, that's what they are.'

Please stop saying claggy, I think.

He carries on, 'So yeah, family, eh? Bloody nightmare. But I love them. I mean, we all love our families, right? But we can't choose them. That's the difference, right. You can choose your friends and your . . . you know, your *lovers*,' he says and winks at me. *Oh God, don't wink at me. It makes your face look even more cheesy.* 'But you can't choose your family, can you? I mean, you're born into them. Unless you're adopted. That's different. If you're adopted. But then, you don't choose them then, do you? I mean, it's not as if a baby can say, yeah, I'll have the rich ones please, thank you very much.' And he laughs and laughs. And I go heh-heh-heh and can hear this fake laugh coming out and I'm thinking, *Kill. Me. Now.*

And now he's off on one about the kids of today and the school run and why can't anyone walk to school anymore like the old days and all the mums in their 4x4s hogging the roads and it's dangerous and everyone should walk to school even if it's raining or snowing or 'fogging' and kids these days and yeah, he knows that some mums have to work after drop-off but not that many mums work these days and they're just lazy most of them . . . and I feel like I've fallen into a local Facebook group come to life, personified in one awful man who will never, ever, ever SHUT UP.

So it goes on. For an hour. I've never heard so many words come out of a person's mouth in such a short span of time. And all those words have no substance whatsoever. I mean, the absolute total emptiness of everything he's saying, the perfect exemplar of verbal diarrhoea, just pouring out of that cheesy-grin mouth. I'm watching his lips and they're so mobile and stretchy and just going on and on and on, forever, till kingdom come and the world will be destroyed and he'll still be there, in the ruins, banging on about fucking nothing. And yeah, maybe he's nervous and he talks too much when he's nervous. But there's talking a lot, which is fine if it's interesting, if it's insightful or philosophical or funny or teaching you something, but this endless drivel . . . I might've had something interesting to say but he's not even pausing for breath, not giving me a chance to really reply, not asking me a thing about myself. Christ, I wish I had a pause button and could switch him off – CLICK – and he'd just be frozen in time with his cheesy mouth open and I could walk away, around the corner, and click him back on and I'd be gone and he'd probably not even notice and carry on talking.

So I keep looking at my watch and the second it hits one hour – which feels polite, to wait for an arbitrary sixty minutes before bailing on a date – I interrupt him and say, 'I've got to go now.' And he's all surprised and disappointed. 'Yeah, I have a . . . an appointment at . . . the hospital.'

'Anything serious? What's it about?'

I think, *None of your bloody business, mate!* But I feel obliged to say something, since he's asked.

'No, it's a . . . boob thing.'

'A what?'

'You know, a boob thing, where they squash your boob . . .' Why can't I remember what it's called?! It's like all his words have sucked all mine out of my head and there's nothing left, zilch, nada. Just words of one syllable like *boob* and *thing*.

'Okay Frankie. Good luck with the boob thing!'

'Thanks,' I say, trying to think up what the hell I'm going to say to bookend this rubbish date and then he reaches in and kisses me, shoves his tongue between my teeth, and I gag and pull back. Bloody hell, that was grim AF!

'Can I call you tonight then? After the boob thing?' And he's standing there with that cheesy grin, utterly unaware of how terribly the date went and how crass what he just did was. I'm so shocked I just say, 'I'll message you.'

And I beat a retreat faster than a chicken who's strayed into KFC car park. Holy SHIT! That's the first time in twenty years I've had another man's tongue in my mouth and it was Lee the garrulous plumber and I didn't even want it there! I mean, there's being spontaneous and there's lack of consent and a very murky grey area in between. And when I get back home, I wash my mouth out – yes, actually, with mouthwash, not soap obvs, but still. URGH. And my phone pings and there's a message from him.

Great to meet you Frankie! You're a top bird! Talk later.

I think a minute and reply:

Good to meet you too. But sorry, I didn't really feel there was a spark between us. So I'm going to say thanks so much for the date but I'm going to move on.

Is that mean? Or kind? I add:

Sorry.

There's a pause, then he replies:

Oh really? I really didn't think you felt that way. That's such a shame and I really like you. Great kiss by the way . . . ;-)

Yeah sorry Lee. But I wish you well.

OK if that's how you feel. Never mind I guess. Back to the drawing board! Not the first time this has happened to me and not the last I bet! Good luck with the boob thing.

'MAMMOGRAM!' I shout. That's what the damn thing is called. And for a second, I think I've actually got a mammogram to go to and my chest tightens in anticipation, then I remember it's a lie and I think, *I'd rather have a mammogram from a steam roller than go on another date with Lee.*

So, that was the first date. I mean, it wasn't the worst thing that ever happened to me but it dawns on me for the first time that this is what dating is: meeting complete strangers in public, having to make random conversation with them, all while sizing each other up, with the horrible implications of what if I fancy them and they don't fancy me, or vice versa, and what if they are boring or weird or moody or annoying? And suddenly, dating isn't so shiny anymore. It's terrifying. I've got another date planned the next evening, at the Wig and Mitre actually. Gerry, the IT bloke. He passed the verification test too, with a nice pic of him smiling, holding a piece of paper with *Hi there Frankie!* penned in a nice swirly hand. Okay, so new plan for this date: watch out for uninvited snog at the end i.e. stand well back, just in case. Also, have a ready-made excuse for after one hour to leave i.e. something I can actually remember the word for. Lastly, if the guy just talks and talks at you, do your best to intervene. Don't just let him rant on. Try to get a word in. At least you'll leave feeling like you haven't had an Acme anvil dropped on your head.

So 7pm comes on Tuesday and I'm going into the pub. I have a good look around and can't see him there yet. I'm bang on time, so maybe he's going to be fashionably late. I sit down near the door and take my coat off. I'll get a drink when he gets here. A couple of minutes pass and I look at my phone, checking out Gerry's profile pic. Shoulder-length brown hair with grey streaks and a great beard, close-cropped, not too bushy, very sexy. He looks good. And his messaging was intelligent and interesting. I'm feeling quite excited about this one. Five minutes pass. Oh no, he's stood me up, hasn't he? Goddammit. And I'm reminded this is the other thing one has to contend with on dates. I've never been stood up in my life. And now I feel righteous anger that a person can talk to another person for a few days and make all the arrangements to meet them and let them leave their house and make their way there and yes, I literally live about twenty steps from here but he doesn't know that and anyway, who does that? Who makes all those arrangements and then doesn't even bother to send a message to say—

'Excuse me?'

I look up. There's a tall bloke standing there with a shaved head and scruffy, five o'clock shadow, holding two glasses of white wine and I'm thinking, *Dude, I'm taken.* Or am I? Not if this wanker Gerry never shows up. But I don't fancy the shaved-head guy anyway and he has two drinks so he's obviously bought one for his companion, wherever they might be, then he says, 'Frankie?'

'Yeah? I mean, how did . . .'

Then it hits me. That's Gerry. It's him, I can tell from the eyes. But . . . no long hair, no sexy beard. He hands me a glass.

'Everyone likes white wine, don't they?' he says and smiles. Do I say, *Bit presumptuous there, Gerry? And also where the hell is your beard and long hair?* It's not exactly catfishing. But it kind of is too. I mean, why not put a recent pic on there? He obviously knows he looks better with the long hair and beard, otherwise he wouldn't have had six pics on there like that. Yes, SIX. And what about the verification pic? Then it occurs to me: Gerry works in IT. He must've photoshopped the Hi Frankie note onto an old picture. Fucking WHAT? The bloody nerve! Manipulative twat!

But of course I don't say any of that, because I'm too polite. Or that I'm not a big fan of white wine and much prefer red. I just sit and seethe, still in shock he'd go to all that trouble to fake a verification pic. And I chalk it up to experience. I'll only ask for videos next time . . .

'Sure. Hi. Please do sit . . .' but he's already sitting down. And I'm already extremely annoyed at him. But after yesterday afternoon's disappointment, I want to at least try to be more positive this time. I must endeavour to give these guys a chance. So he's shaved all of his body hair off and faked a pic and bought me a drink without asking what I want. Not exactly fit for the Nuremberg trials. Let's make an effort to get past this rocky start. But it annoys the heck outta me and I decide to be brave and say something, because it is really, REALLY bugging me.

'You look a bit different now from your photos,' I say, but with a smile, so it doesn't sound accusatory. 'The hair? And the beard?'

'Ah yeah, those pics were pre-pandemic,' he says, with not a hint of apology. 'I shaved all my hair off in lockdown. I mean, every bloke did, right?'

No, every bloke didn't. And also, that was YEARS ago.

'And I just preferred it this way, easier to look after. So much nicer.'

No, it's not. It makes you look like an Aldi Jason Statham. But I can't be bothered to go into it, as he clearly thinks he hasn't done anything wrong by lying about it. I mean, the guy can do whatever he likes with his own hair, but then don't put old hairy pictures on your dating profile, FFS!

We talk for an hour and it goes all right. Gerry is an interesting person. He reads and watches some good, meaty stuff on TV and we can talk about politics. He works in IT and spends a good portion of our hour explaining to me about how he manages different IT systems remotely or at the office in London and it's actually not boring. I mean, I always want to know what other people do for their jobs and what their typical day is like. And I start thinking that dating is also a bit like that miniature therapy session we had at the first quilting meeting last week, where you get a snapshot of some stranger's life and it's quite illuminating. I mean, not always, like the terrible glimpse I got into boring Lee's boring little existence of flapjacks in the caravan. But still, it's all part of life's rich tapestry, meeting these people and finding out stuff about them. So, yes, I can't say it's going badly. We get on okay. But I feel like I'm having a pleasant meeting with my bank manager. Or an uncle. There's just no . . . spark. There's that word again. It's what I'm looking for and it's just not there.

I make my excuses and leave soon after, with no attempted kiss and a very business-like handshake. I go home and pour a glass of red, just to spite him, the white-wine-buying lying git. I don't get a message from him after and I'm guessing that either he felt the same way about me, or that he got the message I felt that about him. Either way, it's depressing. Worse, somehow, than the Lee debacle because it's not even a funny story. So I sit in my flat and feel a bit blue about the whole thing. Two dates in two days and they were both disappointing. I message Bel and give her a precis of both dates. After the Gerry summary, she replies:

Kittenfishing.

What's that?

It's like catfish lite. They don't exactly pretend to be someone else, but their pictures are out of date, or massively photoshopped. Or they've inexplicably shaved off all of their hair without updating their profile pics.

Is it unreasonable that I am really pissed off about that?? I mean, he looked nothing like his pics! Some guys can pull off any look, like Brad Pitt can carry long hair or the skinhead and still look delicious. But some guys just . . . can't. Is that petty?

Of course it's petty. But it's also completely understandable. And fuck that shit, the guy kittenfished you. He knew his pics weren't current. He knew he looked better like that, or he wouldn't have used them. Yeah we all enhance our photos a bit to put us in a good light. That's making an effort. But turning up with a completely different look . . . nah, that's not on. Don't feel bad, babe. Onwards and upwards!

Yeah ok. I feel a bit better now. I'll get back on the apps and see who else is out there.

That's the spirit. Spend some time on eHarmony this week and talk to some nice mature guys. Avoid the weirdos on POF for a while. Luxuriate in some decent company.

OK honey, good advice. You always do the trick and make me feel better.

Hey, I'm ya mate, that's my job.

We chat about Barney and Craig for a while and I give her some tips on first foods for weaning as she's thinking about starting on that soon (the baby, not the husband – Craig eats whole grapes and croutons and everything).

I go on a couple more dates later in the week. One guy sounds fun and interesting by text and his name is Benedict – not Ben, but Benedict. I call him Benny just to wind him up. He also tells me that he owns his own marketing company, he only wears suits by Louis Vuitton, he drives a brand-new Alfa Romeo and has a holiday home on Lake Garda. But when we meet I notice that his sweater has hairs on it – dog hairs? Probably. That's okay. I like dogs. But there are a lot of hairs and he hasn't bothered to clean them off. There are loads of bobbles on it too and his nails are a bit dirty. Actually, looking closer, they're very dirty, with thick lines of black filth under each one. And he's in marketing, not a coal miner. No excuse! Imagine those fingers reaching over and . . . URGH. Oh God, am I being petty again? Or are these legit grumbles? You know what, my feelings are legit. Stuff this, the guy hasn't bothered to even do the bare minimum of wash for our date. And where's his Louis Vuitton suit now? At the end he says he's off to get the bus home. *Where's your Alfa Romeo?* I ask him. *At the garage*, he says. *Is it fuck*, I think. Look, I'm pretty poor myself and I have no problem with meeting someone else who's the same or poorer than me. I don't give a stuff about money. But it's the pointless bragging, I hate. It's the lies. From my dating jargon list I'm starting to compile, I understand this type of fellow is a flexter. Mental note – watch out for flexting assholes. If they sound too 'good' to be true, they probably are.

My other one this week is called Jed and he turns up in a neon-tangerine tank-top showing off his gym bod and head-to-toe fake tan that vies with the colour of his tank-top for orangeness. In the one hour we spend talking, he makes seven jokes about how big his cock is. Yes, seven. I was so bored I counted them. Again, I consult my list: a bonafide peacocker. You can tell them by the brash colours and brasher bullshit.

I've done as Bel commanded and gone on some real-life dates. And I must say, all of them have been about as much fun as athlete's foot.

I then spend the next few days giving some guys in their fifties a chance on eHarmony, not worrying too much about their look, as I'm learning that even when you've seen a bunch of photos that might be accurate, actually seeing someone in real life is a whole other thing. We have some good chats. But . . . a pattern is emerging. By Thursday night it's starting to depress me. Jay rings for a catch-up and he asks me how the dating is going.

'Meh,' I say.

'That bad?'

'Yeah. It's just . . . I don't know. I wonder if I'm being too fussy.'

'Why?'

'Well, two things. I'd welcome your advice on both actually.'

'Hit me.'

'Okay, so firstly, I just don't fancy these guys, any of them. Even when the chat is going well, there's no spark.'

'Ah, you gotta have that spark.'

'Right? I mean, that's what I think. Am I being unreasonable?'

'Fuck no. It's that indefinable thing. You can't force that. It's there or it's not there. You could talk to someone till you're blue in the face but if there's no spark, there's no spark and you can't force it into being.'

How did he get so wise at eighteen? He's right though.

'Urgh, I know. But what if the spark is there in real life and not on the phone?'

'Well yeah, good call. It could be. But if it's definitely not there on first meeting – like with those bozos you met – then it's not going to suddenly come on later.'

'You think? I feel bad for not giving them more of a chance. It feels like I'm being mean to them, these men. And crushes might develop over time.'

'Not in my experience, Mam. Not in my extensive romantic experience of approximately five years of dating, since I had my sexual awakening at thirteen in Miss Jackson's chemistry class.'

'Gosh, she was so pretty. I even fancied her a bit at parents' evening.'

'Are you going to tell me you're bi, Mam?'

'I don't think so . . . I'm not sure. I like the way women look. But I can't imagine . . . doing . . . *things* with them.'

'You're not bi then.'

'I don't know what I am!'

'I'd label you bi-curious then.'

'Urgh, why do we have to have labels? Can't we just be . . . complex?'

'It's a useful shorthand. And it allows people to be confident in their identity. And find others they identify with.'

'Well, I tell you what I don't identify with and that's men my own age. That's the pattern I've noticed this week. I'm fifties-UNcurious.'

'How so?'

We talk about this for a long time. He doesn't really understand it, because he can't get his head round being in your fifties, not in your late teens. It's a stretch, even for a kid as wise as Jay. So it's hard to explain to him. But it goes something like this: after a couple of years of menopausal hell, I finally started to feel about a year ago that I was coming through it (with the help of magical HRT) and that a new, hopeful phase of my life was unfolding before me. But, without exception, when I'm talking with these men in their fifties, I find all of them are looking for a long-term relationship immediately, ready-made. And they're so often bitter about divorce, or waiting for retirement, or treating a date as a business meeting to be scheduled and overall about as interesting as magnolia paint. These men of my age act as if their life is ending, whereas I feel like my life has only just begun. I hate to condemn a whole age group to cliché – I don't want to be that person, because I hate it when society does that to me. I'm a woman in my fifties, therefore I've become invisible. And sexless. And past child-bearing age and therefore pointless. Excuse me while I retire to obscurity and collapse. But THESE GUYS IN THEIR FIFTIES ARE BORING! Even their profiles are boring. So many of them put no effort in to them at all.

'That there is a classic beige flag', Says Jay.

'A what? Ooh, is this one to add to my list of dating jargon?'

'It is indeed. The idea is, if someone has made zero effort with their dating profile and it's really generic or, like, horribly clichéd, then they might not make much effort with their relationships either. So yeah, watch out for beige flags when you're checking out people's profiles. To save yourself drowning in dullness later.'

'Oh my God, some of these older guys are so, so dull. And bitter. And entitled. And Plenty of Fish is sitting there, laden with messages from younger guys awaiting me . . . and they're so tempting. I can't resist.

So, Jay says simply, 'Date younger then.'

'Is it that simple? Are all younger guys more exciting?'

'Nope. Loads of people my age or in their twenties are boring as fuck. But at least they're not bitter. At least they're living life and looking forwards, instead of back. And that's where you are, Mam. You might be fifty but you don't bloody look it.'

'Aw thanks, honey.'

Jay goes on, 'And you just don't look young, you act it too. Not in a pick-me way, but in your attitude, y'know? Like the way you're looking forward all the time, planning your new life. After the hell that was Dad. And that's great. Maybe you're better suited to young, fit guys. And why not, Mam? Get out there and have fun. You deserve it.'

I'm inspired. My eighteen-year-old son has given me permission to have some fun. And how can I refuse? Maybe all these serious dates with serious men my age is the opposite of what I need. After twenty years in emotional and sexual jail, maybe it's the somewhat younger guys that could bring me a file in the cake. I've heard of MILFs – Mothers I'd Like to Fuck. Am I a MILF? Well, well. Maybe I am. Maybe I need to set the MILF in me free. I get straight back on POF and start chatting.

So. Many. Young. Guys. You would not believe how many younger guys want to talk to a fifty-year-old woman. They range from forties down to early twenties. I even get one whose age is set as thirty-seven but he tells me he's done that just to get past POF's age gap limit and he's actually nineteen! Nope, nope, nope to that. Even twenties feels too close to my son's age, which just feels . . . wrong. So I set an age limit in my head. Nothing younger than thirty-nine. Or thirty-eight? Then I start talking to Aaron. He's thirty-five and he's in Lincoln for a year doing his master's in linguistics. And he is fit as FUCK. His pictures are so hot, I immediately assume he's a catfish. But when we start talking, he's really erudite and well-spoken. His messages are fascinating. Would such an intelligent guy use fake photos? His main pic is of him topless, laughing, with the most magnificent chest and abs you've ever seen (on a non-celebrity) in your life. And the pic is a bit grainy, it doesn't seem photoshopped or stolen from a model shoot. The guy in the pic is PERFECT. Floppy light-brown hair and a sculpted beard. He clearly looks after himself exceedingly well. He's a stunner. And intelligent. He's very upfront about what he wants. It's even written on his profile: *Life's too short to get serious; let's meet up and have some good, clean, adult fun.*

Ideal. (Also, use of semi-colon spot on.)

Then below it, he's added: *ENM. One night only with you, so no attachment.*

I screenshot this and send to Bel, asking her, what's this ENM all about? She explains it's ethical non-monogamy. He's saying he's in a long-term relationship and his partner knows he has sex with other women. But they've agreed that he can only have one-night stands, so he doesn't get attached to the other women he sees. What if he's lying about the ethical bit? Maybe she doesn't know. But Bel says, why would he put it upfront on his profile then? His partner could easily see it. (Plus he has his Instagram link on there and I go on it and see lots of pics of him at the gym and with his girlfriend, who is also gorgeous.) Bel reckons he's being completely honest about what he wants. And if that's what I want, one night with this guy, then why the hell not?

I surprise myself by thinking, yes. Why the hell not? I've never hankered after one-night stands. But really, what's the problem? We both get some fun and there's no hassle afterwards. So he asks me, can we meet up this Saturday in Lincoln? He passes the verification test with flying colours. The second I ask him, he immediately sends me a video of himself at the gym, where he is at that moment, and he looks straight in the camera and says, 'Hey Frankie. How's it going?' then he smiles. Holy shit, I think my ovaries just exploded.

CHAPTER 6

Nailing The One-Night Stand

Then it hits me: it's potentially my first shag in years AND my first shag with another person than Twatface in decades. In all the excitement, I haven't actually considered this momentous moment at all. I mean, I've got to get naked with another person. A complete stranger. And a bloody good-looking one at that . . . who's fifteen years younger than me. Am I ready for this? Can I actually do this?! What if he looks at my fifty-year-old body in all its glory (not) and grimaces?! I mean I do, on the rare occasions I look in a full-length mirror (though I don't actually own one – I only check myself out in the bathroom mirror standing on a foldaway stool).

And WTF do people wear these days, to a one-night stand? Do I need fancy-shmancy underwear?? Do I have to shave EVERYTHING??? I'm woefully underprepared. I only have a couple of hours after work on Saturday to sort myself, so no time to go to a professional. Dare I shave DOWN THERE? I've never done that. Oh Christ, I really don't want to. I text Bel:

Does everyone in the world have a hairless fanny these days??

It's up to you, babe. I can't shave as I get a bloody awful rash. I get mine waxed.

Do you?!

Yeah, loads of women do. Times have changed, lady. But only do it if you want to. Any man who turns down sex at an unshaven lady-garden isn't worth the bother anyhow.

Does waxing hurt??

Not as bad as you might think. It's a bit like ripping a plaster off, but one that's been welded to your fanny.

CHRIST

Nah honest it's not that bad.

Oh God, I can't face shaving it. What if I get a rash? What if I slice it and dice it?!

Nah, don't bother for tonight. If you want to get it done in future, I'll give you my waxing lady's name. She's ace and gossips about other clients' sex lives while she's ripping your pubes out. And don't tell her anything personal, or you'll be the topic du jour with her next client. She's dead good at the waxing though!

So, no shaving of the down-belows today, but waxing to consider for another time. I Google it out of curiosity. Would I go full Hollywood and have it all off? Leave a landing strip? That's such a weird phrase and I instantly imagine a

Concorde-shaped cock coming into land on it and I'm thinking this makes no sense at all. It's wildly missed the target if that's what it's aiming for. Or do I get a heart-shape?! I'm not topiary, for fuck's sake. Oh God, I'm too old for this shit. So I just shave every other wanton hair on my body. I go to talc my down-belows, then think, what if the talc's still there when I get naked? I'll look like a freshly washed baby FFS. So I don't talc. Then I finish off with a whole body moisturise, just in case. Then I feel greasy. And hot. Urgh, I open the windows to let the cooling winter air in. I'm getting sweaty with the stress of it all. Then I'm freezing so I close them again. This shag better be worth all this . . .

Okay, next, underwear. Again, no time to go sexy lingerie shopping, so I spend far too long choosing between the only two decent (or even matching) sets of fancy underwear I own: green (sophisticated yet environmentally minded?) or red (full-on sex kitten). I go with the red for Aaron. Oh yes. Now, tights? Stockings?? I don't have any stockings. Another thing for the shopping list. Ah damn, I definitely should've made this date for next week. Do I go bare-legged, in February? Do I wear Spanx?? I do own a pair . . . but no, surely that's just for dates with no shagging. I mean, picture him ripping my clothes off then finding a buff-coloured truss. About as sexy as a hernia. Trousers it is, then. I've got a sexy pair of jeans, which are a bit tight but they look good. A little off-the-shoulder red top I got from Boohoo the other week. Next, make-up. Do I go full-on Katie Price or a bit more subtle? Won't too much make-up just smear all over his face while we're at it? Okay, so I go for a light touch: some eyeliner, mascara, a bit of lippy. No foundation and all that jazz. I've never learnt how to do it properly anyway. I am a stranger to contouring. Fuck it, he's seen my pics. He knows about the wrinkles. Hair is blow-dried and I leave it down. Don't want to be messing with hair clips while we're moving to the bed . . . if we get that far. It suddenly occurs to me: what if he takes one look at me and doesn't want to go through with it?! I mean, we've not had a meet-up beforehand. Imagine the humiliation – one look up and down and a no thank you ma'am and off he trots. Oh Jesus, the mortification! *Don't be negative, Frankie. Look at yourself. You don't look half bad, for a fifty-year-old.*

Just before I'm about to leave, Bel messages:

Are you ready then? What u wearing??

I send a selfie back, high-angle, of course: ***ONS ready***

OMFG babe, he's a lucky fella!!! You look stunning! Enjoy every second! You've earnt it!

I shall report back anon . . .

You bloody better do, biatch <3

Right, time to go. One last look in the mirror. *You look all right, pet*, I tell myself. *And if he's not into you, well then, so be it. Plenty more fish in the sea.*

I lock up, go down the steps and into the street, onto Steep Hill. I feel nauseous, oh God, so sick. I need to pull myself the fuck together. *Focus, Frankie. Think about something else. Think about quilting, think about the shop, think about Steep Hill.* I look around me to ground myself. Steep Hill, lovely Steep Hill. I start walking slowly up it.

I don't want to get all puffed by the time I get to the flat. I look around me at the other businesses that flank my little shop. And I'm looking at each one as I slowly inch by, trying not to get hot and bothered, and I realise, they're not just a collection of shops and small businesses. They are my community. How cool is that?! I've never had a community before, not like this. And it hasn't just landed in my lap either. I've made all the effort myself. And I'm proud of that. Since I moved in just before Christmas, I've met shop owners from all over the cathedral quarter and learnt that we all try to shop locally and give each other discounts. I don't know the other owners too well yet, but it's been fab to meet them and see what a community we have here. I see delightful Sasha at the till through the window of *Lindum Books* – she ordered in some great books on biology for me to give to Jay – and give her a wave. I pass by Amy, the owner of *The Fabric Quarter*, and think about her lovely colleagues Annette, Kayleigh and Emily who all help out in that gorgeous shop selling a myriad of fabric designs that my shop doesn't have room for. Walking up this hill to my terrifying first dalliance with a sexy younger man, for the first time in twenty years, I feel a part of something bigger than myself. Yeah, I alone am responsible for my shop and whether or not it goes under. And that's scary. But I'm not truly alone. All around me are other business owners, trying their best to keep going, recommending each other, buying their veg at the greengrocers, their meat at the butchers and other household goods and refills from the *Lincoln Eco-Pantry*. I think back on the years in the house with Twatface as a weird kind of nothingness, blurred at the edges, with the bright centre of raising Jay. I see now I poured all my love into him and my friends and my job at the school, yet there was a hollowness there from the loveless heart of my relationship with Jay's father. Now, poorer financially and utterly alone in my little flat every night, I feel more a part of something alive and ever-changing than I have in decades. I love my life, I love Lincoln and I love higgledy-piggledy Steep Hill.

I feel a thousand per cent better by the time I reach the Prince of Wales Inn on Bailgate. I'm not too puffed and my mind has been occupied with all my recent accomplishments. *You're doing okay, Frankie Brumby. More than okay.* I pass by a shop window that reflects my outfit for this potential one-night stand – and I don't look too terrible, in fact, I look pretty damn good. *You got this, girl. Go get him.*

Aaron is already there, waiting for me outside as I walk up. Oh my lord, I have been blessed this day. The man is a god. He smiles at me.

'Do you wanna drink? Go in and talk a while? Or . . . can I just . . . kiss you?'

There I am, standing in a street in my home town. Anyone who knows me could walk past at any moment and see me with this younger Adonis . . . and honestly, I don't give a shit.

'Kiss me,' I say and he does. And it's bloody marvellous.

We don't bother with the pub. He says he's booked a room at the Tower Hotel around the corner. And yes, it's bloody presumptuous, but you know what? I'm not complaining. I'm actually delighted he's handled it. And that he'll pay! And the Tower is nice, proper nice. We walk straight there, he gets the key from reception and I studiously avoid looking at the young woman receptionist. Does she know what we're up to? Does she judge me? Or is she a tiny little bit envious? I give her a quick glance and she's smirking at me. Smirk away, bitch! I've got Aaron on my arm! We go up to the room and we don't even speak. It's all bodies and movement and sweat and . . . fun. Oh yes, this is the most fun you can have, it's official.

There's a slightly awkward moment when he opens the condom packets (yes, more than one was used that evening, if ya know what I'm saying . . .) but other than that, I feel like I'm in a movie, a soft-focus sex scene that fades out and this is what you imagine happens after, sex in slow-motion, everything in perfect synchronicity. It's not the most daring sex I've ever had, it's not the best technical lover I've ever been with, but my God: the freedom! The liberation! To see a gorgeous guy you want and just . . . have him! Right there and then! And be had by him, in every which way!

When it's all done, and we've had a shower and got dressed, there's an unspoken mutual agreement that we're going to have a quick kiss and say goodnight. We leave the hotel, have a nice, sensual hug on the pavement, then I walk away towards my shop and he goes the other way (thank God – I mean, imagine the embarrassment of both walking the same way and having to make small talk while I try to avoid letting him see where I live). Perfection. And that was my night with Aaron. No strings attached, good sex. The best fun I've had in DECADES. To think, I've spent fifty years on this earth and only just discovered this now. And I have WASTED MY LIFE! The minute I'm home, I immediately send a post-shag selfie to Bel smirking with my hair all mussed up and she replies, *FUCKING YES!!! GET IN!!!* Then she wants a full-blown report on every tasty second of my night and I enjoy every last word of that too.

She messages: *I reckon you've found your new hobby, babe. Fuckfests with fuckboys!*

Isn't fuckboy a bit . . . derogatory though? I mean, he was 35. And doing a masters in linguistics.

So what?! Any guy would be proud to be your fuckboy, you HOT MILF!

So, the jury's in. I am still desirable, even naked. Any doubts I had about whether this fifty-year-old dame could still cut it in the world of dating are banished. Even a few weeks ago, I could not have imagined any man who looked like Aaron even glancing twice at me fully clothed, let alone all the shenanigans we just got up to. It truly is a revelation. Bel was right: there is sex with gorgeous men just hanging around on dating apps, waiting for you to merely say yes. That's all it takes. And I'm guessing a guy of Aaron's looks must be fussy. I mean, he must get dozens of requests every goddamn day of the week. And he chose little old me. This is the best I've felt in years. Yes, decades. I truly believe I look better now than I did when I had Jay. And it's nothing to do with make-up or clothes or weight or hairstyle or any of that nonsense. It's because I'm happy and I'm confident in who I am. I've heard that again and again on the apps: these younger guys, what they find really attractive is an older woman's confidence. She knows who she is, she knows what she wants. Well, I might give off that impression, but I've still got a lot to learn. But the truth is that at least I am old enough to be myself. I'm not trying to pretend anymore. It's like, this is me, take it or leave it. I can't be arsed with fakery. Another thing I do know is that tonight is the start of something for this MILF. And that something is sex, and lots of it, with lots of different people. How can I find out what I want, if I don't shop around? Suddenly, I see the point in casual sex. It's not just about boredom or horniness. It's about variety. I'm on a mission to learn what I want. Because I've spent the last twenty years denying that I'm even a sexual person, with a husband who pretended he was into sex when we met, but very soon after dropped the pretence and from then on we settled into a largely frigid relationship in the bedroom department. How utterly depressing it was, to go to bed every night and know you weren't wanted. Well, that life is over now, thank God. Everything changes from NOW.

I'm still full of the rosy glow of my night with Aaron when the quilt group night rolls round on Monday. They can tell something's up. They know I'm dating and start asking me about it. I'm not ready to spill those beans quite yet, about the glorious shagging of Aaron at the Tower Hotel. I mean, this is my business and these ladies buy stuff from me. What if they think I'm a bit of a . . . well, a bit of a whore? Am I? Well, he didn't pay me. We were two consenting grown-ups, for God's sake. But still, it doesn't feel right to share right now . . .

So, we're sitting at our sewing table, as well as a sewing bench I have down one side, that I've cleared of stock, so we can put machines there and reach the plugs. Two of the ladies have brought in their sewing machines and I've provided the other two. We're making a quilting square by using strips of material to create a house design. The sound of the sewing machines pootling away in fits and starts is soothing to me, one of the best sounds in the world. The pairs are helping each other and we're all chatting away. They ask me how the dating is going.

'Oh, you know. Dating is a strange and magical world of weirdness.'

'*Tell* me about it,' says Paige sarcastically and sighs. Being in her twenties, I assume she knows all about it.

'How do you meet men these days?' says Linda.

'Online dating apps,' I say.

'Oh God,' says Kelly and visibly shudders. 'I met my boyfriend on one of those a few years ago and thank the lord I've been with him ever since and never had to go back. They're atrocious.'

'What is a dating *app*?' asks Linda. I notice Michelle is listening to all this but not offering a word. Married in her forties with two children, you'd guess she knew nothing about such things, but only Linda is openly clueless. Michelle, however, is sitting there sewing away with a little smile on her face. I'd pay money to read her mind right now.

We explain it all to Linda and she's horrified at the idea of chatting to total strangers online, then arranging to meet these potential madmen. She says, 'My gynaecologist told me years ago that the best way to meet someone is at work. Then you can properly verify them. You have people in common, who know their history. I agree with that.'

'But Linda!' I cry. 'This is my work! A sewing shop! And guys never – literally never – come in here! Unless they're lost. Or following their wives under extreme duress.'

Kelly says, 'But maybe a man will come in here one day, who knows? And if he does, what could be better than a man who sews?'

I reply, 'It's more likely that pigs would fly out of my arse than a man come into my shop on his own.'

And at that precise moment, the bell on the door jingles and we all look up. And the shop door has opened and in walks a man.

CHAPTER 7

Meet-Cute

Everyone bursts out laughing and Linda says, 'Bend over, Frankie. Let's see those piggies fly.'

The guy looks shocked, turns round and heads straight out again.

'Oh no!' we all cry and I trot over to the door, having had enough time to clock that the man who came in was handsome as all hell. I open the door and he's standing outside, holding an iPad and smiling. He's got dark hair, dark eyes, dark beard. Absolutely my type. And a great smile. He's probably early forties, maybe? And he really wears it well. Looks in good shape too, though it's tricky to tell under the thick, long, dark-grey winter coat he's wearing. Holy cow, he's utterly delicious. Who the fuck is this guy?!

'Can I come back in?' he says. 'Or is this a private affair?' Oh and a great voice too, smooth and sexy.

'Oh God, please do come back in. I'm so sorry! We were only laughing because I'd literally just said men never come in here. And then you did!'

We laugh about it and I open the door and the ladies are

sitting there, craning their necks to see, all absolutely agog. As he follows me in, it's all I can do to stop myself from collapsing in hysterical giggles, like a damn schoolgirl. But it's Linda's face that absolutely cracks me up, one eyebrow arched like a matchmaker. The others are smirking too, especially Michelle. *OMG Frankie, hold it together. Don't regress to age thirteen just because a good-looking fella has turned up at your shop*. But really, *what* a turn-up!

'Hi everyone,' he says.

'Hi, Hello, Hi,' chorus the ladies in a flutter. My God, we are supposed to be strong, independent, modern women and we are pathetic. Get a grip!

'What can we d-do you for?' I say. Did I really just stutter? And say '*do you for*'?? I sound like Arkwright in *Open All Hours*.

'This is the quilting group, I take it?' he says.

'Well spotted,' I say and grin. *Deep breath. Relax, Frankie.* Frankie says . . . relax.

'Well, my mum is a local lady. She's a quilter and really wants to join the group. But she's broken her hip. I'm looking after her right now while she recovers.'

'Awww,' goes the chorus and other sympathetic noises. So this guy is caring as well as fit AF?! There must be *something* wrong with him, as he's pretty damn perfect so far. He goes on, 'So I suggested I come and ask if she could join by video, on my iPad.' And he holds his iPad aloft, in case we didn't know what an iPad was. But I'm not actually really focusing on a word he says. I'm just staring at him. I mean, Aaron was gorgeous. But he absolutely knew he was gorgeous. He had that swagger about him. This guy is beautiful but he seems totally unaware of it. Slightly awkward, not cocky or arrogant and zero swagger. And that just makes him even sexier. Then I realise everyone's looking at me and I have to speak now.

'Yes, of course!' I say, hoping that the vague meaning my primitive brain registered was the correct one. 'You'd like your mum to join us on video call. Please, make yourself comfy. You're both very welcome. We'd love to have her join us, however she can.' I mean, of course I said yes. I'd say yes to any damn thing this guy wants. Within reason . . . and even then . . .

'Ah great, thanks,' he says and he's taking off his coat to reveal a dinosaur T-shirt with a T-Rex with its mouth wide open, and a diplodocus saying 'Cover your mouth when you cough!' And the T-Rex with its little arms replying, 'I fucking can't!' OMG it's one of my favourite memes! This guy is into memes! And the T-shirt is just figure-hugging enough to show the curve of his back and the dip of his waist and I really need to stop staring at him like this, it's obscene.

He goes on, 'She's a very experienced seamstress and quilter. She's been sewing all her life. She's from Slovakia and they have a great tradition of embroidery there. She's so talented. And very excited a new sewing group has started around the corner. She lives just down Steep Hill, on Danes Terrace, just along from the gallery.'

'You're Slovakian? How fascinating! I've never met anyone from Slovakia before.'

'No, I'm English. Well, I'm half Slovakian. My dad was English and I was born here. But I do really appreciate my Slovakian heritage.'

I really appreciate *both* your halves, I'm thinking. Top half, bottom half. Both very good halves. Then I realise everyone is staring at us and I think my cheeks are bright red. I glance around and the ladies sense they've been gawping too much and busily start sewing away, like nothing out of the ordinary is happening. Nothing to see here, move along.

'Well, let's get you set up, shall we?' I say and beckon to him to take a seat. I still have a couple of spares out in case we get any newcomers. And what a newcomer! Blimey, I hope he stays once he gets his mum on the iPad. She can watch the sewing and I'll happily sit and fixate on him all damn night, like a dog on a string of sausages.

'Oh and my mum's name is Margita. But everyone calls her Gita. And I'm Stefan. But everyone calls me Stef.'

'Hi Stef,' says everyone. Stefan. Stef. Such a nice name. It's not your common or garden Lincoln man. It's not your Mike or Steve or Dan. It's different. I like it.

'Let me introduce us all,' I say. 'This is Paige, Kelly, Linda and Michelle.' He says hi and they all say hi and nod and then he looks at me and those eyes make me dumbstruck again.

'You forgot about you,' he says.

'So I did,' I say. Yes, I did. For twenty years, Stef. You have no idea. 'I'm Frankie.'

'Hello Frankie,' he says in that sexy voice and I literally just DIE. 'Thanks so much for putting up with all this. You've no idea how much this means to her. She heard about the group from a friend and she's not stopped talking about it since. She couldn't believe it was just up the hill and was so frustrated she couldn't get here yet. So I told her, I'd see if she could do it via video and she had no idea such a thing was possible. So here we are.'

'Here we are,' I echo. 'It's no problem at all. Happy to help. Please, get her logged in and I can have a chat with her about what we do here and she can join in with our sewing projects.'

'Perfect,' he says and begins to set up the iPad. The ladies are sewing and continue chatting amongst themselves, to break up the atmosphere. I really need to stop staring at him, but every time he glances up and smiles, I'm rooted to the spot. Holy shit, those eyes! They are to die for. What a total goddamn honest-to-God SNACK this Stef is. And here he sits, in my shop, at my table! You couldn't make this shit up. If you put it in a romcom, nobody would believe it.

Then a voice emanates from the iPad and fills the room, as the volume is up high.

'Hello Števko!' says the voice. It's an older woman, with a delightful Eastern European accent. 'I can see you, darling!'

Everyone is rapt. What do I know about Slovakia? Absolutely nothing. That's a poor show. I know I'll be Googling my fingers off later.

'I can see you too, Mamka,' says Stef. Or Števko ? What's that about? Sounds like a diminutive. Like Frankie for Frances. How adorable! She says the first syllable with an interesting extra sound, a kind of sh and ch added together. And hearing Stef say Mamka (which must mean Mum or Mummy?) does not have the same weird vibes as MAMA MAN. This time it's cute as heck. 'I'm going to turn the screen round now, Mamka. So you can see everyone and they can see you.'

'Oh thank you, my darling.' And Margita is revealed to us. Stefan must have positioned her camera a little way away from her, as we can see more than just her face. She's sitting in a wing-backed armchair, a sewing project on her lap, with her pin cushion velcroed to the chair arm. Clever. This lady clearly does a lot of sewing. She has a lovely, smiley face, with those same dark eyes she's given to her son. Her hair is white and dead straight, pulled back from her face in a high ponytail, very neat. She's wearing a powder-blue jumper and a string of pearls. She's obviously made an effort. 'Hello everybody! I am so happy to meet you all!'

'Hello Margita!' we all say.

'Can I tell you some things?' she says.

'Yes, yes, of course,' we all say. Stef sets the iPad up at the far side of the table, propped up so she can see us all.

'Ah, what a lovely group of young ladies you are! My apologies for hijacking your marvellous gathering.'

'No, no, not at all,' comes the group reply and I can tell everyone is completely delighted with the unexpected arrival of these two new personalities into the hotbed of quilters. This is top-class entertainment all round. She speaks quite slowly, enunciating everything so clearly. And her English is top-notch. She's a pleasure to listen to.

'I would like to introduce myself. My name is Margita Walker but everyone calls me Gita, so please, you must. My son has told you, I take it, about my hip? Well, it is a nuisance but hopefully only of a temporary nature. When I have recovered and I can walk up the hill, I will be joining you. Until then, we must make do with modern conveniences, eh? Thanks to my son and his brilliant little gadget. My son is called Štefan Walker, but as you probably heard, I call him my Števko, which is a term of endearment in my native Slovakia. I have lived in Lincoln for many years, since the 1960s. I married an Englishman and we moved to this very house and I've been here ever since. I raised my Števko here and this house holds many happy memories. It is on Steep Hill and it is a steep little house with a steep little staircase, that I slipped upon and fractured my silly hip. Such are the perils of age, my dears. Though you all look so young, you will have no idea what I'm talking about yet.'

Linda looks pleased with that! I look around at everyone and they're all engrossed in Gita's speech. Then I glance at Stef and see he's looking at me. Looking straight at me. He gives me a small, sweet smile and I smile back. Be still my beating heart! And my stirring loins!

'Well, my Števko is looking after me, as he is such a good, kind and loving son. And such a handsome boy!'

'That's enough, Mamka,' says Stef and facepalms. *Oh, do embarrass him some more,* I'm thinking. I'd love to see him blush . . .

'If a mother cannot be proud of her son's good looks, then I don't know what the world is coming to. He is a very clever man. He is a designer and has worked in many different countries, learning about their cultures and incorporating them into his designs.'

Could he be any cooler?!

'And he has inherited that talent for the visual from me. We both have a good eye, as one says. So now he is back in Lincoln while he looks after me, but he will be backwards and forwards to Slovakia where his fiancée lives.'

Gah! Fiancée?? I knew he was too good to be true. Ffffffuck. He's bloody engaged. Ah, well. Another dream guy bites the dust. I'm not at all surprised though. It'd be ridiculously unheard of that a man this delicious could be single. Maybe his fiancée will lose her bloody mind and dump him. A girl can hope!

Gita goes on, 'And once they are married this autumn, we will all be moving back to Slovakia to live together in the same house.'

There is a stunned silence at this revelation. Mamka living

with the newlyweds? Maybe it's the norm in Slovakia, who knows? (More to Google later.) Stef has his hand over his eyes now. He's dreadfully embarrassed. But to his credit, he doesn't scold his mother or tell her what to do. She's clearly enjoying herself immensely and he just shakes his head with a wry smile.

'Anyway, I've taken up far too much of your time, my friends. Thank you for indulging me. Now I would like to meet you all.'

I do the honours and introduce everyone. Gita makes a point of grabbing a little notebook and pencil from the table beside her and writing down everyone's names, so she doesn't forget them. I then talk her through the project we're working on, a series of squares in different designs, each of which practises a skill, to which we'll give a backing, then join them all together in a finished quilt. Gita loves the idea of this and then has a chat with me about her own ideas for her squares. Then, as the rest of the group keep sewing and chatting, Stef, Gita and I look through some fabrics together and we hold them up to the camera for her to see. She gets up from her chair with some difficulty, though manages it and although we tell her not to bother herself, she wants to be involved and brings her screen closer, and after putting on her reading glasses, she inspects the materials closely before making her choices, which she'll mix with ones she already has. She's very gracious and keeps thanking me and saying how kind I am.

'But my dear, isn't Frankie a boy's name?'

'Mamka,' warns Stef, as he flashes his eyes at me, then looks at her sternly. Rude old lady alert! She's about to say some controversial stuff and she won't give a shit what anyone else thinks. I remember this from my own grandmother, years ago.

'It's short for Frances,' I tell her.

'Ah, then I shall call you Frances. It is such an attractive name, like the sound of an English rose.'

'No problem, Gita,' I say and smile. I glance at Stef and he mouths, *Sorry.* And I shake my head to dismiss his concerns and smile at him.

'Anyway, dear Frances. I have rather taken over your class tonight and I do apologise for that, to all of you.'

'Not at all. It's been our pleasure.'

Linda says loudly, 'It's super to meet you, Gita.'

Gita glances hastily at her notepad, then looks up and says, 'And you, Linda. And Paige, Michelle and Kelly. Lovely to meet you all. And Frances, our gracious hostess. Thank you so much for your patience and being so welcoming. I shall leave you now and, with your permission, I will attend by video call again next week and that time, I will not talk so much. I will be sewing instead and keep my mouth shut a little more!'

'Not at all, Gita,' I say. 'We have loved hearing from you. See you next time.'

Everyone says their goodbyes and we all wave, then Stef takes the iPad and signs off with a quick couple of phrases in Slovakian. He waves goodbye to her and this time calls her Mamicka – pronounced *Mam-itch-ka* – which he says with real affection. They seem to have such a sweet relationship. It brings up memories for me of my own mum and I have to shake my head to bring myself back to the moment. Something about this man and his mother are giving me the deep-down feels and I have to get a hold of myself . . .

It's not long from the end, so we start to clear away, Stef helping. We're all chatting away about Margita and the ladies are asking him some questions about Slovakia and it's all very congenial. But I feel like I've been punched in the stomach. I'm annoyed at myself for being so affected by it, but meeting Stef tonight has been such a wonderful surprise and then finding out straight away that he's engaged was hard to hear. It was like someone suddenly showing you a steaming delicious bowl of cherry crumble and custard, then whipping it away and giving it to someone else. It's not that you particularly had any plans to eat cherry crumble at that moment, but once you had it there, under your nose and you could almost taste its sweetness on your tongue, it's gone and you want it even more. It's crazy to think that meeting this one guy and spending this short time with him and his mother could have a deep effect on me, but the truth is, it has. And as I watch him chat amicably with the group and be so helpful to them, just as he was with his mother, I realise he's not just a snack, a ride, a nice piece of ass and all that stuff we say about hot guys. He seems like a genuinely nice person. I like him. I like him a lot. And I think, well, you know what, that's good. It's good to meet good people. It reminds you that there are good chaps out there too, not just weirdos or bores or fuckboys. There are flesh and blood decent men out there. Stef is one of them, so there must be more. And that is truly heartening and cheers me up a treat.

The ladies are all done and they're saying goodbye. And I think Stef will go out with them but he hangs back. Linda gives me a quick look before she goes and I know she's clocked him loitering and is amused. She winks at me and I smirk at her and look away. I don't want Stef thinking we're laughing at him. I'm guessing now he's set his mother up, he'll just drop the iPad off next time and come back at the end. I hold the door open, expecting him to pop through it and say goodbye, but he's still standing there, making no move to go.

'I just wanted to thank you for tonight,' he says.

I shut the door – to keep the heat in, obvs.

'That's no problem at all. It really was my pleasure. Your mother is delightful.'

'She's . . . yeah. She's a character!'

'She surely is. And all the more delightful for it. I'm so glad she's joined our group.'

'So is she. I could tell. She was lapping it up.'

'Ah, great! I'm glad.'

'And she'll be buying your shop out, if you're not careful.'

'Fine by me!' I say, rubbing my hands together.

'Have you had the shop long? I don't remember it being here the last time I visited, I must say.'

'A few weeks. It's a new venture. I'm running the group to try to drum up a bit more business. Times are hard.'

'Of course. I wish you every success with it. It's a beautiful shop. Full of beautiful things. You've organised everything so . . . gracefully.'

Never, in all my life, has anyone applied the adjective 'graceful' to Frankie Brumby. I find my cheeks are threatening to flare again. 'Oh God, don't. You'll make me blush.'

'Well, credit where it's due. And the quilts on the wall up there. Are they yours? Did you make them?'

I look up to two quilts I've hung above the cash desk. They are both mine. One is filled with tiny hexagons that form larger hexagons, all in separate materials, themed around the colours of terracotta, lavender and sea green. The other is an art quilt, that follows no style other than its own and my imagination. It's a collection of organic shapes, all in autumnal shades.

'Yes,' I say. 'They're mine.'

'They're stunning,' he says. And I really am blushing now. 'Tell me about them.'

'Oh, well, there's not much to tell. The hexagonal one is in the 1930s style, what we call a Grandmother's Flower Garden motif. It's the very first full-size quilt I ever made, so I'm proud of it for that reason mostly. The other one is . . . well, it's more personal. It represents my grandfather's garden in October, my favourite month. He died when I was thirteen, oh-so-many years ago. And he was my favourite person I ever knew.'

Gosh, just talking about Grandad makes me well up. The kindest man I ever knew, who tended the most beautiful garden. How I miss him still, even after thirty-seven years.

We stand and stare at the quilts and I will myself not to cry. It must be menopause, to get me all emotional like this over nothing. It's silly. *Pull yourself together, woman.*

'Thank you for telling me that,' says Stef and I glance at him. After thinking about Grandad and seeing those deep, dark eyes of Stef's regarding me, I actually feel a little bit weak at the knees, like a bloody Jane Austen heroine, for God's sake.

'You're welcome,' I say and look away, because those eyes kill me, they really do. 'And thanks for the compliments. You're a designer, so I'm glad you appreciate them. What kind of work do you do?'

'Oh, a mixture of projects. I work freelance as a book jacket illustrator for a couple of publishers. I've done wallpaper patterns and designed layouts for museum displays, as well as the usual advertisements and product packaging. That kind of thing. I've even done a few fabric designs, in Slovakia and the US.'

'Wow, really? I'd love to see some of your fabrics.'

'I'll bring some in next time. Oh, and about next time.'

I know he's going to say that he'll just drop the iPad off next time and I'm going to be desperately disappointed and I'll have to hide it.

'Yeah?'

'I don't want to be just sitting there with nothing to do. My mother taught me how to sew, but I've not done it for a few years, only the odd button here or there. And I'd love to get back into it. Could I . . . would you let me join the group and sew a bit? I know I'll be miles behind everyone else, but I promise I won't get in anyone's way or bother you. It just seems a shame to be sitting there twiddling my thumbs, when you're all having fun. I'd like to join in. If that's okay?'

Of COURSE it's okay, man! It's GREAT!

'Yeah sure, no problem,' I say, affecting insouciance. 'I'll help you. If you need it.'

'Oh, I will need it. Listen, thanks again for looking after my mother so well. I haven't seen her that happy in ages. You've really made her night. And mine.'

He looks away before I have the chance to reply and walks swiftly to the door. I follow him and he opens it up, the bell jingling brightly.

'See you soon, then!' he says.

'You're welcome!' I say and he walks away and I'm cursing myself. See you soon . . . you're welcome? That doesn't even mean anything. I'm standing holding the door with my eyes screwed shut, telling myself I'm a stupid fucking idiot and there's his voice again. I open my eyes and there is Stefan Walker, large as life.

'I forgot my iPad.'

'Oh shit, sorry. I mean, yeah. Here you go.' And I grab it from the table and pass it to him. He turns to leave and then stops.

'And you're not a fucking idiot,' he says in a low voice, conspiratorially. 'Far from it.' A little smile and he's gone, off down the hill.

I shut the door and collapse on a stool, nearly toppling it over. What the hell just happened here? I come over all Jane Austen again and feel a bit feeble. Then I realise I forgot to have dinner before the group tonight and I'm starving. I totter upstairs and quickly fashion a banana sandwich on granary bread, my go-to comfort energy food. I eat it ravenously and glug down some semi-skimmed, straight from the bottle. My mind is racing. I'm bloody confused. What am I thinking? What's this feeling? It feels like . . . feels like . . . no. I'm not going there. I've just found my new hobby: fuckboys. This is the new me. Liberated, in control. No attachment, no broken heart. But . . . Stef. Stefan. *Števko* . . . I see those eyes again in my mind and ffffffuck, there goes my tummy again, all butterflies. It wasn't like that with Aaron. That was pure lust. That was all loins and down-belows. This is . . . something else. I like him. I like his gentleness with his mother and the others in the group. His politeness, that he's so relaxed in himself and yet not arrogant – a hard balance when you're that handsome. I like his interest in art and craft and design and that he wanted to know about my work. And that he thanked me for sharing it with him. I like all of that. I like him, very much. And he's so very, very, very pretty . . . *Right, that's enough of that, Frankie. You just met this guy and you don't actually know him at all and what's more, he's engaged.*

This is ridiculous. But also . . . a bit thrilling. I message Bel.

Something ace happened tonight. This very cool man came to our sewing group. And . . . omg I don't even know where to start.

I send it off and see Bel's not online. I put my phone down. I really don't know where to start. I can't process this. Then my phone pings and I grab it, desperate to talk to the only person who gets me about all this guy stuff. My other friends are mostly my age or older, all married or in long, long, long-term relationships. Nobody else I know has internet dated or even been on a date in decades. Bel is the only one who understands all this dating madness.

Sorry babe Barney is off the fucking charts misery guts tonight and has been for hours

Your night sounds AWESOME and I deffo want to hear all about it later

Msg you later when he calms the fuck down if he ever fucking does

Luv u xxx

Oh God, poor Bel. I remember those nights. They were hellish.

Sorry darling. Can I help? Want me to come take him for a while?

Nah but thanks, babe. I've got him in the sling with

the washing machine on full spin and he's starting to calm down a bit. We'll probably take him out in the car in a minute. He always falls asleep in there. Thanks though babe. Catch you later xxx

OK sweetie. Good luck. Call me if you need me.

She hearts my message then goes offline. Bel's shitty evening brings me down to earth with a bump. I'm lucky I'm not standing with a screaming baby and instead I had a fun, interesting evening. And he was a nice guy. With a fabulous mother. And he's engaged. And that's that. Yes, he's gorgeous. Yes, he's a real man I met at work, just as Linda's gynaecologist predicted. And yes, he's not an internet weirdo or bore or fuckboy. Somehow the men on there don't seem half as real as Stefan. It's as if the ether conjures them up. But Stef is a real live man, not one of these online phantoms, but someone I met by accident IRL (In Real Life, as they say). But . . . he's taken. *So, Frankie, you need to move on. Now get over yourself and get back on those apps. That'll take your mind off things.*

So, I finish my sandwich and plonk myself in front of the TV, put some random Netflix murder documentary on for company and get on my phone. I swipe for a while, grimacing at all these gurning nobodies, when a message pops into my inbox from a brand new, bona fide, totally obvious CATFISH. Yesssssss. This'll take my mind of things, off the delectable, delicious, delovely Stefan. A little spot of catfish-fishing before I end my evening with a glass of red and a snooze on the sofa.

This particular species of catfish is well known to me now, the military hero, working either for the Americans or the UN, out there petting puppies and saving lives. This one is called Michael Michael – NO WORD OF A LIE! So crap they named him twice. His profile pic is a muscled masterpiece in khaki, with bulging muscles and a kitten on one shoulder. Yes, an actual kitten.

Hello beautiful

Hello to you! Love the kitty.

Thanks I am glad. Where are you?

I'm in my prime, darling. Where are you?

I am not where you think I am

Ooh, that's intriguing. Where are you REALLY? Be honest, now. Tell the truth, the whole truth and nothing but the truth.

I will tell you the whole truth and that is I am in the US Army deployed to Ghana and I work very hard to stop Ghanaian militants from attacking petroleum pipelines.

I will tell you the whole truth too. I'm a Ghanaian militant who attacks petroleum pipelines. What are the chances?!

CHAPTER 8

Quilting For Two

The following week, on the day of the class, I get an email via my website from Stef, which I open desperately, all fingers and thumbs, to find he's informing me that his mother is not feeling well and so he won't be there that night. God, I'm gutted! I've been thinking about this session all week. I've barely glanced at the dating sites, only engaging in a bit of comedy banter with the elusive Guy, but otherwise, moping around about the delectable Stefan. I hope this isn't permanent, that Gita and Stef weren't put off and won't ever come back and this is just an excuse. I reply, saying how sorry I am she's poorly and really hope she'll feel better soon. He replies again:

Thanks Frankie. But honestly, she's ok, so don't worry. She's only got a cold and is blowing her nose a lot and refuses to be seen by anyone when she's got a red nose, even though I told her nobody would mind and it's not even that red. But she wouldn't have it. She always likes to look her best. So, there you go. Nothing to fret about, as it's more a mild case of vanity than life-threatening, though don't tell her I said so. We shall be back next week, never fear. I'm looking forward to it.

At this chatty reply, I want to answer and start chatting back, asking him things and telling him things, but it doesn't feel quite right yet. So I just reply, ***Ah brilliant. See you then and please send Gita our love.***

I press send and then think, our *love*? Is that a bit over-the-top? I mean, we've only just met her. But it's actually how I feel. I mean, not *love* love; I don't know the woman yet. But I care about her already. I care about all my quilters and about Stef. It's something about being the one who runs the group, feeling responsible for them all, yet it's also about her being Stef's mum, that she feels like a person in whom I have a vested interest. But she's also fascinating and gracious and I'm glad she's in my life, even if she didn't have a mouth-watering son. I wonder if he'll reply and keep chatting, but he doesn't. Of course he doesn't. He's engaged and he can't be chatting away randomly about his life with some female shop owner. But then, later on that day, I do get a reply that reads, *I will and she'll appreciate it. She's very keen to show you her Slovakian sewing designs, based around cross-stitch and other sewing methods too. It's a charming style, seemingly simple yet full of vibrancy and vitality (and probably some other words beginning with v I can't think of). Anyway, no need to reply, as I'm sure you're busy, so I'll see you next time.*

Oh God, I'm so tempted to answer. And I know what kind of style he's talking about, as I've been Googling like mad all week about Slovakia and looked at loads of Slovakian embroidery. It really is charming. I do want to reply and keep chatting with him about Slovakia, but I don't. I feel like I'll get in too deep, too soon. And I can't do that. Because already, after only knowing him a week, I know for sure I'm in danger of falling for him big time. So I restrain myself. I don't hear any more from him. Somehow, that seems right. I mean, there's a part of me that's like, *Make him wait!* Even though, of course, we're not engaging in a mating dance here. The man's engaged to his Slovakian fiancée and they're all moving in together with Mamka when they're married, so . . . I don't reply. Am I being petty? Or just protecting my tender heart? Then, I scold myself. He's just a guy, just the son of a client. That's all. I need to practise being nonchalant. I need to stop being so goddamn *chalant*.

The next week, Stef is true to his word and is back with Gita on the iPad. Seeing him again in the flesh is just as powerful as last time, if not more so. He's wearing black jeans and a puffy navy-blue winter coat that zips up tightly, showing off his shape. He unzips it to reveal this week's T-shirt: a picture of Yosemite Sam saying 'I smell carrots a-cooking!' Oh blimey, he's a *Looney Tunes* fan, just like me. And the carrots quote is so niche, I absolutely love it. And these kind of nerdy connections with another person are gold. He needs to stop being so perfect! Gah! How I would love to take him to Bel's shed and get him high and listen to his whole life story and all that David Copperfield stuff from 'I was born at a very young age' to right now. I want to know everything!

We all settle down again to sew, some at the table, some at the bench on their machines. Kelly's not here yet, but I've had a message from her, saying she's running late. The others are all chatting away about their week, while I am the one who is designated to assist the beautiful Stefan with his incipient sewing skills. Lucky fucking me! He's brought with him two fabrics of which he was the original designer, just as he promised he would the other week. They are proper gorgeous. One is on a dark blue background, with silvery-white moon and star shapes, and a benevolent face on the moons surrounded by moon-rays, like something from a medieval representation of the night sky. It's gorgeous. The other is a great contrast, with bees buzzing between sunflowers, on a spring-green background. There's humour and sweetness in the designs, something ethereal yet grounded about them. Seeing a glimpse of Stefan's art makes me all the more hungry to know him better. As well as him being an absolute goddamn ride of a man. Yep, I've not got over my lust for him. Quite the opposite.

This week we're creating a square depicting a little house – it looks a bit like Bel's house actually – with oblongs for windows and a door, a trapezium roof and a square chimney, with some blue fabric for the sky behind it. I'm showing Stef how to use the templates to cut out the fabric. Most new sewers – or sewists/seamsters/needleworkers/quilters or whatever else you want to call a person who sews – are nervous when it comes to cutting fabric for the first time. Most adults hate the idea of making a mistake. They feel like they've failed if it doesn't go perfectly. Stef, however, gets the scissors and bang – cuts that fabric like a pro – no hesitation, clean, sharp lines. I remember that he's an artist himself and that precision with his hands is the norm. It's a pleasure to watch him. Once we've cut out all of the pieces – using his moon fabric for the night sky and his sunflower fabric for the windows and door – I show him how to put these together using the sewing machine. He's never used one before, so we have to start from scratch. And oh, what a delight that is, to lean over this gorgeous man and help him get his fingers around this fiddly new skill. It's like the pottery scene from *Ghost*, except I'm Patrick Swayze and he's Demi Moore and it's all a lot less claggy. We may only be sewing up a few blocks of material, but I must say, it's the most erotic experience I've had in a long time. It even beats Aaron . . . almost.

Then, Kelly comes in and she's all a-flutter. She announces she has news.

'Listen guys, I've been down at the Usher Gallery because I play music with a friend who works there and she's really nice. And anyway, she told me they're planning an exhibition about quilting in June. And she's asked us to produce a range of quilts for the show! Isn't that fab?!'

'That's cool as fuck!' I cry. 'How many quilts do they want?'

Kelly explains that they want three in total, not too large, 'And she said they can be in any style we like and the overarching theme of the exhibition is the idea of *homeland*.'

Homeland, we all start musing. Hmmm . . . interesting theme.

'If they want three quilts,' says Linda, 'and there's six of us, then we should pair off and produce one quilt between two.'

'Yeah, that's what I said to my friend. Makes sense,' says Kelly.

Paige says, 'I'm bloody glad you suggested that, because I was just sitting here shitting myself about making my first quilt. Can I pair with someone really experienced?'

'That'll be me,' says Michelle, who's generally considered the expert of the group, apart from me obvs. So even though it might sound like Michelle was being smug, it didn't come across that way. We all know how good she is and what a fount of wisdom she is about quilting.

Linda adds, 'Paige, you go with The Oracle then. And I'll go with Kelly.' Then Linda turns her face to me and there's that knowing smirk again. Oh, bless you, Linda, for thou hast paired me off with Stefan, you little beauty! I glance at him to see he's smiling at me and then I remember his mother on the iPad and think, *Dammit, forgot about Gita, bless her!*

'Gita,' I say and go up to her screen. 'Did you hear all that?'

'Yes, I did. How very exciting! But Števko, when did they say this exhibition is? Will we be back in Slovakia by then? Is it before the wedding?'

'Yes, it's months before that, Mama,' says Stef. 'Plenty of time.'

The wedding. It's all really happening then, with this fiancée of his. I didn't realise they'd set a date.

Gita goes on, 'Ah, that is fine then. I would like to work with you, my dear Frances, and with my son. We can all help each other, if that is acceptable to you?'

'It certainly is,' I say and again, see that Stef is smiling at me. Instead of ducking my eyes away like I usually do, I think, *sod it*. I'm gonna be working with this guy on a project for the next few weeks, so I look him square in the eye and beam at him. And I swear down, a bolt of electricity sizzles between us. I didn't imagine it, I really didn't. And this time, it's him who looks away. Hey . . . what's going on here? One minute, the wedding is mentioned and the next, we're making eyes at each other. Or I'm just imagining it. Yeah, he's just a nice, friendly guy and he's getting married in a few months. And I'm just imagining this connection between us. *Pull yourself together, Frankie.*

'That's all worked out very nicely then, hasn't it?' says

Linda and I glance at her to see that smirk again. She's not the only one, as all the other quilters are smirking too and I wonder if they can see the chemistry sizzling between me and Stef and they enjoy stoking the fire . . . I bet they do, the crafty little minxes.

I get paper and pencils for everyone, and we all pair up and start scribbling down ideas and designs for our homeland quilts. Gita says how delighted she is with the theme, as she can include some Slovakian style in our quilt.

'But what about you, Frances? Where is your homeland?'

'Good question,' I say. 'I moved around a lot as a kid, but came here when I was seventeen, so Lincoln is my homeland, I guess, if anywhere is.'

'Same here,' says Stef, 'though I feel like it's fifty-fifty for me, split between Lincolnshire and Slovakia.'

'It'd be nice to incorporate both in the quilt then,' I say. 'I really love the Lincoln Imp, the naughty little chap carved in the cathedral. Maybe we could have him on there.'

'And the big, blue Lincolnshire skies,' says Stef.

We chat more and get lots of ideas down. Everyone's very excited about the new project and we end the group that night all buzzing with plans. I'm particularly pleased that it'll give the shop a bit of publicity. Daily, I worry about the shop not doing enough business to stay afloat. Anything like this that spreads the word to the right audience has to be helpful. And I'm also delighted I'll be working with Stef and his mum. What a pleasure that'll be.

I'm thinking about this during the week, when I see I've got another email from Stef, which gets me all hot under the collar, but then, it starts with a sentence entirely written in capitals:

FRANCES – IT IS GITA HERE!

Dear Frances,

Apologies for hijacking my son's email, yet I do not have my own. I do not like computers. I like writing letters by hand. But anyway, here we are. I'd like to invite you to my house at number 2, Danes Terrace, for tea and cakes on Monday at 2.15pm, as I know Monday is your day off and I would very much like to know you face to face and talk about our homeland quilt and share Slovakian honey cake with you. What do you say?

What do I say? Yes bloody please! What a delightful plan. I can't wait to have a gossip with Gita and get to know her better, and the cake is a bonus. Slovakian honey cake sounds divine. Honey and cinnamon are my favourite flavours ever. Of course, I reply in the affirmative and so it is that the following Monday, I leave the flat and stroll out onto Steep Hill for a little walk down to Gita's house. I wonder if Stef will be there. And I find I don't really mind if he is or not, as I'm just really happy to meet Gita in person, at last.

It's a crisp, sunny, early spring day. There's a chill in the air, but the skies are caerulean, and the sun so bright, Lincoln wears the guise of summer. I look up at the old *Harlequin Gallery Bookshop*, empty now since the business closed, its Tudor half-timbered top floor jutting out over Steep Hill, with its white walls, black beams and wonky profile, the sky resplendently blue behind it. Lincoln is bloody lovely, it really is. Steep Hill snakes down its cobbled street, flanked on both sides by a huddle of historic buildings in long, tall terraces punctuated here and there by side streets and trees, and private houses with window boxes and wisteria. Nowadays, there are a mixture of eateries, pubs, gift shops and boutiques, and other specialisms, from a cat café to antiques and the *Harding House Gallery*, *Timepiece Repairs*, shops selling wigs, leaf tea, chocolate, aromatherapy, fossils, furniture, flowers, artworks and pottery, fudge, ice cream and books.

Halfway down you reach Michaelgate and the church to the right, Christ Hospital's Terrace and the Old Palace off to the left. It's a good job I don't have a car, as there's bugger all parking down here. It wasn't constructed for an age of motor vehicles. I make my way down to Danes Terrace, hearing the cathedral bells above ring out from their burnished clotted-cream-coloured walls, tolling the quarter-hour as I arrive at Gita's house at 2.15pm, just as she requested. I knock on the door and wonder who's going to answer. It takes a while, the door opens and there is Gita, resplendent in a white dress belted at the waist. She might have a dodgy hip but she's effortlessly chic.

Her hip is still healing but at least she's up and about and able to move around her house all right. It's a narrow house with small rooms, and every surface of the walls at eye-level is covered with framed pictures, large and small. Paintings of rural scenes, framed photographs and wall hangings of beautiful tapestry and embroidery, including many in the Slovakian style I'd seen online. There are simple figures in folk dress, the men wearing hats, the women in plaits, making wine or drawing water from a well. There are cockerels and deer and dancing girls with wide skirts, all rendered by needle and thread, surrounded by geometric designs in bold primary colours on white backgrounds.

We sit down in her front room, her bay window letting in the lines of beaming sunrays. She has a trolley with a tray that she uses to lean on as well as bring things to and fro from other rooms. I offer to do it all for her, of course, but she won't hear of it. And she brings in a tray of tea things, as well as two portions of the delicious-looking honey cake she promised, each on a fine white china plate with a gleaming cake fork. The cake is TO DIE FOR. Many thin layers of sponge sandwiched by a honey-cream.

'Did you make this, Gita?' I manage to mumble, between little groans of cakey pleasure as I polish it off far too quickly.

'No, but I can make a wonderful one. This is from my friend who lives down the hill into town and she is Slovakian and visits me but her honey cake is not as good as mine.'

'Yours must be incredible then!'

'I use my grandmother's recipe which she got from her mother and so on and so on. It is the best Slovakian honey cake in the world.'

'I don't doubt it,' I say. 'I feel very ignorant about your country, so do forgive me. I'd love to learn more about it.'

'I can teach you everything about it, my dear!' says Gita, seemingly delighted with this. 'Not many people are interested in my country, especially round here. There is distrust here sometimes, of people from the east in Europe, like we are taking jobs and so forth. I am not taking jobs. I am just a little old Slovakian lady who misses her homeland.'

'What do you miss about it?'

'Oh, so many things . . . where to start? The mountains and the forests – Slovakia is the most forested area in Europe, you know. My village Lúčky Pri Ružomberku is in a valley surrounded by mountain peaks, with a beautiful waterfall. I miss the traditions, like at Easter, the young men and women would dress up in folklore outfits, knock on the girls' doors and sing and dance playing folk music on accordion, then pour bucket of water on them!'

'Are the girls okay with this?!' I ask, the mind boggling.

'It is all good fun, though some do hide, under the beds! Then the boys they use a . . . not sure of the word . . . it is made from willow bound together with ribbons at the end, and they slap the girls' dresses!'

'What?!' I cry. Sounds insane and decidedly dodgy.

'No, not hard, and the girls have many layers on their skirts. It is just for fun, I promise! The girls give them reward of colourful eggs. We decorate them, put a hole in and blow them, and paint the hollow eggs. I miss the dances and the folklore outfits. At Christmas, carol singers go round houses and priest sprinkles holy water and people bring out drink and money and food.'

'Well, if this honey cake is anything to go by, Slovakian food sounds amazing.'

'Oh yes, it is good. We have potato dumplings and cheese – *halušky s bryndzou* – and cheese fried in breadcrumbs – *vyprážaný sýr*. Delicious but not good for waistline, you know. And the alcohol . . . ooh, Frances, is so good. So strong. You will not get up from the floor.'

'Ha! Yes please! What's your favourite tipple? Sorry, tipple is a little drink.'

'Yes, yes, I know. I speak good English.'

'Oh, you do indeed. Sorry!'

'No, there is no apology needed. Well, yes, my favourite is *Slivovica*, a plum kind of brandy and also I love *Čerešňovica* from cherries. But is not just the food and drink, it is the way we live there. Everyone in the village has a small parcel of land with fruit and vegetables and chickens.

A patch and a path through it, with fruit trees – pears and apples – and fruit bushes, like brambles, gooseberries, blackcurrants and redcurrants, raspberries and strawberries. Most people had these. And all neighbours talk outside and spend time together. Whole generation in same house. Grandparents sitting on bench outside. Neighbours would help each other all the time. Go for tea at each other's houses all the time. When I was a girl, my friends and I, we would knock on villagers' houses and offer to take their baby for a walk, just to go for a walk and people would always say "Yes please, gives me a break." Everybody knew each other. Doors were always unlocked. Never burglars. Safe. It is so different here. People can be kind, but they don't care like they do in Slovakia, not as close, you know.'

'It does sound wonderful,' I say, but I do feel she's being a bit harsh on the Lincoln folk, recalling my musings about Steep Hill, about the community feel of this area. But perhaps that's because I run a business and if I didn't, maybe I'd feel as lonely as I did when I lived all those years with Twatface. We weren't close to our neighbours at all, barely spoke, barely knew them. Except Twatface and Melissa Pridgeon, who were obvs getting very friendly under my very nose . . . But yeah, maybe Gita is right about the English. We're not the best neighbours in the world, perhaps? Then again, Slovakia does sound lovely, but maybe old Gita has rose-tinted glasses on. 'Do you visit Slovakia often?'

'When I can, money and health permitting. Stef takes me when he can, work permitting. He has lived all over the world, so he's not here that often. But he's looking forward to settling down for good in Slovakia with me and his fiancée.'

At the mention of Stef and his damned fiancée, I get a

lurch in my tummy and try to cover it immediately by saying, 'I'm very happy for all of you, going back to your homeland.' Lies, lies. But she seems so happy about the idea of going home, how could I begrudge that? I do wonder what Stef feels about 'settling down for good' in Slovakia, if he's used to travelling the world . . .

Margita says, 'I pray you never have that intense longing for home.' Her eyes are clouded with emotion. 'But maybe you already do?'

I reply, 'The Welsh have a word for it, you know: *hiraeth*. A kind of deep yearning for your homeland and its past. I was born down south in Chichester, West Sussex and moved around a lot from my teens. As I mentioned last week, we moved to Lincoln when I was seventeen and in my twenties I met my husband, then had my son and here I am still. But I do remember the village where my grandfather lived, called Pulborough, where he had his garden. It wasn't a very big garden but he kept it beautifully. I think if anywhere feels like home, it's there, in his garden. Never go back, they say, and I wish I hadn't, as I visited it a few years ago with my son Jay and they'd sold off the land where his garden used to be and built another house on it. Broke my heart.'

'Oh Frances, that is tragic. But your memories of your grandfather and his garden live forever in your mind and your son's mind, as I'm sure you've told him about it many times. And in your quilt. Yes, my son told me about your quilt of your grandfather's garden.'

Stef's been talking about me, to his mother? I fight hard not to blush at this tasty morsel of information.

Gita goes on, 'But you say, never go back, but that is what I am doing. I know some things have changed, but the mountains and the forests will never change. They will outlive us all. They are my home, my homeland. And I cannot wait to be back there. We go at the end of the summer, ready for September and my son's wedding.'

And on that word, we hear a key in the door, and Stef has returned. He calls out hello from the hallway and we say hello back. And then there he is, appearing in the doorway. He smiles at both of us and, as ever, it's a thrill to see his handsome face. Today's T-shirt is words written in newsprint, like a ransom letter, that reads: *THE DAILY MAIL CAN GO FUCK ITSELF.* Ohhhhhh YES. Stefan is perfection! It's official!

Gita is so happy to see her son, it's a pleasure to witness her face light up. She says she is tired now and Stef offers to walk me home. It's not necessary at all, of course, it's only up the hill and it's broad daylight, but Gita insists as well. Who am I to argue?

'Thanks for coming,' he says as we set off at a slow stroll. He certainly doesn't seem to be in any hurry to get back. 'I know she was really excited to meet you and looking forward to it all week.'

'Ah, it's nothing. I was excited too. Your mum's lovely.'

'She is, she is. She's a very strong character, very strong-willed. All the women in my family are. She always complained when I was a kid growing up here that her house had too many men in it! She really missed all her sisters and aunties and cousins back in the old country.'

'She certainly seems to miss Slovakia,' I say.

'Yes, absolutely. She can't wait to get back there. She's loved our little house here and her life with Dad, but she feels it's time to go home.'

'You're staying with her here, at the house?'

'Yeah, I was living in New York for a while, and before

that Paris, and London and a couple of other places. It's a bit odd being home in that little house again. I feel like I'm nine years old, except everything feels so much smaller, including my mum.'

So many questions I want to ask – what were his travels all over the world like? I love the fact that he's worldly and seasoned. I've hardly been anywhere, just a few beach holidays as a kid or with Jay, but nowhere really interesting. I envy his freedom and I'm impressed that he's used it so well, getting away from Lincolnshire and seeing other sides of life. I wonder how he feels about settling down in Slovakia? Where does his fiancée live now and what does she do and what is she like and how did they meet? Urgh, do I really want to know the answers? I'm not sure I can deal with hearing them . . . so I change the subject to stop myself.

'Fucking love your T-shirt, by the way.'

'Ah, yeah, thanks! I fucking hate that newspaper.'

'Me too! And that abomination *Femail*. All that shite about *Wow, You Look Considerably Shitter than Our Models*, or *Why You're Failing at Sex, Relationships and Really Everything in Your Life, Aren't You*, or *Stop Eating So Much, Fatty, but Also Here's the Recipe for the Best Cake Ever.*'

He laughs and says, 'You absolutely crack me up, Frankie! You're bloody funny!'

'Yeah, I know,' I say. I'm getting this nonchalance thing down pat, though inside I'm panting with glee.

He says, 'It's gonna be a scream working on this quilt with you. We should get some jokes in there. Slag off the patriarchy or The Daily Fail.'

We laugh as we stagger up Steep Hill. Then we start talking about the quilt design and the different shades that might go together, and this goes on to a discussion of the colour wheel and then we're talking about synaesthetes, how some people hear colours or see smells or whatever, and then we're talking about art and whether art should be beautiful or if it can be Tracey Emin's bed or Duchamp's urinal or whatever and how do we judge art anyway and by what standards and is our quilting art and if not, why not and the snobbery about crafts versus arts and . . . well, we could go on all day. We've reached my shop far too soon, yet we've stood outside it in the street, talking, talking, talking. God, how I'd love to drag him into my shop right now and mount him on the sewing table . . . but actually, I'm realising that despite the fact that he's hot hot hot, there's a lot more to him than that. There's a lot more to being with him than just fancying him. It's a curious thing: I feel different with him than I have with other men I've met. Certainly any of the dates I've been on and – now I'm casting back a few years pre-Twatface – even perhaps before that. And that is . . . how can I describe it? Peace? A sense of peacefulness when I'm with him. I've not known him long, of course, but just being him around him is peaceful. I mean, don't get me wrong. It's exciting too, because of the instant lust he elicits from me, but also, there's this feeling and I've just remembered what it is. I've nailed it – you know when you go to the hairdressers and you sit at the sink and you lean your head back and that first swash of warm water envelops your hair and you close your eyes and succumb to it, the tingly release of all your tension as the water runs over it and the hairdresser is running their fingers through it? That's how he makes me feel when I'm with him. Like I'm tingling all over, I'm keyed up because I fancy him BUT also I'm in that peaceful place you go when you're utterly relaxed. And I can honestly say I've never felt that way with a man before, any man. I just love being around him.

We talk a bit more about the quilt and ideas for it and he's lingering on the street as we're chatting and I'm not really concentrating on what he's saying and just want to invite him in but I'm not going to obvs but I really want to and then he says, 'Maybe we should go for a walk round Lincoln sometime and take some photos and gather ideas for the quilt.'

As soon as he's said it, he looks like he regrets it, but like he still wants to do it, but he's torn . . . Believe me, I can read all this in his gorgeous face. I've been studying it. Then he hurriedly adds, 'Or I can just do that on my own. Or together, if that suits.'

'That'd be great sometime, yeah,' I say and look away down the hill to avoid meeting his eyes, which still slay me. But then I look back and – fuck a duck! – there it is again, that bolt of energy surging between us, between our eyes as we gaze at each other. It's like imprinting, yes, like I'm memorising every shade of brown of his irises, every streak of mahogany, caramel and grey in his hair, every dark swathe of bristles in his neatly cropped beard. And he's memorising me too, drinking me in, in deep draughts, like the thirstiest man on earth . . .

And then he's saying goodbye and see you later and he's off down the hill.

I immediately message Bel. She replies:

GET YOURSELF HERE. Barney is napping! Who knows how long the little hooligan will be out for the count? Hurry!

I pop into *Sanctuary in the Bail* and buy three slices of their delicious almond and raspberry cake (one for me, one for Bel and one for Craig when he gets home) and I hurry along to Bel's house and go round the back. She's at the kitchen window and lets me in the back door. Christ, she looks rough, bless her, in sweats and her wild hair dragged back, massive dark circles under her eyes. She's doing the washing up as their kitchen is too small for a dishwasher.

'Sit the fuck down and rest,' I say and she protests for three seconds then agrees. I tell her to go to the sofa and lie down. I finish the washing up, look in the fridge and find mince and bacon and carrots, so I make a Bolognese or cottage pie filling for their dinner later, then wash up the pots from that. Then I go out into the hallway and see Barney in his pram, fast asleep with his arms thrown up above him. Aww, they are adorable when they're asleep, aren't they? Peaceful and quiet, thank heavens. I edge past him and pop into her downstairs loo and give it a quick spray and wipe down. Back in the kitchen, I clean down all the sides and make a couple of mugs of strong tea with sugar and take them through to the living room, where I find her absolutely flat out with her mouth open. I take a blanket that's folded on the back of the sofa – red with white reindeer on it, for all round Xmas fun – and I lay it gently across her. God, how sharply I remember this, the sheer exhaustion of early motherhood. I let her sleep, as I think about Stef. I wanted her advice, but sitting here, listening to her mildly snoring, I know what my inner voice is telling me to do, and I don't like it one bit. The facts I'm unwilling to hear are as follows: Stef is engaged to a woman in Slovakia, his wedding is in September and his lovely mother Gita is desperate to return to her beloved homeland.

And I know, if there's any chance at all that this man likes me, fancies me or otherwise is lured off his path by me . . . then it'll be a shitshow of epic proportions for him, his mother, his life. It's his choice, of course. He's a grown-up. Maybe he's not happy with this arrangement, maybe he wants to keep travelling the world, maybe he doesn't want to settle down in Slovakia . . . or is that just wishful thinking? Then I picture his face as he asked me if I wanted to go for a Lincoln walk with him. I acknowledge I'm pretty awful at reading men these days. It's been so many years since I've had to. But his face . . . He looked . . . eager and shy and not wanting to seem presumptuous, yet wanting me to say yes – or again, am I just making this shit up to justify my wanton desires for this man?

Urgh. I've no idea. Then, the front door goes and Craig's home. I hop out into the hallway and put my finger to my lips. He starts at the sight of me, then nods slowly in recognition. He's a tall chap with an affable face, mid-brown short curled hair and a cheeky grin. But he's not grinning now, he looks absolutely shattered. We tiptoe out to the kitchen and I grab my coat.

'Thanks Frankie,' he whispers. 'How are you? All right?'

'Yeah, all good, honey. You look like shit though. Go get some sleep yourself.'

'Ach, I can't. Gotta make some dinner for the grown-ups. She'll be ravenous when she wakes up.'

'Dinner's sorted. Bolognese on the hob and cake in that paper bag,' I say and open the back door as softly as I can and sneak out.

He comes to the door and says, 'You're a bloody star,' and I wave him away, as I'm off down the cul-de-sac. I only wish I'd brought them wine too. Looks like they need it, bless them.

On the walk home, I think about this little family of theirs and how self-contained they are, the perfect alliance of three souls. My family is split up now, my husband is my ex, my son is away starting his new life. I don't feel sad about it though, just thoughtful. But it does make me think of Gita and Stefan and the mysterious fiancée, whatever her name might be. A family in waiting . . . Do I really want to split that up? Stomp on it all in my size 8 Irregular Choice brogues and mess it all up? I think of my heart and how bloody tender it is, it really is. For all my brashness, I'm a total goddamn softie underneath. Could I cope with the heartache of messing around with Stefan and losing him? Urgh, I can guess what Bel would say, if she hadn't been asleep: *You've had enough heartache for one life, babe. Avoid like the plague.* And she'd be absolutely spot on.

Back in the flat, I'm straight back on the dating apps. I need a distraction of epic proportions to take my mind off the image of Stef's face as he stood on Steep Hill, his dark hair etched against the blue sky, asking me to go for a walk with him . . . Yep, I need some random fuckboy to cure me. Let's see what we have here then, eh?

I'm looking through the profiles in my likes lists. Here are some highlights:

I am fully committed to every relationship I pursue. If my partner told me to swallow bleach, I would do it for her. I expect the same level of intensity from my woman that I will input myself.

Are men okay? Not this one. You need to work on your pillow talk a bit, mate.

PROFILE sirdom46 'BDSM interest only no time wasters or single mums or benefits scroungers' age 75 Bognor

Black and white photo of woman in a bra and a blindfold, holding a whip in her mouth.

OK I have questions:

1. Do you really look like that?
2. Are there 45 other sirdoms on this dating site?
3. Is BDSM a good idea at your age?

WHY SHOULD PEOPLE DATE ME

WELLLLL LETS SEE IM GREAT IM GOOD MAN I HAVE A WEBSITES I DONT HAVE NO INTERESTS

Please stop shouting at me. Also, punctuation for this guy is the undiscovered country.

Love to get in ur pants

I don't think he'd fit in my pants.

> *You're looking for me. You know you are. And I'm looking for you. We both know it. We've been picturing each other all our lives. When you're brushing your hair, taking a bath, walking to work, putting food away in the fridge, watching a movie, boiling eggs or searching in the fridge in the dark. It's my face you see, my tumescence you seek. Because you want me, you need me to protect you from the slings and arrows of life. It's me you want. Don't fight*

it. Let's talk. Get your head out of the fridge and open your eyes.

RUN AWAY! RUN VERY FAST! Internet dating is a jungle during a game of *Jumanji*. What has the fridge got to do with it anyway? Everything . . . EVERY. THING. The fridge bit is peak psychoing. Is he going to be in the fridge? He is EVERYWHERE!

Wsgh eftr gh sogm tub mkjsd rf emm tyouafdbfkkkg dr ddd bps? Hj wvbs dnmkkslkj dffqi sllp

This makes more sense than most of the dating messages I get tbf. May well be the cat walking on his keyboard. I'd rather date the cat tbh.

Holy cow. Another beautiful day dawns in the world of internet dating. I screenshot a few of those to send to Bel later for laughs, then I go about seeking out the prettiest fuckboys I can find on t'internet and start messaging. There's only one answer to love-sickness and soppy thoughts and keening over some unavailable guy . . . and that is fresh new men. Bring it on, boys!

Once I start messaging with these guys and the intention is meeting for sex reasonably soon, I realise that I still haven't had my Sexting 101 workshop with Bel, as lots of these fuckboys are starting to sext with me and I have no bloody idea what I'm doing. I've managed to completely avoid it so far during online chats, by rapidly changing the subject every time someone starts doing a bit of horny talk. There's no possibility of a shed session this evening, but just as I'm starting to gear myself up to try a bit of sexting, Bel messages that she's awake and so grateful for the dinner and the cake etc etc and I reply, yeah yeah it's my pleasure but is she free for a few minutes to give me a sexting tutorial dead quick?

Fuck yeah. Hit me.

OK so I'm chatting with this accountant guy called Lloyd and he's getting all frisky. What do I say first? How do I start?

She explains to start talking about what I like in bed. Tell him about that and then ask what he likes. Or vice versa.

Then it can kind of morph into talking about it as if it's happening RIGHT NOW. So you start doing it in present tense, like I'm doing this and you're doing that.

Sounds like a Choose Your Own Adventure book.

Get with the plan, Brumby! This is sexy sexy time. Get dirty STAT.

So I figuratively crack my knuckles.

I'm going in, I tell Bel.

So, tell me, Lloyd. If we were in bed right now, what would you want me to do . . .?

Ladies first . . . he texts back, with a cheeky side-eye emoji.

So I tell him some of the things I like doing in bed and I'm feeling dead coy about it, but I remember Bel's admonishment to get dirty and I go a bit more porny and graphic. Well, he loves that.

Bel texts, *What's happening now?*

He's right into it. He's all over it like a rash.

Has he gone present tense?

Yeah yeah he's saying he's doing this and doing that to me.

OK I'm feeling like a third wheel here, texts Bel. *I think I'll retire gracefully. You should be wanking by now FFS*

Urgh no thanks!

Why TF not? That's what sexting is for!

Is it?!

Yes!!

I tell her I'm far too nervous getting the words right to even attempt sexting one-handed yet.

Let's not run before we can walk. And don't you dare retire. I need your guidance! OK it's my go now. He's saying he's going to tell me what he wants.

OK now listen. Once you start doing it for him, believe me, he will be using it for self-pleasure, my dear. So work it up slowly and type in short phrases, then send. Short phrase, send. Do it that way, to eke it out. Give him time to get excited, right? Don't make him wait ages looking at three dots while you're typing some massively long erudite paragraph. You're not Charles

Dickens and he didn't come here to read a novel. It's all about pace and timing. Get it?

Got it.

Great. Get on it.

I'm on it like a car bonnet.

OK so I'm keyed up now. I'm getting myself ready with all my short phrases, send, short phrases, send. I've told him all the stuff I like, which tbh is pretty tame. I've not had enough experience of sex and barely watched porn, so I'm feeling like a total novice. What do men want in bed? I'm fascinated to find out. Here we go . . .

He texts, *We're at home*

All right . . . change of scenery, nice.

And Mummy's still out shopping

Okay?

And we want to be bad

Who's . . . we?

You're a bad bad sister and I'm your bad bad brother and you're going to take my . . .

URGGHHHHHH!! I text to Bel and screenshot the next paragraph, which is the weirdest damn incesty nastiness I ever did see. And I thought MAMA MAN was odd!

ABORT ABORT!!! texts Bel.

Blockety block block block, I go, and Lloyd is gone forever, interrupted mid-flow.

Is that what sexting is like?? I ask Bel, horrified.

Hey I thought you weren't into kink-shaming hahahaaaaa

There's kinks and then there's just . . . weird shit

So you're not into weird shit?!

I'm definitely not into weird shit

Maybe tell them that from the off then!

OK I will . . . if I ever dare try sexting again

Get back on the horse babe. Gotta go. The little terror just woke up again. And hey, thank you thank you for earlier. You're a true friend. Love you so much.

STOPPPITTTT it was nothing. Anyway I'VE GOTTA GO myself because some other guy is starting to sext me now . . .

Bonne chance, mon amie!

And Bel is offline. Now I'm on my own. The next guy up for it is Suveer, an office manager from Leeds, who says he is quite prepared to drive over to Lincoln for an afternoon or evening sometime in the future. Sounds promising, so we get on with it. First thing I tell him is, I'm not into weird shit. And he says, *Me neither!* And we're off . . .

Ladies and gentlemen, I am here to announce that it is never too late in life to learn a new skill. Turns out I'm a goddamn natural at sexting. I harkened well to what Bel told me and I did all the pacing just right and Suveer is well impressed. He's bloody great at it too, a right good tease. If his sexting is anything to go by, we're going to have a fantastic ONS. We shall see then if Suveer is all mouth and no trousers . . . Fun times ahead! Whoop! Now, who else is up for a bit of sexting? I wonder. I get back on the apps for an hour and start honing my skills on random men, who are only too pleased to be my guinea pigs. I'm juggling three different guys and texting them varying degrees of filth, when my dentist texts to ask if I can postpone my appointment next week and I reply:

> ***But I have a filling needs doing and I've been waiting ages for it to be done. When can you fit me in?***

And a random guy replies, *I'll fill you up anytime babe . . .*

Ah, I see what happened there. Well, at least I didn't text my dentist that I need a good spanking.

CHAPTER 9
Bad Dates

I have the class that night and I'm in a great mood after my sexting success. Obviously I don't tell them about it; that's the kind of bragging you save for your bestie, rather than your sewing group (well, not quite yet anyway, not without shitloads of wine). Stef, Gita and I work on our first squares on our homeland quilt. Gita is working on her traditional Slovakian embroidery, mostly in a cross-stitch style. Stef and I are working on a series of squares to represent Lincolnshire, with flat oblongs of green and big blue skies. We're cutting out blocks of blue from different materials to make up the sky and comparing them, chatting about the textures and shades we like. I'm getting that lovely hair-washy peaceful vibe again and it's so, so nice. We chat with Gita about Slovakia and England and the differences, and Stef talks about Paris and New York and his favourite places to go there, but also how some of the worst places he's ever been are in big cities and how they stink to high heaven in the summer and how rude city folk are and how nice they are in Lincoln. And I'm thinking maybe staying in Lincoln most of my life hasn't been such a bad idea after all. When he talks about the places he's been, he doesn't make you feel like he's better than you, like he's showing off. I get the sense he's just a genuinely curious person and likes to sample different lives, and I can appreciate that.

'I just like to wander,' he says and shrugs his shoulders.

I really enjoy the evening, and seeing Stef again, but after my fun with sexting I'm feeling more centred about the whole Stef thing now. I have my sex life and I have a friendship with this nice guy Stef and that's that. It's all good. Yes, Stef is gorgeous. I can't deny, the man is beautiful . . . but I can do this, I can totally do this. It's all about willpower. And meanwhile, I have a slew of new guys to take my mind off Stef.

Now I have one main aim and that is to find new candidates for Fuckboy of the Year. There is a side quest, to go on dates with guys nearer my own age and actually have conversations, but I'm telling you, the odds of finding the former compared to the latter are about fourteen thousand to one. There are so many cute younger guys out there who only want sex, and they're always bloody delighted when I say straight up that's what I'm after. No small talk, no messing around: I'm looking for a great night with a hot guy. They love that. You'll never find anyone on eHarmony who says that up front, plus so many of the profiles on there have no pics at all. Seems like a plea to foreswear the shallow desires of lust and instead get to know someone as a person first blah blah, but tbh I need a picture if I'm going to consider dating someone. I know there are people who fall for personality alone but I know that's not me. I need to fancy them, at least a little bit, before I start talking. That's just the way I am. Plenty of Fish is also frustrating me, with its pointless rule about only permitting you to talk to men with a fourteen-year age gap, maximum. I want to have the freedom to talk to whoever I like, POF. I mean, who the hell do they think they are? The MILF police??

So firstly, I get myself to Bel's waxing lady and I get the full Hollywood. I mean, fuck it, if I'm going to get my downstairs fur ripped out, I may as well get it all done at once, no messing. And it really isn't as bad as I thought it would be. The plaster-ripping simile is apt but it doesn't really hurt much. I thought I'd be awkward about letting a stranger coiffe my privates, but then I realised that this lady must've seen more fannies than Leo DiCaprio. And afterwards, I must admit, it feels pretty great. Then, I download some new apps: Badoo and Hinge. They both have their pros and cons. You can send photos on Badoo, which is handy for seeing more images of someone, yet obviously prone to multiple unsolicited pics of dicks, though Badoo does seem to have a detector of nude images and then lets you decide if you want to see an explicit pic before you view it.

So one evening I decide to have a go at a nude, or at most, a semi-nude. A classy underwear shot. Yeah, I can do that. And if I ever become a famous quilter on telly and the pics resurface, well, I can say, don't I look bloody great?! So . . . sexy pics. How does one take the successful sexy pic? This needs thought and planning. How much do I show – upstairs only? Or downstairs too? Bra on, yes? Yes, for sure. Some nice lingerie has turned up that I ordered after the Aaron night and I try on some of those, sexy but nice and drapey, covering up the saggy bits. Bel rings while I'm cavorting around my bedroom, trying out poses – she's driving and can't text and wants to know where the baby massage class was I'd spotted in the local paper the other week that an old friend of mine runs. I tell her but add, 'Don't hang up yet, I need some nudes advice. Is it just you in the car?'

'Yeah, me and the little man.'

'Not the big man?'

'Nope, you're safe. Fire away.'

'Okay, I'm thinking low-cut bra on, pouting at camera with red lipstick or draped across the bed in silky black teddy thing, looking seductive.'

'Very nice,' says Bel, flatly.

'Boring? Am I boring?'

'You could never be boring, honey. I mean, underwear shots could be boring for some guys, but others'll like it more demure. Leaves more to the imagination. But nobody has the right to demand nudes from you. Only do it if you want to. Look babe, some women are out there popping into the lav at work and taking quick snaps of their hoo-ha and firing them off to all and sundry. Anything goes, believe me. But if I were you, and you want to go further than underwear, always do it headless. Then it could be anyone's body and that'll probably make you feel better about your bits being out there in the world. Blokes don't seem to care so much about that, as most guys are only too happy to show you their bits, face and all. And to be honest, if a guy is sending you random close-up dick pics, there's every chance it's a porn star's, especially if it's particularly massive. Who cares if you're never gonna meet? But if you are, and they're showing you a preview of what you're gonna get, then you may as well ask them for a face in the same pic, so you know it's his! They can say no and you can say no likewise. It's all about choice. Just do what feels comfortable and fun.'

'Thank you, Bel, my filth guru.'

'Always, babe.'

So I spend the next two hours trying on every item of sexy-time stuff I've got, in a myriad poses and expressions and lipsticks and lighting. And then spend another hour looking through the dozens of photos I've taken, sorting the wheat from the chaff and keeping the good ones, then putting filters on each one to get precisely the right degree of colour intensity to show myself off in the best light possible. And I'm dead pleased with those. I am FOXY. I'm getting the usual messages from a few randoms on Badoo, so I ask the cutest one, a brickie called Neil, if he'd like to see more.

Fuck yeh, he replies.

I pore over my carefully honed selection and choose my favourite one: black bra, looking up at the camera with deep pink lippy on, looking all sultry and shit. I send it off.

Wow, he texts. *Bloody gorgeous you are. That is one beautiful pic. You could be a movie star, honest to God.*

Aww thanks honey. How about you? Can I see more of you?

Sure ya can

I'm dead excited to see what he comes up with. It comes through and I tap on it. It's a badly lit, low-angle mugshot of Neil on the sofa, his face gurning like Les Dawson on a bad night, gripping his dick like a can of lager. Holy shit. Disappointment doesn't even cover it. WTF am I supposed to say to that?!

Nice, I text back.

Yeh, he replies. Then starts sexting. As if that shitshow got me in the mood! I make my excuses and leave.

My further adventures in sending semi-nudes and the ones I receive in reply almost exactly mirror that experience. The efforts I went to! Hours and hours of arty modelling and finessing! The guys? Four seconds. Here's my junk. Take it or leave it. And even if it's not a dick pic, their photos are still universally badly done, taken in the bathroom or car, grumpy, often double-chinned and peering. They really don't give a damn what they look like. So many of them seem to have this inner confidence that says, I'm a bloke and therefore attractive and she'll want me cos she's a desperate older woman – yes, I've heard that from a few Neanderthals before I've blocked them. I've seen it on men's profiles, that they're not interested in anyone over twenty-nine, or twenty-five or even twenty, and they're in their forties or fifties. Which is fine, absolutely fine, if that's what they want to say upfront and not waste anyone's time. I mean, I've not put it on my profile, but I'm mostly looking for younger, for the ONSs anyway. But I wonder if it smacks of this weird self-confidence that some straight men just seem born with, whatever they're actually like in terms of what a woman might find appealing. In the messaging sometimes, I get this real sense that the arrogance of some of these guys about their relative worth in the marketplace is unbelievably high, like you'll simply fall at their feet, just by dint of their age, that they're younger than you and that makes them automatically of higher value. This idea that any woman over forty, or thirty even, is on the shelf and therefore up for it with any old Dick, Dick and Dicky. Not this goddess, mate. I'm picky about your dicky. I mean, don't get me wrong. I don't actually give a shit what their down-belows look like,

I really, really don't. But they seem so proud of them, so I try to show willing. I'm much more interested in their faces – their eyes, their hair. That's what does it for me. Yeah, a nice body doesn't go amiss, but if I don't like their faces, if I don't feel any chemistry with their eyes, then it's no way, José.

So, when I'm chatting with these guys, I often ask them to send more pics of their face. And then there's that awkward moment where you get a bunch of new pics, and the one or two images they'd put on their dating profile are shown up to be highly selective and not at all representative. It's a really good idea to get more pics before you get too chatty and certainly before you meet, I reckon, so as to avoid the kittenfishing situation à la Gerry. Like, for example, one guy had these great-looking young, slim shots and then when he sent extras, they clearly showed the profile pics were at least ten years old, if not twenty. I mean, in one of them, he was holding someone's baby and that kid is probably at university now. Or another guy said he didn't have any more pics so I said take a selfie right now then, and he paused then sent me his wedding pic with his wife's face scratched out. Yeah, no. Others are just at different angles from the original flattering profiles, and I just don't fancy them in the alternative pictures. Petty but honest. I just go off them instantly. And yet we've got all friendly. Thus, now comes into play the dating chat etiquette: the moment you see the new pics, the heartless bitch response would be instant block. But imagine that! You send someone images of yourself and they slam the virtual door in your face! My God, the shame! So no, I can't bear to do that, even though that's what my fanny's just done: instant shutting-up shop. Also, Bel tells me this is known as 'ghosting', disappearing on someone suddenly without a trace and with no reason given. So I chat for a few more lines, until it feels polite to suddenly say, there's someone at the door, or my kid has just walked in, or my phone is ringing or whatever and I go. Then later, I block them when they're offline. A hidden ghosting, off-stage. It's kinder, surely than the slow fade? This is where you ghost someone gradually. Doesn't that just draw out the misery? And I really cannot be arsed to have the 'it's not you, it's me' bullshit convo with every single rando I talk to on multiple dating sites, you know? A girl's busy FFS. So yeah, that's the tactical retreat.

Once you get past the additional photos stage and you're both still interested, then what I'm learning next with local contenders for a casual hook-up is that you need to meet for the sex interview. Yes, the sex interview. I didn't do this with Aaron, but I got very, very lucky with that one and it was delightfully spontaneous that way. But with a lot of these guys, I'm not one hundred per cent convinced I actually want to go the whole hog with them but also I can't be arsed to spend a whole evening on a fake date when we're only meeting for one thing. So it's like a first date, but it's much quicker and it's a *Do I fancy you?* outcome that's required and that is all. Very little chit-chat, usually a snog to see if there's chemistry and then, if there is, you arrange a meet at another time and place or perhaps even straight away (usually a cheap hotel) for the one-night stand (or one-afternoon stand – even better – then you're free afterwards to go home and watch *Endeavour* on your own in your scruffs with a glass of red and a mountain of linguine).

Bel wants full reports on every meet. Well, it's a mixed

bag to say the least. Nothing has reached the dizzying heights of Aaron as yet. I'm actually annoyed he had the one-night stands only rule, as I'd love to meet up with him again. Not for the conversation, but for the guaranteed nice evening of sex, thank you very much. And I realise that's what I'm looking for much of the time – guaranteed good sex but no commitment. A fuck buddy, if you will. That's the ideal. But if the recent sex interviews and ONSs are anything to go by, then finding a FWB situation (friends with benefits) is a lot harder than it sounds. You'd think it would be easier, since what I've noticed is, once you put it out there that you're only after a one-time thing, or at the most a semi-regular casual sex thing, then guys will travel a lot further. And I mean A LOT. I've had guys offer to come up from London, down from Newcastle, over from Lancaster or Ipswich, even one from Devon, would you believe. All for one shag. And the great thing is that because these guys are coming from all over the country, there's a much wider range of men than just Lincolnshire's finest and thus you'd imagine a much greater choice. But you could date a variety of guys from every city or town or village in the British Isles and I swear you'd still struggle to find the ideal FWB, or even a halfway decent sex interview, though to be fair, I'd never ask a guy to travel three hundred miles for a sex interview. That's taking the piss. Those are only for the local guys. And they are not going great . . .

One local sex interview begins with the stink of cheap cigarettes. I mean, I could smell it wafting off him the moment he got out of his car. Now, I smoke a joint or two, but I'm no addict and certainly not to fags. And this guy must be a forty-a-day minimum, he stinks so bad. He's an estate agent called Marcus and we meet in a local park and he holds my hand as we walk round, like I'm his girlfriend or something and we've literally just met. I mean, he's nice enough but the ciggie stink is just too much and I message him after to say sorry but no and he says why and I say the cigarettes and he says, *but I don't even smoke* . . . So, yeah, no idea what the hell is going on there. There are three other local guys I meet for sex interviews that are so lacking in anything remotely appealing, sexy or in any way interesting that I can't even be bothered to describe them. They were the very definition of meh.

I do get past the sex interview with Suveer the office manager from Leeds, who was really good at sexting (remember him? If you do, you're doing better than Bel, who says my list of fuckboys is longer than the extras in *Ben Hur*). Suveer and I decide to meet in the Lincolnshire countryside in a secluded lane near a crematorium one Monday afternoon, because he knows that village since his ex-girlfriend lived there apparently. We know immediately we fancy the pants off each other, so no need to mess around making a second date. We climb into the back seat of my car and get rather gropey and hot under the collar and I'm terrified either his ex might show up or mourners are going to start walking by and get the fright of their lives, or alternatively it might cheer up a sad day, who knows? The fear of being seen adds to the thrill a hundred-fold, I must admit. We then go to a hotel to finish and after all the excellent sexting I'm dead excited to see what smorgasbord of thrills Suveer has planned for me. But it seems that he thinks sex is a competitive sport and I swear if he'd gone on much longer our loins would've started smoking like a burnout at a drag race. Wow, that was truly awful. Where's all the hot sexy teasing stuff he bragged about in his sexting?!

Nowhere to be seen. There's a good lesson to never trust sexting as evidence of being good in bed. A master with words, a wanker between the sheets.

Another goes better, at a Travelodge with a Spanish guy called Mateo, who puts on a pretty good performance, though he thinks he's God's gift and keeps interrupting the sex to tell me why Spain is the greatest place on earth and why England is so shit and I get so fed up of it. Not excellent enough to bother arranging a repeat performance. Another this week was rather disappointing: a guy called Kofi whose very lovely body looks like Michaelangelo's David and gets to the hotel room first, where upon my arrival, he opens the door and steps out into the corridor dressed in only his pants and kisses me up against the wall and that was bloody marvellous, but the sex afterwards lasted about four minutes and I may as well have not been in the room. Huge disappointment. At least he paid for the hotel. All in all, as I tell Bel, the casual sex with strangers game is proving itself to be decidedly mediocre.

All I want is a handsome fuckboy who's halfway decent in bed and doesn't finish in five minutes or stink of fags. Is that too much to ask? I message Bel after the last one.

Indeed it is not, my pretty, and you shall have it one day, for I shall grant you that wish, as I am your Fairy Fuckmother.

CHAPTER 10

From Bad To Much, Much Worse

Bel tells me to keep on the apps, keep talking, keep meeting. She says that dating is a numbers game and you just gotta keep looking. I am enjoying my freedom, and the thrill of getting ready for a date and not knowing how the evening is going to turn out is still terribly exciting. And I really do feel I wasted my twenties being in long-term relationships and not trying all this out then. But . . . just hanging out talking about sewing with Stef is a billion times better than any of these knuckle-heads and reminds me that, despite my goal of finding a charming chap to meet regularly, and pursue the ideal-sounding situation of buddies that fuck with no strings attached, the reality is much more messy. Yes, I'm having fun. Yes, you never know if the next shag will be the mind-blowing one with a master of technique. But for all that, teaching Stef how to do an overcast stitch is far more thrilling than any one of these fuckboys. But what choice do I have, when Stef is engaged? By the way, he hasn't mentioned our walk again and neither have I. I think both of us have backed off a bit, as that moment on Steep Hill when our eyes met . . . It all got a bit too heady.

So, February turns to March, the shop is doing okay. I've been developing my website to sell more stuff online and that's starting to pay off small dividends and increase traffic in the shop too, as local people see my ads on Facebook and decide to visit the shop instead of order online. So I'm feeling the word is spreading a bit further. It's still tough though and some days business continues to be slow. The constant worry of running your own business . . . At least the dating game takes my mind off that. The dates and ONSs keep coming and I can forget about money worries for an hour or so. And every Monday, the group keeps meeting and going from strength to strength, working on our quilts for the show. I can see real improvements in everyone's work and it's a pleasure to see. I never thought of myself as being teacher material, but seeing these quilters flourish is giving me the confidence to think maybe I'm not so bad at this tutoring lark after all and maybe I could do more of it, online even. Plus with this group, there's the massive bonus that we all get on so well, which brings a much-needed injection of joy into my life. As the group has spent quite a bit of time in each other's company, we're becoming more like friends than ever and we find our conversations are becoming more personal. I'm a classic over-sharer usually, but there's something about Margita's presence at the meetings that makes me hold back from sharing too much information. I think it's because she's like the matriarch of the group, or even the grand-matriarch, and somehow we don't feel able to talk about really personal stuff in front of her.

But one night in April, Gita decides to leave the video

call early, as she's tired after a long day. But Stef doesn't leave and we carry on, sewing and chatting. And it seems the other group members also feel the absence of Gita has let them open up a bit, because we all start talking about dating. They all want to know, 'How's it going, Frankie?' I do feel rather uncomfortable talking about this in front of Stef. Not just because he's a guy, which doesn't really matter. But, you know . . . it's awkward. I'm keen on him and I don't want him to think I'm a slag. But then I think, the guy is unavailable, so who the hell cares what he thinks? What I'm getting up to with other consenting adults is great and it's only centuries of misogyny that label women as slags, while men get called the decidedly more complimentary studs. So I decide, sod it. I'm just gonna be honest.

'Well, I must admit, I'm not looking for anything serious at all. And I'm looking for a regular guy who feels the same way. And I'm having a helluva lotta fun looking.'

'Ooh, I bet you are!' says Linda. 'I bet you're having the time of your life!'

'Nothing stopping you from getting back on that horse, Linda,' says Michelle, with a twinkle in her eye. This is the woman whose life seems like an advert for the shop she works at, M&S – terribly middle class, terribly nice and terribly dull. But I swear, there's something about her facial expressions that hint at all sorts of naughtiness going on under the surface. One day, I shall get these women out on the lash and we'll see what their lives are *really* like.

'Ah, that horse has bolted long ago,' replies Linda. 'I'm a widow and that's the way I will always be. I found the love of my life, "the one", as they say. And he's gone now. And I'm truly not looking for anyone else in that capacity.'

'That's a shame though, innit?' says Paige. 'I mean, I'm

in my twenties and the thought that there'll only be one man for me in my life and I need to find him . . . That's a bit scary, to be honest. What if we never meet?'

'You will if you're meant to,' says Kelly. 'I mean, my boyfriend is Canadian and he's eighteen years older than me too.' *Ooh*, I think, *that's a new fact*. Didn't realise Kelly was in an age-gap relationship. It suits her though, as she's an old soul, Kelly. And her fella is about my age and I bet that works well for her. I can imagine that some of the young men I've been seeing would bore her to tears. She goes on, 'So, the chances of us meeting in any normal circumstance are slim. But on Tinder, even though he was in Canada and I was here, we just started talking about narrow boats because I had one in my profile picture and soon we were on to talking about Radio 4 and the World Service, and the rest is history. We're soulmates. We were very lucky though. But I do believe in fate. We were meant to meet.'

'I don't believe in fate, I'm afraid,' I say. 'And I've been in a marriage for the last twenty years that nearly ended me, so why the fuck was that *my* fate?'

The room falls quiet. Sewing machines stop. I didn't mean to be such a downer. It just came out. Stef looks up at me, his face concerned, and I look away. Those eyes of his are bloody secret weapons.

'But now,' I add, smiling, 'I'm having some fun. For the first time in years.'

'Good for you!' says Paige. 'And so you should. It doesn't matter what age you are. That's what I think. Some of my mates have kids and they act like old folk. Stands to reason you can be in your forties or fifties or sixties or whatever and be single and have a blast. Why the fuck not?'

'Why the fuck not, indeed!' I agree. 'And luckily, lots of young guys agree with me.'

'You're dating younger men?' says Michelle, interested, not shocked.

'Yeah, some. I'm finding they're a lot more fun than men my age.'

Michelle says, 'Of course they are. Women in their fifties and men in their twenties are perfectly matched.'

'How can that be?' says Linda, aghast. 'I can't think of anything worse than going on a date with someone my youngest son's age. I mean, I love my son. But he's twenty-six and he's an idiot about life and so are all his friends.'

'Well, I'm not meeting up with these guys to discuss Nietzsche or the best way to invest my savings. We're meeting for simpler activities, Linda . . .' I say and smirk. But what Michelle has said has intrigued me and I ask her what she meant.

'Women like you, Frankie, divorced and free for the first time in decades, children off at university . . . Tell me if I'm wrong but you're not looking to settle down, are you?'

'Quite the opposite!'

'Exactly. And lads in their twenties are at the same point in their lives. They don't want a woman who wants to tie them down, who wants to move in together and start nesting and making babies and all that. They want to have fun, just like Frankie does. With no strings, no commitment. Perfect match, if you ask me.'

'Oh my God, that's so true!' I cry. 'And I've never thought of it that way! But that is exactly how it is. Michelle, you're a genius.'

Michelle stands up quickly and takes a little bow, Paige and I clapping.

'But all of this sex with strangers,' says Kelly. 'How on earth are you going to meet someone who really cares about you, who wants to be in your life and you want to be in his, if all you're doing is looking for sex?'

'What's wrong with sex?' says Paige.

'Nothing,' says Kelly and sighs. That's an interesting sigh. I wonder what her sex life is like to elicit such a long, drawn-out sigh at the very mention of the word. 'But sex is ultimately empty, when it's done for its own purposes and nothing else. I can't imagine dating that way. I think I'd hate it. It's all so . . . I don't know . . . soul-destroying, isn't it?'

I catch Stefan's eye and realise he hasn't said a word throughout this whole discussion. He looks decidedly embarrassed about the whole thing. And I'm not the only one who's noticed it.

'You're very quiet there, Stef,' says Linda, giving zero fucks. 'As our honorary man, it'd be very interesting to hear your thoughts on this.'

I will myself not to look at him, but it takes him so long to reply, we find we're all turning his way, wondering what on earth he's going to say, if anything.

He clears his throat and says, 'I feel utterly unprepared for this conversation.'

And we all laugh. 'Well, that's the way things are with a hotbed of quilters,' I say. 'Truths come out while you're sewing that you'd never dream of sharing with strangers elsewhere.'

'You want the truth, then?' says Stef, smiling wryly.

'Fuck yeah,' says Paige.

'Well, at the risk of sounding like a complete sap, I'm a one-woman guy. Always have been. I can't really see the point of sleeping around. I'm with Linda on the concept of "the one" and with Kelly when it comes to soulmates. I do believe true love exists. I certainly believe I've found it with my fiancée.'

'That's good,' says Linda, nodding, and the others make faces or noises that seem to concur.

But I feel sick. Hearing Stef actually say it, actually allude to the mysterious fiancée, brings her to life in a way I wasn't prepared for. It's ridiculous, I know, this visceral reaction to hearing the smallest mention of her from his lips. But she wasn't real until he just said it and now she is. Stef is in love with another woman, the love of his life. Good for him. *He's just a guy*, I tell myself. *He's not yours, he never was and you're being an idiot.*

'That is good,' I say, though it sticks in my throat.

He turns to look at me and it's hard to see those eyes and remember that the gorgeous man who has them belongs to another woman.

'But if I may say so,' he adds, 'I think you will find the one for you, Frankie. Your ex-husband clearly wasn't the right one. And more fool him for that. But that doesn't mean the right one isn't out there. I suppose it's about not looking in the *wrong* places.'

'What are the wrong places?' says Paige, frowning.

'Dating apps, for a start,' Stef replies, putting down his sewing and turning to face Paige. 'No woman is ever going to meet a *serious* man on there.'

'That's not true,' says Kelly, then seems surprised at herself for speaking up. 'I mean . . . well . . . that's not my experience. I mean, I hated dating apps, but that's how I met my man and he's a very serious person. And the love of *my* life.'

'Dating apps are just the way of things, these days,' adds Michelle, who's been quiet for a while. Always keeps her cards close to her chest, that one. 'It used to be getting chatted up in bars or clubs or reading ads in the *Guardian*. Now it's apps on your phone. It's all the same thing, just new technology.'

She's right, of course. But something is really bothering me. The way Stefan said '*serious* man'.

I look straight at him and say, 'And I don't want to meet a *serious* man. No interest whatsoever. My ex was serious, for twenty years. And he treated me like a dog. And all the while saying he loved me. So, I don't believe in love anymore. Not one bit of it. And I'll never trust a man again.'

That got dark quickly. I didn't really mean for that to come out. But it did, so hey. Deal with it.

'But these men you're seeing,' he goes on. 'They'll just treat you like dirt, worse than your husband.'

'What?!' I say. 'What do you know about it?'

Everyone else is quiet and watching us, like they're at a tennis match. And Stef isn't throwing in his racquet any time soon.

'That's what these men are like. They don't care about you. Only about the sex. Everyone who sleeps around . . . They're all the same. It's no coincidence that some of our worst insults are related to casual sex, like slag or hussy or scarlet woman or puta or ho and so forth. That's how these guys see a woman like that.'

'What?! So a woman who sleeps around is a whore and a man is just a jolly bachelor, is that your point? Woke up in the 1950s this morning, did we?'

'No, of course not. The men are just as bad. Our sexist language just hides the fact that it's a bad idea for anyone to have many sexual partners. And the men that do it, they're looking for a piece of meat. It could be anyone, just a warm body. And that allows them to treat *you* like a piece of meat. Is that what you really want?'

The nerve of this guy! And he's sure getting hot under the collar about my sex life. What business is it of his anyway?!

'Listen, it's no crime,' I say. I've stood up from my stool now and I'm staring him down. 'It's two consenting adults having fun and why shouldn't they? This ideal of true love is outdated and makes no sense in the modern world.'

'But some things never go out of fashion. And love is one of them. That's my belief anyway, and so I would never be satisfied with anything other than a long-term, committed relationship, with a woman I love, a woman I know inside and out, intimately. The very reason one-night stands are ultimately unsatisfying is because neither party has any incentive to try and truly know or even please the other person, because they're never going to see them again, so what's the point? There's zero investment on either side. It's all a colossal waste of time and – in my view – only fit for people who can't sustain real relationships. And you're better than that, Frankie.'

Everyone is dumbstruck. It sounds like a compliment, but it isn't really and I'm too mad to back down now. Because, at the heart of it, all I can hear is him being a judgy twat about my dating behaviour. Fuck that shit!

'It's really none of your damn business actually, Stef. And I can do without being slut-shamed by an out-of-touch mansplainer in my own shop, thanks very much.'

If the crowd had been at Wimbledon, they would've let out a resounding OOF at that.

'I guess we'll just have to agree to disagree then,' he says, pointedly.

'Fuck yeah,' I say.

'Okay then.'

'All right then.'

'Let's leave it at that, then,' he says, glaring at me.

'Yes, let's.'

'Good.'

'Good,' I say.

'Last word freak,' I add. And we glare at each other. Then I can't help it . . . I burst out laughing. And so does Linda. And then Stef can't help it either and he starts laughing. Thank God, we're all laughing, as it'd be awkward as hell if we weren't!

There's nothing left to say, really, so everybody starts packing up, as luckily, it's the end of the class. There's still a bit of an atmosphere but I'm not apologising. Screw him and his outdated views. Everyone makes dry small talk and Stef puts on a smile and says, 'See you all next week,' which I'm surprised at, because there's a part of me that thinks he'll never come back. But actually, another part of me is buzzing, because in truth, it feels like we basically just had angry sex with our clothes on . . .

Stef leaves and everyone else is still there and, my word, they are buzzing too!

'Oh my DAYS, he's so into you!' says Paige.

'He absolutely is,' agrees Michelle.

'Head over bloody heels,' says Linda.

'Ohmigod, shut UP! You're such a bad influence, all three of you!' I say, though my cheeks are flared and I'm laughing away. I'm still in shock and the adrenaline is still pumping. I've never liked arguments, especially with Twatface, as they were all about control for him, plus he'd walk out halfway through if he wasn't getting his way. But that argument was a goddamn doozy! I loved every second of it!

'But . . . he's engaged . . .' says Kelly, as if we were all just confused and didn't understand that salient fact, bless her.

'Didn't seem that engaged to me,' snorts Linda and Paige laughs along.

'Listen, you absolute coven of witches,' I say. 'Stop encouraging me!'

'You like him though, yeah?' asks Paige.

'I mean, who wouldn't?' I say.

'Abso-fucking-lutely,' says Michelle, which really makes me laugh. It's so funny to hear her swear, in her terribly nice accent.

'Can I please be the voice of reason for a second, *please*?' says Kelly and her face looks quite upset, so I rein myself in. I don't want to make her feel uncomfortable.

'I'm sorry, Kelly. You're right. Please, tell me what you think.'

I try to regulate my breathing and calm down. But I'm still hyped AF by the sparks that were flying only minutes before. If the arguments are that good, imagine the shagging!

'He has a fiancée, in Slovakia. And he's moving there, with his mother and they're all going to live together.'

'Sounds like my worst nightmare,' says Michelle and I laugh again.

'Right?!' I say. 'But I had a chat with Gita about this and I've been Googling loads of stuff about Slovakia. I think it's much more normal there to have several generations living in the same house together.'

'Fair enough,' replies Michelle. 'But – and it's a big but

– would you want to start married life with your mum sleeping in the next room??'

'No fucking way,' says Paige.

But Kelly is shaking her head now and I feel bad for her again.

'Kelly, carry on what you were saying. Please. I really want to know what you think.'

'Well, it's nobody's business but theirs. He loves his mother and they want to look after her. What's wrong with that? She's obviously keen to go home and Stefan has agreed to it and he's getting married. So he shouldn't really be here at all flirting with Frankie. It's not right.'

'It's not really flirting, really?' I say and immediately the others are shouting me down and laughing, because, of course, we all know what's really going on. 'Okay then, yes. You're absolutely right, Kelly. It's none of our business. And I don't want to be trouble to anyone. That's why I'm staying away from him. He asked me to go for a walk round Lincoln for quilt research and I haven't taken him up on it. And I'm dating a bunch of other guys. I really am trying my best to resist temptation.'

Kelly nods and says, 'Yes, I can see that. You definitely are. I'm more annoyed at him. He needs to control himself. He had no right to judge you like that.'

We finish up and Kelly gives me a hug, I think to let me know she's not judging me, which I appreciate. That night, I lie awake thinking about it all and part of me is still really annoyed at him. Whatever his motive, his judginess has really put my back up. I decide to throw myself whole-heartedly into more ONSs, just to spite him. I'm glad he's let his old-fashioned attitudes slip, because it's helping me to wean myself off my infatuation. Good luck to his fiancée with that.

So, this week, I have another liaison. But, holy shit, it is terrible . . .

It was with an American guy from the deep south called Rich who was basically a self-appointed dom, a guy who wants to dominate you and tease and please and boss you around and make you his slave and all that jazz, which sounded sexy AF when he was sexting me. But in person, he had a really high-pitched voice, so when we were at it in bed, he kept giving me all these instructions in his whiny way and he just came across as bloody annoying. Like, imagine it, a guy with a tone about an octave higher than you, saying 'Do this, do that, turn over' and all I'm thinking is, *He sounds like that tiny woman in* Poltergeist. 'Go into the light, Cay-rol Ay-anne!'

So, yeah, not a great week in the search for a fuck buddy. After the good ones, I think yessss, this is it, the time of my life! And after the shit ones, I'm like, what the hell am I doing here, naked, with this idiot? I keep thinking about that bit in *Raiders of the Lost Ark* (my absolute favouritest film growing up) where Sallah catches the poisoned snack the monkey's died from and says in this deep voice, 'bad dates'. That's the phrase that keeps popping into my head these days, with John Rhys-Davies' accent of Egyptian meets Welsh . . . *BAD DATES*.

The final straw is a young guy in tech called Olly. The messaging goes well, some nice spicy sexting. The sex interview goes even better, a great round of passionate snogging in a pub car park. But then when we meet the next night at a hotel, he starts the sexy talk with a bit of negging – giving me backhanded compliments in order to undermine my confidence – saying I look 'so fucking good for an older bird' . . . I nearly leave there and then, but we've made a start and I think, let's just get on with it, as long as he can keep his dumb ideas to himself and then he says something about how lucky I am to have a hot young guy like him and I'm starting to get the hump and then I realise, he can't get it up. Nothing's happening down there. So I'm super nice about it. I mean, you'd have to be a mean cow to have a go at a guy for that. They literally have no control over it in a moment like that. And I give him a kiss and say why don't we just chat for a while and cuddle and cop a feel and see what happens and it's no problem at all. And then he says, 'It's your fault. Cos I'm not into GILFs.'

Ouch . . .!

'I'm nobody's grandmother, for fuck's sake!' I tell him. 'Fuck off!' And he does, slamming the hotel room door behind him. Then I burst out crying. I know he's full of shit and he was just embarrassed and so he blamed me, but it really cut to the quick. The second he said it, I felt myself age in ultra fast-forward, like that bit in *The Last Crusade* where you drink from the wrong grail and crumble to dust. I message Bel and she says she can do a shed session in an hour or so, if I want to come over. So I shower and wash all my make-up off and look like a panda after a sleepless night and feel like shit. I go over to Bel's and have a good sob in her shed, while she rolls a joint, and soon I'm feeling more human again.

'Was Stef right about all this?' I say, miserably.

Bel takes a long drag, considers, blows it out, then says, 'He's right and he's wrong. You're right it's none of his business. But also, casual sex can be a rollercoaster. It takes a special kind of zero fucks given to get your head round it. Maybe I underestimated that with you, darling, as you're really a sensitive soul, much more than you let on.'

Oh God, maybe she's right. She is right. I am a soft-hearted little oyster inside my shell. That makes me well up again, and fat tears are rolling down my blotchy face as I reach over for the joint.

'Aww, darling,' says Bel and comes in for a hug. I let it all out. Wow, is this really me? Was Stef infuriatingly right, about all of this?

'I'm really sorry I encouraged you, love,' says Bel quietly.

'Oh my God, what are you sorry for? It's not your fault there's so much crap sex in the world. You just wanted me to have fun.'

'Yeah, true. But I am sorry, if I got that wrong. I did want you to have fun after years of unhappiness. Fun and freedom. You deserved that. *Fuck you, Mars*, remember? But maybe you should give up the sleeping around, if it's hurting you, making you sad. It's not worth it. But if you want to carry on, then carry on. And it's nobody's business but yours. Your body, your life. Just make sure you protect that soft heart of yours.'

The next night, I have a date lined up with a guy in his late forties called Ronnie, not a sex interview, an actual *date* date. We met on good old eHarmony, the desert where fifty-something men go to die. But Ronnie is an exception, as he's positive and lively and I like him. We've been sexting a little bit, not full on, just a flirty kind of sexy talk. And I feel like cancelling it after all my recent disappointments and because we've been doing a bit of sexting, I think he's probably just after sex and I'm just not right now, so I message him and say that I'm only really looking for a relationship and that perhaps we aren't compatible in what we're looking for. And he replies that's exactly what he's looking for too. And I get a vibe that he might be bullshitting . . . but he is a good-looking man, funny and interesting, works in social care. I really want to meet him. So I think, sod it, why not? I could do with a nice, stimulating evening with an intelligent man nearer my age. No young'un bullshit, no sex to mess things up. Just a good old-fashioned date. Yeah, I need that.

We meet at a pub and he has really nice big blue eyes and he's sexy, tall and broad. I like him. He's a bit rude to the barman, but he did have to wait a while for our drinks, so I think, *Okay, let's see if he repeats that*. Or maybe he's just had a long day and he's tired, who knows? So he sits down and he's telling me how stressful it is working in social care and how he misses Scotland, where he comes from. So we chat about Scotland a bit and we're getting on okay, chatting away and he asks me what I do, so I say I teach people to sew and quilt and I sell quilting stuff online. I never tell them about the shop, because then I may as well give them my home address on a platter.

And then Ronnie says, 'You've got a shop, haven't you? On Steep Hill? I knew I recognised you. I've seen you come out of there.'

I don't know what to say, as I never tell these random guys where I live.

'Erm . . . well . . .'

'Ah sorry, if that sounded weird. Honestly, I just happened to see you there the other day. I thought it was you from the photos, but I wasn't sure until I met you tonight. It's a great-looking shop. Well done you on running your own business.'

'Ah . . . yeah. Thanks,' I say, but I feel weird about it.

But he's smiling and it's a small world, Lincoln, and I suppose this was bound to happen eventually. Someone would know me from around and about or know someone who knows me. It's inevitable, really.

Then Ronnie says he wants to go outside for a fag and would I mind? No, of course not. So, out we go behind the pub where there's a few benches and it's a cold night and nobody's out there and before I know it, he's grabbed me and pushed me up against the back wall of the pub and he's shoving his hand down my trousers.

I'm too shocked to say anything. I mean, I'm literally letting it happen and I can't say anything. What the fuck is wrong with me?

'No, not there,' is all I can think of to say and I try to grab his arm and I'm trying to pull it out but his arm's so bloody strong, it's like iron, and he's pushing harder and saying, 'Yeah, yeah, there. That's what you want.'

'No,' I say, but it's like it's in slow motion and I can't say it loud enough, just a whisper.

And he says, 'Come on, come on,' and I'm saying no again. And he's not listening to me.

So I say it louder, I say 'NO' and I push him, I shove him. And he takes a step back. And he says, 'Don't you fancy me then?'

'No,' I say.

'Oh, right,' he says, in just the same impatient tone he used with the barman.

'I want you to leave,' I say.

'Well . . . okay. If that's what you want.'

'Yeah,' I say.

'Well . . . do you wanna delete my number from your phone then?'

Why the hell is he asking me that?

'Whatever,' I say, nonplussed.

So, he does this kind of shrug and then he gets his fags out, laboriously takes one and lights it.

Then he says, in a strangely half-hearted way, 'Fucking bitch.'

Then he leaves. I stay pinned against the wall as I hear him walk away, listening to his footsteps recede.

I rush back inside the pub. I sit down at a table and stare out of the window. I don't want to leave, I don't want to be out there on the street while he's out there. And he knows where I live, or at least, he knows where my shop is. Oh God, that was fucking horrible. I think of all the risks I've taken with guys at hotels, total strangers, and nothing like this has happened. Then I go for an innocent drink at a pub, and the guy assaults me in the back yard. I'm shaken up and I sit there for a while, not knowing what to do. Do I call the police? No. I'm adamant about that in my mind. I could call them, I probably should. But the guy knows where I live. And if nothing happens to him, or if something happens to him, but he's not sent to prison, as he probably wouldn't be for an assault like that, he knows where I live. He knows where I bloody live. And it's my sanctuary, my shop. It's my heaven. I can't have him coming round and threatening me if I get him in trouble. I can't have that, I won't. But what about other women he might do this to? I know, I know I should do something to protect them, but I can't risk him coming after me. So I go on the app I met him on and I report him. You can do that on there, you can report someone who's behaved inappropriately. So I find his profile and I send them a detailed report of what he did and I tell them I must remain anonymous and then I block him. I then delete my account. I don't ever want to have anything to do with that app again. And I don't want them to get in touch with me. I don't want to have anything to do with any of this, ever.

I go to the bar and get a nice tawny port and gulp it a bit. It warms me and I feel a bit better. A bit less shaky. And then I realise I've sat in the pub on my own for about an hour. I can't believe it's been that long. I go to message Bel, but then I don't. I'm not sure why. I'm ashamed, I think. I feel like it's my fault. I should've listened to my gut: when he messaged he was into the idea of having a relationship and I had the feeling he was bullshitting; when he was rude to the barman and I made excuses for him in my head; when he said he knew where my shop was and I felt weird about it; when he said let's go outside for a fag and for a split second there was a little tiny red flag fluttering in my mind, like a tiny alarm, but I ignored it, because it seemed silly, I mean, to go outside for a fag, it's nothing. It's a pub I've been in a hundred times and it's fine. It's Lincoln. It's about seven o'clock in the evening. It's fine. But I didn't pay attention to that flag. Or all the other little flags. And now they seem like bigger and bigger red flags, they're massive and they're waving like a goddamn parade. A carnival of red flags. I didn't listen to my gut feeling and it knew. My gut absolutely bloody knew. And I feel stupid. And I don't want to tell anyone about it.

So I knock back the rest of the port and I leave the pub and go out onto the street and I peer both ways down the road looking for that absolute cunt and he's not there, I can't see him. So I turn to run home and a man's voice says, 'Frankie?'

CHAPTER 11
New Guy

It's Stef. He's facing in my direction, hands in pockets. What just happened to me must register on my face, as he looks really concerned.

'Hey, are you okay?' he says, his hand extended but not touching me.

'Yeah, yeah,' I recover myself.

'Sure?'

'Yeah, just . . . a bad date.'

'Okay . . . did he upset you?'

I pause. Do I want to tell Stef about the assault? Something viscerally rises up and says, *No, I really do not want to.* But my face didn't register the command and Stef looks even more worried now.

'I'll fucking kill him. What did he do?'

'Nothing, honestly. Just a really crap date. I just wanna go home.'

He looks unconvinced, yet also nods, accepting that I clearly don't want to discuss it.

'I'm off home too, just been out for a drink with a mate. Can I walk you back, if that's okay with you?'

I like the fact that he asks my permission. I really appreciate it, at that moment.

'Yeah, course.'

We start off and there's an awkward silence. God, I really don't feel able to make small talk right now. But you know what, he seems to get this and we just carry on walking, without saying a word. And for the first time in a long time, I actually start to feel comfortable in the silence with another person. Twatface's silences were so often loaded with menace, because he'd sent me to Coventry or was otherwise seething about something. But not here, with Stef. It's just . . . companionable. It's a cold, crisp evening and we walk past the cathedral, lit up, glowing magnificently against the night sky. We pass down Steep Hill and listen to our footsteps ringing out on the cobbles. We actually reach my door and haven't said a word the whole way. And I didn't feel any pressure that whole time, either. I stop and turn to him.

'Thanks,' I say and try to smile, but my face feels like it'll crack.

'Can I just say one thing?'

'Yeah, sure.'

'I want to apologise for my behaviour in class. I was totally out of order.'

'Oh! Well, thanks.'

'Yeah, I feel like a right tit. Honestly, I don't know what came over me.'

His apology really cheers me. 'We both got a bit hot under the collar,' I say, to be nice. But maybe actually that is the case. I didn't exactly hold back either, but who says I needed to?

'Yeah,' he says and smiles ruefully.

Seeing that smile of his cheers me up exponentially, so much so, I actually fear I might cry – not because his smile is so lovely, but because of the horrible contrast between what just happened to me and this nice bloke standing somewhat awkwardly in front of me.

He seems to sense it, because he adds, 'I just . . . Look, you're a good person, Frankie. And you deserve better than . . . I don't know. Better than whatever happened tonight. And crappy guys in general.'

'Thanks. You're a good person too. To be honest, I haven't known that many good men. My dad was a waste of space and my ex . . . Well, I know people slag off their exes, it's *de rigeur*. But this guy, he really is a piece of work.'

'That sucks. Does your son get on with him?'

'Off and on. His dad is a manipulative person. He doesn't really understand love unless it gets him something. Everything is a transaction.'

'God, I know all about that. Something about me seems to attract that type. I've had a couple of relationships with women who sound like your ex. One of the reasons I've not settled down as yet, I suppose. Most recently, I had a girlfriend for a couple of years like that in New York. Transaction is the perfect word. She'd do something nice for me. Then it would be "Remember I did that nice thing for you" nineteen times a day and you're constantly saying thank you but it's never enough. Then she'd do something shitty and I'd object and she'd say, "But I did that nice thing for you! You're so ungrateful!" Like that, ad infinitum. For two years.'

'That was my life times ten. Exhausting, isn't it?'

'It really is. Sorry you had to go through that. But you

escaped. You got yourself out. That's something to be proud of.'

'You too.'

'I literally had to leave America to get away from her! I'd already moved from New York to Boston and she followed me there. It was insane. It was like . . . she couldn't believe someone would leave her. She talked about herself like she was the Queen and one of her subjects had disobeyed her.'

'How absolute dare you!'

'Right?! The audacity of me! She really believed her own hype. It was pretty terrifying to witness. I just got on a plane and got out of there. Luckily she didn't follow.'

'Is that when you came over here?'

'Yeah, more or less. I came back to see my mum for a while, then we went to Slovakia for a while. Well, you know a bit about the rest.'

Ah, so here we are, back to the fiancée. 'What's your fiancée's name?'

'It's Zuzana.'

'Pretty name,' I say.

'Yes,' he says, with no side to it. Just, yes.

'How did you meet?'

'She lives in my mum's village. I've known about her family for years. They're long-time neighbours and friends of my mum's family.'

'Can I see a picture of her?'

What am I doing? These are the last questions I wanted to ask him, or even know second-hand. It's torture, really, hearing him talk about her at all. But something about tonight has given me the chutzpah to take hold of this infatuation and quash it. If I can talk to him about her, if I can see her, then it won't hold so much power in my head. I don't want to be subservient to these bloody men, either mentally, like with Stefan, or physically, like with Ronnie the Rapist, as I've just christened him in my head. Some might find this a sick kind of joke, but just as I used memes as therapy to get me through Covid, I use humour all the damn time to get through this insane thing we call existence. What else is there? Prayer is out, as I'm an atheist. Humour is always there for me, however dark. So yeah, fuck you, Ronnie the Rapist and sod off, Zuzana with your perfect engagement with perfect Stef. I'm still me and I'm still okay.

Until I see Zuzana's picture, that is.

Damn, she's stunning. Long wavy chestnut-brown hair framing her face, huge dark eyes, just like his. Mine are a wishy-washy grey-blue. But then I realise that Stef and Zuzana have the same eyes. It's weird. They actually look a bit like brother and sister! The banjo music from *Deliverance* pops into my head.

'She's lovely . . . and she looks just like you. How close are your families again?!' I say, with a smirk.

'Not that close! We're not related, if that's what you're hinting at!'

We laugh and blimey, it's good to laugh after tonight's horror.

'Not marrying your cousin then, like the good old-fashioned British monarchic tradition?'

'Fuck off,' he says and we laugh again.

'She really is lovely,' I say and feel a pang right in the pit of my stomach.

'Yeah,' is all he says. No effusing. Maybe he just senses it's not the right time. I think that's the case, as he then adds, 'Look, I think something horrible happened to you tonight and I want you to know that I'm here, if you ever want to talk.'

And there are those eyes again, the ones that slay me. I look away. A screenshot of tonight's experience flashes into my mind, the hand thrusting down inside my pants. Holy cow, I shudder and it's all there again. I don't want to think about it.

'Why are you marrying her?'

I do that sometimes, give in to this crazy impetuous need to ask questions I shouldn't be asking. To his credit, he isn't too fazed by the question, though he certainly looks surprised.

'Wow, okay . . . I love her.'

'Good,' I say. 'Good.'

'It is good, yeah.' There's a silence and then he adds, 'And it's good for everyone. I mean, in the beginning, it was sort of arranged . . . I don't mean formally, but we were introduced with that idea. My mum has always wanted grandchildren and me turning forty, well, it started her thinking. And that's how we got chatting. And it all went from there.'

What? This is an arranged marriage? Okay, I know it works for some people. But it wasn't what I expected to hear at all. He doesn't seem like someone who'd go along with anyone choosing anything for him.

'But . . . is it what you want?'

'Is . . . what?'

'Marriage. Babies and all that.'

'Yes, who doesn't?'

'Plenty of people. I've got friends who knew they didn't want babies from their teens and never changed their minds.'

'Well, that's not me,' he says, but is there a hint of doubt in his voice?

'As long as you're sure . . .' I say, quietly.

'Oh, right. Here we go again.' There's an edge of annoyance now.

'Here we go again, what?'

'Are we going to have another bloody argument?' His voice is a little bit amused, but his face just looks pissed off.

'No argument here,' I say, then pause and my mind is saying, *Don't say that thing you're about to say*, but my mouth vetoes that and ploughs on regardless. 'I just don't think it's a good idea to let your mother organise your love life.'

'Bloody hell, Frankie! You just . . . you've got no damn filter at all, have you?'

'Nah,' I laugh, unapologetically. And because we're not on a date, because he's "safe" somehow because he's already taken, and because I don't have to impress him, or concoct a personality to present to him in that first-date way we so often do, I find I don't give a stuff and I'm just me, in all its horrible inappropriateness. 'Fuck filters,' I add.

He laughs at that and so do I. Wow, it's nice to laugh. And all I really want to do is invite him inside, not actually to ravage him on the sewing table, but just to talk, and laugh. But then again, I'm so, so incredibly tired all of a sudden. I just want to have a shower and crawl into bed.

'I'm gonna get myself to bed, I think, Stef,' I say.

'Yeah, sure. You do that.'

'Thanks for walking me home.' And I feel like I'm gonna cry and I really, REALLY don't want to in front of him.

'My pleasure,' he says. 'Take it easy . . . I mean, look after yourself.'

His face is the picture of concern and it's so tempting to

just blurt it all out but no, no, I don't want that. We say our goodnights and he goes off down the hill and I go up my stairs and get into my flat and close the door and lock it. Then check the lock has actually locked, unlock it again, lock it again, then check the lock is locked again.

Then, I break down.

While I'm sitting on the floor in the hallway crying, I drag out my phone and, punctuated by sobs, I go through it and methodically delete every single dating app. That's the end of that. I've HAD it with dating. Fuck this fucking shit. Then I sob some more.

My phone beeps and I immediately think, *Shit, it's him, it's Ronnie the Rapist.* Then I remember that I've blocked him on everything. So I look and it's Jay, my darling boy. Oh God, how I needed to hear from him at that moment. His presence in the world, just the fact that he's alive, makes me feel such peace and happiness. Thank the stars for Jay.

Hey mam whatchu up to

Nothing much, I reply, wiping the snot from my face. ***You ok?***

Yeh fancy a chat?

Yessssss

So I ring him.

'Heyyyy,' he says and OMG I nearly burst out crying again. Hearing his voice is just the tonic I need, but it's also that thing where you feel shite but you're holding it together and then someone is kind to you and it all comes tumbling out again.

'Hey darlin'. How's life?'

'What's wrong?'

God, he knows me too well.

'Ah, just . . . just a rubbish night, honey. I'm okay though.'

'No, you're not. What happened?'

'Just a crappy date with a crappy bloke. But I'm okay. He can go fuck himself, right?'

'Well, yeah, obvs. But what did he do? Did he hurt you?'

'It was nothing really. I mean, he just pounced on me. In a pub car park.'

'What a cunt.'

'Yeah, he really was.'

'You okay, Mam? I'm worried about you.'

Should I tell him more? Surely I'm supposed to protect him from things like this.

But then he says, 'Does he know where you live, Mam?' How does he do that thing where he reads my mind? He knows me, that's why. Better than anyone.

'Yeah, he'd seen me at the shop apparently. I'm so worried about it. What if he comes round?'

'He won't, I bet you anything. Did you tell him to do one?'

'More or less. I told him I didn't fancy him and said he should leave. He was weird about it, like really deadpan. And just went.'

'He won't come back. He'll be humiliated. He won't want to relive that, I bet.'

'How do I know for sure though?'

'Well, you can report him to the coppers. Do you want to?'

'No, I really don't. He knows where I live and I don't want all the backlash. I just want him to fuck off and die. And if I get the police involved, he probably would never go to prison as it's not bad enough and could just come to my shop any time he likes and threaten me or whatever.'

'Yeah, I get that. Fuck it then, Mam.'

'I'm just so mad at myself for missing the red flags. They were there, from the beginning. Just small things, like he was mad at the barman. And impatient. And said he knew where my shop was. Little things. But they made me uncomfortable and I didn't act on that.'

'You will next time though.'

'Yeah, but I'm so mad at myself for not acting on them this time.'

'Don't be mad at yourself. You're not to blame. He is. He's a cunt. End of story. Don't give him any more space in your brain.'

'That's good advice, love. Thank you.'

I feel so much better having told Jay. I wanted to keep it to myself forever, never tell a soul. I don't even know why, because usually I'm such a bloody gasbag about everything that happens to me. But having said it out loud, it loses some of its power. He loses some of his power, that wanker. And it feels smaller and better and more manageable. Not letting the asshole off the hook, but, as my boy wisely says, just not giving him space in my brain.

'Speaking of which,' adds Jay.

'Speaking of what?'

'Your brain.'

'Oh yeah?'

And then he starts telling me all about this course he's doing on neuroscience. And how amazing it is.

'Mam, Mam, listen. Think about it: your brain is just this thing trapped in darkness inside your skull. And the only way it knows anything about the world is by propelling this meaty thing around and using its senses to find shit out. And it gets all these signals from the outside world from these inputs and turns them into electrochemical messages and creates vision and hearing and touch and all that. Like, the brain just creates this stuff. So what you see out there, it's just how your brain interprets the signals. It's not actually what's out there, or instead, it's not everything that's out there. It's the narrow portion of reality that our sensory organs allow us to experience. How fucking wild is that?'

'Holy shit, boy. That is fucking wild. But . . . isn't there a truth out there, and we see that truth?'

'Nah, we just get a tiny sliver of it, like the slimmest piece of pie. Like, in the visual spectrum, we only see a tiny part of it. We can't even see ultraviolet or infrared. We see so little of it. And compared to dogs, we smell so little of it. And so on. But we get by. Our brain basically creates reality for us, through our equipment. Reality isn't even reality. It's just what our brains project for us, like a movie made in our heads.'

'Stop it, you're freaking me out!'

'Hahahaaaa, I knew I would. But it's kinda cool too. I mean, nothing really matters and everything really matters, when you think of it like that.'

'Like what?'

'Well, we're just these three-pound brains walking around fumbling about in the world, trying to learn shit. That's all it's about. Everything that we do, everyone we meet, every place we go . . . It's all input for our hungry little brains to do wild things with in our billions of neurons. We learn it all and it changes us, every second of every day, our brains are changing and adapting and learning. Your brain, my brain, we all need life's experience to learn from. Even shit things that happen, like that cunt tonight. You'll learn from it and you'll move on and your brain needs all that. You'll know for next time and might avoid a much worse fate, because you had that experience tonight. It's crappy, yeah, but just think what you've learnt. All those red flags. And not listening to your gut. You'll know next time. Your brain has processed it all and retained it, because it's an important memory for the future. Not because he's important, but because your survival is. And you will survive and your antennae will be twitching next time and you'll know what to do. It's all good input, Mam. All of it.'

Well, it's official. My son is a fucking genius.

'You're a fucking genius,' I say.

'I know. And I'm hoping you still feel that way when I tell you I want to specialise in neuroscience and do a PhD in it one day as you're gonna have to help me with the fees.'

'Ha! Good luck with that! Ask your dad! Actually, don't. He hasn't got any bloody money either.'

'The twat.'

'Indeed. Seriously though, pet, of course I'll help you. And there'll be student loans and scholarships or whatever they're called. You're so bloody clever, you'll get stipends or something, I'm sure you will. We'll work it out. Neuroscience, eh? Bloody brilliant.'

'Yeah, neuroscience. It's my thing. I absolutely know that now. Neuroscience . . . is me.'

Then I remember where I've heard the word neuroscience recently. 'I've been talking to a guy who's a lecturer in neuroscience. A bloke called Guy.'

'What, really? You best marry him then, Mam. For me, for your son. Marry that man.'

'For you, anything.'

'Seriously though, Mam, is there anyone halfway decent you've met or been chatting with? Or are they all wankers?'

I think of Stef immediately. 'Well . . . there is this guy at the quilting group . . .' I start. I tell him the whole thing, all about the chemistry, the fiancée, the T-shirts, the honey cake, the argument, everything.

'He sounds like your man, Mam.'

'What?! Really?'

'I dunno, I mean, I've never met the guy. But, it's the way you talk about him. He sounds like . . . you know him. Even though you don't. Know what I mean?'

'Not really. I've always had terrible taste in men. I don't trust my own judgement AT ALL. And this, with Stef. It's pointless. I'm just going to get my heart broken.'

'You don't know that. Maybe he doesn't even love this woman. Maybe he's just trying to please his overbearing mum. And if it's meant to be between you two, then maybe you should be open to that. It doesn't make you a bitch or a bad person, just to leave things open. You don't have to pursue him or anything, but just let . . . you know . . . things unfold. Natural-like. And see what happens.'

'You need to stop being so fucking wise, boy.'

'Well, I am the cleverest person you know, Mam. Deal with it. Now, it's my turn. I've got so much shit to shovel for you, Mummy dearest. Listen up.'

And we chat on like that for another two hours. About his idiotic friends and the mushrooms growing in his bathroom; who's shagging who and who's not shagging who but wants to; his convoluted drinking escapades involving traffic cones and other street furniture; his many, many girlfriends and how many hearts he's broken through no fault of his own other than his beautiful baby-blue eyes and floppy dark hair and I remind him to treat his girlfriends with respect and he assures me he does; his stupid petty lecturers and his cool ones who blow his mind; how he's developed a new low in cooking which he calls CHIPS SPESH which consists of Spar frozen veggie lasagne heated up in a saucepan and smashed up with a wooden spoon then heaped over oven chips and covered in grated cheese; his insane nightly dreams mostly about being lost in a maze with grey walls (he dreams a ridiculous amount – he's always been a terrible sleeper) and I tell him he's dreaming about the brain, his brain, his amazing, beautiful brain. And we send each other about two dozen memes while we're chatting, all really disgusting, hilarious memes that we wouldn't dream of showing to another soul, except each other. He really is the best person who ever lived, my son.

So, after the call, I feel a thousand times better. I have a shower and freshen up, get into bed and look at my phone, with all the gaps on the home page where the dating apps used to be. Maybe I was hasty. Maybe I've just been pursuing the wrong path, or not necessarily the wrong one, but one that I've found isn't really for me. I mean, the sex is fun, and all that, but maybe I should be pursuing love not sex, and maybe I'll find someone who actually cares, like Stef has Zuzana and Bel has Craig. Maybe it's time for that . . . Okay so I Google best paid dating apps. I'm thinking, if you gotta pay for an app, you're more likely to be looking for a relationship, right? Because every weirdo can download a free app for free sex. The results come up and the first two I see are labelled for 'Over 50s only' and they're called Our Time and Silver Singles . . . are you KIDDING ME?! SILVER SINGLES??? No. Nope. No way. I'm not old enough for that yet. SILVER?? I've heard of embrace the grey and

#silversisters and all that and I salute that but fuck this shit. I ain't no grandma yet, thanks very much.

I carry on and I find Match.com. Hmm, no mention of silver here. Says it's ideal for over thirty-fives looking for love. Okay that's me, I guess. Looks good. So I sign up for that. No more fuckboys, no more Ronnie the Rapist, just intelligent, prepared-to-pay-for-dating-apps serious chaps. I put on my profile that I'm looking for a relationship, no time wasters, no bullshit, no scammers, no catfish, no kittenfish, no MILF or GILF seekers, and definitely no fuckboys. Let's see what we have here then.

So, I order a Dominos and once I'm munching on those Red Hot chicken wings, I check my profile and I have a good crop of likes and messages. Okay, time to check out these serious guys. This is what I find:

Your too good to be true, cant take my eyes off you, I thank heaven so much, want to touch you insides xx

*you're

Can we cuddling together? All women I see no trust and no kindness and so much slut hussy bang.

Hey train wreck, this ain't your station.

I am into older women's feet. I want to discuss feet with you and kiss and massage your feet and you look at mine too. Swipe right for feet. Talk to me all night about feet.

I'd rather talk about tax law than this shite.

Whats a quilter

Google is your friend, my friend.

Tell me everything about yourself 1000 words go

Buddy, I've known you all of seven seconds and not enjoyed any of them. I'm not taking homework assignments from you.

You think you know the riddle's answer BUT NO! It is not ham or chicken or turkey or any other meat known to man. It is colour and life and yes! Haha you think you want meat but actually it is all SPAM! Fancy an oyster? Nothing rhymes with oyster. Or does it . . .? Ha!

Taking bets on which Class A drugs this guy is on . . .

Well, holy shit, it seems that paying to be on a dating app makes no goddamn difference at all when it comes to the lunatics and the time-wasters. FFS, it's as bad as POF. Also I see in my likes list Lee the garrulous plumber and Marcus the cheap-ciggie-stinking estate agent, trying their luck a second time. This is depressing. What's the point, if all the sites are gonna be like this?! Is this the narrow strip of pie that I get of all the men out there in the world? Stinky estate agents or '*want to touch you insides*'?! Fffffuck . . .

But then, who do I spy on my list, but erstwhile neuroscientist chum Guy?! So, he's on here too? Makes sense. He's forty-eight and not looking for just sex, according to him anyway. I've not heard from him for a couple of weeks, so I think, yeah, why not? It's actually nice to see a friendly face amidst all these weird randos.

Hey Frankie. How's the cesspit of modern-day dating treating ya?

Not great tbh, chum. Not great.

Sorry to hear that. Same here. It's like some kind of obscene parallel universe where everyone talks bullshit and your job is find the one sane person who tells the truth, like a cosmic game of Would I Lie to You?

Exactly that! And omg the weirdos . . . so many weirdos . . .

Mmhmm. I mean, I'm not one to kink shame. But my word, it's strange out there. One woman I met could only get off if we were listening to Billy Joel. And only Billy Joel. I mean, I don't have anything against Billy Joel – his song Allentown is a remarkable paean to the post-industrial age – but please. Not exactly sexy, so I just can't get it up. So she's mad at me and tells me I have to watch her instead, all to a soundtrack of Uptown Girl and I'm lying there thinking, there must be more to life than this . . .

Omfg hahahaaaa tell me about it. And I give him my weirdo rundown, from ski socks to incesty sexting guy.

Ahahahaaa. Do you think there's something wrong with us? Are we magnets for weird shit?

No, no definitely not. It can't be us. We're cool as fuck, right? I think we're just in the minority.

Well, then, we should meet. How about it? You up for that?

I'm enjoying the conversation, very much. I always do with Guy. He's smart, funny and seems to feel the same way as I do about dating, the madness of it all. But I'm just wondering why we haven't met so far, why he's always been coming and going, chatting like this, then disappearing for a while. I decide I don't want to start anything new with anyone who's going to mess me around. Zero tolerance now of any red flags, even the tiniest ones. So, I reply:

We've been chatting a while now, Guy, and I do enjoy our chats. But I'm just wondering why you haven't asked me to meet before this and why you keep going AWOL. Like, I'm not some nutter who expects your attention 24/7 but I just felt that you weren't that keen, so that's why I've held back. I do like you but I don't want to hang out with someone who's not properly interested. I've had enough of playing around and I do want a proper relationship with someone. So, if you're up for that as a possibility, then yeah. If not, then I'm not interested.

That sounds a bit intense . . . so I add:

So yeah, that's my hill and I'm gonna die on it hahaaa

There's a pause, then he starts typing – then this pops up:

Yeah Frankie look I'm really sorry I've been a bit absent. You know I've got my three boys and the truth is my ex-wife's father has been dying and I've been providing the support for her and the kids. He's passed now and we had the funeral last week. Sorry to lay that on you. I didn't want to be a downer and share that all with you, as I know you've got enough going on in your life too. But yeah, that's a bit of context for you. So I hope that makes sense of why I've been a bit flaky and I apologise for that. But I do really enjoy our chats too. And now things are quieter, I would like to meet, but only if you're up for that obvs.

Ah, well, okay. That makes sense. Makes perfect sense. Now I feel a bit of a dick for having a go at him if he's had all this real-world stuff happening. But then I think, it could be a wildly concocted lie . . . couldn't it? Yeah, I suppose it could be. I thought maybe he'd met someone more interesting than me, and now it didn't work out, he's back on me again, but tbf that could be true of any of us online dating. You try things out, you move on, and so much of this is about timing. Someone asks you first, or not, and someone else waits a bit, then misses their chance, and so it goes. So yeah, he could be full of shit, but he doesn't feel like it. He's telling me stuff that doesn't make him sound exactly like lover of the year and that's refreshing, after all the show-offs whose claims of virility usually end up being full of shit. I like Guy's honesty. And he is the most interesting person I've met online, fact. Maybe it's worth the risk of meeting and seeing if, in the flesh, I believe him. It's always easier to tell if someone's lying face to face, isn't it? Okay, I decide. Let's give it a go.

We arrange to meet that weekend. He lives over an hour's drive away in Chesterfield, but he's happy to drive over to Lincoln to see me, so that's a good sign. We meet at the Wig and Mitre. First impressions are good, more than good. He's tall, much taller than me, maybe six-foot-two and I like that. He has dark-blond thick hair, swept to the side in the way you'd want to run your fingers through. He's forty-eight and he looks it, I mean, he's got wrinkles and pouches and he looks pretty tired. But he's a rumpled kind of sexy and I'm finding I actually like the signs of age in him, that he's lived and he knows about life and parenthood and how bloody hard it is. Three boys . . . oof. That's a lot of parenthood right there. And he has these really big greeny-hazel eyes, like really big. They're quite distracting. And the attraction is instant, I reckon. The spark is there, most definitely there. We're chatting away and every so often we stop, and smile, and glance at each other's mouths. Ohhhh this is the best bit, the anticipation, picturing how those lips would feel to kiss. And here I am, one hundred per cent back in the saddle, loving the madness of the dating game. When it goes well like this, it's like a drug. The highs are irresistible.

And it certainly takes my mind off Stef. Guy makes me feel wanted and he compliments me without sounding fake or thirsty. It's such a laugh to have a laugh with him about sex, with no judgement. We're both really honest with each other about how slutty we've been, sleeping around with different people, sharing our dating disasters and ONS success stories. And it's really refreshing to hear that and not feel he's judging me. Guy seems genuinely pleased I'm like him, playing the field, where some men (including Stef) would condemn me for that. Guy makes it clear though that he's had enough of all the gallivanting and it's time for him to look for a relationship. I agree wholeheartedly and I love that we see eye to eye on this and so many other things.

We have a great evening, talking and laughing and flirting and drinking. He doesn't drink much, as he's driving. I have a few, but not too many. I want to stay lucid. As the pub shouts for last orders, it feels like the whole evening has gone by in a flash, and I don't want it to end. When a first date goes this well, it's a beautiful thing and I don't want it to progress to the next stage, to the sex stage where it could all go horribly wrong. I just want to stay in this flirty, chatty, eyes across the table stage forever. The ultimate high. But, of course, it has to end and then we're outside and people are walking past us and I say I'll walk him down to where his car is parked at the bottom of Steep Hill and we've only walked a few yards and I just stop walking and look at him.

'Just tell me you're not some asshole liar who's out for what he can get or plays games with people's feelings and all that shit.'

'I'm not, scout's honour.'

'Don't fucking joke with me, I'm serious.'

'So am I. You're bloody brilliant, Frankie. I don't want to mess this up with you.'

And I stare at his face and it looks open, it looks sincere. And in this life, what else do we have to go on?

I grab his hand and pull him around the corner into Wordsworth Street and he pushes me up against the wall and he pauses, just for a moment, to see my face and I see his eyes and it's so intense and then we kiss and it's like fireworks going off and it's AWESOME.

CHAPTER 12

Gone Guy

That night, I don't invite him back to my place and he doesn't ask and I'm so glad we don't. It extends that delicious anticipation and also shows him I mean it, that I'm not looking for a ONS. We carry on chatting over the following week and it's going great. But we can't meet up again yet, as he has a fifty-fifty arrangement with his ex to have the boys with him four weeknights, while they're with her Friday to Sunday. Busy life. And when the boys are there, he's barely online and a couple of times we'll be messaging then he says he's signing off for the evening now and he'll check in again tomorrow, but it's only 9pm and that seems a bit odd . . . I mean, I know he wants to spend quality time with his kids, but why the radio silence for the whole night? Then he explains that he has boundaries on his phone to maintain a good work/life balance and tries to switch it off when his kids are around, so they have his full attention. And that seems quite sweet tbh. Makes me feel I might be being too demanding. I was feeling a bit fitted in between his other commitments, but then, that's life, isn't it? If I had three sons of nineteen, sixteen and thirteen, I'd have no social life too. We arrange to meet the following weekend. He has a conference the first weekend, so that's why we can't meet again straight away. It all sounds plausible enough. Why am I doubting it? I just feel so jaded by the dating world, and the scammers and the liars, I think I'm starting to doubt every single person I meet.

So, to attempt to put my mind at rest, I do my research. He says he works in the medical school at the University of Sheffield and so I have a look and I find his name there, Dr Guy Taylor-Jones, neuroscience. There's a bio there and it checks out with what he's told me, about Alzheimer's being his specialism. But there's no picture of him. So I check on a few other profiles of staff there and some have pictures and some don't. So that's reassuring, but still annoying there's no picture to check it's really him. And he's not on any social media. He told me that already, that he hates Facebook and all that and has never been on it. I Google through the main socials just to check he's not lying about that, but he isn't. There's no sign of him. Frustrating . . . and is it suspicious? Yes, but is it impossible that someone could have no trace on socials, on a Google search? Not impossible, again just a bit odd.

Opinion is split on this matter into two camps. Michelle and Kelly think it's fine, that there's quite a few people around that don't have much of a digital footprint, Michelle included, who says, apart from putting her quilting ideas on Pinterest, she's not on any other social media at all. 'I despise it,' she says. Gita says she isn't on the internet either and it doesn't mean he's a liar. Whereas Linda, Paige and Stef – as well as Bel, who doesn't trust anyone who isn't on social media – don't like it. 'What's he trying to hide?' they all say.

So, I go on another date with him, this time to *Gino*'s, the Italian restaurant up the hill. He doesn't mind driving all that way again, but there's not much choice really, as I don't have a car and it's not easy to get to Chesterfield on the train, as it's over a two-hour journey, change at Sheffield. He says he doesn't mind the drive as he loves to listen to podcasts about science and stuff, so he really values the time he gets in the car coming to see me, so he can have an excuse to listen to them. We have a nice meal and there's all that spark there again and it's lovely. I ask him more about his sons and he shows me pictures of them on his phone, playing footie, outside a gig venue, on holiday etc. He tells me all about them, how different they are from each other, yet all the things in himself that he recognises in them and wishes they didn't have or is glad they do. I tell him all about Jay and we talk about neuroscience and he says it's a great field and he's sure Jay would excel. It feels grounding, to talk about our families like this, and I feel much better about him, hearing all this rich detail about his life. He's a real person, with a real life. And after this, I feel ready. We're in the little side street outside the restaurant and I invite him back to mine.

'Are you sure?' he says. 'Because we can take it slow. I know you don't want to rush anything.'

'Yeah, I'm sure,' I say and pull him in and kiss him, deep and slow. We go back to mine and it's so good to be kissing someone I really like, who I really want to know better and who I've spoken to at length and actually want to be around and see again. It's a hundred times better than a ONS, a thousand! We're a bit awkward with each other in bed, but we laugh about it and take it easy and enjoy ourselves. The mood is passionate yet fun, intense yet playful. It's a great first shag! Afterwards, he stays the night and we sleep a bit, then more sex, then sleep a bit more. I wake him up at eight-ish, as I have to go and open the shop soon, as it's Sunday. We grab some toast and coffee, then he kisses me and hugs me and says he can't wait to see me again, and then off he goes. I spend all day in the shop reliving the night before, over and over in my head, and I'm pretty darn delighted with the way things are going. We message a bit that night and on my day off the next day, I'm wishing he wasn't lecturing all day. Shame he has so many damn commitments. And also, I need the distraction, as I spend Monday going through my accounts and it's not great news. I'm simply not making enough money to pay myself a living wage. It's scary stuff and I get a migraine from staring at all my notes and bank statements and so forth and trying to make all the numbers add up. Real life is back, biting me on the arse. All I want is to lounge in bed with Guy, and instead I'm spending hours looking for ways to minimise my expenses and trying to make plans for the future to increase revenue for the shop.

That night is group night and seeing the gang really cheers me up. Stef is there and though I can't deny I'm still mad about him in theory, suddenly I don't feel so desperate about it, because of Guy. It's not that Guy is better than Stef or cancels him out, just that Guy is available and Stef isn't, and that reminds me that I don't *need* Stef. I can be happy without him. And it makes it much easier to be with him, actually, and I really enjoy our banter that night, as the weight of expectation about him has lifted and I can truly be myself and just have a chilled time with him, working on our quilt. The exhibition is less than four weeks away now and we're all grafting to finish our projects in good time. We're nearly there, as most of the squares are done.

We're just busy now piecing them together and creating the finished items. Then Kelly comes in late again and says she has a bit of news about the upcoming exhibition.

'On the opening night, there's going to be all the local newspapers there, taking pictures and interviewing people, so Frankie, you must make sure you talk to the reporter and get the shop and the quilting group in the paper, because I'm sure that'll help your business.'

Bless her, because I've been telling the group recently some of my financial woes and they've all been trying to come up with ideas to help the shop succeed. I thank her. I'm feeling a bit better about everything and maybe this will really help. We have a lovely evening, chatting away. I spend quite a bit of it talking with Stef about his design business and his current projects. He has a real interest in traditional folk designs, not only from Slovakia but from the UK too. He's telling me about a book he's been reading about the Luddites, the textile workers in Manchester in the eighteenth century who broke up the machines that were taking their jobs and it's fascinating, about how textiles have changed over the centuries and yet here we still are, sewing by hand. I love to watch his face when he's discussing something that moves him, that galvanises his mind, and I find his thoughts, his readings, his interests, they galvanise me too and we get pretty excited while we're talking about this stuff and we interrupt each other a lot then apologise for interrupting. The flow of our conversations is a pleasure to ride. At one moment, I glance at Gita and she's watching us talk and . . . well, she's got a face on. And it's not a good face. But then she looks at me and smiles broadly. She says she's tired and wants to go early, so Stef says he'll take her. She does that sometimes, because the full two and a half hours tires her out. And off they go.

And then the rest of us hotbedders know we can talk about rude things, now Gita's gone. We start out listening to Paige's latest date with a guy and how the first thing he says when he meets her is he hates it when women colour their hair crazy colours and how it's almost as bad as women with tattoos or facial piercings and we all laugh at the idiot because of course all her profile pics have her with every colour of hair under the sun, but why do these twats think they have the right to dictate her choice of style to her face, when he could've saved them both time and stayed the hell at home?

Then Stef comes back from dropping Gita off and I'm so glad he does. I mean, he could stay at home after seeing his mum there but he doesn't, he comes straight back here, every time.

Linda immediately asks how things are going with Guy. And I blush, I actually blush!

'Ooh, things are going *that* well, are they?'

I giggle and everyone goes OOH! And Stef is just getting on with his quilting work and I can't see his face, as he's turned away from me.

'Yeah, yeah, it's good. I've found out a lot more about him, about his sons. And it's going well. I do like him.'

'That's good,' says Linda, but she doesn't sound convinced. 'So, you're not worried about the social media thing?'

'No, not really. I just think some people aren't into it and that's fine.'

'Just be careful, love,' Linda replies. 'I don't want to see you getting hurt. None of us do.'

'Damn straight,' says Paige. 'But Frankie's kickass. She can look after herself.'

'Aw, thanks, lovely,' I say. 'But I'm not as tough as I look.'

Stef does turn round and glance at me then, and I can't decipher the look on his face. He looks worried, but then he does a small smile and I do one back.

Linda says, 'You were saying at first that Guy is very charming. And that worries me.'

'In what way?'

'I don't know really, just a feeling I get. We use the word charming a lot to mean something positive, but in my eyes, someone who's charming is often using it as a ploy. As we say, turning on the charm. I just worry about any bloke that's described as charming.'

'Me too,' says Stef. 'You can't trust charming men. I mean, when you think about it, a charm is another word for a spell. Putting a spell on someone, charming them, it's the same thing.'

I laugh and say, 'Guy hasn't put a spell on me!'

'I hope not,' says Stef quietly and looks back down at his sewing. And this annoys me.

'I hope not too,' says Linda and this annoys me too. Can't they trust my judgement, FFS? I'm not a child. Linda adds, 'I do think the silence between his messaging is odd. Why does he go offline at 9pm? It's strange. I mean, I do tend to turn my phone off at night, but until then, it's on and I'll answer messages unless I'm too tired. And I'm twenty years older than this man. I had a friend once who had a relationship with a man and he never communicated with her after dinnertime, and I thought it was odd. Turned out he was married and had two phones. When he got home from work, he'd turn the second phone off and hide it in the car. So he was literally unable to answer messages from that phone. Which explained the absences. I'm not saying Guy's married . . . but he's all the way over in Chesterfield. And you have no way of checking on these things, as he's not on Facebook or anything. It's just something to be aware of, love. Just looking out for you, you know.'

I know she means well. But I don't like this. I'm all aglow after my night with Guy and these guys are really pissing on my parade.

'He's not married,' I say, blithely.

'But how do you know?' says Stef. 'He could be anyone, this Guy guy.'

'Because I'm the one who's spent time with him. I'm the one who's talked to him for hours. I really appreciate everyone's concern but honestly, I've got this. He's not a bad'un. He's just a bloke, who likes me and I like him. Can we just leave it at that?'

It comes out as snappy, but I didn't mean it to come out that way. But I'm defensive, I know I am. And I sound it. But sod it, what I've said is also true. They've just heard snippets about Guy and they haven't got to know him as I have. After that, everyone just smiles and nods and gets on with their work. Then we all pack away and everyone's leaving but Linda is hanging around.

'Everything okay, Linda?' I say, when everyone else has left.

'Yes, love. Listen, I just wanted to say sorry if it felt like we're interfering in your love life.'

'Oh God, no. Don't worry about that. I know you're all looking out for me and I really appreciate that. I'm sorry I was a bit snappy about it. I feel a bit crap about that actually.'

'I understand that. No grown adult wants people

patronising them and telling them what to do. Thing is though, that friend I told you about? Well, that wasn't a friend, that was me.'

'Oh, Linda,' I say, and I'm really surprised. I just didn't think of her having a love life at all, which is daft, of course. Just because she's in her sixties, which is only a few years on from me, doesn't mean she's not a sexual person. I hope I'm a sexy bitch until the day I drop down dead.

'Yes, unfortunately. After my husband died, I went to ground for years, wouldn't entertain the thought of another man. But then I met a man at a delicatessen as we were both buying the same red pepper houmous, and if there's a romantic meeting that's more middle class than that, I won't believe it.'

I laugh at that, then ask, 'So what happened?'

'Just what I said earlier. I really fell for him, I did. He was a lovely man, charming. There's that word again. And highly plausible. Then, over time, things didn't add up. Just odd little things about times he couldn't see me or reasons he gave for absences. His explanations were always very detailed, too detailed, like a story. I grew curious but I didn't have the Googling skills you and the others have. But it resolved itself in the end, as I was in his car and I went in the glove compartment to find some tissues. I found this other phone and I asked him what it was for. His face just blanched. He broke down, cried real tears! I couldn't believe it. And he told me everything. He said his wife had just been diagnosed with dementia and though she wasn't too bad so far, he knew she'd get a lot worse and he wanted to find love with someone else, as he hated the thought of being alone. I couldn't blame him for that. But I couldn't forgive him for lying.'

'Oh God, Linda, that's bloody awful. The lying twat.'

'Oh, I felt such a fool. I was so angry with myself.'

'It wasn't your fault!'

'No, but I had all these little niggles about him. And I didn't act on them. So, I'm just letting you know. I'm sure you've checked all these things out with Guy and it's probably nothing. People have busy lives. And not everyone is wedded to their phone and good on 'em. Terrible things, phones.'

'I really appreciate you telling me that, Linda. And don't worry. I'll keep my wits about me.'

'Good girl. And even though you might think of me as a hundred years old, I remember perfectly well what it feels like to fall for a man. Like the houmous man. He had me well and truly cock-struck!'

Wow, Linda never ceases to amaze me! I love that you never know what she's going to say next. We laugh about that but then she looks serious again and goes on, 'Listen, love. My husband was the best person I ever knew. He wasn't particularly charming or clever. When I first met him, he didn't sweep me off my feet. I didn't have butterflies in my tummy when I thought of him and I wasn't dazzled by his witty repartee. I didn't even think he was that handsome. But we got to know each other gradually, over time. And he was always there when he said he would be, and he was kind and thoughtful. And witty, yes, but in a gentle way, in birthday cards or letters, such a way with words. And what I realised by loving him is this: love can start with a spark, yes, it can. But it doesn't have to. Sometimes it grows over time, slowly, and dawns on you. And before you know it, you realise you love this man. And he loves you. And it isn't about spark anymore, it's something else, something far beyond that. It's peace. A quiet knowledge of love. It doesn't sound very exciting, but it's the most wonderful and precious thing you'll ever know.'

'Wow,' I say softly. 'Thank you, Linda. That really is a beautiful insight.'

'Ah, it's nothing. I just don't want you to fall foul of a liar, like I did. Take care, you,' she says and hugs me abruptly and leaves.

I envy Linda the love she had with her husband. It sounds like once-in-a-lifetime love that, and I can't ever imagine that happening to me. Maybe I'm just not cut out for it, don't attract that peaceful kind of man. I did really appreciate Linda staying behind and sharing that with me. And I'm sorry that liar idiot messed with her. But I'm sure Guy isn't like that. I mean, if he is married, how come he was able to stay with me on a Saturday night like that? Surely a married man couldn't get away with that.

Then he messages me, and it's after 9pm, so I feel like yeah, he's not on the secret phone he's left in the car then. And we chat on WhatsApp for ages and it's fab. I ask him more about his kids and his ex, and he answers in detail and it all sounds legit to me. Then he says how he can't stop thinking about my body and then we start sexting and it's bloody marvellous. He's such a good sexter and he's broken the tradition of being great on the phone and shit in bed. He's on fire when he sexts! What a way to spend a Monday night! Afterwards, I'm lying in bed totally spent and satisfied and I say in my head to Stef, *Beat that, Števko!* I know he's got his doubts about Guy, but there's a simple explanation for that: he's just jealous. Well, good. It's his turn to pine for me for once.

So, the next couple of weeks, Guy comes over on

Saturday nights and we have a great time and it's lovely. He's more attentive on the phone these days and I think maybe he was just a bit distant to begin with, because he didn't know me, he didn't know what this was going to be. He's allowed to be cautious and protect his feelings too. He's had some bad dating experiences and his divorce was hard, he tells me. Men have feelings too, of course. The sex is great and I realise that part of it might be because of his age. He's not inexperienced and gauche, like some of these losers I've had disappointing evenings with. He takes his time and knows exactly what he's doing. Then afterwards, I love the way we lie around for hours talking. He tells me stuff about neuroscience which is absolutely fascinating. Like, how the brain is basically like society, how it has all these different departments that work in concert, yet they're also all in competition with each other for the real estate of the brain, so that's why you're always in two minds about things, because your neurons and all that stuff are actively fighting it out for territory and that's where our constant mental conflict comes from. I can certainly relate to that, as my entire existence seems to be one of mental conflict! I relay stuff like this to Jay and he's delighted I'm learning about it too. Guy recommends science podcasts for me to listen to, like *The Curious Cases of Rutherford and Fry*. And I listen to them and I'm loving it, all this new learning. I'm really digging Guy's brain, as well as his delicious body.

So, it's great sex and great chats and great chemistry. That spark is still there, from the banter and the wit of our chats, to the passion between the sheets. Guy has it all. Can it really be that easy, after a few months of dating, to find a guy as perfect as this? Maybe it can. Maybe I got lucky.

And I deserve a bit of luck, don't I? I've earnt it, after all the miserable years with Twatface.

One Saturday night in late May, Guy comes to my place after we've been sexting all afternoon and we're so goddamn hot for each other, when he knocks on the door, I rush to open it and we fall on each other, snogging and laughing, and he's holding his wallet and keys and he just flings them to the floor and they smash into the wall and I wrench his shirt out of his jeans and he's yanking my skirt off and we do it over the sofa and it's bloody marvellous. This is really living!

Afterwards, we're ravenous and we start pulling stuff out of the fridge and feasting on it. Then we really fancy some wine but I've run out. 'I'll get some,' he says and I tell him I'll come too and he says no, stay in your cute underwear cos I'm coming back for round two after. We laugh and he pulls on his jeans and shirt and I tell him where the offy is and he's out the door. I'm luxuriating in the post-shag, post-food stupor, thinking how great everything is, then I decide to tidy up a bit so we can go and relax in bed after this. I like the sofa and all that, but I much prefer bed for proper sex, where we can really take our time and explore. That's what I want tonight, not just a quickie. So I wrap a thigh-length silky dressing gown round me, feeling great. And I'm folding up the blankets and rearranging the cushions on the sofa, then I see his keys and wallet on the floor that he threw down when he came in. Oh shit, his wallet! I grab it up from the floor and I'm about to text him to say he's forgotten it, then I realise it's really thin and light, like there's nothing in it, which is weird, and I get an odd sensation in the pit of my stomach and I open up his wallet and there's hardly anything in there. There's a couple of quid in coins but no cards in the slots and no driving licence or stuff like that. Except hidden inside a pouch I find a credit card, just one card and it says *Justin Bunch* on it.

And at that moment, he's knocking on the door, and he's saying through the door, 'Let me in, gorgeous, I forgot my wallet.' So I go over and open the door, and he sees me holding the wallet and looks blank and I say:

'Who the fuck is Justin Bunch?'

There's this agonising moment, where he looks gutted, annoyed and shady all at once and my heart sinks like a stone.

'Justin who?' he says, trying to look innocent.

'Justin Bunch, it says it here, on the one card in your otherwise weirdly empty wallet.'

'Can you give me my wallet, please?' he says, his voice flat.

'I could do but it doesn't look like it's yours and there's bugger all in there. Just a few coins and a credit card belonging to Justin Bunch. Who the fuck is Justin Bunch?'

'I just . . . found it, earlier today. That card. On the ground. I was gonna give it in to the bank.'

'Where's your other cards then, in the wallet you came back to get to pay for the wine?'

But he's got no answer to that. He doesn't even try to come up with another lie for that. He's not looking at me and he walks in my flat past me and he grabs his keys from the floor. 'Why have you been searching through my wallet anyway?'

'Don't change the subject, Guy. If that's your name. Or is it Justin *Bunch*?' I say, incredulously. 'So, you take all the stuff out of your wallet that identifies you, except you decide to keep one card for emergencies just in case, then you hide it in a pouch. Talk about malice aforethought, you total lying twat!'

'I'd better go then,' he says as he stuffs his keys in his pocket. 'Now give me my wallet.'

Suddenly I realise there's this man in my flat, and I'm in my silky thigh-length dressing gown, and I've been seeing this man for weeks and he's been inside me multiple times and I've shared intimate thoughts and memories with him. And I have literally no idea who he is. And I'm holding his wallet and he wants it and I'm not going to give it to him. I don't care what's sensible right now, with this stranger in my place, giving me orders.

'No. Not until you tell me the truth, you arsehole. Who the fuck are you?'

'Do I have to come and fetch it? Because I will.' Wow, his voice is so different. He's a totally different person, suddenly. Who the hell is this man? I swallow nervously.

But then I think, *No. Screw him and his threats.*

'Are you Justin? Do you even have three sons, who I've never seen a photo of with you actually in it? Do you even lecture in neuroscience or just get your ideas from podcasts? And are you divorced or actually married?'

He can't look me in the eye. This whole time, he's been staring at a spot in the middle distance that's not me, not the floor, but a spot in between, like there's a person there, because he can't look at me directly. He says nothing. Nothing at all.

'You fucking coward,' I say and the rage is building in me now. 'Say something!'

'I'm just a sad, fucking married guy, okay? My wife has mental health issues and—'

'Oh, don't give me any more sob stories. I don't wanna know!'

'Give me my wallet then and I'll go.'

'Was any of it real to you? Any of this? Us?'

Then he looks at me for the first time. Those huge, pretty eyes of his, that I thought were so open and honest. I was a bloody idiot. 'Yes, yes it was. It *is* what I want. *You* are what I want. But it's too complicated to explain and you wouldn't underst—'

'Ohhhh, it's complicated, is it? Too complicated for my pretty little head to comprehend, is it? Fuck you, you mansplaining cunt. Fuck you and your lies.'

And I throw his wallet at him and it hits him SMACK in the chest and bounces off onto the floor. And he sighs and leans down to pick it up and he walks to the door and opens it and I stomp to the door and as he walks through it, I yell:

'And Justin Bunch is a SHIT name!'

And I kick the door shut.

I'm so fucking angry, I don't know what to do with myself. I'm absolutely RAGING. I'm not gonna cry, that's for sure. I've wept enough tears over men. Lying, secretive arseholes, the lot of 'em! That almost empty wallet, proof that he was trying to cover up his secret identity, like he thinks he's a superhero or some shit. To think ahead that much about your lies and organise them! I bet he empties his wallet out on the passenger seat and shoves it all in the glove compartment, before coming up to mine. Urgh, the absolute wanker.

Then, curiosity gets the better of me about this particular lying arsehole and I go straight on my phone and Google Justin Bunch and there he is, large as life. He's on Facebook and he has a wife called Wendy with a brown bob. He's a science teacher at a secondary school in Rotherham, not a neuroscience lecturer. And he doesn't even live in Chesterfield! He posts virtually nothing on Facebook and in fact the only posts on there are scammers tagging him in bullshit and his wife tagging him in little day trips and meals out they've been on, with their boys (at least the boys are real) or just the two of them. *Twenty-five-year anniversary dinner with my lovely hubster!* posts Wendy, beaming at the camera, while he holds a pint of lager (he never drinks lager with me!) and he's smiling a smile I've never seen him do, a closed-mouth jaw-clenched grimace. Oh God. Poor Wendy. She doesn't *look* like she has mental health issues . . . whatever the hell that means! I mean, what does someone with mental health issues look like?! I've got mental health issues, we've all got mental health issues. A lying cunt like Guy – I mean, Justin Bunch (it really is a shit name) – he's the one with the serious mental health issues, not his poor, long-suffering wife Wendy Bunch. I could message her, right now. I could tell her everything. She might accept the message request, she might not. But at least I could try. She deserves to know, doesn't she? Poor, poor Wendy.

But . . . maybe she does know. Maybe she wonders where the hell he's going on these Saturday nights and doesn't ask, too afraid to. Who knows? I don't know. I don't know this man or his wife or his sad little lying life. And I don't want to. I do have a quick sneak peek at her profile though, and see she runs a business, making little homey things like wooden plaques with a motto on, not exactly *Live Laugh Love* but the same ballpark, inspirational phrases you might get on your tampon packet, like *Grab life by the horns!* and *You got this girl* (no comma). Christ, there she is carving rousing messages for women to adorn their homes, while her husband is out there shagging them. I block him and then her on Facebook, probably pointlessly, but it just feels better. I find him on Twitter with no profile pic and no tweets and I don't even know if it's him but I block him on there too and I find her business on Facebook, Twitter and Instagram and I block her too. Live, Laugh, Fuck Off. Then I throw my phone on the floor. Fucking fucking FUCK.

Why didn't I follow my gut? AGAIN! Why didn't I listen to Bel, who had his number from day one, when she said don't chase him, when she talked about him benching or breadcrumbing me? Why didn't I listen to Linda and the others, who knew something was up? Even Stef knew, but I didn't listen, because I assumed he was heavily biased (which he was . . . but he was still right). This fuckface has played the dating game and beat me, hands down. I thought I was winning the dating game, but Guy – sorry Justin, or now, as I've just re-christened him, Fuckface – has *out-dated* me. I'm so mad at myself too for falling for the same type of man I've always gone for and it always ends badly. Before Twatface, all the men were charming and so was Twatface, when he was Gareth and I first met him. All charm and wit, the same with Fuckface, all spark. I Google 'Why do I go for the same man over and over again?' and get a bunch of clickbait articles that don't give me any answers, except for one, that tells me I'm groundhogging. It's where you keep falling for the same bad guy over and over again and expect it to be different this time. That's it. That's me. I'm groundhogging. And then it hits me. OMFG . . . I have an epiphany. That's where I'm going wrong. That's the mistake I'm making, over and over again. I've chosen these men, these charming guys, because I thought only that spark meant falling in love. And if that spark wasn't there, then it's not love. But love is different than charm, just as Linda told me. She was so right and I didn't hear it at the time. I listened but it didn't hit home, but now I understand it. I was cock-struck! Charmed, under a spell, just as Stef said. I trusted the spark, and let's face it, a spark is bright and vital but it's instantly gone, and gone forever.

But what's the alternative? Feeling that physical and mental spark with someone matters, doesn't it? Fancying someone inside and out matters. However much I like Linda's view of things, I know for a fact that sexual attraction is crucial to me. How could I spend years of my life with someone, if I didn't fancy them like mad? So, is the answer to keep looking until you find the sexiest guy ever who takes it slow and you fall in love over time? How likely is that?! It all feels hopeless and online dating is definitely not the answer. I go on my phone and delete Match.com. I've had enough! Fuck you, Mars and fuck you, men!

I don't sleep too well that night and I have a rotten Sunday. Not a word from Guy, I mean, Fuckface. I message Bel and tell her the basic details. She's at her mum's with Barney for a few days and she's worried about me and offers to call later, so we can talk, but I don't want to bother her. She needs the break. I tell her I'm okay, and I am really. I haven't cried once. I'm just so mad at myself.

Then, on Monday, I just stay in bed all day, moping. I watch *Notting Hill* and torture myself with gorgeous Julia Roberts and nice guy Hugh Grant and their little scene at the end, with her neat pregnant belly reading a book in a garden in London and it's all too perfect and I throw a sandwich at the TV, which I regret afterwards because I have to clean that shit up. I'm dreading the group tonight, because I know I won't be able to bullshit them and then I'll have to admit it all. I consider cancelling it, saying I'm ill . . . but then I think no, sod that. If I do that, then Fuckface wins. They all win, the lying twats of the world, if you let them change your routine, let them isolate you, shame you, embarrass you. *They* are the ones who should be embarrassed, FFS. I've got nothing to apologise for.

So everybody turns up as usual and it's like we know each other so well now, they're tuned in to me and immediately everyone seems to sense something is up. Stef hasn't set up the iPad quite yet, so I take the pre-Gita opportunity to quickly tell them all the sorry tale.

'I knew it!' says Stef.

'All right, fuck off,' I say and scowl at him.

'Yeah, Stef, don't look so bloody pleased about it,' says Paige, and I love her for that.

'Sorry, sorry.' He shakes his head. 'That was a twattish thing to say. Sorry. I just meant—'

'Listen,' I cut him off. 'I don't really want to talk about it. Can we just get Gita online and be normal? I just need to forget all about it and have a nice evening with my sewing homies, okay?'

Everybody's like, yeah, of course and Kelly gives me a hug and we get on with our quilting. We're only days away from the exhibition now and things are really coming together. I get through the evening and Gita feels a bit poorly before the end, so Stef says he'll go home and check on her. Once he's gone, we don't have any girly banter, as I'm clearly not in the mood. All the ladies are lovely with me though, careful and sweet, pats on my arm and helping me clear away even more solicitously than usual. Bless my hotbed of quilters. They're all off home but, this time, Michelle lingers.

The mysterious Michelle. She never has much to say about my love life or any of our discussions really. She makes little barbed comments from time to time, but never tells us much about herself. Maybe she wants to talk about something else.

'Everything okay, Mich?'

'Yes, absolutely. Listen . . . erm . . . I'm not sure if you know about this, but there are dating sites that aren't really dating sites, as such. They offer . . . more bespoke solutions.'

Okay, so this is intriguing AF but tbh the last thing I can face is yet another app.

'Well, I've deleted all the dating apps from my phone. I'm just not in the mood right now.'

'I understand but this is quite different. There are a range of different sites just for sex. Any type of sex. All kinds of kinks, anything you can imagine really. Profile pictures are just body parts and you can view private face pics if you want to ask for them. And everyone on there knows it's just for sex, whatever kind of peccadillo you have, someone out there will cater for it and want it too. It takes all the emotional nonsense out of sex and just gives you what you need.'

I'm absolutely flummoxed by this cosy little speech, from the woman who rarely says more than a sentence at any one time in class.

'Forgive me for asking, Mich, but how the hell do you know all this?!'

I'm absolutely agog to know the answer. She smiles a knowing little smile and replies, 'Because I use them myself, all the time. And so does my husband. We're into BDSM and threesomes. And we have a lot of fun, I can tell you.'

OMFG, Michelle! The dark horse personified!

'I KNEW there was something cheeky about you, Mich! I knew it!'

'It's my private life and nobody's business but mine. And I'd ask you to keep this to yourself and not tell the rest of the hotbed.'

'Oh, yeah, of course. I won't tell a soul.' Though I know I'll be straight onto Bel when she's back from her mum's. How could I not?! It's juicy AF! 'Tell me more about these sites then.'

'There's whole subcultures on there, as I say, for anything you're into.'

'I'm not really into anything in particular. I'm quite vanilla, as they say. I just like good sex.'

'All right, but there will be men on there who'll do whatever you want. And maybe you just haven't explored other types of sex yet. There are swinging groups and sex parties and all sorts. Honestly, anything you can imagine, it exists. And lots of weird stuff you could never imagine. That exists too. And it's all there for the taking. I'm only telling you because I think this dating thing is really getting to you. And I used to be angsty about sex and so did my husband, and our sex life was a joke. Then, one day a few years ago, we were finally honest with each other about what we wanted, and it turned out he was a sub and I was a domme, and then we had some real fun. And after that, we started exploring BDSM porn together and that's how we ended up on the sites. Nowadays, we have regular fun with a range of like-minded people. It's safe and it's good. There's no danger, if you organise it properly. I can give you any advice on it, if you want to and I'm sure my husband would too. We're very open to the right people, my husband and I.'

Wow, there really is no telling with people, is there?

Who'd'a'thunk it with twinset and pearls, M&S employee and mother of two, Michelle? I mean, I knew still waters ran deep with her, but not this deep!

'Thanks, Mich. I massively appreciate your honesty, I really do. And it sounds fascinating. And I'm really glad you found the right solution for you and your husband. Sounds like an absolute scream! I'll think about it. But something tells me I'm not as brave as you. I don't think I could go to a sex party or a gangbang or anything like that. I just . . . I don't know, I just can't imagine myself doing it.' I want to say, I can't imagine not going in and just pissing myself laughing at all these weird-looking folk shagging away and dressed up in crazy porny outfits. Cos that's how it would be, surely, wouldn't it? I mean, they wouldn't all look like Julia Roberts and Hugh Grant, would they? You can bet your life it wouldn't be like *Eyes Wide Shut*, either, all perfect tits and masks. They'd be all middle-aged and lumpy, like me. And I don't want to watch people like me having sex, I really don't!

'If that doesn't appeal to you,' she says and gets out her phone, 'then maybe try this one.' She pulls up a dating app called OKCupid. I have heard of it but just not got round to using it yet. 'It's a conventional dating site in many ways, but when you join, you have to fill in all these questions about what kind of relationship you're after, and you can ignore that, or you can really go to town and list all of your requirements. It's the only normal site I've found where some people will actually say upfront exactly what they're looking for. I remember when we first went on there, my husband and I, and we saw men who said they were cucks and just wanted to watch a man screw their wives in front of them. And we realised that's what my husband likes too, so we hooked up with some men who wanted that and we all had a lovely time. And nobody was ashamed of it. There's so many people out there who love this stuff. There's another app called Feeld which also throws up a range of options and kinks to explore. We really enjoy Feeld and OKCupid and use them often, my husband and I.'

I can't get over Michelle when she says *my husband and I*, sounding like the bloody Queen. Well, she is a queen. Queen Michelle, the dominatrix! Good for her! I love her even more, now I know her delicious little secret.

I thank her again and she is so gracious and yet business-like about it, like she's just given me some Martin Lewis-style financial advice, not tips on how to find the filthiest fuckers around.

After Michelle's gone, I think about what she told me. Is that the answer then? Sex to order. No fuck buddies, no buddies where sex is concerned. No spark, no sex interview, just pure physical transaction with another body. And you order precisely what you want, up front, like toppings on a pizza. No waiting for your ONS to deliver and not knowing what they're gonna come up with, not knowing if you're gonna get stuffed crust or classic, as you've already agreed it beforehand: the sexual equivalent of chicken wings, garlic bread and loaded fries. I'll have those please and some cookies too. Just tick-list sex or dating for love and never the twain shall meet. It would certainly rule out the liars. If you're just meeting for pure sex, no bullshit, no pretence at liking each other and certainly no dating even . . . that could be really liberating. No need to be lied to by a man ever again. Maybe it is the answer. I mean, firstly I wanted sex and lots of it, and got fed up with that. Then I wanted a relationship and got scammed over that. But do I really want a relationship actually? Do I want what Stef has, or seems to have, anyway?

Since I left Twatface, the one thing I've found I love the most about my new life is my independence and my freedom. I get to eat what I want, when I want and watch whatever I want on TV and sleep as late as I want on my day off and I have nobody to answer to for anything in my life. And I value that, hugely. I certainly don't need a man in my house again, moving my stuff around and telling me what to do, do I? But what about companionship and what about loneliness? Ach, I don't bloody know. There are no easy answers in this dating game.

I'm still thinking about it all when I stick the oven on and heat up a frozen pizza (it's Pizza Express pollo ad astra though – I'm not a complete slob). I settle down on my sofa with a glass of red and munch on my pizza and watch a bit of *Game of Thrones* for a laugh (I've seen the whole thing four times, so it's more for company than anything: ultra-violent, soft-porny company, but company nonetheless). I go on my phone and think about looking up OKCupid . . . but decide to check Facebook first and share a few memes to cheer myself up. That annoying little red blob in the corner tells me I have a message and I go on Messenger and nobody I know has messaged me, but I wonder if that means message requests. My heart's in my mouth, because I wonder, for a moment, if it's Guy. I don't want it to be, but also I do. Of course I do. I haven't got over him in forty-eight hours. I was falling in love with the man, FFS. So, holding my breath, I tap on message requests.

But it's not Guy. It's some random Facebook scammer – I can't escape the bastards! They're everywhere!

Hello beautiful. It's so nice to meet you. I tried to send you a friend request but it bounced back to me and didn't work for some reason. I think you and I would get on very well, as you look like a discerning, intelligent woman and I like to think I am a good listener and well read. Your eyes and hair are stunning, I hope you don't mind me saying. I work with Doctors Without Borders as a medic and help people everywhere and in any way I can. I would love to know about your job and your life. Maybe we could correspond every day by email and you could fill me in about yourself and I could share thoughts on my busy life with you too. Perhaps you could give me your email address?

Sure, it's frankie@fuckoffscammer.com

CHAPTER 13

Make An Exhibition Of Yourself

I don't go back on the apps, OKCupid or otherwise. The whole sex to order thing seemed like a good idea, but honestly, I can't face it. I don't think I could ever see sex in that purely, utterly transactional way. I have a deep mistrust of reducing human beings to transactions, probably because that's what my ex is like, not with sex (because he wasn't interested in that anyway), but with people. As much as Michelle meant well, I just know it's not for me. And the dating apps just start to feel horribly transactional, yet a transaction that is the worst value ever: I mean, what other sphere of your life would you enter into a situation where you had no idea whether that person was lying to you, but you have to accept that and go along with it anyway, until you're burnt or they turn out to be okay? The odds of ever finding a nice, honest person on there start to feel like a million to one. And I can't take those odds right now. I'm sick of the game. I go cold turkey. I want to focus on my business and my son and my friends and the upcoming exhibition and not bother with these bloody men right now.

But I'm ashamed to admit that I miss the company of dating apps like mad. I realise they're massively addictive. You can log in anytime, day or night, and have instant gratification, an endless flow of compliments and sweet talk, immediate offers of fun and frolics with a myriad of men. But somehow, despite missing it, I just don't have the heart for it, after Guy's betrayal and seemingly no let-up in my feelings for Stef, which have not abated in any way, shape or form and he's just as tantalising as ever. In short, I'm thoroughly hacked off with my love life and can't even be bothered to think about it right now. The truth is, I have no idea what I want.

One night, with the hotbed of quilters, we're gathering up the finished quilts and about to take them down to the gallery for them to be displayed ahead of the exhibition next week. We lay them out on the table and benches in the shop and admire our handiwork. I'm so proud of us for producing these three beautifully individual and unique quilts. We decide to do a little talk about each one, so we can hear from the quilters themselves how they designed their quilts and why they made those particular choices, all related back to the original theme of homeland.

We start off with Paige and Michelle's quilt. Michelle begins, 'Paige and I opted for a classic rail fence quilt. This involves three different materials, usually in three contrasting shades, from light to dark, laid out in zigzags. We talked a lot about the choice of materials and opted for one from each of us that signified our personal homelands and then a third that represented our shared home of Lincoln. We went for a creamy beige with golden flecks, to represent the colour of the cathedral's stone in the sunshine.'

That's the perfect choice, I think, as that's exactly what

that stunning building looks like on a summer's day. Crème brûlée, as I often think to myself when I see it.

Then Paige goes on, 'And I chose my material from one of my nan's old dresses. She lost a lot of weight when she was ill last year, so she has all these old dresses like tents that are too big for her now. And, like, she says she's thrilled because she was always fat and now she's slim and she loves it. She says, "Nothing looks as good as skinny feels." But I miss my old fat nan, I know that sounds selfish. But I do. And I miss her old dresses, like, they were part of her somehow and her new clothes don't look right to me. Like I said, selfish. But I did ask her could I cut up her old dress that was my favourite, because it had black tulips on it and they're my favourite flower. So yeah, the black and purple bits are mine.'

'And the green sections,' adds Michelle, 'are from the baby blanket I used for my twins. Because I had a boy and a girl, I didn't want to go with the constant blue and pink that these damned shops compartmentalise children into. So I went for neutral colours for them, like white, yellow or green. I liked the fact that when people looked at them in the pram they couldn't guess which was the girl or the boy. It annoyed people. And I enjoyed their annoyance.'

Ha! I love Michelle. She's highly subversive yet does it so quietly!

'I must say,' she goes on, 'I wanted to keep the twins' blanket forever, but then I felt, well, if it goes in a quilt, it will live forever, won't it?'

Yes, it certainly will, we all agree. That's the wonderful thing about quilts. They immortalise their materials. We all give Paige and Michelle a round of applause.

Next is Kelly and Linda's. Kelly explains, 'It's a double

four-patch quilt, with one material from each of us for the large squares, and then we chose four matching colours for the four-patch squares. I chose a blue material to signify my partner's swimming and also the way I feel about handpans, the instrument I play.' Kelly has told us she's going to be playing her handpan on the exhibition's opening night and we can't wait. 'It's a curious sound, like a mini steel drum, but something about its tone always makes me feel it's like underwater music. It's soft and echoey and reminds me of mermaids and darting fish, I've no idea why. So yeah, that's why I chose the blue material with the tiny little silvery fish on them. It sums up me and my man, I suppose.'

That's so lovely, we all agree.

Linda goes on, 'Well, as you know, my father was from India, a village in the Punjab. Every year, he would go back to the shrine at Amritsar and take gifts as offerings, including swathes of fabric. Sometimes, he'd keep some and use them as bedspreads. I chose one of his bedspreads I still own. In a way, it broke my heart to chop it up, but also, I must admit it's been sitting folded up in the airing cupboard for years, as much of it is a bit frayed and see-through these days. But anyway, it's the pale peach colour with the black filigree on it. That's my father's bedspread and he means home to me, even though he died decades ago and I've not spent much time in India. I ought to go back really, shouldn't I?'

'Yes, you should,' comes the answer from the hotbed, and when we see a tear running down Linda's cheek, Kelly leans over and gives her a hug and Linda is saying how silly she's being and we all tell her no, you're not. It's tremendously moving. Another little round of applause.

Now it's the turn of Stef and Gita's quilt, with some help from me, of course. We all turn to the iPad and await Gita's speech, as she sits up straight in her chair and touches her hair, to make sure it's just so.

'As all of you lovely ladies know, my homeland is Slovakia and I'll be returning there at the end of the summer.'

Jeez Louise, I think. That's soon. It's already June. How much longer will Stef be around exactly? The wedding is in September. It's like a goddamn ticking time bomb. I try to block this out and carry on listening.

'My squares for the quilt are all in the traditional Slovakian designs we use for our embroidery, using cross-stitch. There, you can see – hold it up higher, Števo!'

Števo is a new version of his name I've not heard before, so I'm guessing it's the one reserved for scolding her son. Like when my mum used to shout, 'Frances Annabel Brumby, come here!' And I'd always shit myself. Meanwhile, Števo rolls his eyes heavenward and hoists up the quilt, hiding his face, which makes everyone giggle.

'So yes, there you can see the traditional design of two people in folk dress, the man and woman, dancing together. The doves in this other square mean peace, a peaceful life is one we all most desire. Around the borders you see the red cross-stitch design with hearts. These symbolise the victorious power of love, that ends all wars and solves all dilemmas. Love conquers all, as they say.'

Blimey, I wish that were true. All it's brought me is a mudslide of shit. A shitslide, if you will. Call me cynical, but love just leads to problems, doesn't it? Then I think of my love for Jay, which is unbounded and endless, and I realise I'm not such a cynical bitch as I sometimes think I am, and I worry I'm going to tear up, so I blink away tears and get a hold of myself.

Then, Stef appears from behind the quilt. He's wearing a

Ren and Stimpy T-shirt tonight with them standing at a door with a muscly horse holding a fat walrus who's saying, 'Call the police' – OMFG, I used to watch them thirty years ago and they were insane, a dumb cat and his psychopathic chihuahua roommate. And I remember that episode and it was disturbing AF! Stef must have been a kid when they were on telly, as he's ten years younger than me, and they weren't no kids cartoon, or they shouldn't have been. They were hardcore! Another great T-shirt, totally obscure and I love it. He says, 'Your turn, Frankie.'

'Ah, no, no, it's your quilt, Stef. Yours and your mother's. I just helped a bit. Your turn now.'

Stef looks embarrassed AF and like he'd rather have a vasectomy than speak in front of all us ladies about his quilt. But he pulls himself together and I take the quilt from him, so he can point to things.

'Well, Frankie and I had the idea to celebrate Lincolnshire in our squares, but with a Slovakian slant on things, since that's half of me. So we focused on the big blue skies of the county, with its flat lands stretching out to the horizon. It's like that Philip Larkin poem, *Here*, where he talks about "Here is unfenced existence, facing the sun, untalkative, out of reach."'

Wow. Everyone is rapt. He looked like he had no idea what he was going to say, but this sounds like he's planned this speech. Or maybe this is just the way he thinks, in poetry he's read. I can never remember lines from poems, I'm hopeless. Hearing him talk about this poem is beautiful and it really gets to me. I'm holding the quilt but I'm staring at him intensely.

'So yeah, that's the blue squares, and here's Frankie's specific contribution, the cheeky little Lincoln Imp we all recognise, who looks like he's planning all sorts of mischief and won't give a damn about it afterwards, which I think sums Frankie up pretty well, don't you?'

And everyone laughs and I blush madly and tell Stef to shut up, but it's true. I've always been a fan of imps and pixies and brownies (the spindly little thing from A. A. Milne, not the quasi-religious girls' bonding troop) and all manner of elves and gremlins and all those little critters, making trouble and having a bloody good laugh. They're my heroes really. I wish I was more like them, and didn't get the damn feels all the time, especially for this gorgeous man who's standing here smiling at me as everyone watches. *Urgh, pull yourself together, woman.*

'And here,' Stef goes on, 'around the border I've included some traditional blue flowers – well, Frankie sewed those and I helped. And then for my main square I did a multi-coloured cockerel, found in an old Slovakian tablecloth design. He's rather splendid, I think.'

I add, 'So basically, to represent yourself, you chose a picture of a big cock.'

Everyone collapses and I worry that I'll offend Gita, but she's just saying, 'What was that? What did Frankie say?' and I think we're going to fob her off, which feels a bit mean, but Stef says, 'Frankie says I'm a dick.'

And Gita laughs! 'I like the way you tease my son!' she says and wags her finger at me. 'He needs taking down a peg or two from time to time!'

Well, well, good old Gita. If she were here, I'd high-five her (gently obvs).

So, we're done with the presentations and we're all really proud and happy. We pack everything up, as we're going to take the quilts down to meet Kelly's friend at the gallery and hand them over. The others start off down the hill and I've forgotten my phone so I pop back for it, and I'm locking up to find Paige waiting for me, which is nice. I congratulate her on her latest hair colour, which is a glorious concoction of black and yellow, waspish.

'I wanted to ask you, how's the dating going?' she asks.

I groan. 'Don't ask. I'm off all the apps. Sick of 'em.'

'I know what you mean,' she says. 'I've been on and off them for years. They're addictive though!'

'Ohmigod, they are! Nobody talks about this! They are so addictive. I've got withdrawal symptoms! I keep waiting for those beep beep beeps and they're not there. My phone is depressed, I think!'

'Right?! I treat them like sugar, like, you know it's bad and it makes you insulin resistant and all that, but you can't help yearning after it. But also, just like sugar, it gives you a rush, like, a temporary high, but just leaves you feeling hungrier after. It really is so bad for you.'

'Ain't that the truth,' I say.

'Preach,' adds Paige. 'But the thing is, I need them as I'm looking for people of all genders.'

Ah, I didn't realise that about Paige.

'Well, yes, I guess that might well be hard to find on a night out in Lincolnshire, which isn't exactly known for its cosmopolitanism, if that's a word.'

'Yeah, I'm pansexual.'

'Please enlighten me, because I'm old and I'm not a hundred per cent au fait with all of the terminology. So what exactly does being pansexual involve? And sorry for my ignorance.'

'Nah, it's fine. So yeah, it means I'm attracted to people of all genders. So I find it easier to find matches on specialised sites. I use apps like Taimi, Her, Scissr and even Tinder, as there's just so many people on there and it's a lot more inclusive these days than it used to be.'

'Well, that sounds ideal for you. I can see why the apps are properly useful in your case. In my case, they just feel like a cesspool of dodgy males.'

Paige asks, 'Have you thought about dating women or other genders?'

'Not really. I do fancy the way some women look, I mean, women are gorgeous, aren't we? But I can't really imagine doing anything with them.'

'So maybe if you're not sure yet about women, try Tinder and then you can look at men and women.'

'That's good advice, thanks, honey.'

'You're welcome.' She grins and adds, 'Us gals gotta look after each other, right?'

'Fuck yeah, pet,' I say and we link arms as we turn the corner onto Gita's street and there's the gallery at the end of it. Gita says she's going to come to her door afterwards and say hello to everyone. Her hip is healing well and soon she'll be able to come out and join us. It's getting up or down Steep Hill that's not possible for her yet, but she's definitely coming to the exhibition next week. We drop off the quilts and see the others that have arrived from other UK quilters, as well as some from America and they're stunning, they really are. Some have clearly taken months if not years to create, and they're in every conceivable colour and style. I'm in my happy place, surrounded by quilts and friends. Life is good.

The following week the opening night of the exhibition arrives at last. We all bring drinks and snacks, including Michelle's extremely impressive array of hand-crafted pastries, as well as Paige's sparkly cupcakes, a vegan oat roast from Kelly and Linda brings an Indian feast of a dozen or so different dishes, while Gita has brought her very own Slovakian honey cake, which disappears in about five seconds. I don't even get to try some, which I'm right pissed off about! I've been dreaming about that honey cake for weeks. I bring a few bags of crisps and a shitload of wine. Cooking is not my strong point, as you might have surmised. The whole hotbed is delighted to see Gita in the flesh at last, and there is much chatting away and hugs with Gita, who looks thrilled with the whole thing. Paige and Michelle don't bring any partners or friends, yet Linda brings her daughter (sans kids – I mean, we all need a break from the offspring sometimes). And Kelly brings her partner Ben, the Canadian swimming teacher and he's adorable: hugely tall, broad and cuddly with an enormous beard. He looks like he's emerged from the Canadian wilderness, to be honest. He's even wearing a red plaid shirt, which is exactly how I imagine Canadian mountain men, whatever that means. He's quiet yet attentive and talks with everyone in a soft, comforting accent, and when his partner plays music, the way he gazes at her makes me want to cry, it's so touching.

Kelly plays the handpan and it's absolutely exquisite music. As she plays, her face transforms into this alert yet peaceful vision, just as I imagined it would when I first met her, awkward and nervous. But not now. Now, Kelly is a goddess of music, utterly in her element. Paige sings a couple of songs along with Kelly accompanying, and it turns out Paige has a lovely, clear voice, very Lincolnshire accent, very sweet. The talent of these women! With the underwater mood of the handpan and Paige's blue hair (yes, she's dyed it blue again), it feels like a mermaid's siren song. *What a beautiful life I've found,* I think. Who could ever have thought this is where I'd find myself this summer, when this time last year, I was still in my miserable home with Twatface, going through the daily hell of the last throes of a relationship dominated by coercive control. And here I am, under the sea, with my friends. And with Stef, who stands at the side – tonight's T-shirt choice has me reeling because Stef has really outdone himself: it's a picture of the two women from that old TV show about the dressmaking sisters and flapper girls *The House of Elliott* . . . I mean, how obscure is that?! And I loved that show. And how apt for tonight, all about the quilters and sewing and women in the textile industry. I mean, it's perfect, yet again. So I stare at Stef and he is rapt by the music and I'm watching his face drink it in and feel such a deep longing for him, it frustrates me. I don't want to feel like that tonight. I'm in my element, with my craft on display and my friends that my shop brought together. I want to be in control of all that. So, I look away from him and centre myself in the moment. *Remember, Frankie, love should come from want, not need.* I don't need any man. I only need myself. I feel better. Now I can really enjoy myself. I joyously refill my wine glass and inhale a few vol-au-vents. Who the hell makes vol-au-vents these days?! But I'm glad Michelle has, because they're ace, especially the creamy mushroomy ones.

The press are there, or rather a couple of journalists and photographers, from the local newspaper the *Lincolnshire Echo* and after chatting with them, I'm told there will be a feature and picture published soon about me and the group and the shop. Plus there's people from some other local publications and they talk about the possibility of a colour feature in these local glossy lifestyle magazines too, *Lincolnshire*

Life and the *Bailgate Independent*. Lots of photos are taken, of us and the quilts, and it's all looking good for a bit of publicity for the shop and I'm really bloody pleased. Afterwards, I tell the hotbed they're all welcome back at mine for a post-exhibition party and everyone says yes. So we walk Gita home, and I give my keys to Paige and the rest of them go back up to the shop, while Stef sees Gita inside. I'm going to wait for him. Gita asked me to see her home too, as she wants to thank me for the evening and all my help and putting up with her on the iPad and everything, which I of course dismiss and say it's my pleasure. She's beckons me up the step when she's standing at her door and I am treated to a big hug. Stef sees her inside, then he's out and we're off up the hill.

We've both had quite a bit of wine and I say, 'Fuck, I am pissed. The whole of Steep Hill is stretching away from me like a stairway to heaven and I can't make it stand still.'

Stef says, 'Fuck, me too. All those people at the top look . . . really tiny, don't they? It's like that bit in *Father Ted* where Ted's trying to explain to Dougal that cows in a field aren't little, they're just FAR AWAY.'

Then we're laughing like drains. And we start naming our favourite comedy shows and so many are the same and we decide Matt Berry should be given a knighthood or something and then we're onto our favourite cartoons and *Looney Tunes* and then *The House of Elliott* and where the hell did he get that T-shirt and then he reveals that he designs a lot of his own T-shirts because the ones you can buy are all someone else's ideas and they never have the nichey, obscure bits of culture that he likes, so he may as well make his own. And I love this idea and he asks me which TV show I'd get put on a T-shirt if I could choose any and what quote would it be and I say, without hesitation it'd be *The*

Young Ones and the bit where the two rats are chatting by the skirting board about poetry and one of them says, 'Euripides trousers, you mend-a these trousers', then Rik beats them to death with a guitar. And we're howling with laughter at that and Stef is saying, 'Ohmigod I remember that bit!' And we stumble into the shop and the hotbed gives us a little cheer as I trip over the step.

We're all chatting away and Kelly says she's ravenous because she didn't get much to eat while she was providing the musical entertainment and Stef says he could murder some *korbáčiky* and I ask him what on earth is that and he explains it's Slovakian smoked string cheese that's woven together into plaits and it's delicious and I ask him to talk in Slovakian at me and he does and I listen to this beautiful musical language flowing from his gorgeous mouth and I just MELT. But Kelly says, 'Hey, I'm still hungry,' so I say I'll go upstairs and grab some more snacks and Stef says, 'I'll help you.' So off we go up the stairs, and the stairs are difficult and seem too wide, then too narrow, and his hand's on my back to steady me and then we're up the top and going in the flat. And then we're at the fridge and taking out cocktail sausages and those little mozzarella balls that come in a pot with sundried tomatoes and I drop it and it's open and the olive oil goes all over the kitchen floor and I scream and then we laugh and laugh and then we kiss.

Oh fffffffuck. We're kissing and it's wonderful. Christ on a bike . . . His mouth. His mouth feels even better than I imagined it (and I've imagined it A LOT). And my hands slide up his back and it feels so good to touch him, at last, and to feel his hands sliding down to my waist, and pulling at my hips so we bend into each other. Then we're pressed into each other, melting into each other and it's way beyond this space, this little kitchen in this pokey flat and we're floating but so grounded on the earth and it's bloody glorious and then he pulls away.

'Oh God,' he says and takes a step back, wiping his mouth and staring at the sundried tomatoes on the floor.

'Hey . . .' I say. He looks absolutely stricken. 'Hey, it's okay.'

'No, no, it's not okay. Oh God, I'm so sorry.'

'Don't be sorry. I was there too. I was fully involved.' Wow, I've sobered up instantly, as the gravity of what we've done thunks down like a sack of shit.

'This isn't me,' he says and looks at me. 'I'm not this person. I'm not this man.'

'Don't beat yourself up. You haven't killed anyone.'

'But I'm not a dishonourable man. I've pledged myself to Zuzana. What was I *thinking*?'

Okay, have we morphed into *Pride and Prejudice* or *Jane Eyre*, or what?

'You weren't thinking, that's the point. You were . . . feeling.'

And we look at each other and that electric bolt is there again and he steps forward, his boot smushing mozzarella and tomatoes alike and we're kissing again. And OMFG it's even better than the first time and we're moaning with the passion of it and pulling at each other's hair and it's WILD.

'Frankie?' someone is shouting up the stairs to my flat. 'Frankieeeeeeee.' It's Paige and she's pissed as a fart, by the sound of it. 'Where's the fucking snacks?'

We stop kissing and look at each other, our hair all mussed up and blimey, he looks adorable that way. I know now how he'll look after sex, all red-cheeked and hair standing up and blissful.

'I've just thrown a grenade into the middle of my life,' he says and wipes his eyes, like he's trying to rid himself of what he's done.

'Listen, Stef,' I say. 'Listen to me.'

Then Paige's shouting again, 'Frankieeee? Where the fuck are ya?' And I can hear her stomping up the stairs in her DMs.

'Oh for fuck's sake, girl!' I snap.

'I'll go,' he says and grabs the cocktail sausages and a carton of grapes off the side and goes to leave, when he sees his messed-up boots. He stashes the food on the counter, unlaces his boots and steps out onto a bit of the kitchen floor with no food smeared across it. 'It's such a mess . . .' he says and stares at it, but he's not only talking about the floor. Then Paige is banging on my door and he's gone, grabbing the food. I hear him say that Frankie's on her way and he closes the door behind him and they go downstairs.

And this is what my love life is, standing alone in my kitchen with my feet mired in deli snacks. I could stay upstairs and clean it up but I don't. I want to see him. I slip my shoes off and hop out onto an oil-free bit of floor and scoot downstairs. When I get there, Kelly is playing her handpan again, while her bloke Ben, along with Michelle and Linda, are chatting away about something conspiratorial and giggling. Everyone's a bit pissed. Stef is eating grapes and listening to Paige rant on about her job as a hairdresser and how she thinks hairdressers should be categorised as artists just like photographers or fashion designers or whatever and he's nodding and pretending to listen but he keeps glancing up at me. I tilt my head towards the street and he nods and tells Paige he's got to fetch something from his mum's and he'll be right back. I go out of the shop door and shut it and there we are, standing in the street in our socks. It's a good job it's June and not raining.

'We need to talk about this,' I say.

'Yes, yes, of course.'

'Listen, one thing I've learnt in the last few months is that nothing is forever. Nothing is permanent, irreversible, not when it comes to relationships. We can choose our own paths and we can change our minds. It's okay to do that. It's human.'

'Yes, yes, I know, but there are promises made and promises to be kept and that shit matters to me. I know I probably sound like, I dunno, some stupid costume drama . . .'

Well, yeah. Exactly . . .

'But that stuff is important. Oh God, my head.'

He puts his hands to his temples and sways a bit.

'Look, we're both a bit wasted. So, don't panic. Things will seem different in the morning.'

'Yeah, I'll have the mother of all hangovers and I'll want to kill myself.'

'Holy shit, dramatic much?' I say and laugh at him. 'Get a grip, man. You just kissed a girl. That's it.'

Then he looks at me all serious-like and says, 'But that's the thing. It doesn't work like that for me. When I'm in, I'm in. I'm all in.'

'What, you mean . . . you wanna . . . fuck me right here on Steep Hill?'

And he can't help but laugh at that. I mean, the guy needs to lighten up!

'No! Well, yeah. But no. Listen, if I take you upstairs and make love to you now, which is what I want to do more than anything . . . I *will* fall in love with you. I will. That's who I am. But what I fear is that if you make love to me, you won't.'

'I won't what?'

'Fall in love with me.'

'Why wouldn't I?! I've been crazy for you since the moment I met you on this very street, in almost this very spot. Couldn't you tell? Didn't you know that?'

'I don't know, I don't know. I just thought, I was another bloke you fancied. One of many.'

'Oh . . . whoa there. What the fuck are you saying to me?'

Can I be hearing this? This old bullshit again?

'No, I didn't mean—'

'Oh, but I think you did. I think you meant to slut-shame me yet again.'

'Fuck no! I just meant I didn't know if I was just another . . . you know.'

'What, conquest? Is that what you mean? You think I'm racking them up, the notches on my bedpost?'

Jeez Louise, this bloke! What century is he in?! Guy might've been a lying arsehole, but at least he didn't judge my dating history.

'I don't know! That's the point. I don't know you. I want to know you. Christ, I think of little else but you.'

That makes me pause. 'Really?' I say softly.

'Are you kidding? You must know the effect you have on me.'

'Now you make me sound like a femme fatale.'

'Well, you are. To me, you are. I'm hooked, I'm sold, I'm . . . fucked, when it comes to you. I can't see you and not want you.'

And he's saying things I've wanted to hear for so long

but at the same time, it's tainted, with this weird kind of judginess that bothers the hell outta me.

'Look, I feel the same way. But you weren't available. You're . . . not available, are you? So I carried on with my life. You think I should've sworn off dating while you made up your mind and waited at my window like the goddamn Lady of Shalott?!'

'No, of course not. Of course not. I guess I just needed a sign . . . I don't even know what I needed. I don't know what I'm doing.'

'What kind of sign? Morse code? International maritime signal flags?'

He bursts out laughing and looks at me, annoyed but smirking. 'This is serious!' he says, but he's smiling.

'I know but it's all getting a bit heavy, don't you think?'

'But something heavy has happened, don't *you* think?'

'Don't sweat it, honey,' I say and I go to him and put my arms around him. But it's not for a snog, it's for comfort. The guy is so wracked with guilt and shame and all this stuff, he's a wreck. And I feel calm and sober and I feel good. I feel centred. Somehow, I've got to a place in my head where I know I'll be okay, whatever happens next. I've got to that place where I don't need Stef, or Guy, or any guy. I know I'm going to be grand, whatever these guys do. It's really peaceful actually, standing there, holding him. He puts his head on my shoulder and relaxes into me.

'Listen, Stef. You haven't done anything terrible. Nothing permanent. I'm not going to hold you to anything. We don't have to get married, just cos you stuck ya tongue in me mouth.'

He snorts into my shoulder and pulls me closer. We stand there a while and the closeness is wonderful.

Then he stands back a bit and looks at me.

'I made a promise to Zuzana. And my mother. A home, kids. The whole thing.'

'I know,' I say, gently. 'But is that what *you* want?'

He looks into the air, as if the answer is there. He's so cute when he's drunk. So serious and so earnest. I wanna kiss him so bad. But anyway, I'm the soberest one here so I feel a bit protective of him.

'Honestly, I don't know. I thought I did. I thought everything was set.'

'Ah, that's your first mistake. Ever expecting anything to go like you planned. Covid taught me that. You can plan, yeah. But expect? Nah. Expecting is for chumps.'

'I don't even know if I want kids,' he says, miserably.

'Well, they're no picnic. But they're ace too. I mean, they are equal parts horrendous and incredible. It's a fifty-fifty trade-off. Sorry, I'm not helping really, am I?'

'But my mother wants me to have them. And Zuzana can't wait to start trying. She's so excited, already. We talk about it, what we'd call a boy or a girl. How can I take that away from her?'

That's a toughie. I don't know the answer to that. 'Look, I can't comment on that. But one thing I do know is that you can't live your life for others, not wholly.'

'But surely, family is more important than my fleeting wants and needs. Family comes first.'

'Well, to a point, but not all the way there. I did that for years, stayed with my ex for years, to keep the family together. Then I realised that I was disappearing, day after day, another tiny piece of me dissolved, I was . . . eroding . . . over time, like a goddamn coastal shelf. And one day, there would be nothing left. And I owed it to Jay and to myself to get the hell out and put myself first, because I'd never be the mother Jay needed me to be if I had disintegrated away into nothing. That's what you need to do, honey. Ask yourself, *What do I want?*'

He's listened very solemnly to all this. He reaches out and touches a stray lock of hair on my forehead and he tucks it behind my ear, slowly, so slowly. It's a cliché, I know, but of all the ways he's touched me so far, that felt like the most intimate. And it kills me, being so calm with him, when all I really want to do is ask him to kiss me again and take him upstairs and melt into him. I feel so much for him, his dilemma, his goodness, it shines out of him. He's a good man and he hates himself for what he's doing. And that hurts my heart. But it doesn't break it. I still feel strong, I realise, and that feels good to know.

'Why are you being so nice to me? I'm a fucking arsehole.'

'No, you're not. You're a nice guy and you're confused. And you're very, very drunk.'

'Oh God, I don't know. I don't bloody know. Shit, my HEAD.'

We're not going to get anywhere tonight, not with all this wine, and in our socks. I realise the party behind us seems to have gone quiet and I look round and all four quilters plus the Canadian are standing at the window and watching us, holding their wine glasses, like they're at Covent Garden watching the street theatre. They all turn away, pretending they're not looking and I look back at Stef and he's sitting on the kerb now, with his head in his hands, groaning.

'Let's get you home, soldier,' I say and I coax him up. We tramp down the street and I help him find his keys in his pocket and I see him into Gita's house. He turns at the door and looks at me, and he looks pained and sorry and confused.

'It's all right, honey,' I say. 'Go get some rest.'

'I'm sorry . . . for everything. I don't know . . .'

'Go to bed, fella,' I say and he nods and closes the door.

Fuckkkk me, what a mess. I lift up my sock and it's black with street muck. And these are my favourite socks, with the otters on them, that Jay gave me for my birthday because I love otters best (equal with red pandas), and I'll never get this muck out. And then I remember the oil all over my kitchen floor I haven't cleaned up yet. This is what love does to you. It makes a bloody mess of every-bloody-thing.

CHAPTER 14
Back On The Tinder Wagon

I'm back in Bel's shed for a session and it's long overdue. Bel's been away to her mum's a lot as, truth be told, she's not coping very well with motherhood and her mum's been helping her.

'How're you feeling now, now you're back? Are things all right with Craig?'

Bel takes a long toke of the joint, then passes it over.

'Yeah, things are great with Craig. Barney is just so needy and such a bad sleeper that Craig was getting no rest and had to teach all day shattered. And I was crying all the time.'

'I wish you'd told me more. I could've helped.'

'No, babe. You had your own shit going on. And to be honest, I didn't tell anyone. I felt so ashamed, that I wasn't enjoying it. That I couldn't find any joy in it, most of the time. Every time I felt the tiniest bit happy in Barney's company, the knowledge came and bit me in the arse, that later that day or night I'd just be miserable again, because he was crying or not sleeping or whatever. I came to feel like we were enemies, and that made me feel so awful about myself. So I tried to hide it the best I could and there was this massive cognitive dissonance, you know, this ringing in my brain that I wasn't supposed to be feeling that way, but I couldn't stop it.'

'Oh darling,' I say and reach over for a hug. She doesn't instantly dissolve into tears, which is a good sign, that perhaps she's starting to ground herself a bit more. 'Look, this is the hardest bit, I think, when they're babies. Because they're like little aliens. I mean, until the teenage years, but we'll circle back to that! Listen, I've felt like that with Jay, for sure. I told you I remembered hating him sometimes. It passes, though. It passes, I promise you.'

'I know, and it is passing already, especially being at Mum's. She's good, she doesn't just take over. She's always looking for ways for me to bond with Barney. And knowing that Craig is okay at work and he's getting some sleep cheers me up.'

'Is he okay with you being away a lot?'

'He is and he isn't. He misses us. But he accepts that this is what I need right now. I'm not ready to go back off maternity and I'm not ready to be alone with Barney 24/7. So, we're making the best of it and we're okay. Honestly, we're okay. I just feel rotten that I've not been helping you with everything you've got going on.'

'Ohmigod, shut up. As if I'd bother you with my stupid love life when you've got all this important stuff to cope with.'

'It's not stupid and I want to help. And to be honest, it takes my mind of all my own shit, listening to yours!'

'So I'd be doing you a favour, telling you the whole sorry story?!'

'Have at it, babe. Tell me everything.'

So I tell her the whole sorry story of Guy and then Stef and the exhibition night. Bel listens thoughtfully and we pass the joint back and forth and she doesn't interrupt much or comment. Then I tell her that since the night of the Stef kissing incident a couple of weeks ago, we had a talk after that and he told me he had to stop coming to the hotbed of quilters.

'What?! Why?'

'Because he says he can't spend time with me and not want me. And that's not right. He has to sort himself out first and decide what to do.'

'Seems a bit dramatic,' says Bel.

'Well, he is a bit dramatic, but in an adorable kind of way. He's ever so earnest, but he's funny too. He wears the best T-shirts.'

'Well, if he wears the best T-shirts, he must be the best guy ever,' says Bel and rolls her eyes.

'Hey! He's a good guy. And the T-shirts, it sounds dumb, but it's a nerd thing. You know what a nerd I am about cartoons. And movies. My entire wall when I was eleven was covered in movie memorabilia. I'm a nerd and I appreciate another nerd when I find one.'

'Look, I'm not saying he's not spiffy and splendid and all the things you want him to be. But I'm just worried for you, that he's going to break your heart. He just expects you to wait around for him to make up his mind about ditching his fiancée or not?'

'I haven't asked him to ditch his fiancée.'

'Don't you want him to?'

I think about this. It's a good question. It's one I've been considering a lot, these past few weeks. And I've not come to any answers.

'I really don't know.'

'Aren't you in love with him?'

'Probably, but I don't know the guy well enough yet.'

'I knew straight away with Craig. Absolute bolt of lightning.'

'I know, honey, but I'm learning something about myself and that's that I've always made bad choices when it comes to men. I've always gone for charm over substance, so this time, I'm trying to stand back, observe from a distance and let it unfold at its own sweet pace.'

Bel regards me for a moment, then takes the joint from me and grins. 'You've changed,' she says and nods, still smiling away.

'Yeah, I have. I don't know, it's like I've found this kind of inner peace. It's like, I know Stef is a good man. And I have a deep connection to him, that could lead to something incredible. But the circumstances are . . . off. And if I push them one way or another, the whole thing could just shatter. I just have this deep-seated belief that the right thing will happen eventually. I just have to be patient and not analyse it too much. Watched pot never boils and all that. He knows how I feel. I'm not waiting for him, or any man. I'm just getting on with my life.'

Bel nods again, slowly and approvingly. 'You're doing just great, babe. Fucking great.'

'Aren't I?! And so are you, darling. It's been a tough old time, but we're getting through it.'

It's so good to be in the shed with Bel again. We've both missed it. And the hotbed of quilters has missed Stef's attendance these past couple of weeks, me most of all. Whatever I say to Bel about it, the truth is I do ache inside when I think of him. Everything I said to Bel is true, that

I'm not hanging around waiting for him to make up his mind. I'm absolutely getting on with my life. But I'm not made of stone. At my weakest moments, the temptation to run down the hill and bang on Gita's door and throw myself into his arms is overwhelming. But Gita, yeah . . . Gita is a problem. She'd be mortified if she knew what was going on with Stef and me. All her plans rest on Stef marrying Zuzana, and I feel awful about that. Yes, we were drunk and yes, we didn't mean to meet and fall for each other, but this is so much more complicated than just our feelings. This is Gita's future. I mess with that at my peril. And I really care for her. How could I step in and take that life away from her? I can't, I just can't. It has to come from him, or nothing.

The evening after our shed session is Monday and the group night. As I'm waiting for them all to arrive, I'm looking over the week's receipts. The shop got a flurry of orders and new visitors since the newspaper and magazine stories came out, but I'm still sick with worry about money. Also, a nice wooden toy shop next door has closed down due to financial difficulties, which makes me worry even more about my own future and to make matters worse, the shop has changed into a butchers from which the stink of raw meat emanates all the time, which is grim. Sometimes, everything feels like it's moving in the right direction, but now, it feels like my future is creeping along an unknown path and there be a dark wood ahead. Dramatic maybe, but in the witching hour when I can't sleep, it's not just Stef I'm thinking of, but financial ruin. The fear of it grips me, that I might lose the shop and my business and my happy new life I've worked so hard to create. Every time I think of it, it's like a hand around my throat. It terrifies me, truth be told. Then, I hear the bell jingle as the shop door opens and it's Paige, now with pillar-box-red hair, grinning. She says, 'Hey' and I feel better already. My lovely hotbed of quilters is gathering. Thank the stars for them.

Gita is due to come for her very first meeting in person and everyone is looking forward to it but me – except maybe I am a little, because I'm assuming Stef will walk her up the hill to make sure she gets here safely. Will he stay? Doubtful. He made it very clear he wasn't going to be taking part in the group anymore. And I have to respect that. So, the five of us are sewing away on new projects, to make a gift quilt for a friend or family member. And Gita isn't here yet, but I can hear talking and laughing outside the shop and recognise Gita's voice and I look up. And she isn't alone, as I guessed. Beside her stands her son and beside him, stands a woman, long dark hair, big dark eyes. Oh fuck. It's Zuzana, standing there outside my shop, in the flesh.

Stef opens the door and holds it for Gita who shuffles in, looking a bit puffed but absolutely delighted with herself for making it up the hill. The hotbed gives her a round of applause and she nods and motions to Stef and his companion to come in. I can see that Gita is brimming over with pride to introduce Zuzana to everyone, who is even more gorgeous in person than in the photo I saw. Stef looks awkward AF and I'm assuming it was Gita's idea to bring Zuzana, because he looks like he'd rather be playing badminton with murder hornets than standing in my shop right now. Zuzana is smiling away, dressed in casual loveliness in a flowery blouse and a pair of tight black jeans with her long, long legs and her wrinkle-free face – what must she be, thirty-five? Something like that. I could even be her mum, or nearly, if I'd been a child bride. Christ, I want to DIE. She's beautiful.

She's saying hello to everyone in that lovely Slovakian accent and every time I glance around, the hotbed is glancing at me. I'm sure they're gauging my reaction to this horror of social responsibility that I'm having to grin my way through with clenched teeth.

Finally, after what feels like hours of torture yet must actually be about one and a half minutes, Stef says they'd better go as they're late for dinner out, and they bugger off, at long last. Gita is full of it and puts her sewing bag on the table and goes on and on and on about how charming Zuzana is and how good she is for Stef and OMFG I think I'm going to be sick. I focus on helping Paige with some tricky appliqué she wants to do. As I sit down with Paige, she reaches over and gives my hand a squeeze. I look at her and she gives me such a sweet, understanding look, I have to look away to stop the floodgates opening. Goddammit, I thought I was over this. But seeing Zuzana large as life, it's brought it all home and she's too bloody gorgeous to cope with on top of it all and I feel like shit. I mean, I've kissed that woman's fiancé. It was easier to deal with that when she was just a shadowy figure a long way away. But seeing her in the flesh, Zuzana is all too real. I've betrayed her trust and I don't even know her. I've done to her what my husband and Melissa Pridgeon did to me (because, whatever he may say now, I'm damn sure they were screwing long before I left him. The absences, the lies, the spare phone. All tell-tale signs.) And now I've done that to this lovely young woman and I feel like an utter bitch, a traitor to all women. This isn't me. I've never been like this. I hate myself at this moment, truly hate myself.

I get through the rest of the class and I'm nice as pie to Gita, of course I am. She's in her element, having a whale of a time. But then I wonder if she made Zuzana come in on purpose. Could that be true? Could she know about Stef and me, or perhaps have suspected it? Did she arrange this meeting to put me in my place? Maybe she did, I wouldn't blame her. I reckon she's fond of me, but she knows what she wants and it's to go back to her beloved homeland with her son and his healthy young wife of child-bearing age, not a wrinkled old post-menopausal crone (albeit also sex goddess). Gita is lovely, yes, but she's also a clever one. She could well have engineered the whole thing. Well, touché, Gita. You've won. I'm crushed.

The whole thing has to be repeated when Gita is collected by Stef and Zuzana, but it's over much quicker this time. After they've gone, everyone in the hotbed has stayed behind and the first person to break the awkward silence is Linda.

'You okay, love?' she says and everyone looks at me sympathetically.

'Yeah, course. Why wouldn't I be?'

It comes out quite snippy and I'm annoyed with myself. They're being nice. And I'm being obtuse.

Nobody has the nerve to continue the conversation and everyone slopes off with sad little night nights, and I'm crashing around putting things away very loudly. I look up and Kelly has stayed behind. What is this, with the hotbed always hanging around afterwards to give me words of wisdom? Am I some kind of charity case or what?

'Forgotten something?' I say to Kelly with a fake smile. OMG I'm being such a bitch. *Shut up, Frankie.*

'I'm just checking you're all right.'

'Yeah, yeah, I'm just tired. Money worries. You know, the usual drill.'

'Yes, of course. It's just, well, we all know how close you and Stef have gotten.'

'Not really. Just friends,' I say blithely. I really don't want to have this conversation right now, or ever. It's something about the hotbed, that I'm their leader. I want to be the one to look after them, not for them to look after me.

'Okay . . . but it can't have been easy, tonight.'

I don't say a word. I'm intimately interested in this skein of embroidery thread I'm trying to unravel, as if my life depends on it. But Kelly soldiers on.

'And I'm just wondering if the whole sex thing is the problem.'

'What sex thing?' I'm still annoyed but I'm curious now.

'Well, Ben and I don't have sex.'

'What, ever?'

'No.'

Well, well, well. I thought ages ago she seemed a bit funny about mentions of sex. Poor thing. 'Relationships go through these phases, love. It happens. You need to connect with each other again. Maybe go for a weekend away together, somewhere romantic. Sometimes, that's all it takes.'

'Oh, no, not like that. It's what we want. We're both asexual.'

Just like Paige's pansexuality, here's another term I've heard about, but my ignorance is woeful and I admit I am not up on this particular lifestyle either. I make the usual apology and ask her to explain.

'It was very isolating for both of us before we met, because we'd both had negative experiences with people who accused us of leading them on, or just not having met the right person yet who'd convert us, et cetera. As if they understood our sexuality better than we did ourselves. I mean, imagine saying to a lesbian, you just haven't found the right man yet. You'd be homophobic, but that's the same as someone saying to an asexual person, you haven't found the right person to have sex with. It's just the way we are.'

'Okay, so . . . do you cuddle and kiss?'

'Yes, absolutely. We just don't get turned on by it. We enjoy physical intimacy, but not sexually.'

'Actually, that sounds nice!' I say. I think of how one ex-boyfriend of mine, from years back, before Twatface, couldn't do physical intimacy without it being sexual, every single time. Not his fault, I suppose, that he got a stiffy every time we had a hug, but I realised over time I hated it. Sometimes I just wanted a cuddle and nothing more. If I'm honest, most of the time, that's what I wanted from him. I've always liked sex, but it wasn't the be all and end all for me. Cuddling and simple physical affection were just as important, if not more so. But for me, I could never live without sex altogether.

'It suits us,' Kelly goes on. 'Masturbation is very satisfying and then relationships and partnerships with other people are very satisfying too, and the two don't necessarily need to go together.'

Ah, this is interesting. 'So, you do masturbate, if that's not a wildly inappropriate question?' Well, I feel like her mentioning masturbation opened the door to it.

'Yeah, of course. We both do. But generally, not together.'

'So, you have sexual feelings, but not together.'

'That's about the size of it, yeah. It's a new concept to you, I know. It takes a while for people to get their heads around it.'

'Yeah, I'm truly sorry if I'm coming across as stupid about

this stuff but the truth is I am. I was married for twenty years and I am a very late bloomer when it comes to the world of sex.'

She's so nice about it. She just smiles and says, 'No worries. And you're not stupid. You're learning, as we all are. And Frankie, I'm worried for you, for your heart. I know that we probably don't see eye to eye about casual sex, you and I.'

'Oh God, no, let me stop you there,' I interrupt. 'Sorry but I just wanted to update you on that because I'm sick to death of casual sex.'

'Yes, well, I thought that might happen. I don't mean that in a know-all way. I just mean that I think you feel things deeply, Frankie, and I worry about your heart. And I'm just letting you know that asexuality is out there and it's okay. Personally, I think it's something that's part of yourself and you'd already know if you were asexual. But what I am saying is that one way of looking at life is that sex isn't as important as society makes it seem. Sometimes I wonder if all the sex clouds people's judgement and isn't actually what they want anyway.'

'Well, yeah, you may be right about that, love.'

'I mean, maybe being friends with Stef might be the best outcome for you both. If that's not too forward of me to say . . .'

Well, it is a bit forward, but I don't blame her for it. She's coming from a good place. But OMG I couldn't be friends with Stef. How could I be friends with someone I want to mount on my sewing table every damn time he looks at me?

'Maybe, maybe,' I lie and thank Kelly for her honesty and looking out for me. And off she goes.

I go upstairs and fix myself a stir fry with loads of veg

and prawns. I'm trying to eat more healthily these days, give myself some good energy, instead of bingeing on snacks. I've been Googling superfoods like my life depends on it. I even made my own muesli the other day, FFS. I still can't stomach avocado though. It tastes like soap. I settle down on the sofa, glass of red on the table. However healthy my food choices may be, I can't give up the red. Not yet. I'm not a bloody superhero. I think about what Kelly told me and again I'm back to the same old conundrum: what's the answer in the modern world of dating? Navigate the horrors of dating apps or wait around for your true love to show up? Or give up on relationships and even sex altogether? There are no answers at the bottom of my glass of wine, but I have another one, just in case.

The following week, Stef brings Gita to the class again but no Zuzana this time, thank fuck. He still doesn't stay though and I'm sure now that that's that. He's made his choice. I wish he'd told me, actually come to see me and explained it, in some ways, and in others I feel he had no need to, as I didn't say I was waiting for him. And let's face it, being alone with him and hearing him tell me he didn't choose me would be horrible. That's an experience I could do without. But his lack of contact and the appearance of Zuzana said it all. He's over me and he's made his choice. Jeez, it's depressing. I don't feel all peaceful and centred about it anymore, like I bragged about in Bel's shed. Instead I just feel absolutely crushed.

I know red wine isn't the answer, but the night after I see him again, I start drinking. I really ought to give up this poison. It doesn't make anything better. But I need to obliterate all the feels, for tonight anyway. I'll give up wine tomorrow. As I'm starting to slip into that warm buzziness,

I consider what each of the hotbed have said to me about my love life – Linda and her peaceful, quiet love; Michelle, sex with no strings attached; Paige, pansexuality; Kelly, asexuality; Stef, committed serious long-term relationships only. What's right for me? What do I want? I'm so confused, but also I'm lonely. And bored. And horny AF, it's true. I really, really miss sex. I'm stretched out on the sofa, eyeing my phone, lying innocently on the table.

I grab it and download Tinder. Ffffuck, what am I doing? I don't stop to think. I have urges. What's wrong with that? When I'm setting up my profile, I wonder about what Paige suggested and decide, *Nah, I like men.* I wish I didn't, but I do. I like men, and chest hair, and the curve of a man's waist and his long back and . . . I'm just thinking about Stef. I block it out and rush through my profile and then wait for the likes to come flooding in, which they do. I look at a few profiles in my likes list:

> *My ex-girlfriend a very good woman once said to me Steve you are the man of my life and so caring and wrap me in your arms. I feel you in my dreams forever like a Harrison Ford-type and I still sense you deep down in my feet my heart my body I sense you in my teeth*

She could sense him IN HER TEETH??!! Whatever you think about actual internet dating goals, it can't be denied it's tremendously entertaining trawling through looking for nutters I can text to Bel.

> *Why would you bother with a guy like me well let me tell you I am cool and calm and collected as they say and if you dont bother with a guy like me you will not*

know what you are not bothering with and you will take a chance on bothered guys and not me and that will not be bothering to you or me and yes

Can't argue with that searing logic. I'd hazard that these still waters don't run very deep.

I'm royal and man in uniform and caring and rich and looking good sense of humour and much much younger than me

Sounds like Prince Andrew up to his old tricks . . .

Are you the one for me? I live in Goole in my own place and I used to have two kittens but they unfortunately died (separately) in June and July 2010.

Dead kittens aren't the first detail I'd go with on my dating profile, but hey. And note that the cats died SEPARATELY because that's crucial information. It also occurs to me that he dunnit.

I start matching with a few and then the messages begin.

I want to dominate you, make you need and love me so you never will want to go. I will give you tasks, many tasks to do and you will do them and I will task for you also.

I run my own business and I'm a single mum, so please don't give me any more tasks to do. I've got enough tasks going on. However, if you want to clean my house while I go out for a spliff, fair play.

I am good man my mother told me so I was cheated on by ex but never raise my hand as mother was good teacher and raise my right and properly and showed me women break easy and women are soft fruit and must keep in my safe place

Women are soft fruit and must keep in my safe place? Yeah, like your locked cellar.

I am single and like your pictures. Wow hot. I am bored in you.

I'm getting mixed messages here . . .

Urgh, I'm bored already with all these arseholes. It was funny for a while, well, it still is tbf. But it all feels like a colossal waste of time. I feel like a cat who's been chucking a half-dead mouse around for so long, they just get bored of it and don't even eat it. And that's how appealing these losers are to me right now, as tantalising as a dead rodent.

With the vaguely human-seeming ones, I decide to do a straw poll and ask a random bunch of guys of different ages what they think about the conundrum of dating in the modern world. Quite a few immediately unmatch, obviously, since they're not here for a philosophical discussion, they're here to get laid. Some of them say dating apps are weird and a nightmare and the women never talk. They get one-word answers and the conversation is stilted AF. I'm really surprised at this and ask why. One guy says:

Most of the girls on Tinder are only doing it to collect likes. They show their mates how many likes they have and it's a competition. They don't give AF about actually talking to you.

Wow, okay. Sounds like it's not so easy for the guys either. Another tells me:

> *Loads of girls' profiles are scams. They just send you a link to their OnlyFans or whatever. Some dodgy website and ask for money. And when you do get talking to an actual real woman, so many of them are like, I'm a queen, how dare you speak to me. It's fucking annoying. You're not like that though. You're nice.*

Well, you're nice too, I tell him and then he asks me if I'd like to fuck his best mate while he watches. Okayyyyyyyyyy . . ..UNMATCH.

So, it seems that the dating world isn't a bed of roses for men either. I'm swiping through these randos, one after another after another . . . and it's so depressing. What am I even looking for? All my feelings of strength I had in the street on the exhibition night and in Bel's shed have ebbed away. I felt so strong before, so calm and whole. Now I feel so empty, so alone. Why can't my feelings just be fixed, forever? Be strong, forever? But I know that nothing works like that. The river of life and all that jazz. It never rests.

I'm about to delete the whole damn thing when I get a new like and the tiny little thumbnail pic looks like someone I surely recognise. I tap on it. It's Guy. So he's on Tinder as well. And he's a married man. The absolute wanker. Look at him, with his lovely eyes and his cute hair, the bastard. How dare he pop up and like me on Tinder?! I had heard about people doing that zombieing thing where they miraculously send a message out of the blue – as if back from the dead after ignoring you for ages – but I didn't think Guy would ever darken my virtual doorstep again, not after the roasting I gave him. Emboldened by wine, I sit up and click on match. Once you match, you can message, so I'm about to type:

Hey Fuckface. You're a philandering shithead and I hope you get crabs or at least explosive diarrhoea in a traffic jam.

But he beats me to it. A message from him comes through.

Frankie, I'm so glad you matched. I must talk to you. Please.

Fuck off, you utter lying cunt, I reply. I should just unmatch him, but I never got the opportunity to have my say. And he's gonna get it now.

I know I have no right to contact you. But I never got to explain. And there are reasons, there is an explanation, I just need you to hear me. I miss you so bloody much, Frankie. I'm a wreck.

I don't care that you're a wreck JUSTIN BUNCH. And you're not even a Dr or a uni lecturer. You're a lying wanker. And what about Wendy? Your wife, Wendy? Remember her??

I'm leaving Wendy.

Oh yeah, course you are.

I am. I've put a deposit down on a flat to move into. I can show you the paperwork.

It'll just be another scam, cos that's what you are, a lying twatty scammer.

I promise you it's legit. I can get the landlord to call you, whatever proof you need. I'm leaving Wendy and I want to see you again. I can explain everything.

I don't care what your explanation is! Nothing can erase the fact that you lied and lied and LIED. That's unforgiveable, don't you get that, you fucking idiot? Can't you get that through your thick head?

I know the lying was wrong. I know and I can't apologise enough. But I promise you it is complicated and I don't mean that in a mansplainy way, I just mean that it's a long story.

Wendy does have mental health issues, she's got borderline personality disorder. And I know that sounds like bullshit, but if you let me explain I can bring paperwork, I can show you, hospital appointments, the lot.

It's been hell, these past years. I couldn't take it anymore but I couldn't leave her. But I was miserable. We'd not been physically intimate in years. So yeah, I joined dating sites and used a fake name, a fake persona. It was just for sex. Just to meet my physical needs, that's all.

But then I met you. And everything changed. It wasn't about the sex anymore. And I knew I'd have to change my life.

But when you found my wallet, and my identity, I

knew you wouldn't listen. You'd just hate me. So I got defensive and I ran away. I was a fucking idiot.

I should've stayed and tried to explain. I wanted to send you a letter. But I felt I owed it to you to leave you alone, leave you in peace. But I couldn't stop thinking about you.

So, I finally took the plunge and sorted the flat and told Wendy I'm leaving. It's happening, it's really happening.

Please, let me come see you. I can drive over now, I can explain everything. Please. I know I should never have lied, I know it was wrong. But I've been so unhappy for years.

Fuck off and die

I've had enough. I stare at his messages. I screenshot them, to show to Bel. Then I delete him and he disappears forever into the Tinder void of the unmatched. Done. I throw my phone down on the sofa and take another glug of wine. And then I cry. Oh God, not crying over a man again. I promised myself I wouldn't do this! No! I get up and I have a shower. Wash that man right out my hair etc. I put my dancey playlist on – which I've entitled BITCH MOVE – bloody loudly and sing along also stupidly loudly, especially when Dua Lipa comes on with *Don't Start Now*. Yesssss, this is my anthem. *Walk away, you know how, don't start caring about me now* . . . Fuck yeah. Guy and Stef and the lotta them. Walk away, you twats. I come out of the shower and get into my pyjamas and blow-dry my hair. I feel great, clean and comfy.

My phone is sitting there, waiting . . . I pick it up. I go to my Gallery and look at the screenshots. I read them all through. I send them to Bel and say,

Look at this absolute twat of the first order.

Then I read them again. And again. And I pour another glass of wine. And the questions start coming. What if he's telling the truth? What if he's really this guy, who's had this awful life, with a woman he doesn't love anymore? What if poor Wendy really does have BPD and now her husband is leaving her? Do I really want to get mixed up in all that mess? But what if the connection we felt was real, and I let it go, because he made a mistake?

I message Bel again,

What do you think?

And what do I think? I feel completely split, with half my personality going, WTF are you even debating, girl? The man is a lying arsehole. Don't give him a second's further thought. But the other half of my personality is saying it might be legit. And why would he bother, with all this elaborate backstory, just to have another night with me? I mean, I know I'm good in bed, but I'm not the lay of a lifetime, am I? I mean, why would he bother to make all this up with me, when he could get another woman easy online, anytime he liked? I'm always like this, in two minds. Well, I am a damn Gemini after all (not that I believe in any of that bullshit . . . but still). I want to forget him, I want to laugh about it, his pathetic attempt at reconciliation.

More lies, most likely. Or . . . the truth? What if he's telling the truth?

I have another glass of wine. And wish I hadn't, because I feel a bit too buzzy now. I really ought to go to bed. I really ought to drink some green tea or eat something carby or open a window to get some fresh air. I don't know what to do with myself. My head is swimming, not from the wine as much as the confusion, the indecision. This is what love does. It fucks with your head.

Then, someone knocks on my door.

CHAPTER 15

The Three Guy Shuffle

It's late, I mean, not late late, but it's half ten on a Monday night and nobody has any earthly reason to be knocking on my door.

'Who is it?' I shout as I'm standing by the front door.

'It's Gareth. Need to talk.'

WTAF?? What's Twatface doing here??

'I told you months ago, you have no reason to come here, ever. Message or email me or we can talk on the phone if it's one hundred per cent necessary. Otherwise, don't contact me.'

'I'm informing you of something and it's better if it's done face to face.'

This fucking guy, never takes no for an answer. Always knows better.

'No, it isn't. Go away.'

'Melissa has thrown me out.'

Oh well now, this is news. But screw him, it's highly likely it's well deserved.

'Not my problem, buddy!' I shout through the door.

'I'm not asking for a bed, Frankie.'

'Good, because I'd rather have a threesome with *Steptoe and Son* than let you in.'

There's a pause.

'It's about money.'

'Well, I don't have any so you're barking up the wrong tree with me, Gareth. Now can you kindly fuck off please.'

'Well, since you're childishly refusing to speak to my face, I'll have to tell you through a locked door. I'll be instructing my solicitor to sue you for half of the inheritance you received from your great-aunt. I want half, twenty thousand.'

You fucking WHAT??? I unlock the door and fling it open.

There he is and damn, he looks so small again, just like he did in my mum's chair last time, but worse. He looks crumpled and ruffled and all the adjectives you'd never think to use about Gareth on a normal day, the sharp-suited financial adviser. He's let himself go since he pissed away all his own money, it has to be said.

'You must be joking. Tell me you're joking.'

He folds his arms and looks askance. He can't look at me when he says, 'This is not a joking matter, as I'm sure you'd agree.'

'Don't give me that manager talk. Look at me. Look at me!'

He looks up defiantly, chin jutting out.

I continue, 'You know full well that I put all of that money into the business. It was all used up, to buy stock and refit the shop and pay the first quarter's rent and rates. You KNOW that, Gareth. There's nothing left!'

He purses his lips and shakes his head. 'Not my problem.

You unilaterally used that money to start a new business when you could've invested in the family home or assisted me with my financial issues.'

'But I didn't know you had any financial issues because you didn't tell me!'

'And you didn't tell me about the inheritance, until after you'd set up this business, secretly, behind my back.'

'Yeah, because I knew and you knew we were on the rocks. So I had to set up my own future. And it's a good job I did, because as it turned out, your fuckery with the only capital we had lost us everything.'

'Well, my solicitor doesn't see it that way and the courts won't see it like that either.'

The horror of what he's saying dawns on me. It sounds impossible that he'd have any sort of case, not with his own financial mismanagement of our only asset. But Gareth is calculating and Gareth does his research. He's never taken a step in his life that he hasn't thoroughly thought out first. His only and biggest mistake was investing badly, but he isn't alone in that. What if he's right? What if he can take my shop from me?? Because that would be the only way he could get the money, if I gave this up and got another job.

'You can't do this. That's my livelihood gone. I've got no savings. I can't afford to pay you and I'd lose everything.'

'Not my problem. And I'm in a difficult position now I've had a falling out with Melissa. It may blow over, it may not. Women are unreliable.'

'Oh that's rich, coming from you, Mr Bad Investment!'

Gareth's face flinches and then hardens.

'Anyway, I've said my piece and I'm going. I will be staying with my mother.'

I almost pity him when he says that, with a grimace. Mildred, or Granny Smith, as she's known to Jay (in his words – 'looks nice but sour as fuck') is a total nightmare of a nouveau-riche, backhanded-compliment-wielding psychopath in flowery dresses and perfectly ironed slacks.

'Good luck with Granny Smith!' I say and hoot with laughter.

He narrows his eyes and says, 'I was actually doing *you* the courtesy of informing *you* of this face to face, instead of resorting to a cowardly letter direct from my solicitor. *You* would do well to remember that when *you* whine about paying up what *you* owe me.'

My rage is boiling over now. 'What I OWE YOU?? I owe you nothing! You took my life from me! You took my home from me! But even if you could pay me back in any small way for any part of that, I wouldn't take it. I don't want any fucking thing from you.'

Gareth's face twists into a shape I remember when he'd lose his temper at home, all that time ago. It's only a few months, but it feels like a lifetime, a hundred years or more, another life, another person. 'I sacrificed my life for you and James. I had plans, I had dreams.'

'Oh really! What were you gonna do, eh Gareth? Climb Everest? Race Le Mans 24? Please enlighten me as to what adventures you'd have had if you hadn't decided to get married and have a kid, like the vast majority of ordinary people do. And you are ordinary, Gareth. I know your screwed-up narcissistic head thinks you're superior to the rest of the human species, but you're not. You're just a bloke with a boring job like most of humanity. And a bit of a pot belly and coffee-stained teeth, just like the rest of us.'

He takes a step forwards. 'Don't you fucking speak to

me like that.' He's jabbing a finger about an inch from my face. I take a step back and he steps across my threshold.

Then, I hear footsteps on the stairs up to the flat and Gareth whips round.

I hear a voice. 'What the hell's going on here?'

Who the fuck is this now? I peer round the door, and who the hell is it but Guy, large as life, halfway up the stairs. AKA Justin Bunch.

Gareth spits out, 'Back off, pal.' Pal?! Gareth has this blokey voice he puts on when talking to other men, particularly those he considers to be socially beneath him like plumbers and van drivers and he always calls them 'mate'. But 'pal' is a new one on me.

'Frankie?' calls Guy (I still can't think of him as Justin). 'You okay?'

'Yeah, I'm okay. This arsehole is leaving.'

Gareth turns back to me. 'I am leaving but only because I've said all I've come to say.'

'Well, bully for you. But you won't get a penny out of me.' I'm not at all sure that's true, but I'm willing it to be true. It's got to be true, please, please, it's got to be, hasn't it?

I take a step forward so I'm up in his face. Guy's presence has given me a bit of extra courage. At least, I don't think Gareth would hit me with a bloke who's about six inches taller than him standing right behind him blocking his exit. Guy is a lying twat, but he's come in useful at this very particular moment. Gareth never hit me when we were together, but I sometimes thought he'd come close to it, towards the end, and I was desperately relieved I got out of there when I did.

Gareth turns slowly, deliberately and goes to take a step downwards but Guy won't budge.

'Let me pass,' says Gareth, squaring up.

Guy says nothing and folds his arms, staring Gareth down.

OMG, are two men about to have fisticuffs for me? Like *Bridget Jones* but on a rickety stairway in a Lincoln back alley?!

'Just make sure you leave her alone, whoever the fuck you are,' says Guy in a cold, deep voice that I must admit, sounds sexy AF.

'I'm her son's father. And you . . . look like the next in a long line of Tinder fucks I hear Frankie has been indulging in.'

Ooh, someone's been gossiping about me! How delicious!

'Jealous much?!' I shout out from the doorway. 'Go tell Melissa about your thrilling repartee, except oh . . . I forgot. She threw you out, you motherfucking LOSER.'

Guy smiles smugly at Gareth, and steps to one side. Gareth stomps off down the stairs and is at last, thankfully, gone.

Guy turns to me, his face lit up. 'You were magnificent, Frankie! I heard you giving him what for before I came up the stairs. Climb Everest or race Le Mans?! Ha! You're amazing! You don't take any shit from anyone.'

'Including you,' I say and fold my arms. I have to be strong now. But, holy cow, when Guy was standing there blocking Gareth's way, he looked so unbelievably goddamn hot, I could've done him right there on the staircase.

'I know, I know. I had to come. I'm sorry. Can I just explain things, please?'

'You realise you're just as bad as my ex, coming to my place like you have any rights. What is it with you men, you just come and go whenever you please, invading other people's space? No wonder we have so many wars. It's not women who start them.'

'Don't compare me to that wanker! I may have lied to you but I'm not a narcissistic little twat.'

'Yes, you are! That's exactly what you are! You're just a different breed of narcissist. I didn't recognise it at first, because you were so different from Gareth. I thought I knew what a narcissist was, because I'd lived with one for twenty years. But I know now, being a cunt is a very broad church. You fuckers are everywhere!'

Guy says, 'I'll do anything to prove to you I'm legit. I'm not a lying cunt like him. I've left Wendy, now, tonight. I've got an Airbnb to stay in till my flat's ready. I've even applied for a master's in neuroscience, which is what I always wanted to do. I'm gonna be the man I told you I was. I'm not giving up. I'll fight for you, Frankie.'

I've got adrenaline surging through my veins from the Twatface confrontation, red wine surging through my bloodstream from the several glasses I've imbibed and hormones raging in my down-belows for that tall, dark-blond, green-eyed asshole standing in my doorway and those are the only excuses I've got for grabbing that Guy and snogging him so hard we nearly fall down the stairway. And then I climb that man like a tree.

Best sex I've had in a long time, well, at least, since Aaron. I mean, I'm an idiot. And it's the stupidest thing I've done and all because I'm feeling horny and self-destructive. I know all that, as I'm lying there afterwards, panting. And I'm cursing myself for giving into my urges. But I can't regret the sex. It was abso-bloody-lutely great. And he's not even finished. We go in for round two.

And halfway through, we're having the wildest damn time and it's bloody awesome and then KNOCK KNOCK KNOCK. You've got to be kidding me. Did I just hear that?

Or did I imagine it? Guy doesn't seem to hear it and carries on with the business at hand, but I stop and shush him. KNOCK KNOCK. There it is again. It's real.

'That wanker's asking for it now,' says Guy and leaps out of bed, pulling on his pants and making towards the bedroom door.

'Hey,' I snap. 'This is my place, not yours. I don't need you to fight my fights for me. Get the fuck back in bed and let me answer my own damn door.'

Guy holds his hands up and smiles, throwing himself on the bed. I throw on my silky thigh-high dressing gown (the one these days I call my sex gown – I mean, I never wear it unless there's a man around) and stomp to the door. Gareth can get an eyeful of these magnificent thighs before I tell him I'm gonna call the bloody police on him if he doesn't bugger off and leave us alone.

I fling the door open and get ready for battle, but it's not Gareth.

It's Stef.

Tonight's T-shirt has Baby Yoda on eating biscuits and it reads,

THIS IS THE WAY
TO EAT COOKIES

And he gazes at me the way Baby Yoda gazes at cookies. Then he starts babbling.

'Frankie, I know it's late. I'm sorry. And fuck, you look incredible. I'm a bit pissed, but I'm completely compos mentis. And I have to tell you. I had to come here and tell you. You were right. You were right about everything. I've been a fool. Pinning my hopes on a relationship with my mother's choice, I mean, what was I thinking?! Letting my mother direct my love life, just like you said. And meeting you has proved that to me. And changed everything. And I'm in love with you. I'm in love with you, Frankie, and I know I've made you wait and I'm so, so sorry about that, I mean, I really am. But I had to work it out, in my head, in my heart, you know, and all that soppy shite. I mean, I'm a good guy, I don't do shit like this. But you've changed everything and . . .'

'Frankie?' calls Guy from the bedroom.

And Stef is struck dumb.

'Stef,' I begin.

Guy shouts, 'Does that idiot need a bomb up his arse or what?'

'Oh God,' groans Stef and smacks his forehead. 'I'm an idiot.'

'It's not what you think!' I say, despising the fact that it's the worst cliché I could've said.

And then, there he is, Guy, lumbering out from the bedroom in only his pants and coming towards us, and I look back at Stef and he's utterly crestfallen. He's seen a pic of Guy on my phone and he recognises him, I can tell. Disappointed, that's what his face says. He looks at me and he's disappointed, I know it.

Guy sees it's not Gareth and frowns, then laughs. 'It's like King's Cross round here for men, Frankie! Who's this joker?'

'Nobody,' says Stef. He turns to go and he's descending those stairs like Franz Klammer down a mountain.

'Stef!' I call. 'It's not . . . it's nothing!' But he's gone. And Guy's putting his hand around my waist and he's nuzzling my ear and kissing my neck and saying, 'It's so hot you've got all these guys after you. And I'm the one that landed you.'

I push that tosspot away so hard, he nearly slips up on his arse.

'Get the fuck out of my place! Get the fuck out of my life! You've ruined EVERYTHING!!'

I'm raging so hard, I stomp into the kitchen and yell in sheer frustration, 'MOTHER FUCKING FUUUCK!!'

Guy doesn't even wait to get his shoes on. He grabs his clothes and he's out of there. And I'm alone.

Men really are like buses: smelly, unreliable and always make you wait till three of the fuckers show up at once.

I grab my phone and go to message Stef immediately. Then, I think. I totally understand why he ran off. I mean, I would have, in his shoes. But also, I don't feel I have anything to apologise for. I mean, until that moment, he was all set to marry Zuzana and that was that. There was no reason for me to hang around and wait for him any longer. He'd made that very clear. But also, his look of disappointment at my choice to bed down with Guy again . . . well, it's patronising. It's my body and my choice what I do with it.

But to be fair, he would've felt humiliated, I get that. So, I WhatsApp him:

Stef, that was awkward AF for everyone involved. I know I don't have to explain myself to you, but I will say that Guy being here was nothing, less than nothing. Just the result of too much wine and a run-in with my ex that really upset me. That's all.

I see he's seen it with those double-blue ticks. I await the response. But none is forthcoming. I send another one.

I want to talk about what you said at the door. I want to see you and really discuss it. Please don't hold this against me. I had no reason to believe you'd come to this conclusion, as you'd made it very clear that you'd chosen your path. I was just getting on with my life.

I wait. Again, the blue ticks. Again, nothing.

Well, sod him, then. I make up the bed, trying to erase all trace of the idiot who was in it minutes before. If I'd told that lying asshole to leave, as I should've done, it would've been me and Stef in this bed right now and he'd still be here, and we'd be in the throes of passion, no doubt. The consummation of months of yearning. Instead, I'm lying in used, messed-up sheets with sore down-belows and no man at all. I can cope with all that, but the contrast with what could've been haunts me and I'm so mad at myself, and mad at Gareth, and mad at Guy and even mad at Stef. Why wait to make some grand gesture at a moment convenient to him? In that way, he's just another man turning up when it suits him, not me, with no thought that it might be the wrong time for me or that I might indeed have company. The presumption! Fuck this and fuck men – again! And fuck you, Mars!

I look at my phone and think. Okay, we need a plan. I message Stef:

Come to the shop tomorrow at lunchtime and we can talk.

Then I turn my phone off and put it on charge. It's a bold move, because of course I want to see if he replies. But if I leave it on, I'll lie awake all night listening out for it, like a fool. So, off it is. I feel dirty after the shenanigans of the evening and decide to have another shower, to wash it all away. Then I climb into bed and eye the switched-off phone lying innocently beside me. I usually put on an audiobook or podcast to fall asleep to, but I do without it. I must not turn that phone on. If he has replied, it'll do him good to make him wait . . .

I suffer a restless night. In the morning, I jump on my phone and wait an agonising minute until the damn thing decides to load itself up. Straight to WhatsApp and . . . no messages. He's seen all of mine. But no reply. Is he punishing me? He'd better come to the shop today. I remember what Bel said, to not chase these guys. Too true. I've made my feelings clear and suggested a path forwards. There's nothing else I need to say or do right now.

I open the shop up and the first part of the morning is quiet, which is terrible, because then, the events of last night are swirling around my head like a snowstorm. The threats from Gareth, the wild sex with Guy, the sight of Stef retreating down the stairway. I email my divorce solicitor and hope she doesn't charge me another fee just for reading a goddamn email, though she probably will. I hate lawyers for that. Soon, I have a steady stream of customers, thankfully, which keeps me occupied. I'm being asked about putting on another sewing group on a different night and I'm considering it. At first, I wanted to start with one and see how it went. I did wonder if I ought to put on other groups, but I've been enjoying having my evenings free for liaisons or seeing Bel or otherwise resting. But yeah, I ought to start thinking about another group. Meanwhile, lunchtime comes and goes and no Stef. Yet exactly one minute after I shut up shop for the evening, there's a knock on the shop door and there he is.

Blimey, he looks great. In the fog of last night's insanity, I didn't really take him in, but now there he is in all his gorgeousness and I realise these good-looking men are my absolute weakness. And they probably know it. Well, Guy definitely does. Yes, I chose to have sex last night and it was absolutely my choice and my right to do so. But there's always a part of me that feels that the man wins if you give it up, especially if it's a lying twat like Guy. He out-dated me . . . AGAIN. *Mental note: however horny you are, Frankie, however much wine you've knocked back, NEVER give it up for Fuckface again.*

Now, this man is different. He's not a liar, as far as I can tell . . . well, not to me anyway. He's being moody about this and he can be very judgemental, but I still believe he's a good man underneath all that. We need to sort this out, but one thing I know I won't be doing is apologising. I have absolutely nothing to apologise for. I let him in and smile at him, but he's not smiling. This annoys me instantly.

'Lighten up, Stef,' I say as I close the door behind him. 'Nobody died.'

He shoves his hands in his jeans pockets and doesn't laugh. He's not even wearing a comedy T-shirt tonight, as if he knows I love them and wants to remain neutral. Instead, he has an ironed white shirt on which hugs him in all the right places and I really want to feel that cool cotton and his warm body beneath it under my fingers. But I need to concentrate. No more falling into the arms of pushy men. *Get a hold of yourself, woman.* I go to sit on one of my stools and make myself comfortable. Stef, on the other hand, stays stock still where he is. Why do I feel like I'm about to be told off?

'I'm sorry I turned up unannounced last night.'

Okay . . . that's actually a good opening. I'm pleased he apologised.

'Thanks for that,' I reply. 'I'm very glad you did, in some ways. And in other ways, yeah, the timing was definitely off.'

But he won't smile and that bugs me. I've had enough of this already. I get up and walk over to him and I yank one of his hands out of his pocket and I lift it to my lips and kiss it. I want him to raise it to my head, run his fingers through my hair and draw me in for a kiss. But he just awkwardly lets it drop and shoves it back in his pocket.

'Stef, it's me. Stop acting like you're making a complaint at the bank.'

'I'm just . . . confused.'

'Okay. Explain it to me.'

'I know I was in the wrong, making you wait.'

I have an urge to say, *I wasn't waiting around for you,* but I resist it. It's okay to let the man speak. I can make that point later, if needs be.

He goes on, 'And I know it was wrong to be knocking on your door near midnight. But . . . I don't know. It wasn't that you were with another man. You have every right to be.'

Again, I stop myself from saying THANK YOU FOR YOUR PERMISSION sarcastically. I'm the master of restraint right now!

'But . . . *him*? Guy? That liar? That useless piece of shit? Why him? Why would you take him back? How *could* you?'

I feel my hackles rising (whatever my hackles are). I know Guy is a piece of shit and I don't need this man telling me that. Okay, my restraint meter has hit FULL. Time for shit to get real.

'Who I go to bed with as a single woman is my business. And I was a single woman, last night. And I still am this morning. And I do not have to explain myself to you or anyone.'

'I know that and that's why I didn't want to come today. I didn't want to have this argument. Because I don't want to say what I'm feeling about you now. Because it's only going to make you mad.'

'Well, if it's going to make me mad at you, surely that's a sign that you might actually, you know, by some stretch of the imagination, be in the WRONG?'

How he feels about me has remained unsaid but, of course, it's hanging in the air between us like a bad smell. And I have to clear it.

'But, do tell,' I begin, my tone morphing into sarcasm, 'pray, do tell, kind sir. How you feel about me right now. I can't wait to hear.'

'I'm . . . disappointed in you,' he says miserably. He knows it's a shitty thing to say and yet he can't not be honest.

'Oh, woe is me!' I cry and slap the back of my hand on my forehead in a theatrical gesture. 'The mighty Stefan is disappointed in me. What am I to do?'

'Oh, fuck off, Frankie.' He's still not smiling. I've had enough of this.

'No, fuck YOU, Stef. How dare you come in my shop and pass judgement on me. And while we're at it, I'm disappointed in YOU. You haven't learnt a thing these last months. You've lied, you've cheated, you've done questionable things. And have I judged you harshly, even once? No, because you're human. And so am I. And relationships are messy. Life is messy. Get used to it! Get off your high horse.'

He looks suitably shamed. 'I know, I know. You're right. But I can't help the way I feel.'

'Yes, you can. You can give yourself a slap around your judgy twat face and give yourself a lecture on how not to be a misogynist.'

'Misogynist?! Now, that's something I've never had hurled at me. How dare *you*, while we're at it.'

'No, you need to hear this. Judging a woman by higher standards than you yourself are prepared to reach is sexist. You've cheated on your fiancée. I had some rebound sex with a dodgy ex. Who's most in the wrong here, huh? Tell me that.'

'All right, okay, I'm a piece of shit for cheating on Zuzana. Is that what you want to hear?'

'No, I want you to admit you're no better than me. I want you to climb down from that pedestal you've put yourself on and admit you're like me, that you have weaknesses, just like me, just like all of us. You're no worse and you're a hell of a lot better than most men I've known, than most people I've known. You're a good man and you've behaved badly and I did too, by kissing you back, a man with a fiancée. Accept it. We did a wrong thing. But I don't judge you for that. And I won't have you judging me. I'm sorry your little romantic gesture last night didn't go to plan. But don't blame me. You need to get your own house in order before you start criticising other people's. What have you done about Zuzana, anyway? What are you going to do about her?'

'She deserves so much better than me,' he says wretchedly. 'Better than me, than us, than what we've done. She's entirely blameless in all of this.' He's right that he's wronged her. But this still annoys me.

'Look, I don't know Zuzana at all. I've got nothing to base this on. But I also know that she's human too. And maybe this arrangement with her and you and your mother isn't the wisest start to married life. That's not her fault, or yours, or Gita's alone, but it's an unholy mess if you're not one hundred per cent on board. And you're not. Yeah, no good person deserves to be cheated on. And when we kissed, we knew it was wrong. But last night, Stef, you told me you were in love with me. And that changes everything.'

'I can't do this,' he says and he looks around at the door, like he's about to bolt.

'Can't do what?'

'The guilt. It's killing me. I have to sort it out with Zuzana.'

'Yes, you do. You have to tell her about me.'

He looks stricken. 'I can't . . . I can't do that.'

What? 'Erm . . . yes, yes, you can and you must.'

'Are you in love with me?' he asks, his eyes wild.

'Yes.' It's good to say it aloud, finally. But the whole truth is, I don't even know what that means anymore. 'I am in love with you. But these past months everything I thought I knew about love has exploded into tiny pieces and I'm still piecing the jigsaw together. I can't tell the difference between love and lust and charm and manipulation and need and want. I'm just as confused as you are. But something deep down in the pit of my stomach tells me that there is something good here, between us. Something worth pursuing, worth cherishing. But that can only happen if you're free, truly free. And you're not right now, not until you tell your fiancée about us and make a decision. You can't possibly embark on a new relationship until you're absolutely sure that your current one is done, and gone and dead in the water. That's the way it has to be. You can't hedge your bets about these things. You have to man up and make a decision. Are you ready to do that, Stef, for yourself? Not for me, not for us, but for *you*?'

He pauses, he opens his mouth to speak, he raises his hand and wipes his mouth. 'I . . . I . . .' he begins, then falters. Answer me, man!

Then someone is knocking on the shop door. It's a man in jeans and a suit jacket and tie. I've always hated that combo. Smart-casual.

'We're closed,' I call out.

'I'm from the BBC?' he replies loudly through the glass.

What?! Okay, terrible timing. But I can't leave the BBC there waiting forever while I sort out my love life. I go to the door and let him in.

We do the hellos and the guy introduces himself as Mark Richardson, a producer from BBC *Look North*, the local news show on at six-thirty every night. Stef is standing there awkward AF and this guy senses it but soldiers on.

'Sorry to pop by your place without warning, Ms Brumby,' says Mark Richardson.

'I'm used to it,' I say, deadpan. Stef shakes his head. Richardson looks momentarily confused and goes on.

'We've seen the coverage of your shop in the gallery exhibition story. I was passing and about to email you, Ms Brumby, when I thought I may as well pop by. Are you Stefan Walker? I think I recognise you from your picture in the paper.'

'Yes?' says Stefan, looking confused.

'We were hoping to interview Ms Brumby, yourself and your mother, Margita Walker? We'd like to feature the shop, the sewing group you run here, as we thought it'd be a great story about the Slovakian angle, showing a positive spin on the Eastern European immigration issue in Lincolnshire. We're always looking for local interest stories that show the county in a great light, and this story has that in spades.'

'Sounds interesting,' I say, thinking of the great publicity for the shop. Stef looks intensely uncomfortable.

'Ah good, well, here's my card. I'll email you formally tomorrow and we can discuss. If agreed, we'd like to come in next week and film one of your sewing group nights and interview the three of you and some of the . . . sewing . . . well, what do we call a group of people sewing and making quilts anyway?'

'A hotbed of quilters,' says Stef, surprising me. So, he can answer this guy, but he can't answer me about whether he's gonna tell Zuzana the truth.

'Ah, that's a great name!' says Richardson, but then Stef is scowling again and Richardson looks uncomfortable now. I need to pull myself together and attend to this.

'Thanks for your interest in the shop, Mr Richardson. I'd be thrilled to welcome you and the crew. I'll need to ask the other quilters' permission, of course, so I'll contact them all this week and get back to you.'

Then it's all thank you thank you and nice to meet you and he's gone.

'That's good news for you, for the shop,' says Stef, as I close the door behind Richardson.

'Yeah, it is. I don't want to put any pressure on the quilters though. If they don't want to do it, that's fine. What about you? He seemed to want you and your mother to be a key part of the story. Will . . . you be here for it?'

'I'm not sure . . .' says Stef and looks despondent again.

I sigh and say, 'I'm kind of sick of this, Stef. I feel like we're going round in circles.'

'I know and I'm sorry. I need . . . to go to Slovakia. I need to go there and talk to Zuzana face to face.'

'Good, good. That's the right thing to do. You need to tell her in person.'

'I don't know what I'm going to tell her yet.'

'What does that mean?'

'It means, Frankie, that I'm utterly confused. I can't just wipe away the image of that bastard in your place last night. I can't reconcile that with how I feel for you. How you could go back to him . . .'

'Oh, for fuck's sake, *this* again?!'

'Yeah, this again!' He's raising his voice now. Usually, in the past with Twatface, this used to scare me. But with Stef, I cannot lie, it turns me on. I hate and love arguing with him in equal parts. 'I can't get my head round it. Around you. You're . . . incredible, Frankie. I've never met a woman like you. You're a force of nature. But it frightens me, how I feel. It frightens me, the freedom that you embrace. And I don't know you well enough yet to know if that freedom includes me, includes our future. What if I trade everything I've built up with Zuzana, my mother, my new life in Slovakia, everything that was sure and set and decided . . . how can I throw that away for the chance that you're done with your days of freedom, done with your nights of casual fun, and you're ready to commit to me, after twenty years of a bad relationship? How do I know that . . . I'm not just another guy on your list? How do I know you'll commit to *me*?'

My God, I feel like my head's going to explode. The strata of judgement laid down in that speech are deep and solid as rock.

'You DON'T, Stef!' I yell at him. 'Nobody knows anything!

But that's life! And that's being human. I'm not perfect, you're not perfect. We make mistakes, we fuck up. But how we feel for each other, that's not a mistake. It's right and it's real. I don't know what that means or what we do about it. But I'm not going to promise a thing.'

'Well, that's what I need you to do. I need you to promise that . . . that it'll be worth it, that we'll have a life together, you and I, if I give up Zuzana for you. That you'll change your ways . . . for me.'

'My *ways*? No. No, screw you. I'm not promising any man anything. I've fought for years to get away from Twatface and make my own life. I don't need you, I don't need any man. And I don't expect any man to give up his life for me. And before you ask, I'm not a player. If I'm in a relationship, I'm a one-man woman. I don't play around. You need to know that. But that doesn't mean I promise to give my life to you. I will never do that again, I will never say that to a man again. But I am willing to be in love with a man, to truly love a man, to let the separate circles of our lives overlap and intertwine, in whatever ways we feel are right, as the future rolls out. But I can't promise anything, I can't tell the future, I'm not Mystic Meg! And if that's not good enough for you, then maybe you ought to go to Slovakia and make a life there. Because I'm not going to be told how I can act by any man. Not now, not ever.'

'There's my answer,' Stef says simply and with that, he walks out of my shop and shuts the door behind him.

CHAPTER 16

Frankie, Get Your Man

The following week on the first Monday in July, the telly comes to see the hotbed of quilters. They'd all agreed to take part during the week and were dead excited about it, especially Gita, who is over the moon about the Slovakian angle being so central to the report. I'm guessing that Stef had to play along with this and appear to be enthusiastic too, as there's no way he'd tell her why it's going to be awkward as hell. I've not heard from him since our stand-up row in the shop, not a word. I've not contacted him either. I'm sick of explaining myself. I've deleted Tinder too. I don't want to hear from any of these assholes. Someone I have heard from, though, is Guy AKA Justin Bunch AKA Fuckface. I received an email from him, via my website, as the idiot is blocked on everything on my phone. These bastards always find a way to seek you out online. He writes that he is dumping me, citing the fact that he is not happy with the amount of men I'm seeing and that he can't leave his wife for someone who isn't committed to him. OMFG, the almighty NERVE! I speedily reply,

As if I'd ever ask you to leave your wife for me, you utterly delusional lying cunt. Go screw yourself sideways with a broken hockey stick.

Then I block him from my website. Good riddance, Fuckface.

So, it's Monday evening and the whole group are here and then some. Since it's a bit of a special occasion, Bel is here too for a laugh (and to get out of the damn house for once) and my darling boy Jay is back from uni. He dropped in on his dad at Granny Smith's before getting an Uber today over to mine to make sure he's on time for my 'fifteen minutes of Warhol-style fame', as he terms it, the clever dick. Jay and Bel are busy being terribly social – they love all that, handing out snacks and drinks and scarfing as much as they can as they do so, having a giggle and sniggering together about secret jokes. Honestly, those two are like The Bash Street Kids when they get together. Gita is here, of course, and so is Stef. It's the first time I've seen him since the argument and he won't look at me, FFS. Well, he can get on with it. I'm busy.

A chap with a camera and a female reporter from *Look North* are here and they're interviewing people and it's all going swimmingly. We show them the quilts we're working on for friends and family, we talk about what the group means to us. Linda is saying how good it is to share a common interest with others, how when we find a new fabric we love or finish a square and bring it in, how excited everyone else in the group is by these little details of our hobby, which other friends and family members find dull as ditchwater. Paige says that we're all sewing nerds and nobody else she knows really gets that, apart from her nan. It's that nerd thing again, that I was talking about with Bel. Nerd bonding at its best. Kelly tells them that we're all very supportive of each other's successes, as well as our failures, Michelle adding that when we mess up, we laugh about it, not laughing *at* each other but *with* each other and that every time we mess up, we're learning something new. It's all about progress, not perfection. I love that. Gosh, I'm proud of my hotbed of quilters tonight. I also explain how much of a community there is here amongst the businesses on Steep Hill and Bailgate, how much there is for visitors to enjoy in this small but vibrant cathedral quarter, that it's more like a cosy village than a city. Then, they want to interview Gita, Stef and me about the Slovakian angle and the joint quilt that we made reflecting the Lincolnshire and Slovakian heritages. It's awkward AF standing there with him and his beaming mother, pretending everything is hunky-dory, when it isn't. We get through it in one piece though, and while the reporter is doing some extra bits with Stef and Gita specifically about Slovakian sewing, I have a chat with Jay. He's telling me something about his dad.

'Yeah, I need to talk to you about something, Mam, something about the old man.'

'What's up? You okay?'

'Yeah, yeah, I'm fine. It's you I'm worried about.'

'Why, honey? I'm all right.'

'Well, there's two things. First bit of gossip is, he's gonna be moving back in with Melissa tomorrow.'

'Oh right, well, good.' *That's a turn-up*, I'm thinking. Maybe if he's back with her, he won't be so gung-ho about suing me for my inheritance.

'Yeah, fuck knows why she puts up with him. Anyway, when we were at Granny Smith's this morning, I found out that Dad is suing you for your great-aunt's money.'

'How did you find out?' I wasn't going to tell Jay about

this. I didn't want him worrying about my financial future. That's my job to sort out and not put all that on him. I already worry that I put too much emotional stuff on him, from time to time.

'I overheard him on a call from his solicitor, he was arguing with the solicitor and saying he wanted to proceed with it, so I asked him about it after and he explained it, tried to make out you should've told him about the money at the time, as he could've paid off parts of his debt with it. And he said by right it's half his.'

'Ah, love. I'm sorry you had to find out that way.'

'Why didn't you tell me? I could've helped.'

It's at times like these that I look at my six-foot son and can't believe he's the same one who used to pour Ready Brek on his head.

'I didn't want to worry you, honey.'

'But I need to know shit like this. I need to know what nefarious doings my dad is up to. So I can help. He shouldn't be pulling shit like this. It's bullshit. And I told him that.'

'Wow, did you?' Oh, my boy.

'Fuck yeah, I said he was being a dick and that it was his fault he built up all his debts and ruined your livelihoods and all that, and that you had every right to use your own family's money to set up a new business for yourself. He said I was a kid and had no say and I told him he was an arsehole and if he pursued this I'd stop seeing him forever and he said that it was a financial decision that I don't understand and if I reacted in a "childish manner" and refused to see him then that's a chance he'd have to take but I would always be welcome in his new home with Melissa. So I told him I'd rather watch porn with Granny Smith than stay with them.'

I guffaw so loudly at this, the *Look North* camera crew

look round at me in annoyance, and have to record that sequence again. I apologise then throw my arms around Jay and hug him close, saying, 'You absolute star of a boy,' overwhelmed that my son supports me in this way. I've never wanted to be that kind of parent who drives a wedge between the child and the other parent. I'd hate that. I've always answered Jay's questions honestly, like if he asks me how his father behaved on a certain occasion, I've told him my side of it, but always explained that this is only my point of view, and he should ask his dad too and get the full picture. I've always tried to be fair and I've always encouraged their relationship to continue in as healthy a way as possible. But time and time again, Gareth does shitty things like this and there's no way I can put a positive spin on it, and why the hell should I, when he's behaving so badly? I'm glad that Jay's old enough to make his own decisions about his dad and also that we can talk with full honesty about Gareth, knowing that Jay knows full well I'd never try the cheap trick of turning him against his father. And knowing too that Gareth does a very fine job of that himself, at just about every turn, this money business being the latest example. As Bel said to me once about Gareth, 'I bet he thinks he's a great father. But no father can be great when he treats his child's mother like a piece of shit.' Wise words indeed. I hold on to my child – my six-foot son who's the smartest person I know – and despite the icy fear that grips me every time I think about this money, Jay's defence of me to his dad makes me feel so much better.

After this, Jay tells me he's been chatting with all the gang and he thinks they're ace.

'I've had a good old natter with Stef too and I like him, Mam. I think he's a dude.'

'Oh yeah?'

'Yeah, I mean, look at his T-shirt.'

Tonight's design is from *The IT Crowd*, with a picture of Moss saying, 'Let me put on my slightly larger glasses.'

I love that bit from *The IT Crowd*. It's so niche! 'He sure wears a mean T-shirt,' I say.

'Yeah and we had a really good chat about AI and if it's gonna get rid of artists and writers and all that. He's a designer and we were talking about how AI could help or totally fuck up his job in the future.'

'And will it?'

'I don't think so, no. I'm pretty optimistic about it. I think it'll just enhance stuff, not replace it. Human brains will always want to reach out to other human brains. People will still be more interested in other people than machines, or at least, just as much.'

'Yeah, I guess if you think about it, we've had the ways to mass-produce textiles for ages now, yet here we all are sewing and quilting and dressmaking and all that. One doesn't cancel the other out.'

'That's exactly what Stef said! He's clever, like you.'

'Ohmigod, I'm not clever, honey.'

'Of course you are, Mam. Don't do that putting-yourself-down bullshit. We've talked about that, cos that shit's from the past. Anyway, Stef seems a good guy, a clever guy. I like his vibe. Are you . . . and him . . .?'

'Uh, I don't know, honey. It's . . . complicated.'

'God, Mam, that's such a cliché. What are you, Facebook circa 2007?'

'It really is though, love. He's engaged to someone. But . . . we feel a lot for each other. I'll tell you all about it later.'

'Well, he's got my vote. And he's mad about you, everyone says so.'

'Everyone?'

'Yeah, I've been polling views from all the seamstresses. They all think you two belong together.'

'Ohmigod, you didn't ask the old lady over there, did you?! That's his mum and she doesn't know anything about us. She's expecting to move with him to Slovakia with his new wife and start a new life!'

'Don't panic, Mam,' says Jay. 'The blue-haired goddess over there told me all about it. I didn't mess up with the little old lady.'

He glances round at Paige – blue-haired again in an even brighter shade of electric blue with dark blue streaks – and they smile at each other. That's an interesting development . . .

Then, the TV crew say they've got everything they need, and off they go, yet as the wine is flowing and the snacks are still plentiful, everyone hangs around having a good laugh. Gita is chatting away with the other ladies, and Stef looks over at me, then makes his way to where I'm standing. Watching him come over is a pleasure. He's looking snackish as hell tonight.

'Hey,' I say and Stef says, 'Hey' and smiles at me ruefully. Well, a smile is an improvement on last time.

'Thanks for doing this,' I say. 'Much appreciated.'

'I was happy to,' he says. 'I hope it brings you plenty of new business. You deserve it, Frankie.'

He sounds all sad and nostalgic, like he's . . . I don't know. But it sounds odd.

'What's going on, then? With you?'

'I'm going,' he says. 'To Slovakia. Tonight.'

'Tonight?' Blimey, that was quick.

'Yeah. I'm flying from Leeds Bradford. Heading off there after this. And . . . erm . . .' He glances about him at all the people in the shop, within listening distance. 'Can we . . .?' And he gestures towards the back of the shop, where there's a little bit around the corner behind the till, with a mini-kitchenette comprising a tiny worktop with a kettle on and a sink. It can't be seen from the shop floor and it'll afford us a tad of privacy.

'Sure,' I say and we go over there.

'I'm going to Slovakia alone, not with my mother. I need to spend a few weeks with Zuzana. The wedding is planned for September. I'm under tremendous pressure.'

'I know . . .' I say. I want to kiss him, very, very much indeed. I've been yearning for his body all week and then trying not to, because I don't want to be beholden to this man, or any man. But I am cock-struck, to use Linda's great phrase. I am and I can't help it. But it's more than that. I meant it when I told him I was in love with him, whatever that means. But somehow, we just keep fucking it all up and I don't know why.

'I don't know what to say to you, Frankie.' He looks guilty.

'Hey,' I say, gently. 'You don't have to say anything to me. You only have to do what you think is right for you. If you're free, then we can talk. But until that day comes, or even if it never comes, then we will just be friends. And I'll always wish you well.'

'God, you're so nice.'

'I am and I'm not.' I smile. 'I don't take any shit these days. I lived with a man who scared me for far too long and I got whittled down to nothing. Dissolved into barely a person anymore. And once I got myself out, I knew I'd never put up with shit again. I've been building myself back up into a person again and I know who I am now, or at least, I'm finding out.'

He proper gazes at me then. The draw towards his lips is so irresistible, I have to look away.

'You've been through so much, Frankie. And you're an incredible woman. And . . . Zuzana . . . she is a good person. I wish I could . . .'

'What? Have us both?' I say and smile cheekily. I don't want it to get all heavy again.

'No, I wish I could've turned up an hour earlier or a day earlier, before you made that decision to go back with . . . that wanker.'

Seriously?! I sigh, exasperated. 'I'm not going over all that again, Stef. You've got to get past it or we're doomed. I did nothing wrong!'

I know my voice was raised higher than discretion, but part of me doesn't care. We both look round but the hubbub from the shop hasn't abated. I'm getting so mad with this guy though now, I feel like pushing him aside and going back to my real friends and family, the ones who don't judge me.

'Well, I can't get past it. I wish I could. But I can't. But what haunts me is, maybe you are a mistake and mean nothing in my life, just as clearly I meant nothing to you or you wouldn't have jumped into bed with that married man. Maybe this is what you do, mess about with guys who are taken. Maybe that's your thing. And I can't give up my life for that.'

I know this man is gorgeous, funny, clever, great to hang out with and there's a real connection between us. But at that moment, in my own shop on the night of my triumph getting on the local news, my loved ones around me, my patience finally runs out. I'm done explaining myself, I'm done.

'Well, screw you then. I'm done with you!'

'I think you're wilfully misunderstanding me.'

'Oh, really?'

'Yes, I'm asking you to commit to me. What's wrong with that?'

'Because I'm not going to submit to any man.'

'Commit is not the same as submit! They're actual different words, you fucking idiot.'

'Did you just call me a fucking idiot? In my own shop?!'

'Yes, I fucking did, because you're behaving like a fucking idiot. You're so proud you can't see straight.'

'Don't gaslight me! You're just hedging your bets, in case things don't work out with Zuzana. And you're still harping on about Guy. Are you trying to control me or what?'

'I'm about as interested in control as a fish is a bicycle.'

'Well, stop bloody acting like it then. You can't control me. You never will.'

'Sod this, then. You know, I came here tonight to make it up with you, to apologise for being judgemental, and if it went well, and you did the same, then I was going to stay here and not go to Slovakia tonight. I was going to stay here with you. If you apologised.'

'Me, apologise? What the fuck for?!'

'For not waiting for me. For wasting yourself on that loser. For not committing to me when I've told you I'm in love with you.'

'All of those things you've just said? You can shove them all up your arse sideways, buddy.'

'Oh, nice. Very nice. If you can't see that what I'm asking for is reasonable and fair, then it'll never work between us.

And having this talk with you tonight has made my mind up. We're totally incompatible. I was dreading going to Slovakia to see Zuzana but now I'm glad. I can't wait to start planning my new life. Without YOU in it.'

'Good! Zuzana can have you and good luck to her, if she ever puts a foot wrong, with High Court Judge Stefan Walker on her case, poor cow. Off you go!'

'I'm going.'

'Good. Enjoy having a marriage dictated by your mum.'

'Have a nice life.'

'I won't!' I yell, then realise what I've just said, but he's turned around and he's gone. And in that moment, I realise that the whole shop is silent. Unless everyone has gone off home while we've been arguing, then everyone has heard every last word of what we've said. I can't face coming round the corner to see them all standing there, staring at me. I stay where I am, shaking with anger, my eyes filling with tears. Then, Bel pops her head round the corner and I collapse in tears. Bel takes me in her arms and strokes my hair.

I whisper urgently, 'Is Gita still there?'

'No, love. She saw you guys disappear round here and start talking and she looked uncomfortable and she said she was tired, but didn't want to bother Stef. So, Linda took her down, so luckily she wasn't around when . . . it got loud. She didn't hear any of that. Everyone else did though.'

Then Jay pops his head round the corner and says, 'You okay, Mam?'

I start sobbing then and Jay watches, his face looking just like when he was little and he hated seeing me upset.

'You're a queen, Mam. You should be laughing not crying tonight.'

'Hear, hear!' shouts someone from the shop. I think it's Michelle. I remember my hotbed of quilters is still there. I wipe my eyes and thank Bel, and move out of the kitchenette and face my audience. They're all looking so worried and when they see me, they all move my way and go to pat my shoulder or rub my arm, bless them all.

'I'm okay, I'm okay,' I say and feel like a fool. 'I'm just so sorry I embarrassed everyone.'

They're all like, 'Not at all, not at all!'

'I feel like I need to explain,' I say and everyone is saying, 'No need, no need,' etc but I want to. 'I don't want you to think badly of me. We all know Stef is engaged. But it's not what you might be thinking.'

'It's nobody's business but yours, lovely,' says Kelly and smiles reassuringly. Jay hands me a glass of red. I'm surrounded by love and understanding, thank the stars.

Then I tell them, everything that's happened with Stef, plus Gareth's threats (which Jay jumps in on too) and the woeful Guy debacle. The whole sorry mess. I ask them what they all think.

'Fuck him,' says Paige. 'He's asking too much. These bloody men, thinking they can control us. He needs to get in line. Like Jay said, you're a queen!'

Jay looks pleased with this. Is he blushing? There's definitely something brewing between him and Paige. Older woman, eh, Jay? That'd be an interesting pair.

But everyone else is quiet.

'What do the rest of you think?' I say.

Nobody says anything.

'Anyone?'

Bel draws breath in, whistling past her teeth, and says, 'I think you fucked up, babe.'

'What?!'

The others are nodding.

'How?' I ask, agog. I can't believe the vast majority of my support network are not supporting me in this.

'Look, I know I haven't been around much because of Baby Barney blues,' says Bel and I say 'Oh God no, don't worry' et cetera but she insists on going on. 'And I know at first I was a bit sceptical about this Stef fella. But I spoke with him tonight and I've heard everyone else's views on him too. Yeah, we were all gossiping about you two. And now I reckon I've changed my mind about it. For what it's worth, I think Stef seems like a really nice guy, one of the good ones. And he just wants to know he's not blowing up all his plans . . . for a ho.'

'Thanks a bunch!'

'No, babe, look. I know you're not a total ho and Jay knows that too, because we've known you of old. But even these ladies and definitely Stef, well, they've only known you since you started dating and embracing your ho side. And that's fine, we all need to embrace our ho side at various points in our lives – why the hell not? But remember this guy hasn't known you long, and he's coming from centuries of the whole virgin/whore bullshit they have to wade through before the primitive, atavistic bit of their brains can catch up with the rational bit and be all twenty-first century and sex positive. Give him a minute to absorb the new learning, and he'll be with you all the way, I reckon. He just needs a bit of reassurance.'

'So, I was totally in the wrong then, telling him he was asking too much?' I say, flabbergasted. I'm so confused, not about my feelings for Stef, but about the rights and wrongs of what I was doing here.

Linda says, 'Truth is, love, you play with fire if you get involved with someone who's taken. And he's taken in a very serious way. He's not only got a fiancée but also his mother's future plans involved too. It's a lot for one man to carry.'

'I know all that,' I say. 'But what he was asking still feels too much to me.'

Kelly says, her voice kind yet firm, 'I think he was asking for some reassurance, as Bel says. He's only known you these past few months, while you've been . . . having fun. Playing the field.'

Bel adds, 'Yeah, and he doesn't know what you were like before. All he knows is that you've been sowing your wild oats. And that's great and fine and none of his business. But . . .'

Michelle continues, 'Yes, if he's going to give up all of that for you, he needs some assurance that it won't all be for nothing. It's no coincidence that marriages in the historical sense used to be seen far more as a business transaction than anything to do with love. I'm not saying that's the case with Stef and Zuzana. But there is a lot of pressure on him, a lot riding on this. And all he knows of you is that you like to have fun and you're experimenting and you've just come out of relationship jail, after twenty years. Can he give up all of what he's planned for you when, to you, he might just be . . . another lay?'

'But he's not!' I cry. 'I told him that. I told him I was in love with him.'

'Listen, Mam, from a guy's point of view . . .' Jay looks intensely uncomfortable, but he soldiers on, 'I reckon he's probably thinking, well, if she was that in love with me, she wouldn't have gone with that other fella.'

'But that's simply not true. Love doesn't work like that. It's messy and complicated.'

'True that,' says Paige. 'And I still think he's asking too much.'

'Me too,' I say and feel very grumpy that Paige is the only one supporting my side of things. 'But you guys, you really think . . . I fucked up?'

'I think you need to give him some assurance, if you want him to be with you,' says Linda.

'But I've fought so hard for my independence. I can't give that up now.'

Bel says, 'Loving someone will always mean giving something of yourself up. It's inevitable. Like being a mum. Think what we've given to our kids, how much they take out of us.'

'Thanks a bunch!' says Jay and looks fake-mad.

'You're so welcome!' Bel says sweetly back. They're sparring partners of old, those two.

Kelly says, 'But if you're not really in love with him, then none of this matters. If you're not in love with him, then you can carry on, exactly as you are. You can keep your freedom and he can go off into his life and you into yours. Is that what you want?'

I consider this, really consider it. I picture in my mind, Stef Walker driving from Lincoln to Leeds Bradford airport, ready to board a plane and start a new life with Zuzana, knowing that I've told him to go screw himself when he asked me if I could commit to him. Okay, he can be a judgy twat. But was he really asking too much, when he would have to give up so much?

'Oh God,' I say. 'I've fucked up, haven't I . . . haven't I? Oh fffffuck . . .'

'It's not too late,' says Bel. 'Send him a message.'

'Yeah yeah,' everyone agrees. 'Text him now.'

'But what do I say?' I ask, dragging my phone out of my jeans pocket. I tap on WhatsApp.

'Tell him how you feel,' people are saying.

Then I see that his profile picture is gone.

'Oh shit!'

'What?' says Bel.

'He's blocked me on WhatsApp, I'm sure of it. His profile pic has gone.'

'Maybe he just took it off, for whatever reason?' says Linda.

'No, no, his last seen is gone as well. That's what happens when someone blocks you on WhatsApp. I should know, I've blocked and been blocked by so many this year. That's the only way I can get in touch with him!'

'We've got that group chat on WhatsApp we use for the group,' says Michelle. And she goes on there and taps a couple of things and says, 'Oh dear. He's left the group! And blocked me as well!'

'And me,' says Paige. 'He means business.'

The others confirm he's blocked them too. He really does not want to be found!

'He's probably embarrassed,' says Linda. 'Arguing in front of us all. And he most likely thinks we're against him, I wouldn't wonder.'

Kelly says, 'Shall we call Gita?'

'I'd say not!' I say. 'Imagine the conversation. Oh, you know that plan you had to move back to Slovakia with your son and his fiancée? Well, you don't mind if we completely fuck that whole thing up by Frankie declaring her love to him, do you? And can you call him for us to let him know??'

'Okay,' says Kelly, nodding. 'Good point.'

'What am I going to do? He's going back to Slovakia tonight and he's going to sort everything out with Zuzana and I'll be too late. What can I do?'

'Where's he flying from?' says Bel.

'Leeds Bradford.'

'Come on then,' she says. 'I've not been drinking. It makes me sick these days. Let's run back to mine and I'll drive you there.'

It's a crazy idea, like something out of a romcom. Is this my life now? Am I just a movie cliché?!

'Fuck yeah,' yells Jay. 'I'm coming too!'

'And me!' cries Paige.

'Yeah!' says Jay.

So that's how we end up barrelling along the A57, Bel driving, me in the front passenger seat, Jay and Paige getting on like a house on fire in the back. Everyone else was all for it, but couldn't fit in the car obvs, so they went home, demanding we update them with texts. Before we leapt in her car, Bel popped in her house to tell Craig what was going on and he said he had it all under control and Barney was fast asleep anyway and sent her off with his blessing.

'This is insane,' I say to Bel. 'What if his flight's gone by the time we get there?'

'It won't have, we weren't that far behind him. And he's gotta be there two hours early. I haven't had this much fun in years!'

I can't believe we're doing this. But I'm so bloody glad we are. I can't wait to see Stef. I can't wait to run across the airport and grab him and kiss him and tell him that yes, he was a judgy twat but I was also a stubborn twat and we can work it out. Hell yeah, we can work it out. I'm overflowing with optimism and excitement. This is it, the beginning of a new chapter in my complicated love life.

Bel says, 'Everyone was telling me tonight how mad this guy is for you. They were saying every week in the classes they'd catch him gazing at you while you were pottering about and then looking away shyly, and how protective he was of you, when they'd chat about your dating exploits and he'd always get mad or worried about what you were going through. I had a chat tonight with him too about him being a designer and he went on and on about your quilting and how beautiful your designs are, how talented you are.'

'Wow, really?! I had no idea he felt all those things!'

'Oh yeah, seems like he's better at telling that stuff to other people than to you. Sounds like he needs a bit of encouragement to say how he really feels. Strikes me as an introvert, wouldn't you say?'

'Yeah, I reckon. And Zuzana seemed the same, from the very brief meeting I had with her. She certainly seemed quite shy. I'm the opposite though, babe. I'm a gobby extrovert. Does that mean I'm wrong for him?'

'Nah, opposites can attract, remember. It'd be good for you to have a nice, calm, peaceful guy in your life. Although, to be fair, the way he gave as good as he got in your argument shows he can drag out an extrovert side as well when he needs it. He's no pushover!'

'Yeah and I love that, actually! That argument stuff really gets me going.'

'Fuck yeah! I love a good row with Craig. And then the inevitable make-up sex after.'

'Oy!' comes Jay's voice from the back. 'Can you two stop going on about mum sex? It's disgusting!'

'Ah feck off,' says Bel. 'Youse young'uns don't have the monopoly on shagging.'

But during all this banter, I'm thinking about what Linda said about love being a sense of peace. And I'm having another epiphany. I realise that, in my whole life, in all my relationships with men, I've never had peace with love, certainly not with Gareth, who was constant stress and anxiety. I can't WAIT to tell Stef all this, how much he means to me. I will the car to go faster, although Bel is already speeding. What a spectacular night this has turned out to be. And it's only going to get better!

Paige is playing Oasis on her phone and telling Jay why they're the best band ever, so we all start singing along to *Roll With It*, the perfect driving accompaniment.

Then, Bel's phone starts ringing.

'Who is it?' she says and I grab her phone and see it's Craig, labelled as *First Husband* in her contacts.

'Answer it, babe,' says Bel.

'Oy, you two, turn down Liam Gallagher, I can't hear a thing! Hey, Craig, it's Frankie. You okay?'

But he's not okay. 'It's Barney. Something's not right.'

'What's wrong with Barney?' I say and Bel's head whips round.

'Shut the fuck up everyone,' Bel snaps. 'Put him on speaker.'

'You're on speaker, Craig,' I say.

'He woke up screaming. And I couldn't calm him down in the crib. So I went to pick him up and he feels really hot, love. And he's got a rash on his arms and his chest. I'm trying with the glass on him, to do the meningitis test thing, but I can't tell. I can't tell if they're disappearing or not when I put the glass on him. He's bloody hot though. And he's stopped crying now and he just looks all floppy. Fuck, what do I do?'

Bel shouts, 'Take him to the hospital NOW! I'm turning round. I'm on my way. Now, do you hear me, Craig? Now.'

'Yeah, yeah, I'm going,' he says.

'It's okay, darling,' I say. 'Could be anything.'

'Sounds like meningitis,' says Bel, her voice quavering. 'Sounds just like it. I've memorised those bloody cards with all the symptoms on. I've read them a million times, just in case. Where's a turning point?! I'm just gonna do a fucking U-ey if I don't find one soon.'

'Don't panic, babe. Look, there's a roundabout coming up. Turn round on there.'

'Get the hospital on Google Maps, the fastest route,' says Bel and drives round that roundabout far too fast, but nobody says a word, except the Google Maps woman who's telling us where to go in a comforting, patronising tone.

'Listen, darling. There's every chance it's heat rash and a normal fever.'

But Bel's not listening. I know why. She's in emergency mode. I feel so shit I've got her on this hare-brained scheme when she should be with her baby. My stupid love life interfering with matters of life and death in hers. We all sit in anxious silence as she drives like a maniac back down the A57 and then on to the A46 towards the hospital. When we pull into the car park, I tell her to give me the keys and I'll lock the car. She throws them at me and pelts off across the tarmac. Jay and Paige get out of the back and everyone is looking sick with worry.

'It's okay, kids. I've had hospital runs like this with you, Jay, and they all worked out. Babies can often look like death and it be just a little fever or something. Honestly, try not to worry. Paige, do you want me to call you an Uber home?'

'Course not! I'm here for the duration,' she says and I see Jay smile a little smile. Gosh, he really likes her. That's nice.

'Come on, then. Let's go help Bel and Craig.'

We go in and there's no sign of Bel. We're assuming she's found wherever Craig and Barney are. I tell reception we're here for our friends and they say to take a seat. So, then we wait. And wait. And wait. There's no news from Bel and Craig and I'm feeling sick. If it'd been nothing, they would've come out quite quickly, wouldn't they? Then I remember the night-long stays in hospital we had a couple of times with Jay when he was this age, how long it took to be seen, how many hours we sat on a bed holding him crying or watching him sleep, until a doctor could come. Maybe that's what's going on now, or maybe it's not, maybe something fucking awful is going on down a corridor somewhere. All we can do is wait.

I'm looking at my phone to pass the time and take my mind off things, looking at Instagram Reels of cats, biscuit-decorating, sharks, gymnastics, Switzerland and ice skaters (some of my myriad and random interests online), while Jay and Paige are chatting quietly for hours, getting on really well. I keep looking back at WhatsApp to see if Stef has unblocked me. Fat chance. *He'll probably be in Slovakia by now*, I think miserably. I've missed my chance, surely. He's made his mind up about me and that's that. He's with his fiancée now. He'll reconnect with her and realise all the nonsense with me was just like a bad dream for him. And now he's woken up.

Then, I hear a little snort and realise that Jay is actually asleep and so is Paige. Jay's snoring. They've fallen asleep with Paige's head on Jay's shoulder, both a bit worse for wear for the wine. Seeing my boy there, fast asleep, not a care in the world, with Paige, my youngest quilter, to whom I feel very maternal, my eyes fill with tears, for all of it, everything, this mad night, with its uncertain conclusion. Parenthood is a lot, that's for sure, mostly a series of narrowly missed disasters. All the things that can go wrong, all the times you don't feel up to it, but you go on, because you have to. The love I feel for my son is so complicated and yet so simple simultaneously. Love is that way, it's crazy complex and yet so pure, all at the same time.

Finally, FINALLY, Craig appears, coming down the corridor towards the waiting room and I leap up and run to him. I can't tell what his face looks like, I can't tell what he's going to say. He hasn't seen me yet and his face looks like shit. Oh God, oh God, please, please.

Then Craig looks up and sees me.

'He's fine!' he says loudly and holds up his hands, to let me know immediately that I can stop running and calm the hell down.

'Oh, Jesus Christ and the Virgin Mary and the little fucking donkey!' I cry and a nurse passing by smirks at me.

'It's just a heat rash and a normal fever. They've given him Calpol and he'll be ready to go home. We're just waiting to be discharged.'

'Oh, thank God.'

'I feel like a right prick making all this fuss over nothing,' says Craig.

'No, no. Better safe than sorry and all that jazz,' I say. 'You absolutely did the right thing. You know that, don't you?'

'Yeah, I suppose so. Look, you guys get off home. We're gonna drive back in my car, so you wanna drive Bel's home?'

'I can't, I've drunk far too much tonight.'

'Okay, no worries . . . erm . . .'

Craig looks like Rip van Winkle when he's just woken up.

'Don't worry, honey. I'll get us an Uber and you guys can pick up Bel's car tomorrow, yeah?' I hand him Bel's keys.

'Yeah, yeah. Thanks. Appreciate you being here. You didn't need to wait.'

'Course I bloody did. Is Bel okay?'

'Yeah, she is now. She just wants to get him home.'

'Give her our love. We'll sort ourselves. You get back to your little family, mate. And jolly well done tonight. Good call, Craig. Good call.'

'Thanks Frankie,' he says and gives me a wan smile, then turns and heads back down the corridor.

I let out a huge breath, and realise it feels like I've been holding that in for hours. I arrange an Uber and wake up the sleeping beauties. We drop off Paige first at her parents' house on Ruskin Avenue and then the Uber takes us as near as it can get to our place on Steep Hill. Jay and I walk the last bit in silence, arms linked. We pull out the sofa bed and Jay collapses on it, asleep within seconds. I wish I could sleep like that. I'm absolutely wide awake. I wash my face and climb into bed, doom-scrolling through my phone as I try to tire my eyes out. Mentally, I take stock.

So, it looks like things are over with Stef. I can't see a way back now, not now he's out of contact and over there with Zuzana. Maybe it's for the best. Maybe we weren't right for each other. Maybe love shouldn't be this difficult. The important thing is, Barney is okay, Jay is okay, Bel is okay and I'm okay. Everything else is gravy. I think about my dating journey so far, all the weird men I've spoken to, all the dicks I've seen, all the bad nights and the good nights and the meh nights, all the bullshit of modern dating. What's the answer to it all? I haven't got a clue. When it comes to love, at the grand age of fifty, I feel like I know everything and I know nothing, a total beginner and an old pro, simultaneously. And yet I've come to no conclusions, only become embroiled in the unholy mess that is love and relationships. So I go on Facebook to share a few memes to cheer myself up and the goddamn Zuck has been reading my mind and there's an advert on my timeline for Facebook Dating. Oh my God, sod that. Facebook is full enough of catfish arseholes as it is. And again, as if sentient, Facebook Messenger shows me that tedious little red dot even though there's nothing in my contacts, so I check my requests, this time, a very small, very quiet part of me hopes against hope that it's Stef messaging me, telling me he's made a terrible mistake and he's on his way back. We're not connected on Facebook, as we've not had the nerve to make that level of commitment, I think wryly. But no, again, as usual, it's a goddamn catfish, his fake profile pic a handsome young man in army fatigues, smiling with perfectly white teeth. Just think how many poor, naïve women might fall for this bozo and even give him money. What utter bastards these scammers are. And this catfish motherfucker is gonna feel the full force of my wrath tonight.

Good evening I am from Italy original but now deployed in Chile

And a very good evening to you. Is that you in the pictures?

Yes

So you're a doctor?

Yes

What kind of doctor?

I work with Red Cross doctors

Wow, that's impressive! What's your specialism?

My special is surgeons

What kind of surgeon?

Bones I do operations with bones

Ah, so you're a dermatologist.

Yes but do you feel for me as I feel for you? I want to feel your womanhood.

So, you're a gynaecologist??

My dearest I do the both

Gosh, you are multi-talented!

Thank you but let us talk on whatsapp much better give me your number

What's your favourite bone?

I like all bones equal I appreciate your smile and eyes so pretty

Did you know in England we call a bone doctor a 'Boner'?

I did not know this

And a surgeon bone doctor, such as yourself, we would call a 'Big Hard Boner'.

But I will love you and be next to you forever

Can I call you Dr Boner?

If it pleases

It does pleases. I have to go now, but the next time you talk to a lady from England, don't forget to introduce yourself as Dr Big Hard Boner.

OK

Good. Don't forget!

I wont now give me whatsapp

I'm only on Snapchat, I'm afraid.

Ok whats your snap

I'mRoastingYou

This is correct?

Yes indeed. But you could also try this one: StopLyingtoRandomWomen

I cannot find messg me whatsapp now

You don't get to give me orders, Mr Nobody. Truth is, mate, you're a waste of breath. Somewhere in the ocean, there is a vast cloud of plankton producing oxygen that allows you to breathe, and you need to apologise to that plankton. Get control of your life and do something with yourself instead of trying to scam people. Have some goddamn self-respect. Wankers

like you are a scourge on society and social media companies do fuck all about it, so it's up to people like me to deal with you. I can mess you about and waste your time, just like you're wasting the time of countless women all over the world. But in the end, you're just gonna keep creating new profiles and looking for vulnerable women to scam. You're scum and I'm sick to death of the lot of you. I hope you find yourself one day alone, miserable and poor, with no friends, no family, no lovers, no security, no home and no life, because those are the seeds you should be sowing, instead of this poison. And you're salting your own fields, buddy, so good luck with that. So, no, I won't be giving you my WhatsApp. I'd rather shit in my hands and clap than spend another moment of my life even thinking about you. In fact, I've already forgotten what you said and who you are. Goodbye forever, you utter cockwomble.

CHAPTER 17

The Whole Package

Summer in Lincoln. It's a sight to see. Ice creams and frozen yoghurt and fudge portions on Steep Hill abound, masses of international tourists line the streets in pottering huddles, in and out of every gift shop and café. It's a seasonal peak for *Sew What?* I've many, many customers every day due to summer tourist footfall in the city, including a ton of orders for new materials and tools. After our feature on *Look North*, I got a slew of interest in classes. I'm going to start two new ones in September, one on a Thursday evening and another on a Wednesday afternoon (as I've realised I can still serve customers while the group get on). And of course, I'll be continuing with my original hotbedders on a Monday night. Gita still attends, as do the rest of the gang. Gita never said a word to me about what happened with Stef that night, as thankfully Linda got her out of there early. But I do wonder what she knows about me and Stef, yet she never gives an inkling. She's nice as pie to me. But I have noticed she never mentions Stef anymore, not a word about him. That's unusual and I'm pretty sure it's deliberate.

Life moves on . . . And I'm relieved she never mentions him, because I just don't want to hear his name. It's too sad. It makes me blue and I'm riding high right now and I don't need the negativity. Or to question things too much . . . or to ask, what if . . .? No, I'm done with that.

Back to business, I've also had requests from people not able to make it to the shop regularly, asking if I might consider doing online tutorials on YouTube. Plus I'm looking into home-made quilts as gifts, perhaps as a separate business with Michelle and Linda, who are up for that. And the cherry on top is that the butcher's next door is closing down (only because he's moving to a larger location) and a patisserie will be opening up soon. The aroma of freshly baked bread and cakes?! Yes please! Now that's a turn-up. I'm damn proud of the progress my business is making and I'm starting to feel a little bit more hopeful about the future. I'm not seeing anyone right now, I haven't spoken to any sort of romantic interest since the airport run three weeks ago. I'm just not interested. I want to focus on myself, on Jay (who's got a summer job at the castle, just up the hill) and on my business. My life is busy and full and I don't need the added aggravation of dating right now. I don't even want it. I'm in control. Neither my loins nor my emotions are directing me right now and that feels great.

Until the postcard.

One morning, late July, the postie drops in my mail, and I'm working through the pile when I find a singular postcard. It's a picture of a house with a gable end painted all black, with white figures painted onto it in the shapes of hearts, crosses, dots and geometric birds. A bolt of recognition judders through me. It's Slovakian. I hurriedly turn the postcard over. The name of my shop is written on the other side and my address, but that's it. No other words on there. I don't recognise the handwriting, but then I've never seen Stef's writing. And surely, it must be from Stef?? What does it mean? I pull my phone out of my back pocket and check WhatsApp. I'm still blocked by Stef on there (and yes, I haven't had the heart to delete his contact. I'm not quite ready for that yet). Why would he send me a blank postcard and no message? And if he was reaching out, why hasn't he unblocked me on WhatsApp? But then I wonder, what if it's from Zuzana?? She came in here, after all. Maybe she gleaned something. Maybe Stef told her about us. Maybe the postcard is a threat . . . Urgh, I've no idea. I turn it over and over in my hands. What could it mean? Whatever it means, it's given me a squirming feeling in my tummy and a tingly sensation in my down-belows. And as much as I've tried to shut all that nonsense out of my life this past month, the excitement that feeling brings is not unwelcome. In fact, it feels rather good to be alive with electricity again. I hadn't realised until now how much I've missed it. But then, I start thinking about Stef, and Zuzana, and their life in Slovakia right now. I mean, maybe the postcard is just to say hello, no hard feelings and this is his life now. Maybe that's what he's trying to say, if he sent it. The Slovakian postcard is saying, 'I've made my decision and it's here, not with you.' Maybe he's making love to the beautiful, young Zuzana right now and Christ on a bike, the thought of them in bed together tortures me. I literally feel sick about it. And, oh God, all the old feelings of yearning return and I miss Stef. God, I've missed him. I've missed his quiet presence in the group, the talks we'd have about fabrics and designs and the colour wheel and art and history and culture and cartoons and books and poetry and comedy and movies and, oh, everything. I miss his eyes, his hair, the curve of his back. His mouth. His T-shirts.

All this comes flooding back while I'm standing there holding the postcard. I haven't even noticed the rest of the pile of mail I have to sift through. So I carefully place the postcard to one side and try to ignore it as I get on with the bills and junk and other ephemera I have to sort. And the last in the pile is an official-looking letter and I see from the stamp that it's from my divorce solicitor. Oh, fuckkkkk, I hate getting letters from her. Something else to pay for. Or maybe, news about Gareth's claim? Now I feel even more sick, but for a totally different reason. I'm sick with fear. I don't want to open the letter. But I force myself to and I rip it open and read it dead quick, trying to get past all the formal solicitor bullshit language and I get to the meaty part of the letter, the bit it's actually about and it's saying . . . is it, can it be? Gareth is dropping the suit?? He's goddamn DROPPING IT??!! Oh my fucking stars, he's dropping it!! Reading between the lines of the legal jargon, from what I can make out it seems that his solicitor will have advised him that the fact he kept it quiet when he re-mortgaged so recklessly is tantamount to misconduct, so because he bankrupted the marriage, he won't be entitled to any share of my inheritance. The divorce can proceed as planned and no more claims afterwards, no more bullshit, we can finally move towards the final decree and be free of each other, legally, forever! WHOOOOOOOOOOP!!!!

I grab my phone and message Jay, then Bel.

Jay's at the castle so he doesn't reply straight away but Bel is on it and she sends a message saying:

GET YOURSELF THE FUCK ROUND HERE TONIGHT & WE'LL CELEBRATE! BRING WINE FOR YOU! AND CAKE FOR ME!

Jay replies later:

Yaaaaaaaaay!!! :) :) :)

Cant believe old bastard did smthng right 4 once

Maybe my threats held water 4 1st time eva

Thrilled 4 ya Mam

I spend the rest of the day on cloud nine. I even put the Slovakian postcard up on the noticeboard in the shop and make peace with it. Whoever sent it, whatever it means, it's okay. Because I'm okay. My business is okay. I have a future, without this existential threat from Twatface hanging over me. Holy shit, it's like coming out of prison, again! It gives me the strength to deal with missing Stef and get on with my day, secure in the knowledge that my world has opened up again with new possibilities. Oh, the joy of freedom, and the only somewhat lesser joy of beating Gareth at his own game. Victories like this are seldom with arch narcissists, but fuck me, they feel good.

Jay comes home from work and I invite him to come with me to Bel's, but he's off out with Paige again. Yes, again. Are they dating? I've no idea. It's . . . complicated, as I tease him. I don't mind, as long as he's happy. And he is happy and they have fun together, so it's all good. I get myself round to Bel's and we're in for a sofa session tonight, as Craig is out with his mates and Barney is there, healthy and bouncing and gorgeous, and then Bel lets me give him his milk and cuddles. It's such a joy to hold a bairn again and feel that warm package of love on my arm. She puts him down and after a bit of gurgling and babbling, he drops off and we're in peace. We sit on the sofa and eat cake and I drink wine and we're talking nineteen to the dozen, as ever. I'm eager to tell her about the postcard, but I want to hear how she is first. I worry about Bel since Barney's come into their lives and I hope she knows she can always talk to me. So I make sure I always ask her how she's doing, just in case nobody else has asked her for a while.

'Yeah, I'm good, you know. Actually, better than I've been in weeks. Or even months. It was the hospital thing that did it.'

'How so?'

'I don't know, but it worked. Something to do with a moment in your lives when time stands still, when everything comes into focus. And at that moment, when I was racing through A&E and searching for my baby, and then I found him and held him and he was okay . . . something just clicked in my head. Like a cog, slotting into place. It was odd. And it was great. I just felt like a cloud had lifted. This heavy bastard thing of motherhood I'd been carrying . . . I don't know. The weight's not gone, but it's shifted, somehow. To a better position, to something I can carry more easily. Lighter, somehow.'

'Wow, that's fantastic, babe. I'm so, so glad to hear that!'

'Well, yeah! Me too! It's been a ride these past months. I dunno, that moment in the hospital when I took him, I bonded so deeply with him in that moment, it's like we get each other now. We understand each other. I'm more relaxed, he's feeding better and sleeping better. The colicky stage seems to be passing. I actually feel ready to go back to work in September now. I'm not fearing it anymore. I just feel . . . yeah, it's all gonna be okay. I've even started gardening again. I've really bloody missed it. I'm starting to feel . . . like myself again.'

I move over and give Bel the tightest hug. I'm so delighted she's feeling this way.

'I'm so proud of you, darling.'

'Ah, fuck that. I'm just a mum. Women have been doing it forever.'

'Yeah and it's been bloody hard forever. And that's why it takes a village to raise a kid and all that. But we don't have villages anymore like we once did, and we don't have elder matriarchs living in the house with us, ready to take our babies when we need a nap.'

'Unless you're living with Gita, like Stef and Zuzana . . .' says Bel and lifts her eyebrows.

'Oh God, I've something to tell you about that. I got a postcard today.'

I tell her about it, what little there is to tell.

'What could it mean?' I say.

'Wow. I don't know. I wasn't expecting that. It's a bit cute, if he's sending you a message. I mean, why can't he just be honest, if he still feels for you?'

'Maybe it's not from him, maybe it's from Zuzana.'

'Well, that would be weird. And stalky. And *Fatal Attraction*-y. Good job you've not got a bunny.'

'Should I . . . do anything about it?'

Bel considers. 'Still blocked on WhatsApp?'

'Yup.'

'What about Facebook?'

'We never actually became friends on there.'

'But you could send him a friend request? Or a message request?'

'I could . . .' I cogitate. 'I dunno. Why . . . well, why should I? Like you said, sending a blank postcard is a bit bloody coy. Why can't he just be straight with me? That annoys me, actually.'

'Yeah . . . or he's just confused, and he's reaching out . . . but doesn't know what to say. Because he doesn't know what he feels. Which is annoying. I mean, I like Stef a lot, you know that. But the guy needs to make up his mind.'

I knock back a gulp of wine and say, 'Hell yeah. No, I'm not gonna message him on Facebook. I'm gonna wait and see.'

'Good for you, babe. That there is strength. Muscles you've built up after months of love gym!'

We have a laugh about that and chat on about other stuff, gossiping about the folk I used to work with at the school Bel is planning to return to in September. As we talk away and eat cake and laugh, it occurs to me that both Bel and I have been on an odyssey this year. We might be at different stages of our lives, but we've both had to cope with massive change and, with each other's help, we're getting through it in one piece. More than that, I'd say, we're killing it. Thank the stars for friendship and thank the stars for Bel.

That night, I'm lying in bed thinking about all this, listening to Jay snoring in the next room. I put my earphones in to listen to an audiobook. It's one that Jay has recommended, by a neuroscientist called David Eagleman. He's just discovered this guy and he's been reading everything by him that he can get his hands on and he's been telling me over and over I should get into it, so I bought one of his books on Audible and I've been listening to it the last few nights and it's great (plus I realise that loads of ideas that Guy passed off as his own, he totally stole from Eagleman, the utter cock – Guy, that is, not Eagleman. I'm sure he's very nice). Anyway, so Eagleman is going on about brains, obviously, I mean, the whole damn book is about brains. And he's saying that brains aren't hard-wired, they are still developing and malleable and they adapt and change throughout your whole life. And it occurs to me that here is a very good argument for being flexible in life, for bending with the wind, for changing your mind. There's no point in making one decision and saying that's it, like, I'm never going to love a man again, I'm never going to live with a man again, because of the shit I've been through before, because I have no idea what's coming. Yeah, I might give up my heart again and I might have it broken, but I might not and that's what life's all about, accepting the uncertainty and embracing it and moving on.

And actually, I realise that Stef and I are very similar, but just at different poles, both as stubborn as each other: I won't commit because I don't trust men and he won't agree to a relationship unless he has absolute assurance that it will last forever. And both extremes are untenable. Because he's saying he can't take a chance on anything unless it's going to be forever, and I'm saying I can't take a chance on anything because men are unreliable, but actually there are no answers, no certainty, everything changes. Then, I realise I've not listened to a word David Eagleman's been telling me for several minutes, so I tune my mind back in and then I hear him say this: 'The best way to predict the future is to create it.' Hold on a goddamn minute. I press pause and slide it back a few seconds and listen to that again.

The best way to predict the future is to create it.

My new best friend David Eagleman has given me my third epiphany of recent times. I pause the book and think again about that line. And I realise it is the best argument I've heard yet for trying things out, going on adventures, not waiting for disaster but instead taking risks and leaps into the unknown. That life is frightening and full of pitfalls and unpredictable trips to midnight hospitals and meeting graphic designers with great T-shirts and all this stuff, this madness of life, it's all about discovery and trial and error, while fixed ideas, entrenched decisions and stubborn beliefs are the opposite of what your brain needs, every moment of its existence. And it's not just your brain, but your heart too, and your very soul.

Wow, that got deep real quick. But it's TRUE. Thanks, David Eagleman. And thanks to my brilliant son Jay, for sharing his obsessions with me.

So, what do I do about this? Nothing, really. Stef has gone and I'm alone. And that's okay. I'm okay, being alone. But if I meet another Stef – if there ever will be another Stef – I'll know what to do. I'll know to leave things open, to embrace the new, to explore and adventure. What's the point of life otherwise?

The next day, I'm back in the shop and feeling stronger. I eye the postcard on the noticeboard from time to time but I resist the urge to go on Messenger, even though I keep thinking about what I thought last night – will there ever be another Stef? I mean, there will be other men, of course. There are so many men, lining up on all those apps, to speak to women, to have sex with women, but also there's a few who want more than that. Yes, there's no shortage of fish in the sea. But they won't be . . . Stef. There's only one Stef.

I'm not saying he's the one, because I don't believe in The One. But Stef . . . and his brain . . . and the way he thinks . . . To misquote the immortal line from Olivia Newton-John and John Travolta (and how I wanted them to get married and him to break with tradition and take her name and then he'd be John John) in the song that was number one for-fucking-ever which I used to sing along with every Sunday for weeks when I was a kid in my dining room eating boiled eggs and listening to the top forty on my mum's radiogram, *He's the one that I want.*

And my brain does that random rabbit-hole thing where one memory leads to another and another, and I suddenly have a flashback to when I was about thirteen, chatting with my grandad in the greenhouse in his beautiful garden. He was a chemist, my grandad, not the kind who doles out condoms and piles cream, but a chemist in a lab. That's where Jay gets his scientific mind from. And there I was in pigtails and school uniform and I was complaining about some girls at school and how mean they were and how life would be much easier if there weren't other people in it and why are people so bloody complicated and they really do my head in and why can't people just be nice and simple?

And he said to me, 'What is the most complicated thing in the world that a human brain will ever have to deal with?'

And I said, 'Erm . . . a big computer. Like Deep Thought.'

And he said, 'Nope. It's another human brain.'

I can see him standing there, with his shock of white hair (he slicked it down for work, but at home, in his garden, he let it stick up at all angles). He was wearing denim dungarees and that's where I get my love of dungarees from. I wear them a lot, especially when I'm sewing. I can see him there, in my mind, with absolute clarity, with a little knowing smile, then he carried on trimming shoots from his tomato plants. I needed to hear that, right now, Grandad. I needed a reminder that the best thing about being a human brain is the luck of stumbling across another human brain and connecting with it. And how rare it is, really, in this life, to meet someone and have that pure connection with them, that's so good and so true. My grandad knew that. So . . . maybe, at the end of the day, when the shop is shut, I'll swallow my pride and take a leap of faith and reach out to Stef on Messenger and tell him how I feel. Maybe . . .

The shop is busy again, then a lull comes near to closing time and I'm sorting out some fabric deliveries when the bell rings as my shop door opens and I look up, ready to serve another tourist who's hopefully come to spend some of their lovely money. But it's not a tourist, it's Gita.

'Hey Gita,' I say. I've seen her at the class just under a week ago and she's been fine with me. Since Stef has gone, we've got on far better. But she looks pretty serious right now and I'm wondering what's up. 'Everything okay?'

'Hello, Frances. How are you, my dear?'

'I'm fine, Gita. But, how are you? You look worried.'

'Would it be all right with you if we had a little chat? I came at this closing time of your shop for such a reason, so you might not be too busy.'

'Sure, no problem.'

What the hell is this all about? I'm curious though . . . I set up a couple of chairs for us, even though I was actually desperate for a wee just before Gita came in, but I figure I can hold it for a while; it seems too rude to leave her when she's looking so worried. So I sit down with her.

'I want to explain something to you and then I want to ask you a favour, my dear.'

'All right,' I say, already a bit freaked out. Does it have something to do with Stef? Jeez, I hope not. 'I'd always like to help you whenever I can.'

'Okay, thank you, Frances. And I would ask that I say all the things I have to say and you could listen, please, and not interrupt, only because I have practised it and I need to say it all in one go and then it will all make much more sense, if that is agreeable to you.'

Okay, I'm thinking now this *must* be about Stef. But what is she going to say? I'm agog. But I pretend this is the most normal thing in the world. 'Absolutely. Fire away.'

'So, I was planning on moving back to my beloved Slovakia in September, as you know. My flights have been booked and I am busy packing up my life here. And all is go. But a few days ago, I have my son call me on the iPad, you know, on the video thingy as we used to use here. He calls me that way regularly to check on me, though I do have my Lincoln-Slovakian friends who check in on me too, but I like to hear from him, you know. So, he calls me and he tells me that the wedding might be off.'

Ffffffuck . . . I want to react so badly. I want to say, YAY! I knew it! I knew that postcard meant something! But I have to stay calm. I can't start celebrating while Gita is sitting here with a face like thunder. And I adhere to her request to not interrupt and I literally bite my lower lip to stop myself from blabbering out what I really want to say at this momentously good news. I say nothing.

'We discuss it at length. He says he is confused, about his feelings for Zuzana, that she is not everything he hoped she might be, that spending time with her has shown him that in many ways they are too different, not compatible. He says they gel on certain things, on how they want their house to be, how they might raise their children. Zuzana is a neo-natal nurse and she is very knowledgeable about children and this is a very good thing for a mother for your children, is it not? And he knows that. And I tell him that he knew her well enough before this and all couples go through their ups and their downs but he loves her and that's the most important thing. But then he tells me that he doesn't know if he loves her now. Because he's in love with you, Frances.'

Oh, holy cow. Am I allowed to speak yet? Obviously not, as she continues straight on with the next bit.

'So he says that he wants to do right by Zuzana and right by me. But he cannot help the way he feels about you. So I tell him, that this is all normal. This is all the nerves that we have in the last-minute time of things. You know, as they say, the jitters? I think that is the word. And all men have this. Giving up their freedom. It is a big thing for them. And that's all this is, I tell him. The wedding is all planned for a few weeks' time. And we have found the house we want to buy to live in. And the sale is imminent and we need to get things sorted. And I tell him to grow up and get a hold of himself and I will talk to him again when he has pulled himself together. And I end the call. I have not spoken to him these last few days. I am waiting for him to get in touch with me. And I have been beside myself with worry and so far away from him that I cannot counsel him as I would want to, in the same room, beside him, so I can explain these things properly, not on these damn screens. So I decide there is one thing I can do from here. I can come to see you, Frances, in your shop, and I can beg you. And I will beg you. That if my Štefan gets in touch with you, you turn him down. You say no to him. I am asking you, do the right thing for me, for Zuzana, but mostly for him. He has always been a bit of a lost soul, wandering the earth, feeling caught between two cultures, this one and his real one, his Slovakian home, and it has only got worse since his father died. He needs to choose his home now and that is in Slovakia with Zuzana. I know you agree with this. I know you will do the right thing.'

And that's the end of her speech. WTF do I say to that? I take a moment and breathe.

Gita says, 'Has he been in touch with you?'

'No, nothing, not a word,' I lie and think of the postcard. Well, I've no actual proof it's from him. It's not a proper lie, not really.

'Good,' she says and looks pleased with herself. 'But if he does, you know what to do. Tell him, his home is in Slovakia, not here.'

I could just go along with it. I could say whatever she wants, to please her. I could message him later on Facebook. But something about the way Gita has done this, the way she has presumed to not only speak for her son, but to speak for me . . . Look, I get where she's coming from. Her lovely retirement plan might be out the window. And that's shitty and I feel crap about it. Having had a hand grenade lobbed into the middle of my life this past year – what with not only leaving Twatface but also finding out my retirement plan is up the Swannee due to his debts – I really, truly get that it'll be rotten for Gita. I get that more than most, I suspect. And I don't want to be that person, the one lobbing the hand grenade this time. That's not me. I think about Gita's request and I think maybe it would be best for everyone involved if I just retreat. If I just do what she wants . . . and then, she'd be happy, and she'd like me again, and nice Frankie prevails. But . . . is it nice to live your life denying what you want, just to please other people? And is what Gita wants her right to want in the first place? Does it give her the right to organise her son's life to suit herself? To even organise my life, and she's not even my damn mother? Does it fuck. I'm going to be polite though. I can act the lady, even if I say fuck a lot.

'Okay, so, Gita. I understand why you came here. I understand why you feel this way. But surely, this is Stef's decision to make, not mine, not yours. And you may feel his spiritual home is Slovakia, but maybe he doesn't. I mean, he's half English too, so why does he have to choose?'

Gita says, 'You do not understand because you are English and the English are so very different from the Slovakians and do not feel the same way about home as we do. My boy's soul is Slovakian and he's spent enough of his life here and it's time to go home.'

'But what if this is his home? Or somewhere else? Surely our home is what we make it, as the cliché goes. Either way it's not your job to choose for him. He's a grown man.'

Now she purses her lips and looks daggers at me. I must admit, it might well've been tough for that lad growing up with this look whenever he messes up. Now I know where he gets his judgy side from, but it's far less pronounced in him than it is in his redoubtable mother.

Gita says, 'I said to him, even if he thinks he's in love with you, you're not in love with him, you're not in love with anyone. You are playing the field, as they say. And you have been married to one man for many years and you've had your baby, so you don't want what he wants, you cannot give him what he needs. So even if you are in love with him, you know that the best thing for him is to give that foolish idea up. And anyway, the point as they say is neither here nor there, because you are not in love with him, are you, Frances?'

Okay, so we've been skirting around the main issue, as I couldn't face it head on. But now we're here and I have to put my cards on the table. And what are they? What do I really feel about this man, with his judgy ways and his interfering nightmare of a mother? Do I love Stefan Walker enough to deal with all this fallout, all this hassle, all this shit, just when I've fought to escape from a hellhole of a marriage and my life is just starting to come together? Do I love this man enough to take all of this on now?

I close my eyes for a moment and before I know it, I've blurted out what I've known deep down for a while now.

'Yes, I am. I am in love with him. I love everything about him, even when he's judgemental and unyielding and we disagree horribly, even then. I love him. I'm sorry, Gita, but I do.'

'No, you don't,' she says with such certainty, shaking her head and closing her eyes. I almost believe it myself, she's so sure! She continues, 'And you are not to tell him that. Because I know the truth, that you are not ready for another serious relationship, not now. You have your business and your friends and your men you date and you are happy. You are not ready for this commitment to my son and he is not the one for you. You need to tell him that, to tell him to make the right decision about his life.'

Wow, okay. Gita seems to know me better than I know myself apparently. This is not okay.

'Gita, look. I'm sorry but it's not up to you to speak for me. Or to speak for your son either. It's up to Stef what he does with his life, not you. I care for you and I don't want your plans to be ruined. But I need you to know I've had no contact with him at all and I haven't encouraged him, not recently. So whatever decision he makes is his alone. I've had no undue influence and I've not spoken to him since the night he left and I've not messaged him.'

'You'd better not try,' she says, firmly.

Right, that's it. My patience is at zero. She may be nearly eighty, and the mother of the man I love, but I've had enough of this bloody woman.

In fact – it dawns on me now – I've had enough of anyone telling me what to do and how to live my life. I've had enough of men like Twatface and Fuckface thinking they can control me. I've had enough of men like Ronnie the Rapist thinking they're the ones with power over women like me. After fifty-odd years of living for other people, I, Frances Brumby, have absolutely, categorically, had enough. It's time to take matters into my own hands. I inhale. *The best way to predict the future is to create it*, I think to myself.

'I'll do whatever the fuck I like, Gita.'

She looks at me and I look at her. It's the battle of the ages. Who will blink first?! I do. Jeez Louise, that woman has eyelids of steel. Then, she stands up and with great dignity, she walks slowly across my shop, opens my door, walks out of my shop and leaves the damn door wide open, like a duchess. I have to give it to her, she's regal as all hell. But she doesn't get to tell me how to live my life. No one does, anymore.

I walk over to the shop door, shut it and lock it. It's closing time, more or less. And I've had enough of this day. I've had enough of interfering mothers and of being told what to do. But now, I have to decide. Do I go on Facebook and message Stef? It seems like the thing that I want, more than anything. But, even though Gita is out of order, I mean she obviously is . . . is it right, what I'm contemplating doing? And what if I'm wrong about my feelings for Stef? What if we don't last? What if he blows up his life for nothing? What if he's just infatuated with me, but soon realises I can't give him what he needs, I can't be Zuzana or Slovakian or everything he's got set up with her, this new life he was all ready to plunge into? What if I'm not good enough? And what if he's not the right one for me? If only I could see him, right now, I think I'd know. I'd look at him and I'd know. But I can't, so what do I do?

Well, the first thing I urgently must do is go for a wee. I've been holding it in since Gita turned up and it'll be running down my leg if I'm not careful. I pop out the back and up the stairs to the flat, piss like a horse and that's a relief and a half, then come down again to finish tidying up. I'm feeling pretty low and looking forward to Jay coming back from work, so we can chat. Then I remember he said he was going out with some old school mates tonight, straight from work, and then I feel crap, that I'll be all alone, without my boy to cheer me up.

So I mope about the shop and clear away the last of the stock I was in the middle of when Gita invaded. I ruminate, I look at my phone on the side. I pick it up and hold it. I stare out at the street and consider my next step. Then, I see that there's a little package shoved through the letter box in my door and it's stuck there. When did that come? When I was having a wee, I suppose. I bet it's that thread from that nice online shop I buy from, electric-blue thread for Paige for a quilted bag she's making. I shove my phone in my dungarees pocket and go over and pull it from the door and open it up, ready to pop it away in Paige's drawer. All my quilters have their own drawers in a colourful plastic unit I got for the purpose. But it's not thread, it's fabric. I pull it out and it's a quilted square. The background is sky-blue and there are quilted clouds at the top. There is a green strip of fabric for the ground. Above it float two figures in black cross-stitch, two geometric birds, beak to beak. In each corner is a sewn red heart. It's hand-sewn and the sewing is a bit wonky and I know that hand, I know that style. It's one of my quilters, one of my hotbed, someone who loves the big, blue skies and the green flat land of Lincolnshire, someone who loves the folk embroidery of Slovakia, someone who loves cartoons and comedy and books and films, someone who loves to talk and to be silent, who loves to be right and loves to argue with me and challenge me, someone who wants to protect me yet loves my independence and my spirit, someone who loves me.

I turn the package over urgently and there are two words written on it, in the same hand as my address on the Slovakian postcard and it says,

FOR FRANKIE

Then I shove my hand inside the package and find a slip of paper in there and there's the same handwriting on there and that reads,

I know my sewing is shit.
But my heart's in the right place.

Oh God, it's corny as fuck. But it's so him.

I rush outside into the street, even though the package

was left half an hour ago. Is he there? He must be around here somewhere, unless he got some passing urchin to drop it off. Then, my phone in my pocket goes off. I drag it out, open it up and it's a WhatsApp message. From Stef. He's unblocked me.

It's just a photo of him in a T-shirt. Blimey, he looks good. There's no picture on the T-shirt, just words. And they read:

SORRY
I'VE BEEN A
JUDGY TWAT

Hahahaaa!

I reply:

I was a stubborn twat. So if you can forgive me that,
I can forgive you for this.

Then it says, *Stefan is typing* . . . at the top and I've never been as happy to see those words in my life till now.

He replies:

FYI I am now officially unengaged.
If you've moved on, I'd quite understand.
But if you would like to see me, would you meet me at the imp?

I know exactly what he means. Underneath the statue of the Lincoln Imp in the cathedral! I close up the shop and look down at myself, wearing my scruffiest dungarees, and haven't washed my hair in a day or so and I look okay for customers but not for a hot date and I think, who cares? Stef won't! And I hurtle up to the cathedral. It looks bloody marvellous against the blue July sky and I rush in through the door and get to the front and there is the beautiful interior, stretched out before me, the diagonal lines of coloured light slanting down from the sun beaming through the stained-glass windows, as I stand there panting from the run. There's a rehearsal going on for an orchestral concert with a piano. The orchestra are playing and the conductor is waving her arms about and the pianist is waiting and then he starts playing and I know that piece. What is it? It's from some movie . . . Holy cow, it's Rachmaninoff's 2nd Piano Concerto. My grandad used to play all the classics on his gramophone. It's the very piece they play on the railway platform in *Brief Encounter* and here I am, about to experience the most romantic moment of my life, and fucking Rachmaninoff is my soundtrack, in real life! If you put this in a romcom, nobody would believe it.

I can't see Stef yet, and I have to pay to get beyond the first bit of the cathedral, so I pay and nearly rage when the card machine takes ages and they say it's always playing up and I'm like, 'Yes, yes, anyway, goddamn let me through,' and then it goes through and I hurry forward. People are milling about, and standing in clumps listening to the music and it's gorgeous and lush, flowing over me as I rush forwards through the nave to the side of the quire and I'm running now, to reach the far end of the cathedral and get to the bit where the Lincoln Imp is carved up above in the cathedral roof, looking down at me cheekily as I scan the crowd for Stefan Walker.

And there he is! Large as life, standing in his *JUDGY*

TWAT T-shirt, those dark eyes, that thick, dark wedge of hair and dark trimmed beard, the long curve of his back to his hips. He's looking so bloody good, I could jump him right there and then, on the cathedral floor. He catches my eye and grins and comes towards me and we meet in a glorious hug, our mouths finding each other and we're lost in a fabulous kiss, while the odd pilgrim or tourist walks past tutting and whispering.

'Let's get the fuck outta here,' I whisper and he nods. We hold hands and it's simply wonderful, just feeling the strength of his fingers looping around mine. And we hurry our step up to the cathedral entrance and we're out into the sunshiny evening.

'I've got so much to tell you,' he says. 'So much, I don't know where to start.'

'Me too, me too!' I say.

And we're laughing and it seems neither of us know where to start, so we don't and we just keep glancing goofily at each other and giggling as we rush down to my shop. We're round the back and up the stairs and the key is in the door and we don't reach the bed, we don't even reach the sofa, or the flat as the door is open, we just fall on each other there and then. We're half on the top of the stairway and half inside the flat and we're dragging each other's clothes off. And then we're kissing and grabbing at each other and we shove ourselves over the threshold and he slams the door shut with his foot and he's on top of me on the floor and we move together and it's the clumsiest and funniest and stupidest and sexiest and just all round the absolute BEST sex I've ever had in my life.

Afterwards, we climb into bed and just stare at each other

for ages, laughing and touching each other's faces and hair and not saying a word. And it's not even weird or awkward, it's just intense and dreamlike yet real, utterly real. Naked and honest and us.

'I love you,' he says.

'I love you,' I say.

And then, we talk.

'Zuzana actually dumped me,' he says, 'before I had a chance to tell her about you.'

'Oh yeah?'

'Yeah. I knew once I got there I didn't love her, not really, not like she deserved to be. And not like I deserved either. I knew I'd done the whole thing to please my mother and her side of the family. They all wanted it. When Zuzana saw me, well, even though the right feelings weren't there between us, she knew me well enough to know I'd changed. We skirted around it for ages, talking about the plans, ignoring awkward silences. Then, one day she said, "Do you want to marry me?" And I paused, and she said, "Because I don't want to marry you." She said she'd become convinced I was only doing it for convenience and she was worth more than that, anyone should be.'

'She's right,' I said.

'Yeah, indeed. And I said I had some stuff to tell her and she said, "I don't want to hear it. I don't need to know." And she said it all seemed a good idea at the time, but love can't be arranged.'

'She really is a wise woman,' I say. And oh God, the relief I feel, of knowing that Zuzana felt the same as Stef, that she knew it was all a farce. Or maybe she was just saying that, to make him feel better or out of pride? I ask, 'Do you think she meant it? Or was she just saying, I never liked you anyway, nerrr. You know, because she thought you were about to dump her.'

'No, no, I honestly don't. She told me, she's moving to Bratislava to live with her sister and she'll get a new job. She had it all planned out in her head. She was having as many doubts as me. And she was relieved to hear I felt the same way.'

'That's good, that's good,' I say. 'I'm not gonna lie, I'm glad she dumped you. It feels better that way round. I felt shit for messing up her life plans.'

'You didn't mess up anything,' he says softly and kisses my shoulder. 'You just . . . existed.'

'Well, I'm just glad Zuzana had the agency and made the decision. The last thing I want to do is drive people apart or be responsible for someone else's unhappiness. Which brings me to . . . your mum.'

'Oh God, I know. I haven't told her for sure it's actually properly over between me and Zuzana.'

'Well, she knows something's up for sure. She came to see me.'

I tell him the whole sorry tale and he's fuming.

'I can't believe she did that! I mean, I can. But that's totally out of order!'

'Look, she's hurting. She had this beautiful plan and, the way she sees it, if you'd never met me, it would all be going ahead. No wonder she's mad at me. I get it.'

'Yeah but she's still no right. And I'm gonna tell her so.'

'So, you haven't seen her today?'

'No, I haven't even told her I'm back here in England. I got in early this morning and I sent you that package on a same-day delivery, and then I've just been wandering around Lincoln, down the hill in the shopping centre, drinking far too much coffee and thinking about what the hell I'm going to say to her. And I didn't come straight to you, even though I was desperate to, because I was terrified.'

'Of what?!'

'That you'd tell me to piss off. That you'd say no. I knew I'd be okay, alone. I always have been. I like my own company. And I was quite prepared to start a new life, without Zuzana, without you, if needs be. But while I was still wandering around Waterstones or yet another café or wherever down there, I knew that there was a universe before you said no and I was still in it. It took me all day to muster up the courage to come see you. I wanted you to get the quilted square first, to conjure up some tender feelings for me, I was hoping. And then I'd have the nerve to finally come to you and ask for your forgiveness.'

'You don't need forgiveness and neither do I. We were both just being stubborn twats.'

'True, very true.'

'Listen,' I say, and I kiss him very tenderly on the mouth. We nearly fall into our passion again but I must say this, before the moment passes. 'Listen. I've had some big epiphanies these past few months. And one of them is this: I want to thank you. For making me see that proper love might still exist. I know that sounds corny but I honestly thought that was all made-up shite from romcoms and love stories. I'd never known it, never actually felt this thing . . . Linda told me, it's peaceful. Love is peaceful. Yeah, it's passion and lust and all those things too, don't get me wrong. But it's a quiet kind of knowledge. And that's how I feel for you.'

'Yes,' he says. 'Yes, that's it, exactly.'

'Well, I've never felt that before. In the fifty years of my life, I've never felt that for anyone. Except my mum. And my grandad. But I've never had it with a man I'm in a relationship with. Never. I didn't know it really existed. Until I met you. So I want to thank you. For showing me it exists. And whatever happens, even if you and I don't make it, even if it doesn't work out, I'm glad I know you, I'm glad that you're in the world. And that's huge for me, it really is. So thank you.'

He kisses me lightly yet lingeringly, and then we hug, like a friend hugs you, tight and loving. It's so good to feel that from my man. I don't think a lover has ever given me such a loving hug.

'Then I want to thank you too,' he says. 'For challenging me, for making me realise I judge too easily, that I have these deep-rooted views I need to dig up. Thank you for opening my eyes to my life and the mistakes I was making. Thank you for being incredible and thank you for loving me.'

'Jeez Louise,' I say, 'we're cheesy as fuck!'

But cheesy as it is, something feels very right for the first time in the longest time and, as I look into his eyes and we smile at each other, I get that exquisitely warm hair-washy feeling sweeping over me and I think, *This is it.* This is what love feels like. Thrill and spark and tingle and knowledge and peace, all at once. I found the guy I want to hang out with, talk for hours with, cook with and watch telly and have a laugh with, stay up all night baring our souls or messing about all day in bed with, chill at home and cuddle and go on adventures all over the world with, share my whole, true, authentic Frankie self with and . . . oh yeah, fancy like fuck.

Reader, I shagged him. Again. And I'm not telling you a

thing about it, because that's my damn business and you lot can just fuck off and imagine it, every last delicious moment.

Epilogue

AKA THE LAST LITTLE BIT BEFORE THE END

'Stop hogging that joint, Frankie.'

We're in Bel's shed, freezing our arses off. There's no picturesque snow so far this January. It's just icy and colder than a witch's tit. I'm wearing my usual wonky bobble hat and duffel coat and a new quilted scarf Stef made for me and the sewing is terrible but it's the best present ever and I love it.

'Oy, I'm due a big long toke,' I say and take one, then pass it over. 'I haven't had one for ages. You can come out here whenever you like.'

'Not for much longer. Back to school next week. Why did I think it was ever a good idea to go back to work?'

'Because you need the money.'

'Oh yeah. I forgot we weren't Elon Musk there for a minute.'

'Christ, I'm glad I'm not Elon Musk. He looks like Kathy Bates.'

'Hahahaa he fucking does,' says Bel, wheezing with laughter. 'I mean, I love Kathy Bates though.'

'Course you do. We all do. She's great. But if you're a guy, you don't wanna *look* like Kathy Bates.'

'True. She's so good in . . . you know . . . that film.'

'*Titanic*?' I say. God, I love that movie. But I can't watch past the iceberg. In my version in my head, Jack and Rose stay in love on a boat forever and she never shoves him off a floating door to his icy doom.

'No, no, no.'

'*Fried Green Tomatoes*?' Another favourite, and KB is great in that, but I like the bit in the past best. I always wanted to be a bee charmer like Idgie Threadgoode.

'No, although yes. But no.'

'*Dolores Claiborne*?' I try. Fuck knows where I dredged that up from. Have I even seen it?

'What the . . .? No. Is that a real film?'

'Yeah. I think. Or is it . . . the girl from *The Wizard of Oz*?'

'No, that's Dorothy Claiborne.'

'Is it . . . Claiborne?'

'Yeah,' says Bel, nodding wildly, like her life depends on it.

'No, it isn't. Her name is . . . something to do with . . . wind?'

'No, that's the tornado. And the house whizzing around in it. And the little dog. Toto.'

'I miss the rains down in Africa.'

We snigger at that, then hoot and fall about. Wow, I've really missed Bel over Christmas, while she's been doing all her family duties and so have I. This is our first shed session in two weeks and it's long overdue. It's been a wonderful Christmas though. My second in the flat, with Jay. And not just with Jay. Paige came too, after she'd had lunch with her folks. And Stef was with us, of course. He cooked the turkey in his oven down at his mum's house and carried it up the hill like Scrooge's remarkable boy. We had crackers and cranberry sauce and pigs in blankets and proper roasties and all that jazz. It was great. He brought a kind of Slovakian potato salad that they have on Christmas Day and that was damn tasty actually, a mixture of diced potatoes, eggs, carrots, gherkins and a spicy mayo sauce. Jay said it was grim as fuck, but that's fine because I loved it so it meant all the more for me. I was shovelling it down by the tablespoon-full before we even carved the turkey.

We did presents (not many, because we're all a bit skint, but my best one from Stef was a T-shirt he made for me with the *Young Ones* Euripides rats on them! He remembered! Even though he was pissed as a fart that night!) And we pulled the crackers and put on hats and told jokes and all that and then inhaled my traditional Christmas trifle. Then, once we could barely move, we forced ourselves to do our pre-planned post-prandial iPad call to Gita. She's living in Slovakia now, very happily, with her cousin in her home village. We went out to see her in November. She was mad as hell when Stef first told her the news, but then fate intervened and her cousin's husband died, which Gita was delighted about, as she'd never liked him ('He had long nose hairs and preferred Russian vodka to *Slivovica*, the idiot,' she told me). So, the cousin didn't want to live alone and invited Gita to move in, which she did very happily as the cousin was pretty well off and it was a much nicer, bigger, posher house than the one she was going to live in with Stef and Zuzana. Stef's ex did indeed move to Bratislava and get a new job and a new fiancé by all accounts, all within the space of four months. Nice work, lady. Once Gita was ensconced in her new home, she forgave us and invited us to visit. I loved it, the country.

Very pretty, very mountainy and foresty. We went to that village where the decorated houses are, the same ones on the postcard Stef sent me. We got pissed and ate oysters in Bratislava and I got the shits in the hotel and Stef got the shits too, and we were fighting to get to the loo to throw up or spatter the toilet. So yeah, you really get to know whether you love someone when it's coming out both ends. We managed though, and we bonded over it. There's nothing like being ill away from home to make you cling to each other like Rose and Jack on the deck of the Titanic.

Which reminds me . . . where were we?

'Dorothy Gale!' I cry.

'Yes! Is it?'

'Yeah, she's called Dorothy Gale. In the book anyway. I don't know if they say it in the film.'

'What film?' says Bel and yawns elaborately, stretching her arms up to the shed roof and inadvertently scattering ash on her beanie hat.

'Come on you,' I say. 'Time for you to hit the hay.'

'No,' she says and looks directly at me. 'No, I have things to say.'

'Say them then but give me the fucking joint before you drop it.'

'Did you realise,' intones Bel, steadfastly serious, 'it's almost exactly one year, since we sat here, in this very shed, and you started online dating?'

'Fuck . . . is it really?'

'Yep, almost exactly three hundred and sixty-five days ago!' cries Bel, triumphant. 'And look how far you've come! Look at ya, look at ya!'

'All right, missus, calm down. Look at *you*, while we're at it. Mother of the Year. I mean, you always were, but you didn't believe it. You're so much happier now. It's so damn good to see.'

'Aww babe, what a year it's been. An odyssey and a half.'

'It really has,' I say and I look out of the shed window and I see snow is falling, pretty fast, a lot of it swirling around in the breeze and I can't stop watching it. And as I'm staring at this symphony of snowflakes, I start talking, just talking and talking about this year and my epiphanies and all the madness of it, like it's all coming to me at once, everything that's happened to me, my words carried on the snowflakes themselves.

'Holy shit, babe, so much has happened, hasn't it? So bloody much! All that dating app madness. I don't even know what I think about it all now. Does it work? Is it all bad, or can it be freedom-ing? I mean, liberating. I mean, I met Stef through work, just as Linda's gynae said I would. But that doesn't dismiss dating apps. After all, you and Craig met through one, babe, and you two are a true, bona fide love story. But you know, one thing I've learnt is this. The idea of true love might seem *outdated*, but the truth is, it really does exist. However you meet someone, the thing I've learnt is to take your time, let things blossom and flower, let the layers peel back at their own sweet pace and reveal themselves. Then you'll know each other more deeply and truly appreciate the person they are. And that's what I've learnt about love: that's it about quiet joy as much as it is about passion and lust and . . . spark. Yes, the spark, that I thought was love. But the peace that's actually love . . . well, that's something that dawns on you gradually, never straight away, not in the early banter and flirting and nonsense of new relationships. And I've learnt that playing the field can be fun, as well as shite. I've learnt a hell of a lot about sex, what I want and what I wouldn't touch again with a ten-foot bargepole. I've learnt that slut-shaming is bullshit and that sex for its own sake can be a double-edged sword, one that is freeing, yes . . . but could just as well leave you feeling empty as all hell. But maybe that suits some people, you know? And that's just fine. You know, Bel, you said to me a year ago, in this very shed, that dating apps are one big game and you have to play to win. You have to *out-date* the dating apps, you said. That's brilliant, by the way. You should copyright that. Anyway, that's true BUT what I know is that if you're really looking for love, then you just need to have some patience, a lot of savvy, a . . . a little tiny sprinkling of romance and a bit of faith. And a community of friends and support definitely helps too. You and Jay, and my hotbed of quilters, and my Steep Hill friends and my internet friends and my long-ago friends and all of them. They all help. And my man. My man, my family, my friends. And my tribe.'

I look at Bel to see her reaction to this deeply heartfelt speech I have just crafted and she's fucking well asleep. Hunched up on the bench with her arms crossed and her mouth wide open. Poor, tired lamb.

'Come on, you,' I say and stub out the last of the joint and gently nudge her awake. I help her off the bench and link arms tightly so she doesn't fall over and walk her to the house and shove her in through the kitchen door, where she wakes up properly and looks round and grins at me. Then, her mouth drops open and she yells, 'MISERY!'

'What?!'

'Kathy Bates was so good in *Misery*!'

'She was goddamn terrific!' I say. 'Now get thee to bed, you nutter.'

'Thanks babe,' Bel says and puts her arms around me. 'Love you.'

'Love you,' I say and nod at Craig as he comes through to the kitchen. He blows a camp kiss at me and off I go, into the snowy night. I'm off home, back to the flat above my shop, and there will be nobody there, but that's cool. That's fine as fuck. Jay has gone back off to uni early, to get some essays done before term starts. Stef is working on a new contract down at his mum's house, where he now lives, renting from her so she's got the money to live off in Slovakia and he doesn't have to find some dodgy landlord in Lincoln. And very handily, just down the hill from me. I must say, it's pretty much the ideal scenario. My man nearby, but not under my feet, and I'm not under his. I need my independence and my classes and my friends. And he needs his mates and his introvert quiet time plus he needs to wander the earth at will. Gita was right about him being a nomad but wrong that he was lost. He just loves to travel and I'm happy to be home and see him whenever he gets back. Or maybe we'll go on adventures together as well, one day. And that suits us just fine. I'm tramping through the snow just starting to lay itself snugly on the ground. I make my way along Bailgate, past houses with yellow squares of light pouring warmth onto the street. Along I go into Castle Square, where I look up at the stunning West Front of the cathedral, glowing ethereal blue tonight, spectral in the moonlight and the swirling snow. And as I start to descend Steep Hill, I think about this time last year when I slipped up on my arse and lay on my back, scared and sad and alone, an uncertain future ahead of me, a miserable past behind me.

You've probably been there yourself, staring into the

swirling abyss of a future like that, when shit goes down in your life and you've no idea what's going to happen next and you're bloody terrified. I know, it's the pits. But you've gotta get up off your arse and say, *fuck you, Mars*. Don't beat yourself up, but get a hold of yourself instead. You might want to hide behind the sofa of life forever, but you can't. You've got to get out there and live again. Be careful, yes, be safe. But also, be willing to re-enter the game of life and have an adventure. Novelty is good for your brain and your soul, so don't fall back into the same old sad routines forever. Challenge yourself and be willing to fuck things up. As Thomas Edison said about failure . . . erm, well, I can't bloody remember what he said exactly and it's too cold to get my mittens off and Google it, but anyway, it's something about I haven't failed, oh no, I have simply taken ten thousand steps to success or something like that blah blah blah. ANYWAY, look, more importantly, as I, Frankie Brumby, say, go forth and fuck up. Because change is terrifying but it's also necessary. Change is life. Leaving a crappy marriage is hard, it can be petrifying, literally, turning your life into stone. But staying in that barren place is a kind of death. And anything must be better than that. Being single after years of marriage can be scary, going out into the unknown is always scary, but it'll never be as bad as being in a bad relationship. And let me tell you, instead of staying a day longer with soul-suckers like Twatface or even Fuckface, I'd rather talc my twat with chilli powder.

GLOSSARY of Dating Terms

Asexual = A person who experiences rare, little or no sexual attraction to others. Not to be confused with celibacy. Celibacy is a choice to abstain from sex, whereas for some asexuality is a lack of sexual attraction. Sometimes people might refer to themselves as being 'ace'.

BDSM = Bondage, discipline/domination, sadism and masochism, manifesting in sex which involves roleplaying around control and power.

Beige flags = Elements of a dating profile which seem boring, generic or clichéd, suggesting a dull person who'll probably make as little effort when dating as they have with their profile.

Benching = Keeping someone on your 'dating bench', which means texting someone just often enough to keep their interest but exploring other more interesting options simultaneously.

Bisexual = Someone who is sexually or romantically attracted to both men and women, or to more than one sex or gender.

Breadcrumbing = Where someone won't move forward beyond the flirty texting stage and has no intention of meeting up or having another date i.e., they are giving you breadcrumbs and nothing more.

Catfishing = Pretending to be someone else online, often with the intention of defrauding others.

DILF = Dad I'd Like to Fuck. A term used to describe sexy men old enough to be your father.

DMs = Direct messages. These are private messages on social media platforms such as Facebook or Instagram which can only be seen by the sender and recipient.

Dominatrix = A dominatrix, or domme, is a woman who takes the dominant role in BDSM activities. The male equivalent would be a dom.

ENM = Ethical non-monogamy. Having a loving and healthy main relationship while also having sexual relationships with others, with the main partner's knowledge.

Flexting = Exaggerating one's sense of self and being arrogant about accomplishments, looks or charisma that turn out to be false on meeting.

Fuck buddy = Similar to 'friends with benefits', i.e. a casual sex partner with no strings attached.

Fuckboy = A male sexual partner who is interested only in casual sex. Sometimes this can be used as an insult.

FWB = Friends with benefits. Similar to a 'fuck buddy' i.e. a casual sex partner with no strings attached.

Ghosting = Suddenly disappearing from someone's life, for example by blocking them on social media and becoming a 'ghost'.

GILF = Grandma I'd Like to Fuck. A term used to describe sexy women old enough to be your grandmother.

Groundhogging = Dating the same type of person over and over again and expecting the results to be different.

Hey-ter = Someone who refuses to answer any first messages on dating apps that start only with a single, solitary 'Hey'.

IRL = In Real Life, meeting someone in the flesh.

Kink shaming = Mocking or insulting someone for their sexual preferences (particularly those that might be considered unusual i.e. a kink).

Kittenfishing = Not full-on catfishing, but subtly misrepresenting oneself by exaggerating youth or other features through little white lies on a dating profile. For example, using old photos from when someone was younger, editing photos or lying about their height or age.

MILF = Mother I'd Like to Fuck. A term used to describe sexy women old enough to be your mother.

Negging = Giving someone backhanded compliments and

other put-downs to lower their self-esteem so that they become more attracted to you and desperate for your approval. Often used by men to hit on women.

ONS = One-night stand, i.e. a one-off sexual meeting. A successful ONS could develop into FWB, if repeated often enough!

Pansexual = A person who is sexually attracted to all genders /attracted to a person regardless of their gender.

Peacocking = Dressing or acting in an ostentatiously arrogant or preening manner while on a date.

Red flags = Signs that a person is bad news, often felt as a gut reaction to small, sometimes seemingly insignificant events or reactions.

Sex Interview = A brief meeting to ascertain whether two people would like to then proceed to sex at some point later (or not.)

Sexting = Engaging in full-on sexy talk by text.

Slide into DMs = Start private messaging, usually with the intention of flirting.

Slow Fade = To 'ghost' someone but in a more gradual manner.

Snap = Related to using Snapchat for messaging purposes.

Swipe right/swipe left = How to choose people you like on Tinder and some other dating apps i.e. often you will swipe right to tell the app you like someone's profile, or swipe left to get rid of their profile.

Thirsty = Desperate for sex.

WYD? = 'What You Doing?' Often used as a generic opener to dating messages on apps or websites.

Zombieing = When you think the relationship couldn't be more dead, an old flame rises up from the grave you dug them in (or they dug themselves in), begging for that one last chance.

Acknowledgements

Rachel Hart, editor-in-chief, for believing in this romcom, in Harper Ford and in me. And for not only counting the exact number of 'fucks' in the first draft (545) but exhorting me, quite rightly, to reduce those by at least 300. Thanks, wise and wonderful ed.

Maddie Dunne Kirby, Gaby Drinkald and the entire brilliant team at Avon, who took this book to their hearts and finessed TF out of it.

Laura Macdougall and Olivia Davies – my marvellous agenting team at United Agents – for believing I had it in me to write contemporary comedy, for shaping the early submissions and plot, as well as putting up with my ridiculous sense of humour.

Sasha Drennan of *Lindum Books*, Lincoln, for fascinating information on running a shop in Lincoln and small businesses in general. Also, for supporting all of my books, whatever the author name or genre.

Sarah Todd Taylor, splendid writer of children's books and also a very keen quilter, for kindly reading and advising on quilting bits and bobs.

Liz Beeson, my mum, quilter and seamstress extraordinaire, for inspiration and also memories of her beautiful and highly organised quilting room. And for Poppy's ark quilt, a thing of hand-sewn beauty.

Suzie Greenbeck – of *Suzie's Sewing Studio* (in Waltham, North East Lincolnshire) and *Love, Suzie* – for agreeing to an interview and inviting me to her group, where I was delighted to meet and interview this wonderful team of talented women: Sarah Huteson, Jo Jacklin, Heather Mathias, Sarah Louise Snow and Alison Wintein.

Iveta Drabekova – for all things Slovakian, excellent research help given on names, places, food, drink and traditions, as well as your valued friendship. One day, I would love to see your beautiful country . . .

Early readers – Lucy Adams, Melissa Bailey, Lynn Downing, Jo Lancaster, Pauline Lancaster, Fiona McKinnell and Louisa Treger – for encouragement and enthusiasm. And letting me know which jokes were too dodgy or not . . .

Amy Claridge of *The Fabric Quarter* (Steep Hill, Lincoln) for very helpful shop information and advice about sewing shops, quilting and quilters.

Helen Fields, author and legal expert, who kindly spoke to me on the phone about money, mortgages, investments, debt and divorce. Superlative legal advisor, who also happens to be a brilliant novelist.

Debbie Cowie, for help with sons and covers and fabulous hair.

Claire Newman-Williams, photographer of incredible author headshots and boswams talk.

Kate Kelvin, make-up artiste and stylist of big hair extraordinaire.

Lu Corfield, for recommending Claire and also just being you, Lu. Thanks for the honey cake, tea and chats in that there London.

Louisa Treger, for being the lovely hostess with the mostest, during my London adventures.

Tim Marchant, web designer, for an excellent new Harper website (and putting up with my preposterous colour-scheme odyssey) and Alison Marchant, artist, for fabulous line drawings of Frankie, Stef and Harper.

Hamza Jahanzeb, for excellent editing skills, much appreciated.

Lincs Inspire, Cleethorpes Library and all the staff at Waterstones Grimsby, for supporting the publication of this book and throughout my writing career and many names.

My family in its entirety, from whom I inherited their wicked sense of humour, which not only gave me the confidence to try writing a romcom but also keeps me going in the darkest days, because in the end, what else do we have but sarcasm to save us from the abyss?!

My Facebook fam, for celebrating this new genre I'm writing and laughing at all of my nonsense every goddamn day. And to the invisible, unsung inventors of memes, wherever they may be, who keep this novelist sniggering at 3am when sensible people are asleep.

Poppy, for her patience while I was writing and editing this book, all while we juggled exam revision and housework with minor inconveniences like food and sleep. Also, I'm glad to see she's inherited the same family wit and so now there are invariably two of us laughing inappropriately.

The little café in Prague, twenty years ago, that served me my very first taste of Slovakian honey cake and set me on the path of finding the best recipe for this delicacy. I never found the recipe, but I did find a chef who can make it for me . . .

Clem, for encouraging my dark sense of humour with

regular harvesting of the finest memes known to humanity. And your incredible honey cake, which is the only one that's ever matched the first.